SHIFTING GROUND

A Novel

A. Z. Zehava

Copyright © 2013 A. Z. Zehava

All rights reserved.

ISBN: 1493523090
ISBN-13: 9781493523092
Library of Congress Control Number: 2013920899
CreateSpace Independent Publishing Platform
North Charleston, South Carolina

for my husband

They were careless people…they smashed up things and creatures and then retreated back into their money or their vast carelessness, or whatever it was that kept them together, and let other people clean up the mess they had made….

–F.Scott Fitzgerald, *The Great Gatsby*

For the last ten or fifteen years, the immense and proliferating criticizability of things, institutions, practices and discourses; a sort of general feeling that the ground was crumbling beneath our feet, especially in places where it seemed most familiar, most solid, and closest to us, to our bodies, to our everyday gestures. But alongside this crumbling and the astonishing efficacy of discontinuous particular and local critiques the facts were also revealing something… beneath this whole thematic, through it and even within in, we have seen what might be called the insurrection of subjugated knowledges.

–Foucault, Society Must be Defended, 7 January 1976, tr. David Macey

Hope is for people who wait. And I don't want to wait no more. I'm not scared anymore.

–Concha Buika

Prologue

I shifted from foot to foot on the unnaturally green and spongy grass, the acrid damp scent of insecticide in my nose, and stared at the casket. We were all sweating in the low glare of the December sun as we waited for it to start and to be over.

Finally, the old priest arrived and took his place as we watched him. Looking down, he stepped up unsteadily onto the AstroTurf-covered hillock next to the grave. A sturdy matron nearby offered the old man her arm, but he refused it. He stood at the head of the casket without looking up, took off his eyeglasses, wiped them and his brow, and then attached two sunshades to the lenses. He had a Parkinson's tremor in both hands and I wasn't sure if he was going to be able to get them back on, but then he did.

It was only after he had pleased himself with the position of his glasses and taken out some notes that he acknowledged us and opened his mouth to speak. He began in a low rumble, appropriately mournful but authoritative, and built it up. I had the sense that he had performed and perfected this speech over many years and now considered himself to be quite good at it. Did he really know anything about the man in the box beyond the usual disclosures, added up and formed by what this priest supposed he knew about all of us? I doubted it. On the other hand, I thought, many here would be surprised to learn what I knew of him.

Someone explained to me long ago that in a relationship between two people there are six: The person I am, really, the person I think I am, the person you think I am, the person you are, really, the person you think you are, and the person I think you are. Each of them with a piece of the action. Now that my friend is dead, three of these are dead also, including the man he thought I was. A part of me lies in that casket. There was something in that.

Perhaps this explains the ephemeral joy one sometimes feels in the face of someone else's tragedy, that tiny unconscious smile. We hear that a village was put to the torch, or that a coast was leveled by a tsunami, or that a co-worker has brain cancer, and before we can quash it, there is sometimes this strange instant of inexplicable joy. We feel guilty about it because we think it's some sick kind of *schadenfreude*, but it's not. It's the recognition that it was I who was put to the torch, I who was leveled by the tsunami, I who face the wasting away. We are all longing for the transformative power of death. The trick, as they say, is to die before you die. That is quite a trick—especially to work it so that it feels okay.

The old priest kept right on talking and so I turned my eyes to him. He was telling us what this means, he was cementing his own authority, he was spreading his own thoughts and opinions, like sticky marmalade upon us all. That's when I noticed that whenever he paused for effect, he would glance down at the trembling sheaf of notes in his hands and look up at us again. Each time he bobbed his head in this way, the hard sun refracted from the lenses of his glasses and sent skittering a hundred points of light that jiggled across the black dresses sunbleached gray and the gray suits, as if a child were hiding somewhere, playing with a mirror, just to mock him. I imagined that it was the man in the box, now childlike again, giving us one last silly salute. That made me happy.

The casket gleamed as they dropped him in, and the handful of dirt sparkled as it scattered and fell. I walked away alone.

I drove across the Golden Gate Bridge to go home, but then I realized I couldn't. The slanting rays of the setting sun, fractured by the cables, seemed to blink urgently, and, it seemed to me, in code, as I changed lanes, deciding where to go. Open to these sorts of messages, wide open now, I decided that I needed to go somewhere with an edge. The Haight was too full of cheerful tourists. I went to the Mission.

In the Mission I wanted to walk off that ache in my chest that started when I left the funeral alone, but the walking didn't help. I wasn't hungry. I didn't want a coffee. What I wanted I couldn't have right now. I was making peace with that, and letting go of the wanting, and feeling a little better when I found myself in a large group of people stopped on the sidewalk and spilling out into the street. Someone was tearing up an old building and other people didn't want it to come down. Two pieces of dirty yellow construction machinery towered above the crowd, sullenly silent, while their operators slumped in their seats. The protestors were packed tight on the sidewalk outside of the construction fence, and several people were holding signs saying, "Gentrification No!" and "SF needs Affordable Housing."

In the center of the group was a tall, skinny youth in a Che Guevarra t-shirt speaking angrily to a silent hard-hatted foreman with a clenched jaw and giant hands that curled impatiently on his hips. Next to him, a young woman scribbled in a notebook. These three were surrounded by a tight knot of people who glared and interrupted. One heavyset elderly woman was crying. Off to the side, a slouching cameraman filmed the scene. As several police officers arrived, the reporter and cameraman retreated, and after some scuffling, the crowd was moved back and we were all deafened by the ignition of the giant engines.

Everyone turned and stared at the building, shoulders aligned and brute eyes unblinking. I knew that I should feel sympathy for these people who were obviously suffering, but instead I recognized something in them, in their faces, that I found repulsive. There was something in this all too focused attention, however motivated, that was unwholesome. These people reminded me of soldiers leveling their weapons, of football players squaring off at the line, of politicos shouting each other down, of police officers storming the poor tenement. These all are indistinguishable in character, in sound, in energy. In all, the people stare like this, with their eyes front set in predator faces, facing forward. In all, it is nothing else but the will to dominate.

I stood there, at this other funeral, for lack of anything else to do and interested in seeing the building come down. Yeah, let it come down! In gratitude to the great tear down of 1906, whole neighborhoods are now built where a handful of mansions of breathtaking beauty once stood. As the building pancaked to the ground, the protestors held rags to their noses and mouths against the dust. I breathed it in. I was learning not to resist death. I was learning that inside me was an old building that must come down.

The man in the box never went in for this line of thinking. The man in the box viewed my uncertainty, my struggle, my instability as the worst species of unmanly weakness. That shouldn't have come as a surprise. From the perspective of a man breaking down, a man gathering himself up seems to be going in the wrong direction. How amazing it was to me that it was only one year ago that Henry Buchanan had everything under control, and how in only one year, that building pancaked down.

Unto The Breach

The rising sun broke over the rim of San Francisco Bay, skipped over the rippling water, climbed up Yerba Buena Island and sent an eruption of cormorants scattering skyward. It reflected, then burst through my office window, washing my white walls golden. I turned in my chair. The bay glittered with the frisson of new aurora. I watched as the water scintillated in solitary enjoyment until a lone skiff interrupted its surface and skimmed across it. I turned back to the blinking cursor on my computer screen and the stack of open books resting in the small pool of light cast by my desk lamp, now superfluous. I switched off the lamp and continued working for an entire hour before I heard the secretaries chatting in the hall and people coming in. I heard rather than saw Henry walk by. He called to me as he went, but I didn't respond. He would say to my secretary that Mikey was in one of his moods, and he would be right.

Some time later, Henry reappeared in my doorway, occupying almost the entire space of it. He was talking to another partner at the firm. An associate waited patiently at his elbow, but Henry didn't acknowledge him. Henry was accustomed to other people, drawn by his magnificent aspect and volume, approaching merely to watch the spectacle of Henry being himself. Henry cut his eyes to me, pointed in the direction of the Ferry Building and then to his watch. I nodded. We'd have lunch later. I turned back to the screen but couldn't concentrate.

A decade and a half ago, I'd known Henry in law school. He was a happy puppy who played pranks, loved to hear himself talk in class, and threw a Frisbee on the lawn. He crashed one of our parties with his foxy young bride. I didn't know them well then, but I could still see them clearly now: Atlanta coquettishly perched on the back of my couch, gesturing with her cocktail for emphasis and puncturing the polite conversation with her quick, sharp wit. The party collected itself around her. I never got close enough to hear exactly what she was saying, but it must have been mildly shocking because after she spoke, she would smile a sly smile while the men brayed and the women covered their mouths. Meanwhile, he worked the room, arguing free marketeer philosophy with anyone who would. I remember dismissing him as naively idealistic, and I suppose he has remained so ever since. However, idealism solidified goes by other names.

It wasn't until years after law school that I saw him again when I came to work here. I almost didn't recognize him. His long pleasant face had grown fleshy and ripe with large boned self-satisfaction, in that way a certain breed of Southern men have. He was heavier, both in body and in character, and seemed to be the kind of man who felt he represented something.

I turned to the window again. The solitary skiff was replaced by a small army of retired people skimming across the Bay in their sailboats. An airplane crossed over them. How much of the last hour could I actually bill? I asked myself. Fifteen minutes? Maybe I could bill fifteen minutes.

At noon, I was pulling on the sleeves of my jacket as I walked to Henry's office and it became one of those rare, disorienting moments of déjà vu. I was about to say something to him about it, but the words stopped in my throat as gooseflesh crawled up my spine. Backlit by the bright, plate glass window, Henry was standing in the middle of the room, his eyes wide in panic. His palms were raised in front of him, his gaze not fixing on anything, but seemed to be focused on a landscape beyond the walls, a landscape containing dangers unseen by me. I felt a wave of nausea as Henry was pulled away from me, becoming smaller in the warping expansion of the space in front of my eyes, like a man lost at sea. I nearly leapt at him to support him, hold him against whatever it was that held him in its grasp.

The vision evaporated as his gold, tiger's eyes fixed on me.

"Ready?" He grinned.

I shook myself and grinned back, looking at him twice to make sure.

Too impatient for the elevator, we ducked into the stairwell. I was winded by the time we finally burst through the doors on the ground floor. Henry bounded across the lobby and opened the heavy glass street door, putting his arm around my shoulders lightly as I passed in front of him. The laser directness of the California sun was blinding. It burnt away the stale office air and evaporated the office emergencies, which now seemed trivial. I laughed out loud at the vision of the lost Henry. We both began to walk quickly, in step with one another.

Henry opened his arms wide and yelled into the street, "What a beautiful day it is!"

Henry said this looking directly up at the sky, and the people walking toward us skittered from the path of this distracted leviathan.

"Say, do you still see that girl at all? That one you brought to lunch that time…the blonde?" he asked.

"Kate, uh, not really. I've run into her once or twice. She must be out of art school now. She was working on her final project when we split."

"Hmm. Yes, she was interesting," Henry said. He had used that word, and the word, *lovely*, also, to describe my ex-wife, an opinionated and childless woman devoted to market analysis. In his eyes, my relationship with Esperanza was the product of a poorly thought out early marriage and he, no doubt, thought that it was just as well, or at least, not surprising, when she left me for another man two years ago. He wouldn't ask if I was dating someone else, so I filled the space myself.

"I think I dated Kate because she was as different from Esperanza as could be. And it was flattering that she was so much younger. I'm a walking cliché, actually. It's embarrassing."

"How does a divorced man meet women without humiliating himself?" I rambled on. "That's what I'd like to know. I haven't dated since I was a teenager, and I wasn't good at it then. Ez pretty much took me in hand."

I stopped abruptly, feeling myself become maudlin.

"There's those websites," Henry said, "women from Thailand and Russia. Not that I know about it, but a guy I know shopped for his wife like out of a catalogue."

"I don't know," I said archly, "Things aren't as bad in Thailand as they used to be...maybe Afghanistan would be a better bet at this point?"

Henry replied, "Well, that's a market that's not quite open yet."

"Hey, school started last week, didn't it?" I asked before he could continue.

"Yes! The kids, they're all in school now." He paused reflectively. "You know, it would be madness to have another child, but since the little one has started school, I miss having a baby around the house."

Henry's face softened. "No, I tell you that there is nothing sweeter than laying in a hammock on a summer day while a toddler climbs all over you."

Despite what some said about Henry and his marriage, the picture he painted of it had a stable wholesomeness that I found attractive.

"I'm the opposite," I said, laughing, "I start to like children when they are old enough to engage in rational conversation."

I was playing the happy bachelor again, and it made me feel happy. I laughed again. "Once, when Ez's sister and brother-in-law were in town with their first, Esperanza and I agreed to babysit while they had an afternoon to themselves sightseeing. That baby cried from the moment the door closed until the moment they came back. Hours. I think that was the day she became sure she didn't want any babies. I was trying to convince her that we should adopt an older child…."

I trailed off, feeling wretched that I had already lost the happy bachelor. I tried to make it into something else, and added, "there are so many older children needing families, you know."

We stepped into the cool shade of the Ferry Building and sat in front of the big windows in the back of the restaurant with a fine view of Pier One and a slice of the Bay. We ordered iced drinks to dispel the pall of gloom cast by the invocation of Esperanza's name, the specter of needy children, and my own terrible aloneness. My drink had bourbon in it.

Sweating glasses in hand, we both looked around in a comfortable silence, but something occurred to me.

"I know you don't like to hear about Esperanza," I started.

Henry interrupted, "It's not that I don't like it. I have listened, hours and hours, as you have talked about her, about," he paused, avoiding my eyes, "what happened."

"I listened because I thought it would get it out of your system." His pale green eyes were gilded and reflected the light as he fixed them on me. "It isn't helping. It's an obsession."

A moment of silence passed as I dropped my eyes and I tried it on, right there in front of him.

It didn't feel like an obsession. It felt more like a longing. And it wasn't even a nostalgic longing, but rather a forward falling longing, which was curious because I hadn't seen or heard from Ez since the divorce was final. She had just vanished, and no one would tell me where she was.

"Well," I said, "what I was going to say is, except for elementary school and the last two years, all of the events of my life are connected with Esperanza. If I can't talk about her, I have to kill off most of my life like…some head injury victim."

Henry was silent.

"Wouldn't you miss Atlanta if she left?"

Henry looked up sharply, "That's scarcely possible."

"Hypothetically. If you were to remember, say five years from now after a divorce, Joshua's first day of school, wouldn't that memory have Atlanta making his lunch, standing next to the bus wiping away tears? Would you efface that whole memory? Or rewrite it, so that her part is written out?"

"I can't imagine it."

"Yes, you can," I said, piqued. "Try! You feel like you've been killed, but at some point you realize that you are not actually dead and you have to start off in a new direction." I was warming to the subject, trying it out on myself as I spoke. "Although you are a new person, your old self is still a part of you, in the same way that your childhood isn't you but is a part of you."

Henry seemed to be trying to imagine it, or at least pretending to.

"Do you refuse to talk about anything that isn't present tense?" I asked him.

"But it would."

"It would what?"

"It would kill me. I would be dead," Henry said without emotion, and placed his glass squarely on its bottom.

I was too annoyed to be moved by the vulnerability in his gaze.

"Forget it!" I lost my patience. "I just won't talk about her anymore. You're stuck with the last two years, which is too bad for you because you know as well as I do how pitiful they've been."

Henry was strangely silent and the silence disturbed me, but he was looking away, sipping his tea. He was staring at the bolus of tourists waiting for the next pleasure boat, their many broad butts massed in front of us out on the pier. I took a gulp of the bourbon.

"We got married on a pier," I said to Henry's profile. He didn't turn around. "The wedding wasn't actually on a pier, but on the beach. Everyone followed us to the Port."

Henry ignored me. Ez was as tiny as a doll in her flouncy wedding dress and we walked onto a cruise ship immediately after. She threw the bouquet right before we got on. Cheesy, but we were nineteen and had never been abroad.

Esperanza scared the crap out of Henry. I smirked as I studied his backlit profile. She was half his size but she didn't take shit even once from anybody. I missed that.

"You ever been on one of these things?" Henry jabbed a thumb at the tour boat outside the window.

"Once," I said absently, "with...."

"I never have," he interrupted, "in all this time, I never have."

I had pressed her to get pregnant right away. Her mother, all along skeptical of this too young gringo boyfriend of unknown prospects, was soon overwhelmed with baby lust and called Ez regularly for an estrus cycle update. This update was then duly relayed to all the female members of a wide and only semi-related Cuban-American family, all of whom desperately wanted a new one, cousin Josephina's being born the last year and already walking.

"You guys moved out here pretty much the same time that we did, right?" I asked Henry.

"Yeah, but I went straight to law school," he said.

"Right. And had the kids."

"Right," he confirmed, "while you guys were 'finding yourselves' or whatever. Did you ever find yourselves?" I looked at him, his smirk fell, and he turned away again.

Ez did not get pregnant. Despite the *monton de candelas* that Josephina burnt, the young man declined to marry her and the college plans were put on hold. Ez decided that we'd wait until after we had both graduated. We joined forces to fend off importunate questions with the giddy good humor of people not yet denied anything.

By the time we had graduated, Josephina was still living with her mother, working nights. And Esperanza's college educated older sister was home happily cooking, cleaning and washing for three kids and a husband, but in Esperanza's eyes, completely enervated. She called it the dirty secret of educated womanhood.

I wanted kids now, I thought, as the waiter laid our plates in front of us and Henry turned around to face me. I desperately wanted them now, especially with Ez gone. She probably wouldn't even be gone, at least not so completely, if we had kids. I just got older and more alone while I watched my friends' kids, coworkers' kids, Henry's kids grow, get smarter, funnier, more beautiful or strange, each in their own surprising way, and I wanted them.

I was trying to think of something to say to Henry when I saw a partner at the firm, Nell, come in with Jane, an associate firmly on partnership track.

"Hi, Nell," I mouthed silently at her when she glanced at me and waved.

Nell was a woman of supreme confidence and tremendous gifts as a litigator. In addition to these qualities, she had a large, relaxed physicality and an air of self-satisfaction that animated every gesture, much like Henry. It was no coincidence that, also like Henry, she too was married to someone who remained at home to care for their children and smooth the details of daily life for her. Henry hated her with an intensity that challenged his composure.

Henry ignored them and attacked his lunch.

Nell was trying to catch my eye again but I pretended not to notice. She probably wanted to come over. Nell and Jane enjoyed kicking Henry. They never behaved in a way that anyone could call reproachable. They merely saved accounts of victories, or demonstrations of power to be savored between themselves in Henry's presence. They dropped stray comments, appended like red ribbons flying from the continuity of their speech that flowed quickly by him. They held open doors for him and paid for his lunch. And Henry, in massive bovine confusion, could never obtain purchase and only pawed the ground in helpless fury whilst the *picadores* nimbly gored him.

"Nell just settled the Bertram case," I said to him.

"So I've heard," he replied and continued to shovel food into his mouth.

"It was a huge multi-million dollar divorce and it came out very well for us," I said defensively.

"For the wife, you mean," Henry added and slurped his tea.

I rolled my eyes.

"How can you stand listening to them crow about ruining a man, knowing that our firm resources are complicit, and be fine with that?" Henry asked.

"You're talking about it as if they were doing something unethical. That's the law, Henry, that's how it is."

I took another bite before talking again with my mouth full. "Married couples are expected to share, and frankly, I don't think it's such a bad idea. Do you really want a bunch of women and children living off of your tax dollars so that their rich ex-husbands can go clubbing in Baja with twenty-year-olds?"

"So, just because some handful of men abandon their family responsibilities and chase younger women, I've got to...," Henry paused.

"You've got to what?" I demanded.

He didn't answer.

"This Bertram fellow," he started again, "is he chasing twenty-year-olds?"

"I really don't hang around with the litigation people that much. I don't know anything about the guy except that his ex-wife thinks he's kind of a jerk."

"All I am saying," Henry asserted again, "is that a person should keep what they earn with their own hard work. Atlanta is a maid without a commute. I'd never say it to her, but it's the truth. No one would pay her much to do what she does."

"So, everything comes back to money as the standard of worth?"

"We live in a market economy, Mike. She's support staff. Am I going to pay my secretary the same as myself? No. If people get divorced, the wife should get compensated at support staff rates."

"Not everyone agrees that people should walk around with price tags on their heads, you know. And if the price tag were based on individual character or a person's contribution to society, the rich guys wouldn't always come out so well."

"Anyway," I said, taking another bite, "Equality in marriage is the best support for the so-called family values your fellow partisans are forever blithering about."

"Oh, you're a fine one to lecture me about marriage," Henry scoffed.

"So, if a guy stays home with the children, and she's supporting the family, is it the same?"

"If he's stupid enough to put himself in that position, he deserves what he gets."

"So if everyone were smart, no one would have children."

"If people got married, stayed married, if men did their duty, and women raised the children, we wouldn't have any of these social problems."

"Yeah, and if everybody went to bed early, got up and punched their time card, mowed their little lawns, and waved a flag on the Fourth of July while they ate their homemade apple pie in front of cable TV, we'd be living in fucking Brave New World land and I would need something much stronger than Prozac."

"You're on Prozac?" Henry asked.

I shrugged. "Thinking about going off it."

I could tell that he was shocked.

"There isn't anything wrong with apple pie, of course," I said, "What I object to is conformity to a military style lifestyle in the name of economic productivity and world dominance. What good is living if twenty years from now, you're just an older version of this self? That scares the shit out of me, until I take another Prozac with exactly the right amount of single malt."

So self-indulgently maudlin, I could hear Esperanza saying it.

"Well, I like apple pie and all the rest, and I don't have to take any Prozac."

"So you never wonder what your life means, agonize, second-guess yourself, long for…something else?"

Henry wouldn't admit to any of it.

"What about Atlanta? Is she blissfully ensconced in your self-delusional paradise, as well?" I asked mockingly, getting angry now.

"What?"

"I'd bet anything Atlanta takes more Prozac than I do."

I didn't know why I said it, or how I knew it, I hardly knew her, but I had one of those moments of perfect clarity and I knew I was right. Henry was stunned. That I would venture such an comment on his wife's mental state, that I would have such an attitude about it, that I would be right, was all too much for him for about ten seconds.

"You don't know what you're talking about," he said.

I didn't, but that didn't change the fact that what I said was true. Thus, we sat quietly in the presence of this impasse until we stood up to leave.

Henry claimed he had some errand to do and walked off in the other direction. I walked out to the Pier One

Promenade and stood with my hands on the cold, metal railing and stared at the Bay. It felt good to be close to it, the water plashing gently in front of me and a stiff breeze blowing steady from behind.

A pleasure boat heavily burdened with tourists motored steadily away while the sailboats continued to skim across the water. Then from around the piers, the monstrous black hull of the *Yang Ming* appeared, towering like a moving island bearing a city on top of it. It passed behind the sailboats, causing them to bob about its hem like bathtub toys. The Chinese freighter proudly bore shipping containers the size of semi tractor-trailers rising seven high and sixteen wide along its length. Only a stack defiantly belching black smoke into the blue sky was visible over the top. As it turned and motored under the Bay Bridge and away, I could see that this city of boxes stretched twenty or thirty wide across the stern. This seemed to me the perfect example of the produce of our age: impressive and monstrous both. I was looking at these piled up human dreams, unnecessary goods stuffed into boxes and filling up not only this ship but countless others, each of them another nail in the coffin of this world, when a scruffy-haired elderly vagrant on the bench behind me began to mutter something to himself. His ramblings echoed with the same monotonous, helpless fury as my own thoughts. I turned to look at him. His eyes were the same washed-out blue color as my father's, but these were both vacant and wild. I walked around him and back toward the office.

I sat down at my desk and picked up a memo, subject: our bank's fervent need to get around bank regulations. The bank that fueled this department needed us to earn our keep and find it more money. I tried to make myself care, but couldn't.

Maybe it is an obsession, I thought, as I laid the memo back down on the open file in front of me.

Every time Ez and I talked about kids it always came back to time. If we had kids, we wanted to enjoy it and do it well, but if you place caring for your family ahead of making money for the people who own your time, you are not meeting the necessary standard of commitment. So you have to do both. When would we get to live? Was one weekend day, maybe two per week, plus a vacation once a year all you got to live your life, to grow? I tapped a pencil eraser on the file in front of me and remembered how we spent many midnight hours on our balcony, or up at the top of Twin Peaks getting slowly sloshed and discussing revolution.

We never said anything out loud, but we found a house in a neighborhood sandwiched between Noe Valley and the Castro, without any regard to the school district it was in. You had to climb dozens of steps to get to the front door. Esperanza, who valued her privacy, called it defensible space, loved it, and painted it a color she called Cuban Yellow. It had no yard to speak of, but an amazing view. It astonished me when she let me buy her out of it in the divorce. It was not only a house she loved, but as she well knew, a continuously, steeply appreciating asset. Although she made mountains of it, Ez cared nothing for money. Something had happened in her, something had made her want to break everything she had, and she did.

And now, as I looked out of my office window, my mind's eye travelling over the tops of the buildings, flying a bird's trajectory past the financial sector, over the Mission and up toward the hills where that house was, I realized that summer was gone and Christmas was coming. It was the season of harvest, of cutting down. It was not a good time for me. Esperanza left exactly one year after I had bought into the partnership, right before Christmas, and then Kate dumped me the next year, right after Thanksgiving.

"What will this Christmas bring?" I asked myself and immediately regretted it.

"I'm going home," I mumbled to my secretary, who glanced at her watch. It was only one thirty.

"See you in the morning," she called with mechanical deference.

Christmas

I rounded the curve at twice the posted speed and my too-tight tuxedo bit my neck. My BMW was the only car on the dark road up Twin Peaks and I felt strangely liberated, unaccounted for, out of bounds. I felt dangerous. My body wedged backward into the creaking leather seat as I accelerated savagely upward, out of the second curve. I had started out driving downtown to the firm Christmas party, but had turned and found myself driving up the steep winding curves of Twin Peaks instead. It was my third Christmas alone. It was just too much to have to go to this thing and pretend to be so self satisfied and magnanimous. Shaking all those limp wife and girlfriend hands. Talk and talk and talk without ever saying anything. I ground my molars together and gunned the engine around another curve. I could feel my blood pulsing hotly in the front of my head. Did nothing ever get any better? I gripped the steering wheel tighter as the tires squealed. Was there no way out? As if in answer, the tires skidded out beneath me, sending the car sideways. Eyes wide, grunting, heart pounding, I fought the steering wheel and brought the car to a skidding stop at the top of the last curve. I sat there panting and staring at the spot where Ez and I used to get out and sit at night. I accelerated and rammed the front wheels up over the six inch curb, bottomed out hard and then motored upwards until I stopped between two of the three cedar trees standing sentinel at the edge. I sat there gripping the steering wheel, my tensed thigh holding the brake firm. I was breathing hard as I stared out at the carpet of light coruscating beyond the precipice. I didn't blink or think a single thought for a long time.

Then, I pressed my right foot against the accelerator. Yes. I gunned the engine and it sounded good. My eyes traveled from Market Street, which stretched like a dark runway dividing the sea of light in front of me, decorated with a parade of shining crosses enclosed in a circle that reached upwards as a vast chandelier, to where those lights halted at the base of this wild hill. I dropped my eyes to the band of darkness immediately below me. I turned off the airbags and unbuckled my seatbelt. The dash began to beep insistently at me. It was beeping like a time bomb set to go off. Beep. It was egging me on. Beep. Just a shift of weight from one foot to the other. Beep. I breathed hard as both thighs tensed against the obedient machine, listening to the roaring engine and creaking brakes. I said goodbye.

I was blinded in the glare of headlights as a car rounded the curve, coming slowly down the wrong way from the parking lot. I took my foot off the accelerator as the car stopped in the road next to me.

"You okay?" the man yelled through the closed glass of my window. A woman craned her neck from behind him.

I opened my window enough to assure them that I was fine. I sat there, sweating and breathing hard, while they turned back onto the road. I exhaled.

Shifting Ground

"Fuck it," I muttered to myself as I watched their taillights turn to go down. I backed around to follow. Disgusted with myself, I stopped the car in the middle of the empty road and looked again at the spot between the two trees where the hill dropped off into the dark. I didn't want to go back down with my tail between my legs, but I had lost the will to vault into the darkness. Staring at that dark edge, I made a promise to myself: If I were still this miserable next Christmas, I would do it. I would die in a tragic car accident and Esperanza would get the insurance check. Wherever she is, the check would find her. When they told her where the car was found, she would know.

I was still in denial that I was actually going to attend the Christmas party when I handed the valet my car keys. I walked quickly through the wide double doors, dragging in the night air with me, walking unseeing, nodding mutely to the people who turned and spoke to me as I passed. I quickened my stride, swinging my arms, the breeze from my coat stirring the air and settling the tiny, snapping particles of cold evening around them like stars: impotent, tiny, exploding stars.

They didn't call it a Christmas party anymore, but it was, in fact, a good old-fashioned secular American Christmas, all types invited. I passed the enormous "holiday tree" and got a scotch first thing. I found an empty table at the back of the room and sat down against the wall where I could survey the entire room, but remain in shadow, separate. From this shadow, on the periphery of the shining sea of smiling faces, I saw the people I had passed in the hallway begin to wander through the ballroom. I slumped down casually, trying to remain invisible, but not resorting to making myself look ridiculous, should I be spotted. At least, not yet ridiculous.

Jesus. They were coming over, and soon they'd all come. Defeated, I put both hands on the table, sat up. They all came. The habit of place soon took me and I found myself spewing the same stock phrases, smiling the same smile, swallowing myself. And the evening was only one hour gone. I attacked a second scotch as I simpered and smiled.

That's when I had the brainstorm: I'm a partner at this firm, I'm the boss, and a white male to boot! If I'm half as powerful as everyone says I am, then by God, I shouldn't have to do anything I don't want! I don't want to be polite, I don't want to make small talk, and I'm sick of lying and listening to other people lie. Yes! I thought, now feeling lively, sitting up straighter. I will be completely and honestly myself. I will sit here and drink my own liquor and I will subject anyone who dares approach me to the spotlight of Sincerity and Truth. I capitalized the S and the T. I was now the only sincere person in the room! One is better than none! I thought giddily.

I looked out at the crush of people in front of me, all silk and sequins and expensive liquor. It has been said that there is a class of people who feel entitled to smash up things and creatures and then retreat back into their money. As certainly as that is still true, I thought to myself, it is now a new aristocracy of bankers, lawyers and CEO's who imagine they turn the levers of the world. Their whims are the highest law, consequences fall where they may for the great mass of people who don't matter.

I looked at the women in front of me trying to look casual in expensive dresses with the tags freshly ripped. I watched their affected sincerity that belied the constant stream of comments holding spears that carried the true meaning of the words. The outstretched fingers and quick speech that announced a moment of bonding through excoriating one not present. Aggression as art form, aggression as fluid as water, as subtle as mist, and just as easy to grasp. Then, the over-loud laugh that dissipated competitive tension, should it build past the customary level, and the little touches that brought the woman closer after she unconsciously recoiled from a passive-aggressive barb. The rule was that you hurt her, but not too much. Small numerous wounds, they, *picadores*, all.

Men were much more direct. Blue-collar men punched each other until the police came. These white-collar men talked money: whoever had the most, won. Their aggression was boring, ritualized. They stood still, talked in even tones, offered each comment without affect, like a card in a poker game. I watched them from my perch of Sincerity and Truth, watched them so busily engaged in the petty violence of everyday speech. I watched them, twisted my lip, and drank.

I now looked forward to the herd. Let them come, if they dare! I will expose them all.

Just then, materializing before me as if they had risen out of the floor like spooks, was a little associate and his even littler girlfriend.

"Merry Christmas, Mr. Davis, or rather," he caught himself and backpedaled, "Happy holiday season to you. We tried to catch you in the hall as you came in, but you were moving like a man on fire."

He laughed at his own joke, and kept the smile stretched across his face, tight as a canvas, long after he was finished with it. His skinny girlfriend smiled then, wrinkling her nose as she did so as if she were sniffing out a foul odor, as if it offended her sensibilities to have to smile.

"Ah," I thought, "Young Jones has gone slumming. She's not one of us." I smiled at them then. It was a slow, menacing smile that they, inexplicably, found encouraging, and they smiled even wider.

"Good God, look at him," I thought, "pretending he doesn't smoke pot."

Young Jones continued to babble about something, I didn't know what. They continued to smile their strident, stretched smiles. Look at him, I thought. Pretending that he wouldn't rather be an artist, a stand-up comedian, a farmer, anything, but a securities hack at the bottom rung of a law firm. Money, money, money. Acrylic paint and a black beret won't pay off that six figure debt sitting in the hand of a too fit, orange tanned New York banker, now will it, buck-o?

"Hey Bill," I interrupted him, "you smoke pot, Bill?"

He blinked his eyes several times in utter confusion before stammering, "Uh, no sir. Uh, why do you ask?"

"You're lying." I said it dispassionately, as a simple fact.

"Why don't you just admit to yourself that this was a huge mistake?" I continued, "Why don't you just admit that you never should have gone to law school in the first place? So what if you're in debt? The bank doesn't own your soul. You can pick that up and walk right out of here. Be an artist, be a bum, go to an ashram. Live an incredibly long time and die with forty grand still to go and tell them to go fuck themselves. Put it on your gravestone, Bill: 'Fannie Mae, go fuck yourself.'"

His little girlfriend was staring at him and then at me and back at him again, her eyes wide with alarm, and that sniffing smile still plastered on her pointy face, forgotten.

"I really don't..." he stammered, looking to his right and to his left, to orient himself, to try to play a game that had gone completely out of bounds and into dangerous hinterlands.

"Why did you do it?" I interrupted him again. "Why did you go to law school, in the first place?"

"I wanted..." he was on solid ground here, and started to repeat the same drivel he had parroted during his interview.

"Trying to please a too authoritarian father?"

He didn't respond.

"You wanted to be a rich guy. Bed more women? Because you just didn't know what else to do?"

He blinked after this last.

"Ah!" I said, and celebrated the solved mystery by grabbing another scotch from a passing waiter's tray. "The *raison d'être* of the vast majority of the legal workforce!" I toasted him. "You're smart, you want to do something with your life, college is quickly coming to a close and you must, you *must* maintain the illusion of industrious purposefulness that marks the successful man. You must not give up that hard won social dominance you had so carefully, so dutifully, worked for." I lowered my voice to a conspiratorial whisper. "People would have talked about you if you took a job in a coffee shop and went soul seeking. Can't have that, huh Bill? People. Talking."

I took my eyes from them. They were dismissed. I took a long swallow of my drink, and watched them out of the corner of my eye, watched them stand there three more beats not knowing what to do, before finally slinking away. I laughed.

Harvard, Stanford, Stanford, Yale. I labeled the lawyers I saw as they passed. I didn't tell you that all of these people were white; you just assumed it, I told the audience in my head. You always assume that unless you are told, specifically, otherwise, although in this context, it's understandable. All Caucasian with a handful of handpicked exceptions. I surveyed the room packed full of rich, pale people, all of them laughing at the same joke. Columbia, Yale, another Stanford. How many of these schmucks wrote long, sappy law school application essays about how they had each overcome a thousand species of handicap and hardship so that they could go to law school and change the world? You don't get into schools like that unless you can. I wonder if anyone ever wrote an essay declaring simply: "I've always done well in school, I've always managed to hold an advantage over others, I'm competitive (hooray for me!) and aggressive and I fully deserve to get everything I think I want. And what I think I want is to make a lot of money so that I can fuck around and have fun being one of the ordained elite and powerful of this society. I'll become a dutiful producer of wealth for a while in the hope that one day—very soon, mind you—I will be the beneficiary of that pyramid scheme that sits atop all of the other dutiful producers of wealth." I wonder if anyone has ever had the balls, or the ovaries, the whatever, to at least write that once, ball it up and throw it away before they brought on the tears.

After the triumphant cross examination of Young Jones, my company became a continuously moving transient population who, lured by the sea of empty seats around me, alighted, only to flee moments later, unable to bear the frightening and undeviating spotlight of Truth and Sincerity. I was feeling merry and proud of this, my courageous attempt to rise above the petty banality of superficial relations, to be completely honest and sincere.

I saw Alicia approaching from a distance, coming to pay her respects to the guy who had taken her under his wing, her source of manna. She was wearing a simple, black number hardly a shade darker than she was, and with her hair up and liquor-loosed muscles, she looked like a jazz singer. She had no little man in tow. She would at least spare me that, the awkward introduction to her sexual partner.

Trivialities were tripping off her tongue. She seemed happy and it annoyed me. I saw Henry standing across the room, waving his arms at a gaggle of sycophants gathered around him.

"Hey Alicia, ever wonder why Henry doesn't give you any work?"

She wasn't yet sure whether this were some kind of joke, and she narrowed her eyes at me before glancing at Henry.

Henry saw us looking at him. He stopped talking and shifted from one foot to the other.

"I really don't think this is the time or place," she said to me.

She wasn't afraid of me. I secretly congratulated her, but not even Alicia would escape the spotlight of my Sincerity.

"The black middle class isn't all it's cracked up to be, you know. Just because you see hoards of white guys stampeding after something, you shouldn't assume that it's something *good*. Maybe they're all idiots. You should really take a look at what it makes them," I swept my arm in front of me, "before you decide to go chasing after them."

She was looking straight at me.

I congratulated myself on my perfect, honest sincerity before adding, "By all means, use me as a perfect example. Alicia, you are going to end up just like me."

She pursed her lips.

"Oh that's right!" I knocked the heel of my hand against my forehead, "*You'll* be different. You'll just pay off your law school debt and then serve the underclass, go back *home*. You won't be corrupted, and you'll change the system *from within*."

She regarded me with a pitying affection that surprised me. "I never was a member of the underclass, Mike. My dad is a doctor." She bent down to me as if she were talking to a child.

"Shall I get you a cab?"

I waved her away. Esperanza's gesture, I thought. After realizing that I had been thinking about Esperanza for a while, I looked up so I could apologize to Alicia. The table was deserted.

Henry came over then with sycophants in tow.

"How are you doing there, Mike? I hear that you've been chasing away people in droves." He addressed me jovially for the benefit of his audience, then lowered his voice as he sat down next to me.

"If you insist on staying in your condition, I'm going to sit here and chaperone you until I see you in the back of a cab."

I responded by ordering another scotch.

I was watching her, Henry's wife, who was standing nearby. I was disappointed the first time I had seen this sucked-dry phantom of the woman I remembered from that long ago party. It had been years now since I had paid her any attention at all. Now it surprised me to notice the way she stood out in relief from everyone around her. Still. Her curling, jet-black hair was drawn up loosely, and her simple violet colored dress fell from her shoulders in a slim column that just grazed her hips. Her posture was imperfect, a deferential comma, rather than the assertive exclamation mark of those around her, but her grace made the effect charming. Her smile was shy, her every gesture drawn back before completed, and she stood back a step, ready to be dismissed. She had a full mouth built for pleasure, but she pressed her lips shut, only opening them in bursts, accompanied by nervous laughter and hands fluttering, promising self-effacement. Her undisguised insecurity, her passivity, her shyness should have made her disappear, but it didn't. Watching her made me think of the Byron lines that started, *She walks in beauty, like the night.* I couldn't remember the rest.

Henry paused in mid-sentence. I felt the arc of his eyes land on her, and it seemed to disturb the very air around her.

Henry hoisted himself out of his chair.

I looked back to where she was standing and noticed for the first time that she was talking to a small group of heavy hitters, all women. A woman of her kind broke the rules. They left her alone, except to use her as a break against the sea of aggression between them all.

Henry's back obscured her from my view, like an eclipsing moon, and then he came alongside her. He laid his palm on the small of her back and bent to speak to her softly, alone, inquiring. Her diamond earring swung back as she lifted her chin upwards, nestling her profile under his. Henry's eyes were heavy-lidded and warm, focused only on her as she responded. He slid his hand across her body and brought her hips close as they turned to face the other women. He talked for them both while caressing her waist. He made the other women laugh as he wrapped his arm around her. He broke them all up and then he came away with her.

The tense comma of her posture had been caressed lithesome, and when she turned to me, her lashes fell down over her irises in a way that loosed my joints.

"Mike, you remember my wife, don't you?" Henry said by way of introduction.

"Atlanta," she murmured as she extended her hand to me, palm down.

I nodded dumbly as I took her hand. She gave me a limp wife handshake. Her hand, enfolded trustingly in mine, both pressing and yielding, opened a door in me. Because the yielding hand was hers, I couldn't distain it. Because it was hers, I finally understood that this world would be better if we all touched hands like this. How silly and fearful now seemed the challenging grip I had always associated with strength!

"Don't pay any attention to Mike," Henry wiped me away with his eyes, and then, cocking his head he said, "Darling, why don't you come over here next to me? Mikey will move for you, won't you Mike?"

I stood up, and two associates stood up. The chair opposite was the only empty chair at the table, and we all needed to move around to make room. The second man nudged a third, who was talking, and pushed him into the empty chair.

"There you go," Henry said.

Atlanta sat down between Henry and I.

Now I was embarrassed about the Byron line, and undone by her nearness. I looked at her critically, from the side, to steady myself. She was studiously avoiding looking in my direction, thus, all I could see was her olive toned profile, illuminated by the flickering candles on the table. Tiny lines at her eyes broke the smooth plane of her face. She had a Greek's nose. Her diamond earring was askew, tangled in one loose corkscrew curl.

"What do you do?" one of the new associates asked her.

"I have children," she said, and her hands fluttered like little birds.

The new associate asked her the common questions about her kids, but then became drawn into the election year political conversation Henry was having with the other men. I was still stealing glances at Atlanta and she was watching people pass by until she finally decided that social protocol demanded that she look at me. Without understanding why, I dreaded her gaze. I ran away from her into the safety of my sincerity. As she opened up her mouth to say something, I interrupted her.

"You don't have to be polite to me. I'd just as soon you skipped it, actually. I find it annoying."

"You find politeness annoying?"

"Very." Then I added, "Feel free to ignore me, if you prefer."

She seemed to consider it, and then said, "I'm not sure I know how to affect the impoliteness you prefer, but I'd rather not ignore you."

Her words, her tone, was formal, self controlled, her very slight Southern accent now pronounced, as if she were channeling her very proper Southern grandmother. I jabbed a thumb in Henry's direction and lowered my voice to a conspiratorial whisper, "He's ignoring both of us, you know."

"Oh well, they are deep into something from before," she smiled.

"See. That's what I'm talking about," I said as her smile faded. "Why did you smile? Nothing is funny, nothing is pleasing. You smile because it's expected, you smile to be non-threatening, you smile because we're not talking about anything."

"Smiling is annoying?"

"Very." I gulped my scotch, avoiding her eyes. Instead I watched Henry, who was fending off carefully controlled and politic challenges to his dominance from the younger men.

"Like a pack of little wolves challenging the alpha male," I muttered.

"Pardon?"

"I think it is rude that he is ignoring you. It's unforgivable," I declaimed, making a fist and bringing it down on the table, mockingly. I left my gaze on my fist.

Out of the corner of my eye, I saw Henry incline his head in our direction.

"I thought you preferred rudeness," she said archly.

I looked up sharply to see her laughing eyes regarding me.

"I think you should say something," I declared, looking away from her again.

"Say something?" She seemed to consider this. "I don't know anything about banking law or politics." Her hand fluttered.

"Do you really think they are saying anything that matters? I think you should just break in and give some opinion. It doesn't matter what it is, so long as it's loud."

"She has better manners than you, Mikey," Henry interjected, and swiped the full glass of scotch I had in front of me. He smiled at me indulgently, like an older brother.

Atlanta made no response to this other than to close her mouth.

I reclaimed my scotch and listened to Henry and his Chicago Boys, muttering a running critique to the audience in my head. Finally, I tired even of this and turned to Atlanta again, this time turning on her the full glare of my spotlight.

"Why do you come to these events when you so obviously hate them?" I asked her, knowing that I could ask myself the same question.

Instead of throwing the question back at me, she bowed her head. I immediately felt like a bully. She was pausing reflectively as I was sitting there, sipping my scotch, pretending that I was still sincere and not, instead, uncomfortable and dissembling. She was taking her time, and in the moment of that unselfconscious pause, I felt her strength, that deep-rooted, solid strength in the center of her that made her weakness surprising. From that place, she raised her gray eyes to mine, so matter-of-factly, so nakedly, that my eyes ran away from hers, retreated, and settled, unfocused somewhere in the center of her face as she spoke in carefully measured phrases.

"Henry needs me here. Although I don't seem to say anything or do anything, I do seem to help him invisibly in some way. I know that women don't always stay home nowadays, but if she does, it should be her joy to support her husband in whatever way she can."

"But it's not your joy, is it?"

"Yes. Good for you, Mr. Davis." The reply was instantaneous, but delivered with a quietude that stilled the air rather than stirred it, "You have successfully smoked it out."

Before I could say anything, I felt her hush me, silently, as she swallowed.

"I just don't understand why it seems so necessary to him," Her eyes rolled around the table, settled on Henry, for just one moment. "To everyone, that I come, yet once I am here, no one seems to notice or care, like I'm a box that needs only to be checked off." She found my eyes, opening hers as wide as a horizon, "Do you know what I mean?"

I bowed my head, speechless. I felt the sweat on my body. I felt my stomach bulging obscenely between my separated cummerbund and pants. She had burst the bubble of my sincerity, leaving me naked and exposed. We're cannibals, I thought to myself, but we don't consume our own kind, if we can help it. We were both sitting there looking away from each other, silent, though I could feel her waiting for me to say something. Poor thing, I thought, don't you see? We need your tacit promise of subordination to the rules, to the pyramid scheme that makes us what we are. Your slender shoulders hold up much of the weight of this monstrosity, but if we acknowledge that with any but the most condescending, patronizing, and empty gesture, we reveal too much. Somehow we have convinced you that this pyramid scheme has a genie inside it, a god that is worthy of your sacrifice of self. We know that if you opened those mystified portals and saw that it is only a created beast, a maw with legs, you would turn away in horror that you had ever given away anything at all.

I said nothing, for who was I to say anything to this woman who was so much better than I was in every way.

She raised four fingers to her throat in alarm, "Did I say something to offend you?"

"What did she say?" Henry interrupted, his tone insecure. He was upset that he had been distracted, had missed it.

"Nothing," I said, smiling my most sincere crocodile smile. "She was just telling me that she felt that the recent Supreme Court opinion regarding arbitration due process was not so entirely wrong."

"Oh, please." Henry sighed.

I ignored Henry, who was trying to start a conversation with me over her head to reassure himself.

"Is your family from Georgia, is that where your name comes from?" I leaned in towards her so that she could hear me over Henry. Our shoulders were almost touching and the nearness created a warm envelope of frisson around us.

Her face brightened. "Yes, an obvious guess, I suppose. My mother liked the idea of naming me after the first thing she saw after I was born. It was nighttime, and as she raised her eyes from childbed, she saw the lights of Atlanta spread out below."

"Your mother is a romantic," I said, and Henry rolled his eyes at me.

"Is your mother still there, in Atlanta?" I asked, ignoring him.

"Yes, yes she is."

Atlanta folded her hands together on the white tablecloth, and I felt her draw away.

"She must not like being so far from her grandchildren?"

"The kids and I go out to see them every summer for two weeks."

"And that is quite enough!" Henry laughed.

I was confused about why she was so far away now.

Atlanta glanced in Henry's direction, "Since Henry and I were married…."

"After we were married, we moved out here, and it's just too far to travel with the kids," Henry said.

"Henry and my mother do not get along very well," she explained.

"Heathens, the both of them, just like you, Mikey," Henry laughed.

"My father is Jewish," Atlanta said quietly, "and he still celebrates some of the holidays."

I wanted to ask about that, but Henry launched into some story I wasn't really listening to. I was watching her. The bones of her shoulders slumped forward and the plane of her face winced in the outside corner of her eye, even as she maintained a congenial expression. Henry was teasing her, making jokes about her parents. She responded good naturedly after each riposte, admitting all, pausing after each spoken phrase as if speaking the words required her to dredge forward stores of latent strength, like a flame that pushes upward one final burst of orange flare before it is extinguished. His story finished, Henry turned to talk to someone else.

It made my heart ache to watch her retreat into herself. I tried to think of something to say but couldn't. I leaned in close to her to reach a napkin, and then left my thigh next to hers. She looked down and stared at her fidgeting fingers curled around her empty glass, but didn't move away. I gazed at her while she looked at her hands. I traced the line of her glossy lips to where they met plush and indecent at the crease. I memorized the small freckle hovering above her jaw. I wanted to reach out one finger and release the diamond earring.

As our two legs became warm there together, I felt again between us that envelope of silent intimacy that made me want to be better.

One of the younger men had said something about his girlfriend who worked at another firm and they were all laughing. I wasn't listening anymore.

She had profoundly unsettled me, but it wasn't just a sexual attraction. I wanted to restore her. I wanted to be the one who laughed when she said something mildly shocking.

Henry was going after the associate with the lawyer girlfriend. He asked him whether he was the dominant or the subordinate, because he had to be one or the other.

"Ez was probably the boss," I mumbled to myself.

"Pardon?"

Atlanta's face was in front of mine. I didn't know she could hear me.

"Esperanza, my ex-wife. You probably don't remember her. She never came to these things. I was just saying that if anyone had to be the boss, it was probably her."

"Oh," she said. She turned toward me, but left her thigh next to mine.

"We were still kids when we married…though it wasn't because we had to. No shotgun wedding or anything. We never had any kids," I babbled without being asked. My mouth seemed to move slowly, but the words came out too fast. I could no longer feel the tips of my fingers on my glass.

"Yes, that's why you could be equal," she said, "Having children changes everything. The woman stays at home with them and then she's no longer equal."

I didn't say anything. This talk of children cut too close. A new level of drunkenness had settled upon me as the scotch sitting in my gut metabolized. This, my nervousness, and my unstable mood imploded at a spot just below my sternum.

"It's because people work too much," I said, "All the rich people who control everything have got everybody lower down in the pyramid scheme convinced that making their bosses more money is the highest calling! They make everybody work harder and harder, until they don't have any time to do anything but work and sleep, and enjoy rare three-day holiday weekends!"

Having said this with a straight face, I laughed out loud at the monumental, monstrous irony of my diatribe against all the rich people. I couldn't stop laughing and had to lean my hand against my forehead.

She had moved her thigh away from mine.

"They aren't equal," she said with purposeful seriousness, "because he makes the money. I work around the clock, but I don't have anything to show for it."

We were talking about *her* now, her and Henry. She's a maid without a commute, Henry had told me. I pushed away my glass.

"Why does the money matter?" I demanded, "Why does the money make him boss? Money is just a thing. Is it more important than intelligence, spirit, wisdom?"

"Well no."

"If one person is stupid as a post and immoral to boot, does money redeem him? Do you place him as master over your life just because you have none?"

I had passed into that zone of drunkenness when the brain is completely fogged, but the mouth could still somehow speak with an intelligence that mystifies the speaker.

"Marriage is different," she objected.

The alcohol had opened me up, and I remembered that this was why I drank. I could feel her frustration. I could sense the wall of feeling she held in check behind her mild words. I felt her need. I desperately wanted to be her champion. And then, I caught the glimmer of something important. I wasn't sure of it yet, but she was still waiting for me to say something.

"Let me put it to you this way." My head swam and I temporarily lost track of it. I shook my head in frustration and then caught it, "Yes. Yes," I said to myself approvingly. "Let me put it to you this way. Money is like air or water, it just flows around. Manna, you know? All manna comes from…well, your God, say. If all manna comes from God, and is only distributed by men…."

She nodded her head, leaned her body toward me and met my eyes. The impact of her grey eyes, staring unblinking and attentive into mine, and the once again nearness of her thigh, completely unbalanced me. I had lost it again, and started over.

"If we are all one," I began, focusing intently, "If all of us are one in the human family, then we should very naturally want everyone to be happy. We should want to share everything, all the manna that comes from one source…your God, if you will. It's only because we're all split up into these primitive tribes with allegiances, and we hoard and vie for power with each other. It makes so much waste, you see?"

It was becoming clearer. It was the waste. The waste of destruction, of competition, of hoarded assets.

"Everyone could have plenty," I said, sure of it, "So, if you think of it like that, like we are all one, and manna is all one, it seems so natural to share, to direct it together. There would be no reason to pile it up for yourself, guard it from others."

"That's a nice idea, Michael," she said, "but in the real world, you can't do anything without it, and therefore, those who have it have more bargaining power, as you lawyers say. They can say, I have something y'all need, and I'll only give it to you if y'all do what I want. People do that all the time."

I was deep in my vision, I could see so clearly how people would naturally give things to each other, not feeling like it was theirs, like it was divinely appropriated, in the first place. I clearly saw how manna wanted to flow like water, how it hated the dam. I clearly saw that economies were spoiled by the fear of scarcity.

"If I weren't afraid that I would be penniless at retirement, I would give away everything I have sitting idle and useless in the bank right now, today!" I declared wonderingly. "It's a species of faith!"

As I said it I realized that it was Truth and almost wept with joy. I saw her trying to get it, trying to take me seriously, when one of the associates nudged me, laughing.

"Are you going to let him get away with that?" he asked me, still laughing.

"What?" I demanded impatiently, mentally scrabbling at my fading vision.

"Henry is impeaching your manhood," another chortled.

"Henry seldom has anything better to do," I mumbled, trying to ignore him, trying to repeat the words, resurrect the feeling I had while saying them.

"Seriously," Henry said, still smiling from whatever it was he said before, "women and men are different biologically. Women are nicer," Henry chuckled, "and they are just exhausting themselves swimming upstream when they try to take on the male role."

"Thas' a load of crap," I bawled loudly, not even bothering to look at him, murderously furious at them all for interrupting me before it became solid, something I'd remember tomorrow.

I noticed that Atlanta was sitting up straight, and her thigh was gone.

"Women are perfectly good leaders in any environment, but especially in those they change to suit themselves." I raised a finger as I said it, thinking of Atlanta's gentle hand. "Which is just what is happening, and that's what you're afraid of. As for myself, I like having the gals around."

The younger people laughed approvingly.

"I know it offends you to hear the word God, Mikey," Henry said, "but He created this environment, as you call it, and the way it's being changed is not natural. That's why we're having so many problems."

Henry sounded composed and reasonable, and this I could not tolerate.

"So God hauled his fat ass down here and published himself a book, did he?" I grabbed the scotch I had pushed away before and drained it by half.

Henry turned red, before smiling at me indulgently again, cocking his head on one side. "His truth was given to divinely inspired saints who wrote it down, and people have been using those sacred writings to guide their lives for two millennia now."

An associate started to argue with Henry about whether God was male—wasn't the creation of new life more naturally the province of a great mother God?

Big Dada in the sky, Big Mama in the sky, what does it matter, for crying out loud? I didn't really care about any of it, but I desperately wanted to beat Henry. Beat him at his own stupid game.

"Him and his circuituitous arguments," I mumbled, my head swimming now, but no one was listening to me anymore.

How does one defend against such fantasies? I silently fumed. It's the same as saying that I'm right because space aliens who live on Uranus and eat green cheese know everything and they dispense this wisdom through laser beam transmissions to the telepathic brains of crazed and celibate schizophrenics, who then dutifully write it all down for us. They support my every opinion on everything. How do you argue about the—past, always in the distant past—existence of men who raised the dead, performed magic, got up from their own deathbed, sprouted wings and flew up to heaven? Yeah, the Big Daddy in the sky told me that I get to dominate women, children, animals, weaker men, the environment, and the New York Stock Exchange, by God. Those Uranus dwelling, green cheese eating wiseacres gave me everything, and I wrote it all down very carefully so I can justify anything.

My head swam and I burped out one word.

"Bullshit."

"Now that's an intelligent argument," Henry announced jovially.

I saw a smile playing on the lips of Atlanta Buchanan and I wanted more than anything to make her smile like that again.

"And the aliens gave all the power to only one kind of person, too," I continued out loud the conversation I had been having with them inside my head, "the ones who were already pushing everyone around."

They were all staring at me.

I burped again, and then spoke slowly and clearly. "Don't you think it's a little too convenient that the space alien wisdom is exactly what you want to hear? Huh?"

I sat back, satisfied that Henry's circular and hypocritical logic was exposed for all to see.

"What?" Henry's jaw remained open in amazement.

I could tell by the way they were all looking at me that I hadn't gotten it out just right.

Later, I found myself on the sidewalk, revived by a bracing, cold wind. Henry was hailing a taxi. I looked around for Atlanta, but she was gone.

"Where'd everybody go?" I demanded.

"They're all going home," Henry said, still waving one hand at the passing cars.

"Where's my coat?" I mumbled, turning around in a circle.

Bright lights erupted from the undulating pavement. I stumbled forward.

"I've got it." Henry seized my bicep. "Just stand still or you're going to fall down in front of everyone."

A taxi pulled up, but I was suddenly very happy and didn't want to get in.

"Jus' you and me, Henry. Le's go out, jus' you and me."

"I'm not going to try to suggest that you go to my church," Henry said.

"Oh, good."

"And I'm not the type to go running to a therapist, myself," he continued.

"That shows!" I shuffled my feet in a little jig.

"But you can't go on like this, Mike. By next Christmas, we're gonna find you a wife."

I fell into the cab backwards, and Henry put in my feet.

"Oh!" I laughed. "You think this is about Esperanza." I leveled my wobbling gaze on him, "It's not about Esperanza."

Henry And The Boys

"How was your Christmas?" Henry asked me as he settled into the visitor's chair opposite my desk.

It was my first Monday back after a week in Miami for Christmas. It was a new year, although nothing about it felt new to me. I guess I should have been grateful that nothing bad had happened this Christmas, for a change. But then, nothing happening was another species, or a cousin, of something bad.

"Miserable," I confessed, "I broke down and went back to Miami. Stayed at my father's apartment on the fold out." I shrugged. "Saw some old friends. We were all just sitting around not talking about You Know Who."

I raised my voice, "And I know they know where she is, and they know I know, and I know that they won't tell me and so I don't even bother to ask."

Henry dismissed the mention of Esperanza by closing his eyes.

We were interrupted by my secretary who came in without looking at me and wordlessly left a folder on my desk before marching back out.

"She's not talking to you?" Henry smirked.

"Something I said to her at that damn party," I said, "I don't remember what it was and she won't tell me."

Henry laughed.

"Someone is gonna do an intervention on you," he warned me.

"It's been a whole week since I've had a single drink."

"You in AA?"

"No." I shrugged. "I just decided I'd quit for awhile. Seeing firsthand what a miserable wretch my father has become made me lose my taste for it."

"He drinks?"

"Always has, though when my mother was alive, she made him moderate, both the booze and the horses. Now, all bets are off." I was indulging in a grim chuckle when I saw Alicia in the doorway. "Hey! There's someone who is still my friend."

Alicia raised one eyebrow at Henry.

"Good morning," he said, only turning his head to glance at her.

"What's up?" I asked her, "Henry and I were just gossiping like a couple of schoolgirls."

I said it to annoy him. He drummed his square, manicured nails on my desktop.

A sardonic smile kissed the corners of Alicia's lips, but she squelched it. "It's not that urgent. I'll be in my office when you're ready."

"I'll be there in a minute," I said and she smiled at us both and left.

"Well Mikey, I'd better let you get to it," Henry slapped both of his thighs as he stood, "But, we gotta get together. There's someone I want you to meet."

"No and no."

"Atlanta picked her, not me."

That made a difference and because I didn't say anything, I left the question open and Henry knew it.

"I'll set it up," he said gleefully and left.

"I didn't promise anything!" I yelled after him.

The days of the week passed just like that, each like the orderly, regular tick of a clock, and the empty detritus of daily life got bagged and hauled to the street with the garbage on Friday. Everyone knew Friday was different. Any other day of the week I could work until seven or eight without really noticing it, but on Friday, I started feeling restless by three. It was the agitated feeling that something might happen. It was both threat and promise. It was the train you ran to catch without even knowing where it would take you.

After another week slipped silently by, I found myself staring out the plate glass window at the fading sunset, wondering what I would do with Friday night. I could go to the gym, but I'd already thought about going to the gym every day this week.

Getting into my car, I thought about going to a bar. I always felt at home in a bar. Bars were bursting with that strident frisson of expectation, all that bright sharpness mixed with pride, dissimulation, and despair masquerading as a good time. All of it dimmed and drowned out by loud sounds and alcohol. I always loved going to bars. Then, I drank, I stumbled home, left my clothes on the floor, slept face down, and woke up disappointed on Saturday. Whether I went home with someone or not, Friday always felt like a one-night stand, the empty and discarded husk of potentiality.

Nah, I said to myself, going out to drink is that name in your address book you don't want to call. Beside it you have written, Do Not Call This Person. But you don't rub out the name entirely, do you?

No, I didn't rub it out, I said as I poured myself a scotch and walked out onto the balcony. It'd been two weeks, after all. I had never before realized how women were the key to everything. In middle age, if you didn't have a woman, you were a lost soul. All of our old friends were home with their children, or out having dinner with other couples. Was there anyone in this entire city who would read to me as I lay in the hospital, the AIDS hospice?

Then it occurred to me that Henry would. Henry would read to me, I was sure of it.

"Atlanta?" I asked the woman who answered the phone, and I realized that I was unaccountably nervous.

"Mary."

"Oh, uh, Mary, could I please speak to Henry?"

"May I ask who is calling?"

"Sure, Mike," I said, and then unsure, added, "from work."

I heard her yell at Henry, "Mike from work!" It made me feel ridiculous and sorry I called.

"Mikey!" Henry's voice, fulsome with pleasant surprise, steadied me. "We're not doing anything much. The boys picked out a video and we're just sitting down to watch it. Atlanta will read a book and only pretend to watch it with us. We can hold off until you get here."

Henry understood perfectly why I was calling. I was hoping that Henry and I could go out, maybe to his club. I tried to picture myself there at his house, sandwiched between Henry and Atlanta with her book on the couch.

"Thanks, Henry, I, uh, don't think I can make it tonight, but, what are you doing this weekend?"

"I'm playing golf with the boys tomorrow. I know you don't play golf, but why don't you come anyway? Neither of the boys is any good either."

I heard the boys protesting in the background, and Henry laughed at them.

"All right. You want me to meet you there?"

"Yeah, meet us at two-thirty, our tee time is three."

"We're having tea first?" I don't know why I had to be an asshole, but it made me giggle silently like a teenager.

"No," Henry exhaled, exasperated, "the tee is…it's part of the game. Just be there at two thirty, okay? And Mike?" Henry paused, considering, "Let's not meet at my club. Don't go to the Olympian. Let's meet at the Presidio. Yeah, the Presidio will be perfect."

The next morning, I awoke with the feeling that something might happen. I woke up hungry. Pawing around in the empty refrigerator in search of the makings of a big, sizzling American style breakfast, I realized I had to go to Bell Market.

Bell Market was only four or five blocks around the corner and it felt good to walk. I hiked up to the top of 22nd, and then stopped and turned around, winded, for a look at my corner of the city. I loved this view. From here I could see the palms of Delores, Guerrero, Valencia, and Potrero and then the hills rising beyond stretched out in front of me. I stood there on the corner, my hands on my hips, breathing hard, and watched all the cars speeding through the intersections, the people walking purposefully across them. I sighed deeply, bid them good morning, and turned down Sanchez.

From across the parking lot, I saw the row of regulars panhandling outside the front doors of the market, and I steeled myself for that gauntlet. The first one was probably about my own age but of course, looked much older. He had a round, red cheeked face, bleary, alcoholic eyes, and unusually large hands with deep, dirt filled cracks running across the palms and fingers. Hands that had seen a lot of rough use.

"Spare some change?" he asked while the others watched.

I frowned and shook my head. We're not supposed to give them money, I reminded myself. He'll just use it to drink himself to death. The other men looked down, but as I passed the last one, feeling helplessly discomfit, the man held out his hand.

"Fuck it," I swore, "go buy yourselves a twelve pack."

I handed the man a bill.

"Wow! Thanks!" the man grinned.

"We ain't gonna drink," the first one slurred.

"Okay."

"Really, we ain't."

I passed through the automatic doors into the soothing coolness of the market, feeling that peculiar release always attendant upon bold and useless action. I picked up sausage, coffee, eggs, a loaf of bread, orange juice, butter and jam. Every item seemed to me to be fulsome with vitality, every item an answer.

"Find everything alright?" the doe-eyed cashier asked brightly, automatically.

I nodded when she glanced up at me. I didn't want to stare at the large, machinery metal stud protruding through her lower lip, so I looked away. My eyes rested instead upon a large, cheerful sign announcing that it only costs $2.49 to feed a hungry person. As I watched my own largesse pass in front of me on the checkout conveyer belt, I pushed a bill into the can underneath the sign.

"Does it do any good?" I muttered.

The cashier glanced up, and shrugged, "I think so. I mean, it's the difference between eating and not eating for some people."

"Does it do any good, though?"

She stared at me for a moment and then said, "Thirty-four ninety-five."

Outside the market, the men were on their feet, trying to look casual. They all nodded at me, saying good day, have a good one. As I turned the corner of the building, I looked back and saw them jostling each other through the automatic doors, which admitted them into that coolness.

I chuckled to myself.

Back at home, I watched the playoffs and ate until I couldn't anymore. Then I got myself a beer and walked out onto the balcony. The fog was completely burned out of the low places now, and I could see the crown of hills all around me. This city was one of the brightest stars in the constellation of cities across the globe. It occurred to me that it was rather like a white dwarf that burns brightly by consuming everything around it. Was it possible that this wealth could expand the city infinitely or would it go supernova in a cleansing blast and burn everything away? Right now, the only thing it seemed to be burning away was the credulous, the struggling, the middle class, who already had to commute forty minutes to serve authentic chain store burritos in the Mission for minimum wage.

Yeah, the dot-com industry and all his minions came in smooth, like a lover, knocked her up and then left as quickly as he came, leaving the city with a cheap commodified electroplate patina that rubs off. Everything that brought us here, Ez and I, was no longer apparent, dominant, but has been driven out or underground. It was franchised, normalized, and bureaucratized. The genie of San Francisco was now available in bottles and cans for on-line purchase. It was a tourist's Disneyland simulacrum, and for the first time I thought about leaving.

I thought about this as I drove to the club. Maybe I needed to get back to my roots. Was it really me who was driving a BMW across town in order to stand around on acres of poisoned grass all day and then dine at the club? When did I start wanting to? I just took what was offered, what was easy.

"You remember Mr. Davis," Henry said to the boys as I walked up.

Henry handed me a soda from a small cooler and Matthew huffed as he started dragging Henry's golf bag behind him.

"How are you?" Henry asked with mechanical good humor.

"Never been so obsessive, self absorbed, and disoriented in all my life," I said with mechanical good humor.

The boys just stared at me.

"Oh, so it's gonna be a day like that," Henry said.

"I'm fine."

"Please be fine," Henry said, "At least for today."

"What is so special about today?" I asked.

Shifting Ground

"Nothing," Henry drew a curtain across his face, "It's a nice day. We should have a great time."

As the cart silently rolled over the grass to the first hole, Henry was talking to the boys. He was asking them golf questions like, what is a duff? What is that patch of grass you knock out of the ground called? The boys were yelling, vying with each other to be the first to answer, and so, as we approached the hole, Henry had to quiet them. We were early, and there was a foursome ahead of us. Henry stopped the cart a polite distance away and retrieved a soda for himself.

Henry was talking about golf. He was telling the boys how golf started in Scotland, and then was appropriated by Great Britain. As those Kings reached their grasping fingers Eastward, the game was then deposited by that great conquering empire, like cowbird eggs, in the clean, flowering fields of the other nations it conquered. It was the sport of conquerors, Henry said, and the boys should approach the game with a respectful attitude.

Joshua gleefully teed up first, and then looked at us smiling.

"Focus!" Henry commanded, "The wind, the grass, the distance are your enemies. Stand against them and conquer."

Joshua's features drew themselves up into a kindergarten scowl as he squinted into the sun, sighting the hole. His sturdy body flexed and swung, and he hit it quite a long way for a little boy.

"Well done!" Henry exclaimed. "Go, Matthew," Henry said.

"Nah." Matthew avoided Henry's gaze as he anxiously smashed the back of one hand across his freckled nose. "You guys can go first."

"Go," Henry said.

Matthew reluctantly teed his ball.

"Now remember what I told you. Focus. And don't break your wrists like you always do. Keep them straight," Henry exhorted him, "and relax! Keep your swing relaxed!"

I could see that Matthew's hands were shaking and I found myself angrily pressing the dented golf ball in my pocket.

Matthew prepared to swing, broke off, prepared again, but decided to sight the hole again.

Henry huffed impatiently.

Matthew glanced up at us, Henry and I standing there together watching him, nervously exhaled, steeled himself, and swung. Though six years older, Matthew's ball flew only as far as Joshua's and veered sharply right, kicking up almost to the rough.

Henry sighed ruefully.

Drawing himself up to his full stature, Henry walked to the tee and sighted his shot. He then looked at the three of us as a man looks at a crowd some distance away, aloof and challenging. Henry wiped away everything else and looked through us to confirm that he had done so as he positioned his body. He glared at his enemies, the impediments, and became more dense as the very air around him was drawn into him by gravitational force. Then he swung.

It was a remarkably lovely swing and the ball did exactly what it was asked to do. It flew to the right of the bunker and rolled to a stop. One drop more push on the drive and it would have been on the green.

"Caddy this, won't you?" Henry said to Matthew, handing him the club.

Henry turned away, but I saw how Matthew hung his head and then complied.

My hand shook as I placed my warm ball on the tee. There was nothing I could do about it now. I exhaled my aggression and looked down the fairway. It was a par four. I absentmindedly reached into the bag for the two iron.

"You can't use just any club, you know," Henry told me, "you'd better use this one."

He handed me a three wood.

I shrugged and made a face at the boys, who giggled.

God I hate this game, I thought. I had taken it up when I was a kid, mostly to annoy my father, who called it a sissy's sport. That went pretty well until I started winning and he and his friends discovered that they could bet on my rounds. He came to every competition, stalked my practices, and gave me second or third hand advice on my form. He called me the Florida Hurricane. While I had always craved his attention in my youth, by adolescence I was far too jaded to be flattered. That man would bet on a dog's bowel movements. By the time I was a medalist at the NCAA regionals, I was sick to death of it, and swore I would never play again.

I squinted into the sun, spotting the flag off to the left of the green, close enough to a bunker to be trouble. It was possible, even out of practice, that I could have a birdie. With the club Henry gave me, though, the best I could do was whack at it for a par. Did I retrieve the two iron? If

Henry knew I could play, he would be forever after me to play with him, and, of course, he would be manic about beating me. He would become unbearable if he couldn't. Anyway, I didn't care at all about impressing Henry, and I sure as hell didn't want to play into his sport of conquerors bullshit.

I assumed poor posture, cracked my wrists, and made faces at the boys, who giggled. All the while, Henry was trying to instruct me.

"Bend over the ball!" Henry said, "Without sticking your butt out. No! You're sticking it out more!"

The boys giggled at my slapstick golf parody but Henry remained clueless.

"You know, Henry," I said, "I've seen on TV how guys will snuggle up behind someone to teach them how to swing." I batted my eyes at him.

The boys laughed.

"With girls!" Joshua laughed, "They do that with girls!"

"Good God, Mike, just hit the damn thing."

"Here goes!" I said, and hacked it like a credible first timer.

"Hey Mikey, not bad," Henry said, his impatience gone.

Henry gave the boys no quarter, so getting to the putting green took some time. Joshua was playing well with a charming childish insouciance, while Matthew struggled. As for myself, playing a game like this took skill, and club selection was everything—wood on the putting green, the putter to get it out of the rough. I carried around the three wood damp in my palm and used it for everything except drives. By the fifth hole, I was exhausted and just wanted to go home.

We were on the putting green of the fifth hole when Henry got a phone call.

"Yeah," he said, glancing up at me, "we're here. We're on the fifth, the putting green. Okay, that's perfect."

Henry gave me a cat's smile and then put away the phone, smiling to himself.

"What?" I asked him.

"Nothing," he said, "Atlanta."

I glanced at Matthew, who then turned away as he attended the flag, waiting for me to putt. He knew something.

"If you use the putter, Mikey, instead of being so stubborn, you'd do a lot better," Henry said, extending it.

Glancing again at Matthew, I said, "I like this one. It's prettier."

By now, Henry was onto me and he had become completely exasperated, trying to bully me into making an effort. But now all of that was gone, and he just shrugged and gave me that same cat's smile.

"Suit yourself," he said.

I looked at Matthew, who looked away again. I was too impatient to goof around anymore, so I just putted it in, three wood and all.

"Onward!" Henry yelled exuberantly, extending his club ahead of him.

Driving to the sixth hole, Henry was inspired to sing "Onward Christian Soldiers" the entire distance in his loud baritone, which almost put us all into a good mood.

He was equally gleeful as he teed up his ball, so that he almost forgot to set the example of Darwinian predatory competitiveness for his sons.

When we had all teed off, Henry suggested that we stop for a snack.

"Won't the other people catch up to us?" Joshua asked.

"Nah, there's no one behind us," Henry said, taking a sandwich out of the cooler and tossing it to Matthew.

When we had finished eating, Henry was looking around, getting annoyed. The boys and I packed the cart, and Henry reluctantly stood up. As we were getting in to leave, Henry stopped and smiled.

"I think I see something we left," he said, jumping out.

The vinyl seat was sticking to the backs of my sweating thighs and I was getting impatient, when a cart drove up and parked right next to us.

A fuzzy haired woman with bright lipstick hopped out next to me.

"Are we moving too fast?" she asked.

"Uh, we teed off, and dawdled, I'm afraid," I told her, putting one leg out of the cart and half standing, by way of apology.

"Oh, so you haven't putted yet." She frowned toward the fairway.

It was then that I noticed that the woman in the passenger seat was staring at me. She had very blonde hair that darkened at her scalp, a color I knew came out of a bottle, and bright lipstick. She got out and came around to stand in front of me so that it was difficult not to notice that she had large breasts and well-honed biceps. I didn't want to stare back, so I focused on the fuzzy haired woman.

Henry came striding over and extended his hand, "I'm Henry Buchanan."

"Hi, I'm Amy," she said as she shook his hand, "and this is Carol."

"Are we in the way?" Henry asked.

"Oh, no!" Amy said, "Don't think of it. We could all just play together."

"We were just playing the front nine," Henry said.

"Us too!" she squealed, "It's fate!" she squealed again, looking at me.

Carol, the blonde woman, was still staring at me, but looked away when I noticed.

I glared at Henry and he smiled at me in return.

I was then obliged to stand up and introduce myself. Henry squared his body in front of the boys and put his hands on his hips. "Boys, you'll have to become spectators at this point, okay? It's only three more holes."

Joshua said, "Yes sir," and then dropped his gaze to the ground.

Amy teed off first.

"You don't mind too much, do you?" Carol whispered into my left ear.

I was startled, because I didn't notice that Carol was standing so close to me.

I silently shook my head and smiled.

"I warn you," she said, "I haven't played golf in a really, really long time."

She giggled and smiled coquettishly as Amy hit her ball.

We all watched it, a decent drive, land, bounce and then rest square in the fairway.

"Don't worry," I smiled at her, "the boys were beating me."

My initial annoyance was wearing off and I was starting to relax, but there was something else too. I looked at her again, and she smiled brightly before nimbly skipping to the tee.

She was very light, I thought to myself. I'd never paired with light, but maybe it would be good for me. She hacked a drive that flew a wayward trajectory, though it flew farther than I expected.

She giggled and shrugged.

When we all arrived at the putting green, the women parked next to us and we all got out, chatting about the hole. Joshua sulked in the cart until Henry turned, fixed him in his eyes and jerked a thumb toward the pin.

"Joshua, attend the flag."

Carol smiled at me before she putted her ball, which rolled straight to the cup and dropped in.

"Wow!" Amy exclaimed.

Carol smiled at me again.

I used the putter and dropped the ball in the cup. I pretended to be amazed at my luck.

Henry was scrutinizing the grass, running his hand over the top of it, when I leaned in next to Matthew and whispered, "Henry knows Carol, doesn't he?"

Matthew drew a curtain across his face in excellent imitation of Henry.

"I don't know. Maybe you should ask him," he said.

"If I get it on the green on the seventh will you tell me?"

Matthew looked at me and laughed.

"You're not gonna get anywhere near it," Matthew snorted.

"But if I do."

Matthew waved one hand through the air. "I'll tell you whatever you want. I'll turn into a big yellow bird and fly away."

Matthew began to flap his arms and Joshua, only half understanding our exchange, began to imitate him.

Henry was preparing to putt and quieted them with a warning gaze.

Henry watched his ball roll across the green and drop into the cup. He rubbed his hands together.

We all jumped in the carts and bounced over to the seventh hole.

When it was my turn to tee off, Matthew was smiling to himself as he stood unobtrusively aside. I walked out to the tee and surveyed the course. I had noticed when the others had teed off before me that there was a little breeze that vaulted over the trees and pushed the drives from the left. The power drive had always been my strength, if I still had it in me.

I took the three wood out of Henry's bag and teed up my ball.

"The three wood is actually a good choice here," Henry said with a smirk.

Just like riding a bicycle, I told myself as I gripped the club. I extended it in front of me and felt the muscles of my shoulders resist, then give and relax into position. As I gazed down the fairway, everything became silent as I fixed the pin with my eyes and made that energetic lock on it. Looking down at the club face addressing the ball, I could feel it, the pin. The solidity of my body gave way to the hum of the golf genie pervading my limbs and it filled me with electric body memory. I knew I would do it. I drew back, swung and hit a perfect drive that flew straight to the hole along the trajectory of my gaze. It not only landed on the green, but rolled and rolled and then dropped from sight into the cup.

Both women jumped up and screamed.

"Oh my God!" Carol threw her arms around my neck and I could feel the soft crush of her breasts against me, "That was great!"

Henry stared at me.

"I've never seen anything like that in my life!" he exclaimed.

Matthew was staring at me and then he nodded knowingly.

At the putting green, I leaned in and whispered to him, "So?"

"Henry made my Mom call her."

"And?"

"She doesn't have a boyfriend. She goes to our church."

"And?"

"That's all I've got."

"She's not one of your Mom's friends?"

"Nah, we just see her at Mass."

I nodded as I watched Carol putt.

"So, you play," Matthew said to me.

I nodded again, still watching, and then turned to him to share a confederate's smile.

"That was cool," he said.

I modestly played the rest of the course and wasn't miserable at all. I was even a little sorry that we weren't playing the back.

Henry was grinning like a fool the whole time. When the last putt was played, Henry announced that he was starving, and that we should all go to dinner. The women readily agreed.

Henry called Atlanta, pretending to the boys that he was asking her if they could eat with us.

"Your mother says that she has already made dinner and she is already on her way here to pick you up," he told them.

Henry and I stood out in front of the club with the boys, while the women went inside to get a table. The boys were challenging each other to jump off rocks and benches in front of the building and Henry and I just stood there talking as we waited for Atlanta.

"So, what do you think of Carol?" Henry asked. "It seems like she likes you and she isn't wearing a ring."

I considered confronting Henry with his duplicity and putting an end to these ridiculous lies. Somehow, though, it was more fun to be the only omniscient person among us. It gave me distance, and it was amusing to watch Henry scheme.

"I like her alright," I said.

Henry looked up as we heard a car circle around and park nearby.

Atlanta, slim in a pair of chinos and her face hid behind a pair of Jackie Onassis style sunglasses, stepped out of a silver Mercedes and looked right at us.

"Go on boys, see you later," Henry called to them both.

"Bye, Mr. Davis," they called to me dutifully as they ran to the car.

It seemed unnatural to stand here staring at her, within calling distance, saying nothing. I wanted to speak to her, but I wasn't sure what it was I would say. So I just stared and she stared back and Henry watched the boys. Henry took a step forward and I followed, shielding my eyes from the sudden glare of sunlight reflecting from the car's windshield. Henry raised his hand and waved. I raised my hand in an awkward salute. She paused, looking at us, before she waved back at the two of us. Joshua crashed into her at that moment, knocking her off balance, and she shooed both of them into the back of the car. She looked at us one more time before disappearing behind the windshield's mirrored face.

Henry and I went in and found Amy and Carol at a table, both of them with drinks half gone.

The conversation at dinner quickly became an interview moderated by Henry and lubricated by a constant stream of alcohol. After only an hour, Amy looked at her watch and announced that she had to leave. On cue, Henry said that he had to get home also.

"You don't have to leave, Carol," Henry said soothingly, "Mikey can drive you home, can't you Mike?"

Carol looked at me briefly before saying, "No, I'm okay."

"You haven't even finished your dinner," Henry said to her, while staring at me.

"I can take you home," I said, and everyone exhaled.

"Thanks," she said, and then smiled nervously at Henry and Amy as they got up and left.

She and I sat in silence for some minutes, looking around. It was dark outside now, and Carol brooded as she gazed at the large, cold windows next to us that reflected back the obscure interior of the room. I drummed my fingertips on my knees as I turned to watch a waiter light a fire in the large fireplace. Another waiter came over to light the candle on our table and to tell us that happy hour was almost over.

Almost as if she had come to a decision that would determine the course of events, Carol took her eyes from the window and looked right into my face. She began to talk in animated tones about the last two holes. She asked me questions about myself, and I found myself answering them. Our conversation became more frank, more intimate, without Henry's moderating presence. Maybe that was part of the set up, like good cop, bad cop. Nevertheless, I liked her better now. We didn't order dessert and coffee, but instead, more drinks and bar food.

Then, I had to stop drinking.

"Henry thinks I drink too much," I told her.

"What do you think?" she asked me.

"I think I probably drink too much," I confirmed, "though, if it helps my case, it's not a habit that's normal for me."

"You have a case?"

I felt myself flush. When she looked at me, I noticed that her eyes were a lovely shade of brown with gold flecks. That probably meant that her hair was some shade of brown also. I imagined her hair a chestnut brown, a little longer, to her shoulders. The effect was pleasing.

"You should let your hair go back to brown," I mused aloud before I could stop myself.

"Oh my God!" her hands flew to her head, "Are my roots showing that bad?"

"No, no. I just thought that you would look very pretty with brown hair."

She smiled a dazzling smile as her cheeks colored.

We both looked down at our hands.

"I know I'm not supposed to do this," she started, and I couldn't imagine what she was about to do.

"I know that the books say that I'm supposed to be cool and hard to get and all that, but so much of modern relationships is don't ask don't tell, and it's just too exhausting." She sighed, sat up straighter, seemed to fortify her resolve, but looked at her drink as she spoke. "I'm in my thirties now and the truth is that I want to get married." She glanced up at my face and then back down at her hands holding her drink, "I want to get married and have children."

She met my eyes for a long moment, challenging me to object. I didn't.

"I'm not saying that I want to marry you. I don't even know you. And I'm not desperate."

She challenged me with her eyes again.

"But, I've followed all the relationship advice out there, you know—don't scare him off, don't say what you think. Then I end up spending six months, or three years with a guy before I find out that he doesn't want to get married and have children, or not with me. I'd rather be honest and say what I want in the beginning so that if we want different things, we can part friends and keep looking. I'm in my thirties now, and I just don't want to waste any more time being dishonest."

She looked down at her hands, fearing my silence, and then again met my eyes. I held her gaze. Something that was not possible became possible then. My hands were shaking.

"I was at my best when I was married," I said, "and although I say I don't want kids, I do."

"That's wonderful," she said. She paused and stirred her drink. "You know, while we're being honest, I have a confession to make," she leaned forward, biting her lip while I nervously waited for it. "I know Henry. He goes to my church," she said quickly.

I was relieved.

She babbled on nervously without waiting for me say anything, telling me all about Henry's machinations. She stopped speaking, finally, and looked at me, gauging my reaction.

"I already knew all that," I said as her mouth dropped open, "I got it out of Matthew."

Her nervous tension exploded into laughter so ringing that other people looked around at us.

"So, you're not mad?" she asked, looking at me with coquettish penitence.

I watched her as we talked. In these last hours I'd learned that she worked, but not too much. She wasn't a picky eater, and she had excellent table manners. She obviously exercised, but playing golf today had just been a ploy. She was a cafeteria Catholic who said she was pro-choice and probably used birth control. She would probably stop bleaching her hair, if I asked her to. She would be a kind and sensitive mother. And the way she handled Henry spoke of personal resources that were impressive.

Sure, there was still a lot of personal history to unload, a lot more dates, weekends in Mendocino, long discussions about tax reform or environmental protection, but the truth was clear, right now in this moment. I could marry this woman and it wouldn't even be that hard. All I would have to do is to say yes and she would move into my house and decorate it. Her mother would plan the wedding. They would tell me what to wear. She would fill my refrigerator. The house would have life in it again. All I would have to do is continue to work, pay the mortgage, pay taxes and come home at a reasonable hour. Hell, I already did that. I needed only say yes, and by next Christmas I could be a married man with a baby on the way.

When I drove her home, we sat in silence in the womb of intimacy created by the phosphorescent glow of the dashboard instruments that pushed back the night. We listened to jazz and she directed me. The streetlights flashed a gentle strobe as we drove, and out of the corner of my eye, the intermittent flashlight glow on her thighs was mesmerizing.

I parked right in front of a white building the shape of a layer cake. She pointed to the bottom level of a tower of bay windows that stood on the corner of it. As we walked up the interior flight of stairs, the tension kept us silent. I wanted something to happen, didn't I? Was this it?

She walked ahead of me the last couple of steps, swaying her body in a way that told me that she had come to some conclusions. I stood close behind her as she unlocked the door, breathing on the small hairs on the back of her neck. When she opened the door, she didn't turn on the light. She pulled me into the doorway and I pressed her against the wall. I ran my hands all over her body, stripping her of her clothes. I looked at this woman, still stranger, and wondered, Is this it? Is this how the rest of my life starts?

Atlanta

I dreamed I was walking in my desert, barefoot and wearing the nightdress I had worn as a girl. The cool silt I walked upon in this dead place was made of countless crumbled ancient vessels turned to dust. They were, long ago, colored terracotta, ochre, hematite, charcoal, but they were now the color of bleached bones. This silt stirred in tiny eddies around my feet, pushed by a fitful breeze, then dashed itself against implacable rocks before settling quiescent once more. I walked for miles with no view ahead of me except this stirring settling silt that stretched vast and flat to the horizon before blending with a pale sky and curving in upon itself again. Behind me I saw rock mountains, their summits cleaved and eroded, slumping against the horizon, and by a swindle of perspective, dwarfed by the singular dark silhouettes of cacti that rose like sentinels in front of them, puncturing the sky. Where is it? I kept asking myself as I continued to push forward.

My alarm startled me awake, parched, at five. I rose without disturbing Henry, who was sleeping heavily with his back to me. Shivering in the darkness, I dressed and went down to the basement with a full laundry basket on my hip.

I tossed the clothes in the machine, and while they washed, I went across the hall to run on the treadmill in the exercise room. It felt good to sweat in the cool and quiet privacy of the basement, listening to the cheerful hum of the lovely machines.

As I began to run I started thinking about how I wanted to remodel my bathroom. Someone had done a fancy remodel two decades ago, and it was holding up, but it was dated. That was our argument, mine and Henry's. He didn't want to fix it if nothing was broken. It was orange and green. Henry called it "kinda cool," and said that if we waited long enough it would come back into style. I didn't care about style. I would hate it in any decade. I wanted to take the big sledgehammer off the neatly organized garage pegboard wall and smash it to bits.

When the washing machine switched off, I stopped the treadmill and put the clothes into the dryer. Upstairs, I chose one of the many white shirts hanging in Henry's closet and brought it into the kitchen. There, I opened a cabinet that concealed the ironing board, turned on the iron, and started the coffee. I listened to the sput-sput sound of the coffee maker and inhaled the moist singed cotton smell of Henry's shirt under the iron as the first glimmer of silent aurora outlined the bare trees and shimmered across the fog rolling in from the bay. The furnace clicked on and began to hum. I replaced Henry's shirt on the hanger and hung it on the back of his closet door before I passed again down the hall to wake the boys.

"Joshua?"

He rolled over onto his back and rubbed a hand over his sleep-creased cheeks. He opened his eyes and blinked twice before he smiled. Joshua always greeted the day with this tiny aubade, and I gathered him into my arms, kissing his eyebrows, before continuing to Matthew's room. Matthew loved his sleep. I took one of his hands and drew him upright. He sat on the edge of his bed, eyes still closed, but yawning. As I passed her bathroom, I plugged in Mary's hot rollers. She went to school with a friend who drove and had the luxury of sleeping an extra half hour.

I was scrambling eggs when the children straggled into the kitchen and sat down, Mary in hot rollers and a housecoat.

Henry followed, fully dressed and smelling of cologne.

"Morning kids!" As he sat down at the breakfast table he cocked one baleful eye at Mary.

"She goes with Jen, now," I reminded him.

"Coming to the breakfast table undressed sets a bad example for the boys."

"What's the use of going with Jen if I can't sleep late? That's the whole point," Mary objected.

"You can sleep as late as you want so long as you come dressed to the table."

"Can I roll my hair after breakfast?" Mary looked up cautiously.

"Hair rolling is outside my jurisdiction," Henry smirked.

I sat down at the table with my second cup of coffee and a half slice of toast. Joshua was already absently stirring the remains of his breakfast as he stared out of the window, watching a grey squirrel.

"Lookit, he's thinkin' that there might be some breakfast in that flowerpot." Joshua cupped one hand over his mouth and giggled as the squirrel dug in the bottom of a big, empty flowerpot, only its flipping tail visible above the rim. "He's silly, momma."

"He's probably out there looking in here at you, thinking the same thing!" Henry told him. Joshua giggled again.

I smiled as I carried my half empty coffee cup to the sink with a stack of dirty plates. When I returned to the breakfast room to give Joshua his lunch box, Mary had already disappeared.

"Come on, Matthew, or you'll be late," I said.

Matthew sleepily shoved the rest of his breakfast into his mouth, one eye on Henry, and, still chewing, got up from the table. As the front door slammed shut, I mused that it was always Joshua who walked Matthew out rather than the reverse.

This thought caused tears to spring in my eyes. I turned my back to Henry and began to wash the dishes. I heard the newspaper crackle open and Henry shift in his seat.

The branches of the ornamental plum planted on the side of the house reached across my kitchen window. My hands stopped washing. The bare branches were covered in a bit of frost, and silhouetted against the gray fog in the quiet stillness of my kitchen window, they made a pleasant tableau. Year after year, I look at these branches—bare, flowered, green, and bare again. If I were a Buddhist, this would be a haiku. But I am not a Buddhist. Joshua is already gone and all I can do is stand here and wash dishes.

After fifteen minutes of silence, Henry mumbled bitterly, "Women only care about their abortions. Jobs, wealth, and national security are all subservient to abortions." He folded the remaining sections of the paper savagely and got up from the table, still talking, but in a more subdued tone, as he prepared to leave.

I stopped listening as soon as I heard that the subject of his diatribe was a familiar one. Occasionally, he would stop mid-sentence and demand some statement of agreeable support, and I automatically, unconsciously prepared such a statement and held it in the back of my mind as it wandered.

It seemed only yesterday that I had tears in my eyes as Matthew left the house for kindergarten. Now I was already waving goodbye to Joshua as he climbed on the school bus. There was a tightness in my chest that sometimes made it hard for me to breathe. The first time it happened I thought it was a heart attack and almost called the paramedics, but now that I was taking pills for it, the pain merely pressed upon me with dull, betrayed insistence until I busied myself.

I heard, distantly, Henry change the subject to something about school prayer.

"That's it. Don't you think?" Henry was looking straight at me, and my panicked mind scrabbled for the prepared response that wasn't there.

"Prayer is good for children," I offered uncertainly.

"It is, by God!" Henry exclaimed, "We really should have sent Mary to St. Agatha's. Why we left that decision to a child is beyond me."

My attention snapped into focus. We had already gone through all this with her two years ago. I knew that forcing Mary into a new school would rip apart her fragile, adolescent equilibrium. However, I also knew that an argument based on contract theory would sway Henry more than concerns of the heart, which he felt were distaff, and therefore, of little importance.

"We already decided this with her in her freshman year." I said, "She's doing everything we asked, she's making straight A's…."

"Yes," Henry agreed gravely, "but we know what is best. We'll talk about it later."

He kissed me and left for work. I was dismissed. I now realized that he had been thinking about this for a while, and the decision had already been made in that first wave of immoveable, convinced righteousness.

I stood fretting in the kitchen doorway, biting my cuticles I didn't know how long, when a car horn splintered the air and Mary came running through the living room.

"Your lunch!" I called.

Like a gazelle, Mary corrected her path nimbly in a full run and leapt past me into the kitchen. She reappeared, her arms full, the lunch bag swinging from two fingers, and swept past and out the door.

Like a sleepwalker, I dumbly trailed behind in that stardust wake of juvenile ebullience until I reached the front window. I watched Mary smile at her friends as she jumped into the back seat of Jen's waiting white convertible, and pitied Mary her loss. Mary, ordinarily so sensitive, her adolescent antennae so attentive, so attuned to the slightest disturbance around Henry, the slightest concern reflected in my face, was today in her rush blithely ignorant that she was to lose all.

A keening wail broke free of my throat. And then before I could stop it, tears came hard, tumbled out of my eyes, the pain in my chest crushing my breath, my mouth gaping noiselessly. I gasped finally, "She's just like me." I sobbed out loud to no one, "Oh Jesus, Oh God, my daughter is just like me."

I sank to my knees and cried with my forehead pressed against the cool marble of the entry hall floor. Then I began to pray. I couldn't help wondering as I prayed my prayers, set up next to Henry's, contradicting Henry's, if God would listen to mine.

The radiating cool of the floor calmed me as I breathed softly. I lay crumpled with my wet cheek pressed against it, my mind empty of thought for what seemed like a long time. Finally, I brought the back of my hand to my face and struggled to my feet, feeling foolish and disoriented. Was this really my house, my life? I raised my eyes and saw the huge painting of daisies on a blue background over the hall table strewn with my art glass collection, I smelled the cooked protein dampness that lingered in the air from breakfast, I heard the pipes hiccup as the dishwasher cycled to rinse. I willed myself to move.

I wondered what Michael would say. Although I hadn't seen him since that Christmas party, I often heard him in my head, like a confederate, commenting on annoying things Henry said, or repeating things he had said to me that night. With a flush of heat, I remembered his thigh pressed warmly into mine, but then pushed the thought from my mind. He had never suggested that we go out to the stairwell together. I flushed anew at the image this thought called into my mind, of his large hands upon me in the salmon colored back stairwell of the ballroom. I had noticed that he had large hands.

I shook myself like a flustered horse and walked to the kitchen, pushing my hair from my face with a motion that tried to be careless. The kitchen gleamed spotless before me.

It's not a sexual attraction, I said to myself, not exactly. I remembered that it was Michael's quiet supportive touch that had wrecked me. It made me realize how completely alone I was. No one, for instance, would ever know that I cried today, and Henry would never understand why. Michael would.

A momentary panic was quelled by the welcome avalanche of a dozen things that needed doing. I walked in the direction of the first necessary thing.

"We're going to Jack and Steven's," Matthew yelled to the house, generally, when they got home.

I picked up the boys' book bags from the couch where they threw them, grateful for a task to soothe my agitated nerves. I smiled at the construction paper puppy Joshua had brought home, made of pre-cut pieces from the teacher's day planner. Instead of dutifully gluing the pieces where the teacher had marked, Joshua had glued the ears straight up, the eyes close together, the tongue more lolling, so that he was so much more alert, alive. I glared at the tiny penciled hash marks on the puppy's face where the pre-cut pieces were to be glued, those innocuous looking, but insidiously dangerous pre-cut enemies to my little boy's spirit, and taking Joshua's pencil eraser in hand, I carefully and completely rubbed them out. I hung the puppy face in the center of the refrigerator.

"He looks like he's on crack," Mary commented when she got home.

"Mary!"

"Well, he does." She shrugged and poured herself a glass of milk.

I sat silently, struggling for the words that would make Henry's decision something less than devastating, and Mary immediately became still and alert. I could feel Mary's eyes on me, but it was several moments before I could bring myself to meet her gaze.

"I need to talk to you, now, while the boys are out."

Mary's face paled slightly as she sat down, and I could see the thoughts scrolling quickly across her eyes.

"I was going to clean my room after school today. The only reason it's been messy so much lately," Mary went on, "is because we've had so much homework lately and I'm trying out for the school paper staff and Jen and I have been talking about running for school office for next year, you know, because it's good for our college applications."

It was painful to see Mary, ordinarily so precociously articulate, babbling like a middle school child. I tried to calm her.

"You aren't in trouble, Mary, and nothing is final yet, really. I just wanted to tell you before your father gets home that he is thinking about transferring you to St. Agatha's."

"That's not fair!" Mary shot up beside her chair. "I'm doing everything! Nothing is slipping! I'm actually doing more!"

I looked at my hands curled on the table next to my coffee cup.

"Can't you talk to him? Can't we vote? He's only one and we're two. Doesn't what I want matter to anybody?"

"You know this isn't a democracy, Mary," I said calmly.

"What about you?" Mary demanded, "Do you want me to transfer?"

I knew I couldn't win with Henry when it came to something like this, and so disagreeing with him openly would only fuel Mary's opposition.

"This is between you and Henry," I said weakly, feeling my weakness.

"You are useless!" Mary screamed and ran to her room, slamming the door.

I wasn't even offended by Mary's outburst. A heavy fatigue bent me down into my hands, but I didn't even bother to cry.

"Maybe I'll lay down," I thought.

I took a casserole out of the freezer, put it in the oven, and set the computer controlled temperature, timer. Another lovely machine.

I was asleep in a moment. When I woke, the room was dark. I sat up with a start, nervous, wondering what could have happened in my absence, and I hustled out into the cavernous great room.

Illuminated only by the saucer of light hanging over the dinner table, Henry and Mary were sitting alone, the empty casserole dish in the middle of the table, a pile of dishes leaning askew at Mary's left elbow. Mary's eyes were red and swollen, and they looked at me with dull and lifeless accusation. Henry was sitting at attention, his hands on the table next to Mary, assiduous, placating. Henry hated tears. He looked at me.

"Are you ill?" he asked.

"I'm not sure," I said looking from one of them to the other, waiting for them to tell me.

"We were discussing what you and I decided this morning," he said.

Mary's eyes were baleful slits when she again turned them to me.

"How we feel that it is in her best interest in the long run, how she may not understand it now, but it's the best possible choice. Mary and I have talked about it and I've decided that it probably isn't a good idea to wait until her senior year. St. Agatha's doesn't even start again until next week, so she even gets an extra week of winter vacation. It really works out perfectly."

"Perfectly," Mary said with a quiet fierceness that Henry pretended not to hear.

"Where are the boys?" I asked, remembering them in a momentary panic.

"They're already in bed," Henry paused, cocking his head at me, "Why don't you go to bed early. There's something going around."

I turned away. I crawled back under the covers and closed my eyes against them.

The next morning, I got up, ran on the treadmill, woke the boys, made breakfast, made the coffee. Everything was the same, as if nothing at all had happened, except that Mary was not at the breakfast table.

"She's on vacation," Henry said to the boys.

My neck ached. I rubbed it with one hand as I sat down with my coffee.

"So, you'll go over there today and get her registered?" Henry asked.

"Me? I thought you had already done it." I tried to look at him, but my neck was so stiff, I had to turn my shoulders to do it.

Henry exhaled, "I made phone calls, but we need to go over there and sign papers, write them a check. It's around fifteen grand a semester. You can take it out of your checking and I'll make a deposit later."

This was not my doing. He should have to do it. Rage welled in my belly, but I checked it as I cut my eyes at the boys, who were watching our conversation intently.

"I don't know how you expect me to accomplish this," I said with a completely false, bright insouciance, the tendons in my neck tightening, "with everything else I have scheduled today."

"Perhaps you would like to go to my office instead, and deal with the mountain of work that has been piling up since my best associate quit and we had to lay off a couple more. I can't do everything, Atlanta." Henry got up, leaving his breakfast half eaten. "I gotta go."

My angry, racing thoughts were rent by the impatient blare of a horn.

The boys grabbed their book bags from me as I shivered on the front porch, and they ran towards the bus waiting in front of the house. I could feel the silent accusation of the bus driver as her reaching, waiting silhouette stared out of the open school bus door.

I waved at the dark row of windows that dumbly reflected the fog back at me as the bus rumbled away. I closed the front door behind me. The house was absolutely silent, but Mary's presence was heavy in it. It bowed the walls, it pulled with an inexorable gravity, it filled the empty spaces in each atom, even to the atoms within my own body. Mary's impotent rage, her righteous indignation was a dull hum that thumped inside my own head. *Useless*, it said, *useless*.

I put my ear to Mary's door. I heard no sound. I quietly busied myself, willing Mary to wake, to rise. As a silent hour passed, I busied myself less quietly, making the noises casual, unintentional, but this too produced nothing. At last, I had to leave to get across the Golden Gate Bridge to St. Agatha's and back in time for the bus.

I stood outside Mary's door for several minutes listening.

"Mary?" I called, quietly, timidly. "Mary?" I said with feigned confidence, "I'm leaving now. I left your breakfast in the warmer."

There was no sound from inside the room. I gingerly tried the door, but the knob was locked against me.

"Is there anything you need?" I called into that expanding, pulling, throbbing and silent vortex of adolescent rage.

I heaved a defeated sigh and left the house.

When I returned, the house was still silent. I tried Mary's door and found it still locked. "Mary!" I pounded on the door, demanding an answer, but received none.

I put my ear to the door and heard a small sound, like a page turning. Encouraged, I tried again.

"Henry will not stand for this, you know."

My voice was firm, indignant and convincing, but still, there was no sound.

Later, Henry called while I was making dinner. I heard a click on the line as Mary hung up her extension.

"As I predicted, I'll be late tonight. I'm sorry about dinner," he said, sensing my irritation. "What are you making?"

"Chicken and rice," I said sheepishly.

"That's interesting," he said.

"She hasn't come out of her room all day," I said.

"So you make her favorite dish? It's best to wield a firm hand in situations like this."

"Oh? What do you suggest?" I said with irritation, pulling helplessly at the tendons in my neck.

"I'll be home in a couple of hours," he said.

I stowed Henry's plate in the warmer, got Joshua ready for bed and asked Matthew to read to him. Then I sat down on the couch and flipped magazine pages as I watched the illuminated crack of Mary's door. I could hear Mary's voice murmuring into her cell phone, I could see her shadow cross the door's threshold.

I threw the magazine back onto the large shelf under the mahogany coffee table, which was already stuffed with hundreds of issues of home design magazines. The magazine slipped out and fell on the floor. Quelling a frustrated rage that stopped in my throat, I carefully placed it again on the pile, and it again noiselessly slipped off. A bolus of heat shot into my head and hot tears welled in my eyes as I grabbed the magazine and crushed it in my fist and forcibly shoved it again and again into the pile of magazines until it stuck. Crying now, I kicked the mass of glossy paper, which tumbled out onto the floor in a heap.

I picked up a magazine and threw it at the mantle of the vast fireplace with all my strength. It crackled open and tumbled slowly through the air until it thwacked quietly and impotently against the bluestone facade. That small noise made me want to scream.

I stood in the middle of the room my fists and teeth clenched, tears burning, eyeing the stairway leading to Joshua's room where the boys were quietly reading together. I sat down, buried my face in one of the overstuffed silk couch pillows and screamed, then screamed again, and screamed a third time until my throat ached and saliva dripped from my bottom lip onto the shiny smooth surface of the pillow.

Wiping the pillow and my eyes, I straightened myself and then calmly retrieved each and every magazine, putting them back on the shelf in neat piles. Then, taking one, I sat on the couch again, and opened it, flipping the pages.

It was last month's *Architectural Digest*. A dog-eared page caught my eye. It was a picture of a shower, muted stone tiles surrounding a little round window. I turned the page and realized why I had dog-eared it. The big soaking tub rested against the shower stall, tucked into a corner space. In my mind, I was placing the tub so that it sat beneath the bathroom window with a view of the bay visible over and between rooftops from our second story perspective. I had that vision before my eyes when Henry walked in.

"Has she come out yet?" he asked.

"Not even for the boys," I told him as I laid the magazine down on the tabletop.

Henry sighed, tossed his briefcase on the couch and stalked to Mary's door.

He pounded on the door. The murmuring within stopped, but there was no answer. Henry pounded again.

"Mary Frances Buchanan, I want to see you in this doorway immediately."

There was no answer. I stared in breathless amazement.

"Mary Frances, if you do not open this door immediately, there will be consequences."

"Like what?" Mary yelled from within, "Prison? What else can you do to me?"

"You won't see your friends for two weeks. Let's start there," he said.

"I already don't see my friends," Mary said, her voice sounding nearer, close on the other side of the door, "I'm going to be bussed all the way across the Golden Gate Bridge. I'll never see them anyway."

"That phone you are busily talking on will be taken away."

"Possession is nine tenths of the law!" she yelled, farther away again.

Henry turned red, then amazingly, he just walked away.

"She'll get hungry," he said, pouring himself a scotch, "and I'll just cancel her phone account from the office tomorrow. That will get her attention."

"Great. I'll be the one here all day with her after you get her attention."

"She's a child. How bad can it be?" Henry said, stirring his scotch with a finger. I closed my eyes. It seemed only a moment later that Henry was shaking me awake. The sliver of light beneath Mary's door was gone.

The next morning I awoke to find an open peanut butter jar with a butter knife upended in the middle of it sitting in a lake of crumbs on the counter. Mary wanted me to know that she had not touched the chicken.

Neither did she appear for breakfast. Henry winked at me and ate his breakfast, unperturbed. The boys pretended not to notice that anything was wrong and left for school as usual. Everything was as usual, except the pressure of Mary's silent presence. Right before lunch a deep throated yelling scream came from Mary's room followed by the splintering thud of an object breaking against the wall. The shock of that scream in the perpetual silence of the house almost knocked me to the ground.

Henry had cancelled Mary's phone. The event, however unpleasant, at least felt like some form of communication with Mary, a release of the pressure in the house, and I hoped that Mary's rage now would be directed at Henry.

"What did Mary say when her phone went dead?"

Henry asked me the question with amused relish, as he ate his dinner, late again, at the kitchen table.

"The iPhone is now iJunk."

Henry laughed.

"How can you be so relaxed?" I said, "Doesn't it bother you at all?"

"Why should it? She has engaged me in some kind of power struggle, except that she has no power. The rest is theatre."

On the third day, Henry arrived home early and in good spirits. I stared at him. Henry smiled, raised one finger to his lips and watched out the front window. After some moments, he nodded at someone outside and chuckled to himself.

"What's going on?" Matthew wanted to know.

"I have no idea," I said.

Joshua wandered out of his room and stood next to Matthew.

Henry opened the front door before the bell rang and admitted a man carrying a large toolbox. A small tuft of graying hair stood unkempt on top of the man's bald forehead and he smelled of stale cigarettes. I turned away.

"Where's this problem door?" he asked Henry.

"Here," Henry said, walking quickly, leading the way.

We followed them as the man pulled a gold doorknob out of his box.

The new doorknob didn't match the others in the house. I pressed my lips together.

The man set to work immediately with a large power drill, drilling out the lock.

A large object slammed against the door from the inside, just as the man pulled out the doorknob entirely.

Henry gleefully pushed himself into the room. From where we were watching, we could see Mary standing defiantly in the middle of the room, her fists clenched, glaring at Henry. Henry ignored her, and instead retrieved the stereo and her iPod and carried them out of her room.

Appearing again some minutes later, Henry carried out Mary's new television. While the man installed the new doorknob and cleaned up, Henry carried out Mary's phone extension, her games, controller, laptop and Blu-ray player. He paid the man, smiling.

Mary was sitting on her bed now, staring at the floor.

"Your door no longer locks," Henry told her, "but we all knock before we come in, so I really don't see how that could be a problem. You are grounded to the house for the rest of the week, with no phone calls, until school starts, except for when you go with your mother to buy your new school uniform. Do you understand?"

"Yes, sir."

I looked up with a start. Mary had never called him 'sir' in her life, except as a joke.

"Problem solved," Henry said when we were alone together on the couch.

He was right. Mary did seem to buckle under completely. I no longer felt the walls bowing outwards with the pressure of Mary's presence. In fact, the house felt positively still.

"I know this has been hard on you," Henry told me with an amused, indulgent expression, "but tomorrow will be better, I promise."

Tomorrow was better, at least in the way Henry meant it. Mary was at the breakfast table, eating little, speaking when spoken to, looking at us all with hollow eyes. Henry was delighted and left for work as usual.

Mary helped me clear the dishes without looking at me.

"I'm sorry this all had to happen," I said.

"May I go to my room?" she asked.

"Of course," I said gently, "You can do whatever you want."

"Except leave," Mary said, "except listen to music, or talk to my friends."

"Well, yes. It will pass. I really appreciate your cooperative attitude."

Mary looked up. "What alternative do I have?" she asked, looking directly into my face, "drop out of school, give up my chances of getting into a good college? Get a job as a waitress, or a prostitute? Live on the street and get raped?"

"Mary!" I said, shocked.

"Seriously. What alternative do I have? None. I need him to protect me from men, and in return, I have to do what he says. That's the point he was trying to make and he made it." She turned away.

As I watched her leave the kitchen, I tried to think of the right thing to say, but nothing came.

Later, as I left the house, I went to Mary's room to check on her. The door was open and Mary was asleep, face down on her pillow. I shut the door and ran my fingers down it as tears welled in my eyes.

On Monday morning, we all had to be at the table early so that Mary could make the carpool van that took a dozen or so Sausalito kids across the bridge to St. Agatha's. Maybe it wouldn't be so bad. My new morning schedule was compressed, and I set my watch when I climbed onto the treadmill. I shook myself out as I ran, tried to breathe more deeply, relax.

It was that convertible, of course. Jen's white convertible. Henry had never trusted that car, and I was sure that it was the sight of Mary jumping gleefully into it every morning that started Henry thinking. Where was my own convertible now? My Beauty, I had called it: my white 1968 Buick Electra convertible I'd bought with my summer money. She was probably rusting in some gearhead's garage now, wearing a crown of beer cans.

That car was the most beautiful thing I had ever had. My mama, Ms. Mara, got me that fantastic summer job as a research assistant right after freshman year and I had saved every penny. The old used car dealer was sweet on me and saved it for me. It sat there on the lot all summer long and

I bought it on layaway like a pair of pants. I almost drove away from Henry in that car.

There was a photo of us with that car somewhere—me smiling behind the wheel, him standing next to the car with an arm resting possessively behind me along the seat. Somehow, he had steadily ingratiated himself, made me need him. I had always been alone growing up, and I remembered how good it felt to be swallowed up by his largeness, his friends, his church, his plans. That enclosure felt hollow now.

"This whole morning has felt like a fire drill," Mary moaned in a depressive monotone. She sat down at the table in her new creaseless school uniform, her wavy black hair pulled back into a severe ponytail. There was no evidence whatsoever of the powers of hot rollers.

Everyone was seated at the table by seven ten.

"Not bad," I said, drinking my coffee at the sink.

"Eat," Henry said to Mary, who was staring at her French toast as she sipped her juice.

"I can't," she said.

"The van will be here soon," he said.

Mary dutifully began to shovel bites of toast into her mouth, grimacing. Several minutes later, the color left her face and she started up from the table.

We all stopped eating as sounds of retching reached us from the vanity bathroom under the stairs.

"It's just nerves," Henry said.

Mary stood at attention next to the table.

"Are you okay?" I asked her.

"Does it matter?" she replied.

A car horn sounded outside.

Mary's limp body turned in a slow arc and she left. She closed the front door so quietly that no one heard it.

I walked to the front door, drew the lace curtain aside and looked out.

The side door of the van was open and Mary was standing outside it. The entire van was full of teenagers wearing blue and white and sitting in rows. The nun in the front seat said something to Mary and Mary shrugged before climbing into the back row. The door shut and the van drove away with her.

I let the lace fall back into place and went back into the kitchen to start the dishes.

As the boys were leaving, I grabbed Joshua and held him tight against me, tears welling in my eyes. I didn't want to let him go. I rocked him back and forth and then finally released him. He blinked twice in that way of his before he turned to go out the door.

I had abandoned myself to sobbing on the couch when Henry walked in holding his briefcase.

"What in the world is wrong?" he asked, alarmed, sitting down next to me.

"Nothing," I said, wiping my eyes, but the tears kept coming.

"Are you still taking the pills?" he asked.

I nodded and I tried to will myself to stop crying.

"Maybe you should do nothing today and just go out to lunch, go shopping?"

My eyes fixed on the magazines bulging from the coffee table at my feet.

"I want to remodel our bathroom," I said without thinking, immediately feeling how ridiculous it was.

"Is that all?" he laughed, "If it means that much to you, by all means, tear it to shreds," he said.

He kissed my hair and stood.

"Gotta go," he said.

"I don't really have to remodel the bathroom," I said.

"I want you to remodel the bathroom. We'll have the prettiest bathroom in all Sausalito," he said, laughing, as he left.

The Furies

I.

I was sitting at the kitchen table surrounded by tile, or rather, images of tile that spread themselves to the edges of the table and beyond to the chairs and floor. After four weeks, I was finally closing in on a decision.

"Just choose something!" Mary said as she stepped over a pile of magazines, holding a handful of cookies.

"Choosing tile isn't like choosing a rug, Mary. It's permanent. Fifteen or twenty years from now, I don't want some woman to have to rip it out."

"Of course someone will hate it later. But maybe the next woman who lives here will have more important things to think about. She probably won't even notice that you chose hideous tile."

"You know, Mary," I said, sighing deeply, "I really don't need your help right now."

"Okayfine," Mary chewed a cookie and then squirreled it in one of her cheeks to speak. "But if you make us go to one more tile place or home store or anything else, we're going to mutiny. We're gonna take illegal drugs and vandalize churches."

"Mary!"

"And when the judge takes us away," Mary said, "I'm going to make sure that everyone knows that it's because of you and the tile."

I threw a magazine at her, and she skittered away laughing.

"I'm serious!" Mary yelled. "Get a life!"

That last bit stung, but Mary was right. It was hideous tile. I shoved the catalogues to the floor. I plucked one of the three yellow apples I had placed as decoration in the centerpiece and bit it. I was trying to be artistic. I wanted everyone who saw the bathroom to be amazed at my hidden talents. I wanted to have hidden talents.

All of the patterns were making my head swim. I retreated to a stack of *Architectural Digest* magazines. I wouldn't copy anything exactly, but there was a famous designer bathroom, a remodel of a Parisian flat, that I admired. It was daring. It was black and white with splashes of red. That's it, I thought. I would make the bathroom into this black, white and red Paris confection, but I would change the red into a muted, sophisticated red and I would arrange it according to the rules of feng shui. I would learn feng shui, and I would design it all myself and it wouldn't be hideous at all. It would be fabulous and full of my hidden talents. Henry would hate it, and that would be even better.

Mary seemed to respond to my good spirits and helped me clear the dinner dishes without being asked. She was telling stories about her new school and I couldn't help but laugh at things I knew I shouldn't.

Since she started at St. Agatha's, Mary's humor had become sharp. It revealed a penetrating intelligence mixed with a sardonic wit that referenced a broad and sophisticated knowledge of the world. Where did she get it?

I looked at Mary, now silent. There was still so much about my own child I didn't understand. It wasn't only her unexpected, untutored intelligence, and strange, defensive privacy, but also her protean, shifting personality that completely baffled me. For instance, was this really the same girl who, only a few weeks ago, was boiling with adolescent rage and rebellion? She was so full of strength and determination, but then, she just buckled under to Henry's demands finally, as if it were nothing. Here she was now, helping with the dishes as if none of it had ever happened.

Mary paused her dishwashing and cocked her head.

"Some guy wants to go out with me, apparently," she said finally.

"Do you like him?"

"Maybe. His name is David something. Dave."

"That's a nice name. If you decide you like him..." I started to say.

"I know, invite him to dinner first."

That explained everything. Mary was sweet on a boy, and that had smoothed everything out. I would remodel the green and orange bathroom, Mary would get a nice boyfriend, and everything would smooth out.

On my way home from Matthew's school the next day, I stopped at the public library and checked out a stack of books on feng shui and Asian design and spread them out on the kitchen table.

"*Feng Shui For Dummies,*" Mary read aloud and rolled her eyes.

"Why do you have to be so rude to me?"

Mary raised her hands. "I didn't mean anything by it. No need to get your martyr complex in a twist."

I closed my eyes, hoping that when I opened them, she would be gone. She was.

"You haven't learned anything," Henry told me later. "She wouldn't dare speak to me like that, but she does it to you because you allow it."

"So, I should punish her for every comment?"

The idea of policing everything Mary said to me seemed more of a burden than the comments themselves.

"And," I added, "what if she's right? What if I am pathetic and have no life?"

Henry just shook his head in exasperation.

The following day, I steeled myself for Mary's arrival. I didn't want to make her behave, but rather, I wanted to find a way to inspire in her a natural respect for her mother.

When Mary came in, it sounded like the boys were with her. But when Mary came around the corner I saw that she had with her a dark-skinned girl in a St. Agatha's uniform, her dreadlocks pulled back into a neat ponytail at the nape of her neck. They stopped talking when they saw me.

"Hey Mom, this is Monique."

"Hi Mrs. Buchanan," Monique said, politely smiling.

"Well, hello there. Do you live in Sausalito, Monique?" I asked.

"Yeah, in a house kinda over the hill."

"How long have you lived there?"

"My parents moved over here from Oakland two years ago because of my brother."

"Oh really?"

Monique exchanged a look with Mary. "My parents thought the schools would be better over here, but then they ended up sticking me in St. Agatha's anyway."

"You don't like St. Agatha's?"

"Enough with the cross examination!" Mary interrupted.

I drew myself up as Henry does, and addressed Monique, "Did you feel that I was cross examining you?"

"No, ma'am," Monique replied dutifully.

Monique came to the house every day that week, apparently having decided that she liked me. Monique liked to hang over my shoulder and look at the design books, or chatter to me while I cooked dinner. Monique's parents both worked long hours and her older brother was already grown and gone. Neither of the girls said anything specific about him, but I supposed that he had gotten into some trouble. Monique hinted that it was her brother's fault that she got transferred to St. Agatha's, but I never pressed for details.

At first Mary was annoyed by Monique's attentiveness, but over time she seemed to accept it. I hoped that Monique's admiration would set a good example, and inspire in Mary that natural respect I craved. Whether or not that was happening, the end result was that Monique had become a bridge between me and Mary, and I loved her for it. Monique basked in my approval, and every day became more bold, more relaxed, more herself. Monique could do things, talk about doing things, and use inappropriate language in a way that I could never tolerate in Mary. If Mary noticed or if it bothered her, she never said anything. Indeed, it seemed to me that Mary and I attended Monique in an almost sycophantic way that was not entirely explained by Monique's personal charm.

One Thursday, the girls came home late.

"We missed the van," Mary said.

Monique elbowed her and smiled directly at me.

Mary rolled her eyes and acknowledged, "We got a ride."

"From her boyfriend," Monique said, unable to contain herself.

"He's not my boyfriend," Mary quickly insisted, "but maybe we should invite him to dinner?"

"Alright," I said, suppressing a smile, "Friday would be most relaxed."

I stood behind Monique and began absentmindedly arranging and rearranging her crispy soft locks while I listened to them talk. Monique stood still for these attentions and was pleased enough to forget about harassing Mary.

The phone rang and I jumped to answer it. It was only Henry making his customary mid-afternoon call. I silently fumed. Another day had passed without a single call from a contractor. The design was finished and I was entertaining bids. None of these men took me seriously. Of course, I could have Henry do it and they'd call with alacrity. But it was my my project, and I didn't want to give up any part of it.

"You could have my brother's crew do it," Monique suggested.

The one who got into some unmentionable trouble? I silently wondered.

"They do good work, really. My brother works for this guy who does remodeling all over town, nice houses."

I withdrew into the study to make a call to the contractor's board before I called the contractor himself. I was surprised when someone answered immediately and agreed to stop by the following day to give me an estimate.

"I told you," Monique said.

The next day when the contractor showed up, it was Monique's brother who stood in the doorway. He was her own image—the nose with the round tip like a cartoonist's caricature of a perky person, the thickly lashed dark eyes that crinkled in the corners, the sharp fashion model's jaw—except that he was larger and his dreadlocks were short and spiky. I was speechless.

"Hi, I'm Marcus Wilson, Monique's brother," the man said, smiling broadly.

I gave Marcus my sketches and showed him the bath.

"Wow, you're really organized," Marcus said, "and this is a really cool design."

His approval was like sweet iced tea on a hot day.

"I have to make some calls and run the final numbers before I can give you a solid bid," Marcus said as he scribbled on a pad of paper, "By the end of the week for sure."

I was becoming excited now. The idea of the new bathroom was no longer abstract, but something that was becoming solid, imminent. It had become almost like a living entity, burgeoning, pregnant, waiting for its transformation. I stood there in the doorway noticing all of this with excitement that was mixed with a strange and strong nervousness that I could not explain.

I could hardly wait to tell Monique. Although the girls were pleased, they didn't stay, as I thought they would.

"We're going for a walk, maybe to the coffee shop," Mary said as she and Monique filled their water bottles. Mary won this round, I thought. They were leaving.

II.

The setting sun hit the girls full in their faces as they shut the front door behind them. Mary sat down on the steps and lifted a hand to shade her eyes. Monique sat down beside her.

Why do you like hanging around her so much?" Mary asked, piqued.

Monique squinted and pursed her lips.

"It's hard to explain," Monique started, "it's like she's a jewel before they cut it to make it shine. And you can see that she knows it, that she longs to become what she is." Monique paused. "Yeah, I think that's it. It's the sadness and the longing. She wants so much, but asks for so little."

"Oh, please," Mary said, "She's got plenty, believe me. That little bathroom remodel isn't free. Just because she doesn't like the color of her bathroom, she's going to spend as much as some people make in a year to change it."

"I'm not talking about stuff, Mary. I'm talking about soul. Your mom has a beautiful soul and she just washes your socks, takes Matt to soccer, and shops."

"Lots of moms do that."

Monique grimaced and pushed out her lower lip, revealing the fuscia-colored inner plumpness. Like the ripe inside of a fruit, Mary found herself thinking. Then she drew back and averted her eyes.

"I'm not gay, you know," Mary said.

"I know. You're sweet on that dork, Dave."

"How do you know you are, anyway?" Mary asked her.

"When I'm sweet on a dork, it's a girl."

They shared a smile.

"So you don't think my Mom should wash my socks."

"Oh, I don't know!" Monique threw up her hands, "I guess I think that she should be able to do something else too. Something that's hers."

"She's got the bathroom."

Monique shrugged, "You wanna get a mocha or just walk?"

"We can walk that way, maybe get one."

The girls walked at a desultory pace, their hips loose in their sockets.

"So why aren't you going out for anything?" Mary asked Monique.

"Like yearbook and class officer and all that? I'm not the type. I'm too much of a fringe dweller, I do my own thing."

"What's that when you're not down here with us?"

Monique smiled, "Oh, there was a group of people over by my house I used to hang with. We hung out, smoked, talked, mostly. And then there's the gay ghetto."

"The gay ghetto?"

"Yeah, it's a great place to meet girls, but why hang out with people just because you have that one thing in common? It's almost like joining a gang."

"A gang? I mean, I can imagine wanting to find a place where I could be comfortable with other people who are like me. What's wrong with that?"

"Life isn't about comfort, Mary. No one is ever comfortable, even if it looks like they are. Life is about pushing the envelope, man. I want to be in people's faces, I want to be out there mixing it up and if someone doesn't like it, that's their problem and I'm gonna make them deal with it. I'm proud of who I am, and in every encounter, I want to be a walking invitation to engage."

Monique delivered this speech as if she had said it before, or had it written down. She wasn't even looking at Mary as she spoke, but looked instead at the undulating horizon of the city, visible over the rooftops of the buildings down the hill.

"You wouldn't feel that way if you lived under Henry's roof."

"Oh yeah? Bring it on. You know I'll bring it, and that's why neither you or your Mom has ever invited me to dinner. All this time I've spent at your house, and you haven't ever asked. I'm always gone or going when Henry gets home."

Mary said nothing.

"I feel like an illicit lover, getting hustled out the back stairs."

"Oh please."

"I call it like I see it. We have family meals sometimes, and if you were there when we did, you'd be invited too. Here, everything gets shut down when Henry gets home. You've got The Man living right there in your house, and everyday you run from him like a coward. You kiss his ass and pretend."

Shifting Ground

"Maybe you like living in a war zone, but I don't."

Monique shrugged and started to look around, disengaged.

The girls walked in silence until they reached the coffee shop.

"If I am such a pathetic coward, then why are you here?" Mary asked.

Monique smiled again, "You have that same pressed down diamond sadness that your Mom has, but your sadness is angry and that's something I can relate to."

Mary flushed scarlet. Her mouth worked silently for two whole seconds before a loud string of words finally rushed out.

"You don't fucking know what you are talking about. You don't know me at all. I'm nothing like her."

Monique raised her eyes at the obscenity, so foreign and renegade in Mary's mouth, but said nothing.

Both girls walked, Mary with lips angrily pressed, Monique with tilted head and rolling eyes.

"Isn't it the pressure that makes the diamond?" Monique asked while toying with the fringe on her jacket.

Mary didn't respond. Monique ignored Mary's pique entirely.

"Yeah, I think it is," she said, musing to herself, "I like that. I'm gonna write that one down."

"You and your juvenile poetics."

"All great poets have to start somewhere," Monique responded, unperturbed.

"I thought you were going into politics."

"Political activist, poet, and lesbian extraordinaire."

They stopped at the coffee shop and ordered their mochas without speaking to each other, and then settled on a bench. They leaned back against the storefront and stretched their legs out onto the sidewalk.

"Anyway," Mary said, "It's only another year, a little more, and then I can do what I want. Why stir up everything now?"

"I'm not saying that you should fight just for the sake of fighting. I'm just saying that you should be yourself, be who you are. Your parents don't even know you. You think that identifying myself as a lesbian in a Catholic high school is easy? It's not, but it's worth it to be able to be myself, comfortable or not."

"The teachers don't know you're gay. I heard about it as a rumor."

"So? Do you walk around telling the nuns that you're a heterosexual who fantasizes about sex with a skinny, ugly boy? Being myself doesn't mean I have to go around giving every person every detail about my life."

"I thought you wanted to be in people's faces? You never stand up to them about anything gay."

"Whatever!" Monique held up a hand and loudly sucked the foam off the top of her drink.

Mary knew that she had no real cause to be mad at Monique, but she was anyway. She avoided Monique the rest of the week. She was probably over the hill smoking with her old pothead friends, Mary supposed maliciously. It was easy to spend Friday alone after school; she was strung so tight about Dave coming over.

Then, Dave arrived and everything else fell away. It was as if a missing piece of puzzle fell into place and smoothed all of those rough edges. He joked with Henry, flattered her mother, played with the boys. At the table, she discovered that it was great luck to sit at Dave's left, because when Henry talked, and he did talk tremendous volumes, Mary could look in Henry's direction, pretending rapt attention, while studying Dave out of the corner of her eye. She loved the way his wavy blonde hair was just a little too long in the back and bent itself into shiny curls, like a toddler's. He had a strong jaw and a jutting chin that asserted itself in front of Henry's talking face. And every now and then, he looked at her with a winking expression, just to show that he wasn't really listening to Henry either, that he was on her team. She loved him so much, she could hardly stand the interminable chewing, talking, clearing, before she could finally have a few unsupervised moments alone with him outside as he was leaving.

"Come over here, by the garage," she told him, pulling his hand, "they'll watch us out of those windows."

Then, she threw her arms around him, kissing him furiously on his mouth, his face, his neck. It wasn't the first time they had kissed. They had found several places and times during the school day when they could be alone together. It was when these periods of time strung together were no longer enough that Mary invited him to dinner. Dinner opened the door to time, legitimate, long periods of time together.

The boy was panting, but he stopped her.

"Oh!" Mary held him for one last kiss, before pulling back to a respectable distance as they walked out into the arc of driveway visible from the front windows.

Mary could hardly wait to call Monique, who sounded sleepy when she answered the phone.

"I'm totally in love with him," Mary said at once. "Everyone loves him. We're going out tomorrow night."

"I guess that means that I've got to scrounge up some chick soon, or I'll be hanging with my English book every weekend."

"You want to come over tomorrow?"

"I'm distributing candidate flyers for NARAL all afternoon. You could come." After lunch on Saturday, they were walking along the residential streets of Pacific Heights, placing a rolled up flyer on the doorknob of every house, chatting as if their argument the previous week had never occurred. Mary talked only of Dave, until Monique made her stop.

Mary walked silently for several feet, and then cocked her head.

"So, because you are a lesbian, I guess you'll always be a virgin, huh?"

"You don't need a penis to have sex, Mary. It's all in the tongue," Monique said, and flicked her tongue through the air.

Mary screamed and hid her face in her hands. Mary looked at Monique timidly. "So, you have? You've had sex with girls?"

"Sure, lots of times. No worries about getting pregnant, that's for sure."

Mary let this sink in.

"I think I might have to get on the pill," Mary choked out.

Monique laughed out loud.

"I'm glad you find it all so amusing." Mary grimaced. "I'm sorry I told you."

"I'll introduce you to Planned Parenthood," Monique said with a smirk. "We're old friends."

Mary just looked at Monique silently, in wonder.

They hung several flyers before Monique spoke again.

"So, I guess I'm on my own tonight, and probably every weekend until who knows when."

"We could hang out Sunday. You could see if you can go to St. Agatha's with us Sunday, and have lunch with us afterwards."

"Lunch with your family? Lunch with Henry after church?" Monique asked with mock incredulity.

"Yeah," Mary said defensively, "You said you wanted to so bad, so here's your chance."

Monique eyed her, smiling impishly. "My, my," she said.

Monique arrived at Mary's house Sunday morning, precisely on time, dressed for church. Mary wasn't sure what she was expecting, but she was a little surprised to see Monique in a skirt. They sat in the back seat of the minivan and whispered about Mary's date the night before, while the boys elbowed each other and drew comments from Henry. When they crossed themselves and settled into a pew, Mary's parents seated themselves between the boys, and the girls ended up on the end next to Matthew. The church was full, and there seemed to be more than the usual number of priests milling around. When Monique mentioned it, Mary shrugged. As the altar boys passed them, walking down the aisle with the priests, Monique snickered to herself.

"Chesters and Chesters in training," she whispered.

"What's so funny about them?" Mary thought she had said "jesters."

"You don't think it's funny that the religious institution that rules every aspect of our waking lives is riddled with pedophiles?"

This non-sequitur baffled Mary.

"Like Chester the Molester," Monique whispered loud enough to draw a stare from Atlanta, who leaned in front of Matthew to deliver it.

Mary smothered a smile. She understood now.

The girls remained silent until Mary saw Atlanta relax back into the pew and pat Matthew on the knee.

"I've always thought that Father John was creepy," Mary whispered without turning her head. "He's so old and he has those long, skinny fingers."

A slow smile spread across Monique's face.

"It's a new game," she whispered, "Find the Chester."

Mary had to squint and lower her head in a penitent, prayerful gesture to hold in the laughter that was backed up behind her teeth. After the storm had passed, she continued to look at her hands folded in her lap for several moments before attentively facing the altar again.

"I'll bet on the pudgy one, Father Dan," Monique whispered. "Those big lips and beady eyes. He's always licking his lips. He's probably thinking impure thoughts right this minute."

"He's in charge of the Youth Group for regular church," Mary said.

Monique squinted and pressed the back of her hand hard into her mouth. Atlanta shifted in her seat, and Mary nudged Monique hard in the ribs.

Monique tried to say, 'youth group,' but couldn't before she again had to press the back of her hand to her mouth.

Atlanta leaned around Matthew and whispered, "Girls!" The two straightened up, and faced forward.

"I can imagine sitting in one of those confession booths and those fat fingers trying to shove themselves through the little grate," Monique whispered, and screwed up her mouth to stifle a giggle.

"You're gonna get us in trouble," Matthew whispered to Mary, as Atlanta shifted again and whispered something to Henry.

The girls sat attentively through the rest of the Mass, but cast glances at each other every time Father Dan moved.

As they all filed out of the pews to leave the church, Atlanta raised her eyebrows at the girls, as if to say, *Almost.* Monique looked back at her with an exaggerated, penitent expression.

"You have plenty of time to talk after church," Atlanta said to them.

Atlanta put a hand on each of their shoulders as they walked out. Her hands left their shoulders as they reached the crush of people stopped at the double doors, separating to file past one or the other of two priests who flanked the opening. The girls drifted to the center of the stream, away from the waiting lines in front of the priests.

Matthew waited in line behind Atlanta. The girls floated next to him, whispering to each other. When Matthew shook the priest's hand, the girls erupted in a fit of giggling and skittered along the edge of the line, out of the priest's reach.

"Ew! You touched Chester!" Monique taunted him and punched Mary in the shoulder.

Mary and Monique were seized again by a fit of giggling.

"Who's Chester?" Matthew asked, annoyed that, as usual, he had no idea what they were talking about.

"Oh, you mean the priest? His name isn't Chester, it's Father Dan," Matthew told them with authority.

This comment brought on a renewed fit of giggling.

"No, dummy," Mary said, "Chester, like Chester the Molester."

"He's not a molester," Matthew objected.

"How do you know?" Mary asked him.

"Yeah, that's the point, you don't know," Monique said, "He might be. We have studied him, and we think of all the priests in this church, it's probably him."

"Father Dan is the nicest one! He wouldn't do that."
"That's what they said about the guy in Boston, and he chestered hundreds," Monique said.

"Mary! Matthew! Let's go," Atlanta called.

"Henry has an early tee time today," Mary told Monique.

Atlanta had turned her back on them, apparently caught in a conversation with a man and woman who were smiling at her and Henry. Mary, Monique and Matthew watched them for a couple of minutes, and then turned to each other.

"They're not even going yet," Matthew said.

"We could check on my gardening project," Monique said to Mary with a grin.

Mary looked back at Atlanta and Henry.

"We'd have to hurry, it's all the way behind the school," she said.

Monique shrugged.

"If you don't tattle, we'll show you something," Mary said to Matthew.

"Okay."

Mary drilled him with her eyes until he repeated, "I won't. I said okay."

The two girls led him around to the back of the school building to where the nuns maintained a vegetable garden.

"See that tall plant by the fence? The one next to the sunflowers?" Monique asked. "That's pot. I got a seed from my brother and planted it. They just water it with all the other stuff. I go and pinch off some whenever I want it." Monique was beside herself with pride.

Matthew turned his eyes to Mary, without blinking.

"Mary's body is a temple," Monique said to him in response, rolling her eyes.

"I only do things that are healthy," Mary said. "I don't smoke cigarettes or weed, and I only drink in moderation. Studies have shown that drinking in moderation is good for you."

"Well, studies have shown that marijuana makes you better looking," Monique said, mimicking Mary's tone of authority.

"Maybe if the other person is stoned," Matthew said, "Real stoned."

Monique punched him and Matthew laughed at her.

"Actually," Mary said, unmoved, "studies have shown that people who smoke age seven years faster than people who don't."

"You said that study was with cigarettes," Monique said.

"Smoking is smoking," Mary insisted, "And anyway, you're always talking about how black people are getting left behind and how such and so percent don't go to college, or make a high income, but look at yourself."

"What about me?" Monique demanded, her features darkening.

"You could get better grades if you didn't smoke so much."

Monique didn't say anything. The two girls just stood there looking at each other, and Matthew shifted his feet.

"So what if I got good grades and got into a good college? Then what?"

"You could be one of those people that increases the percentage of black people who graduate from good colleges, of course."

"Yeah, and then what?"

"Get a good job and a good income, and all that."

"So some old white man can rig the stock market and steal my pension and refuse to promote me? Great." Monique looked at her feet. "I want to be successful, but I want to be successful in a different world," she said, "I don't want to spend my life working for this one."

"Be successful and change the world. That's what I'm going to do," Mary said.

"Everyone says that, but they never do."

The girls stood for several moments, looking at each other.

"I think they should legalize it," Matthew said, affecting for them a sophistication that was beyond him.

"Amen to that," Monique said, "but they never will. Drug laws are how The Man controls black people."

Matthew nodded knowingly, but then his curiosity overcame his pride.

"What do you mean?" he asked her.

"The police concentrate in black neighborhoods, and harass black people. Anybody they catch with drugs, they throw in jail. Once you've been in jail, your life is over. And you can't vote while you're in jail, and sometimes not even after. The white man gets rid of a lot of black votes that way. Permanently."

"But if those people are breaking the law, they gotta go to jail. That's not the police's fault," Matthew said.

The girls looked at each other.

"White people do drugs too, Matthew," Mary said patiently. "They just get away with it. The police really do concentrate on every little thing black people do."

"Yeah," Monique said, "A black guy jaywalks, and a cop is right on him, frisking him for drugs he doesn't even have, while some old white dude who has stolen millions of dollars from old ladies on the stock market walks wherever he pleases with his after lunch coke lift right in his pocket, no problem."

"Well, that's not fair!" Matthew protested.

"No shit, Sherlock," Monique said.

"What are you kids doing?" Atlanta demanded from across the lawn.

"Nothing," Mary called, "We're coming."

Lunch was rushed and completely uneventful. For the most part, Henry ate quickly while glancing at his watch, and ignored Monique. Mary couldn't help feeling disappointed.

Deconstruction

I moved the heavy wooden handle in my hand, testing my grip as I stared at the broad sea of orange tile in front of me. I felt the weight of the iron juggernaut pull my shoulder out of its socket ever so slightly, and I smiled. This would do.

"Do it Atlanta!" Sally urged me.

"Bash it!" Susan said.

Uncertainty gripped my belly.

Susan sighed with exasperation, "Bash it!"

"Bash it! Bash it!" Sally and Susan chanted together.

I took aim at the patch of tile next to the vanity. I swayed the sledgehammer back and forth gently in front of my knees. It slipped a little in my grip on each swing, and I was unsure that I'd be able to swing it up high enough to make contact. How pathetic it would be to get it up only halfway and then to feel my spaghetti arms go limp and have to let it drop! I wanted to be bold and do it properly the first time. My insecurity and frustration with my insecurity beat at each other with their fists until, in a surge of rage, I swung the hammer around behind me, over my head in a perfect arc and smashed it into the wall. The splintering ceramic exploded all over us and the floor.

Susan and Sally jumped backwards with a scream, while I held my ground, feeling the tiniest splinters still falling, stinging my face, my closed eyelids.

"Wow!" Susan said, examining the crater that reached all the way through the plaster to wood underneath. "Way to go!"

"It's official," Sally said. She took the red-ribboned sledgehammer from my hand and placed it ceremoniously, like a trophy, on the bathroom countertop.

I brushed my face with my palms, shook my hair out.

"Let's eat. I'm famished," Susan said.

I had prepared a ladies lunch that I had cribbed out of a fashionable magazine.

"I've died and gone to heaven," Susan said, eating loudly and talking with her mouth full. "This is a fabulous end to my days of leisurely lunches."

"Oh, yes, you start work on Monday, don't you?" I said.

Susan had always said that she would start working again once both of her kids were in school, but the idea always seemed remote, even as Susan sent out resumes.

"The medical software thing, right?" Sally asked.

"Yeah. I really think it's a good idea. Maybe that's just what I'm telling myself because it's a good job in a bad economy, but," she waved her hands, "anyway, right now I really believe that it's going to revolutionize how hospitals are run."

"I can't imagine going back to work," Sally said wistfully, and then started upright in her seat, extending a hand. "Not that it's bad, or anything. I just can't imagine myself doing it."

"Why not?" Susan asked her.

"Well, it would be too stressful."

"Stressed might be better than bored. Don't you miss the challenge?"

"I guess I always had too much money and too little ambition." Sally laughed. "And then Jeff and I started with the kids right away...there wasn't that much to miss."

"You're a lot younger than I am," Susan said, "You'll still be young when they're in high school. You've got lots of time to figure something out."

"Why do I have to figure something out?" Sally's face tightened. "I think I'm just a housewife. Maybe you don't want to be a housewife, but then, I don't want to be a computer start up whatever you are."

"Okay, whatever." Susan raised her hands.

"I want to be home when my kids get home, until they are out of the house. And then, who knows? Technically, I'll be retired and so I guess I'll do what retired people do—whatever I want."

"I'm not saying that you have to be like me. But the proper career path of housewife is similar to that of a fashion model. You've got maybe two decades tops, and then you have to find something else to do. Fashion models, pro athletes, and housewives need a back up plan, that's all I'm saying. As soon as the kids go to school, you should too."

Sally made no rejoinder, and instead asked what was in the quiche. The three of us politely finished our lunch.

When Susan had to answer a text, I got up to clear the dishes. Moments later, Sally came into the kitchen and began to load the dishwasher.

"I think it is selfish to go back to work." Sally hissed under her breath. "Who's going to be there for those kids?"

"The kids are pretty busy with their friends after school, I think." I wasn't really wanting to take sides. "She's got a nanny to take them around to their lessons and such."

"Will that nanny love them as much, though? Our nanny is just a helper. I'm always there. I can't imagine how those kids feel about her going back to work."

"The kids seem pretty positive about it, Sally. I think they're okay, really."

"You just wait until they're older. They'll be the first on the block to get in trouble."

"Do you think I'm deaf?" Susan demanded from the doorway.

Sally didn't turn around, but continued to load dishes into the machine with pursed lips.

"Statistically speaking," Susan said to Sally's back, "It has been conclusively shown that children who are in quality childcare after age one are actually better off on a number of different scales, including intellectual development and emotional health. And I don't know the statistics about troublemakers, but my high school was full of delinquents and back then, almost all of them had stay at home mothers."

"My mother worked all the time," I said, relieved that I actually had something to say.

This admission had the effect of exploding the expanding bubble of aggression between the other two women.

"Really?" Sally turned to me

"I'm not sure if she took any leave at all," I said, "but she's a professor, so she had summers off."

"What does she teach?" Susan asked.

"She started out in Anthropology, but she does this inter-disciplinary stuff with Mythology and Feminism. She's very devoted. I think she's written twelve books, maybe thirteen, if the last one is out."

"Wow, why didn't I know that?" Susan asked.

I shrugged, pleased that I broke up the brewing battle.

"See?" Susan declaimed to Sally, "Is she a delinquent? Was she the first on her block to get an abortion?"

Sally started.

"Yes, I know that's what you say about daughters of working mothers, don't try to deny it."

Sally said nothing.

I bit my lip and turned away again. I began to rinse the glasses.

"Why are you so angry that I'm going back to work? What do you care?" Susan said to Sally. "I'll tell you why you care—you're jealous. You're mad because you're making all these sacrifices and I'm not, and you think I should be punished for not sacrificing myself. You want me to get divorced, or have bad kids so you can say, See? That's what you get, Susan, for thinking that you can have a life of your own. You want my life to fail so that you can justify yours. When you say that my daughter will be the first on the block to get an abortion, it's because you hope she will. And that is sad, and ugly, and I feel sorry for you."

"Well, don't you feel sorry for me," Sally said angrily. "I'm perfectly happy to be there for my kids, out of love."

"Fine, Sally, you just keep saying that. But count the hours, Sally. During these grade school and middle school years, the kids don't hang around with their mommies. They play with each other. They run around. They don't need a full time mother now—they just need a chauffer and someone who knows how to apply a Band-Aid and arbitrate disputes. Any intelligent young adult will do. Your kids are ten times more daring and independent than you are, and every year, I see you becoming more habituated to it. It's only because I care about you that I say anything."

"You're wrong, and you can keep that kind of caring to yourself from now on."

"Fine! Suit yourself."

I was silent through this exchange, desperately trying to think of how to stop it. Then I saw Sally, smiling in a satisfied way to herself, and I wondered what she could be thinking.

"It's not over until the fat lady sings," Sally said after Susan left.

"You make it sound like some kind of competition."

"You don't think Susan is competing with us? Please! She sat there all afternoon, saying look at me, I'm so great and successful and you two aren't. I've got this great job and you have no life. Her whole life is about competition. She belongs in business, and it's just too bad for those kids."

"She didn't actually say that we had no life," I said, thinking aloud.

"She implied it. She practically demanded that I get a job. Actually, she did say that because my kids are in school, I should be in school too."

"Like working at a job is so great," Sally added, sneering.

I didn't want to say anything more about it. The pressure of all my thoughts was giving me a headache.

"The kids will be home soon," I said.

Henry came home late all the time now. He appeared in the kitchen, smirking and holding up the forgotten sledgehammer while I was cleaning up after putting Joshua to bed.

I blushed, dried my hands on my pants and took the tool from him.

"Susan and Sally were here, and we had a little ground breaking event." I grimaced. "And then Susan and Sally had an argument. The lunch was spoiled by it, and now I'm not sure they're going to get along very well anymore."

Henry smirked again. "It'll pass, I'm sure."

I wasn't so sure and I fretted about it when I didn't see either one of them all weekend. Sunday I was worn out with worry and decided to go to bed early. Mary and her boyfriend, Dave, were watching a movie.

"I'm going to bed, Mary. Don't stay up too late, or you won't get up."

Dave gave me his most charming smile.

The boy was easy to get along with, and had all but replaced Monique in Mary's affections, at least on the weekends. That worried me. I would appreciate it very much if the romantic intensity would level off just a little.

The next morning, I saw Susan across the street in the foggy half light, standing in her driveway in a pantsuit and pumps, watching the bus drive away. When she noticed me looking at her, she turned and waved. I thought that we could talk for a few minutes, but Susan opened the back door of her car and stowed a briefcase. She smiled, pantomimed nervousness, and then gave me a thumbs up before getting into the front seat. I smiled and waved and then shut the front door. Henry kissed me on the cheek and left.

"It's cold this morning!" he said, shaking his shoulders as he closed the door behind him.

I cleared the breakfast table and loaded the dishwasher. Count the hours, Susan had said. I counted one. The workmen arrived promptly at eight, and by ten, I could not remain in the house any longer. I was relieved when I called Sally and found her home.

"Will you allow a remodeling refugee to invite herself over?"

"Of course!" Sally laughed. "Demolition today?"

"My God, they are tearing out the inside of my skull with that pounding."

"Come on over. You can have some stale coffee and half a doughnut."

Sally's house was always warm. I shivered gratefully as I entered. Sally claimed that it was passive solar from the big Southern windows, but I knew that Sally had no compunction whatsoever about turning on the heat, any season of the year, if there were a chill in the morning.

"Maybe this wasn't such a good idea," I moaned as I allowed the steam from a deliciously fresh cup of coffee rise around my cheeks.

"Remodeling is like childbirth. It's painful, but afterwards, you're so happy that you don't remember the pain. Let's just hope that it goes quickly and they don't find anything. They always seem to find something."

"Don't even say that."

"Termites, dry rot, water damage, cracked foundation," Sally went on, teasing me.

"At least they're upstairs and won't ever see the foundation."

"It's not necessarily a bad thing, you know." Sally took a sip of her coffee. "If your foundation is going, you want to know, right?"

"That darn entropy," Sally chuckled to herself in response to my silent cogitation, and then looked out the window at the trees shivering in the fog. "Anything that moves rubs something, so you've got friction causing some kind of decay. Everything passes away to make room for other things. It's the nature of life to grow like that."

"You make a damaged foundation sound so romantic," I said drily.

"Maybe that will be my backup plan…dark, romantic poetess," Sally cracked.

"Are you still thinking about what Susan said?"

"Yeah," she admitted, "You know, I think our problem is that housewives have some kind of martyr complex sometimes."

My whole body vibrated hard like the too taut string of a bow. That's just what Mary had said. *Don't get your martyr complex in a twist.* I exhaled several times as Sally babbled on.

"Martyr complex," I interrupted, "what does that mean, anyway?"

"Well, no one says it out loud, but there's this idea that we're second class citizens. We're dismissed politically. Everyone assumes we're dumb. Everyone imposes on us. When was the last time you said no? When was the last time you made some big financial decision you found necessary?"

"Well, Henry mostly manages the money."

"It's not just about the money. It's about feeling like you matter, even though no one else thinks you do."

I watched the steam rise from my cup.

"Last weekend, I took out all of our financial papers and studied them. It made John very nervous!"

Sally laughed.

"I think he thought that I was thinking about divorcing him, he was asking all these questions. The whole thing led to a very interesting discussion about how we invest our money. I think John was glad that he could talk to me about it. In fact, I think he found it very exciting to listen to me talk about technical financial stuff."

Sally smiled in a way that made her meaning plain.

"Oh he didn't!" Atlanta laughed.

"I respect myself plenty. I don't have to work at some job to do that," Sally said.

She laid both palms on the table. "Now you," Sally said, "you are going to go to the gym with me. You are going to stop ironing Henry's shirts. That is just ridiculous. We'll drop his dry cleaning on our way to the gym. And we'll have nice lunches out together after."

"Oh, don't you fret about me," I deflected. "I've been ironing his shirts since we were babies just starting out, it's part of my routine. When you send them out, they come back all stiff and creased in funny places. Henry hates that. I let the housekeeper fold our laundry, but letting someone else wash your clothes, well, that's just gross."

"Atlanta!" Sally sighed, exasperated.

"TMI, as the kids say," I put up one hand.

I did start going to the gym and having lunch with Sally. Henry teased me about being a princess. It was all good humored, but I always felt that there was something about the way he spoke to me that was offensive. He indulged me, but only after making me feel it, how I needed indulging, like a small, spoiled child.

Sally, on the other hand, bloomed with the new, more rigorous regimen. She started dropping pounds and dropped provocative comments about the sexual renaissance she was enjoying with John. These revelations made me uncomfortable. It had been a long time since I had had the energy to want that kind of renaissance. As I watched Susan wave from her driveway in the morning, and as I watched Sally bounce around, red cheeked and handsome in our neighborhood, I just felt tired.

I didn't talk with Susan at all anymore. I really didn't even care how her job was going. I was very surprised, then, when Susan called and woke me from a long afternoon nap, chattering at me as if nothing had changed. I listened to her without saying much of anything, sitting on the edge of my bed, trying to clear my sleep fuddled brain.

"So I really hate for this to be the reason for my call, it's so rude. But you and I know each other well enough to impose, right?" Susan's laugh was loud and ringing.

"The thing is, my babysitter has called in sick and the kids are due home in an hour...."

"I can take them," I said.

"That would be so fantastic," Susan gushed. "I'll try to get home early. I really appreciate it. Sally says that you two are having lunch out now. Maybe I could meet you one of these days."

Later, on the phone, I couldn't help quizzing Sally.

"I didn't know that you were still talking to Susan," I said.

"Well, I don't talk about it because you always seem so negative when I mention her. I thought that maybe you were still a little mad about that lunch and what she said. I figured I would give you a chance to let it blow over."

"Me? I'm not mad," I objected.

"Maybe not mad, but annoyed…something, right? It's okay. I don't even think she realizes it. She's totally into the new job."

"Yes, she doesn't have much to talk about except for herself," I said.

"See? That's what I'm talking about. You're still mad."

I was starting to wonder if I should be setting the table for five kids instead of three when the doorbell rang.

I opened the door and the cool evening air rushed in. Susan smiled.

"Hey! Sorry I'm late instead of early. Traffic was unbelievable," she said brightly as she entered the foyer and unwrapped a broad, red and gold silk scarf from her shoulders.

She seemed happy and out of breath.

"What a day!" she said, "How were they?"

"Oh, no trouble at all. They played with Joshua in his room all afternoon. Joshua!" I called, "bring Alex and Andrea, their Momma is here!"

She laughed and babbled playfully with the kids, who were now hugging her knees. As they all bounded out of the front door and across the street, I thought to myself that it was a good thing for her that I didn't have a life. What would she have done today if I had a life?

That question was running around and around in my head when Susan stopped by the following evening with a bottle of wine to thank me for my help. Finally, Susan said something that made the question irresistible.

"Anyway," Susan said, as she moved to the front door to leave, "I don't know what I would have done without you."

"Oh," I tried to sound casual, "You probably have all kinds of backup plans."

Susan smiled and extended her fingers, one by one, "My backup plans are named Jeff, Atlanta, and Sally. After that, I just take off work."

"I guess if Sally and I got jobs now that our kids are all in school, that would leave you with only one backup plan."

Susan cocked her head, "I never thought about it that way. It is really nice to have someone in your neighborhood that you can count on. Well, anyway," she smiled and raised a hand, "I'll let you guys eat dinner. Good night!" I sighed.

"So," Henry asked me at dinner, "are those remodelers ever coming back, or are they only a destruction service?"

"They said this week, but it looks like it might be next week."

"If it were me, I'd fire them tomorrow," Henry grumbled. "In this economy, there's a lot more where they came from."

"They've got another house they're working on too. They'll be back as soon as they can."

Mary took my plate and her own to the kitchen. The boys pushed past her to dump their plates into the sink before they went into the living room to watch television. Cleaning up after dinner was now Mary's job.

"Henry?"

Henry looked up and I fingered my water glass, composing my face into an expression I hoped was both confident and insouciant.

"Where do we keep our financial records? I think I should know, just in case."

"In case of what?" he asked, as he chewed his last mouthful.

"Well, you could end up in the hospital, or something."

"I'm not going to end up in the hospital, and anyway, even if I did, I could still take care of everything, or call my accountant."

"I just want to know where it all is," I paused to steady my resolve, to resurrect the illusion of confidence, "I would like to see it all."

"I take care of it all at the office," he said, pushing his plate away.

"You could bring it home," I insisted.

"There are a lot of files, Atlanta, and I don't want them to get lost. I feel like I am catering to enough of your whims for now, and I have more important things to do." Henry shook his head in disgust and stalked out of the room.

Is he going to take away my stereo and cell phone now? I thought and then put my fingers over my tired eyes.

Mary appeared to clear Henry's plate, and I sat up, startled and embarrassed. Had she heard it all?

It was on the same day that the remodelers came back that Monique reappeared also. I was sleeping. I was walking in my desert, looking for something, hiking to the tops of those eroded hills but seeing nothing more from the tops of them except another stretch of desert. Then, as I sat dejected on that silt, my teeth began to fall out into my hands. I woke up, my hands flying to my face in horror.

"The guys are back," Mary said, impatience in her voice.

"What?" I shook my head and ground my teeth together to assure myself that they were all there.

"Marcus is back and he wants to do something for the shower."

I rubbed my face with cream, brushed my hair, and pulled my body up straight, as if I felt refreshed. When I entered the living room, Monique and Marcus were in animated conversation and didn't even notice that I came in. Mary was standing aside, eyeing me.

"I was just giving Marcus shit for abandoning you this week," Monique said, laughing.

"You were giving him trouble," I said automatically, still sleep numbed.

"Yeah, I was giving him that very particular kind of trouble called shit." Monique laughed again and punched Marcus twice in the shoulder.

"Do you allow all of your contractors to be abused in this way?" he asked me, laughing, while fending off Monique's pushing hands.

"I'm really sorry," Marcus said to me sincerely, but he had to pause to grab Monique's upper body and hold her between his muscled arms as she struggled to topple him.

"I'm really sorry," he said again, smiling to demonstrate that he had Monique immobilized, "but our other job blew up on us, and we had to take care of some unexpected problems. These grand old houses, you know."

Just then, Monique succeeded in getting behind Marcus' knees and they tumbled to the floor together, laughing.

"Jesus, Monique, I'm working!" Marcus exclaimed as he picked himself off of the floor.

Monique was already on her feet, stretching out her arms with catlike satisfaction.

"Still the champ," she said.

I put my fingers to my forehead.

"I'll just be a couple of hours today to prepare for the tile," Marcus said, breezing past me, "Tile next week!" he called as he went upstairs.

I sat down on the couch.

"Are you alright?" Monique asked.

Mary was still silently eyeing me.

"I just woke up, I guess. I laid down for a few minutes, and I'm just waking up."

"Matthew's school called," Mary said. "They thought you were supposed to be teacher's aide this afternoon."

"Today is Friday," I said, my stomach clenching with embarrassment.

"We did the dishes in the sink," Monique said, "Joshua is in his room, and Matthew is over at Jack's."

"Okay, okay. Thank you," I said, still unable to focus. "Well, girls, I need to go down and check the laundry."

Once downstairs, I closed the door behind me and sank down onto the laundry room floor to get my bearings. I had spent every spare moment that week sleeping. All I could do was sleep, and if Marcus hadn't been hammering in the bathroom, I'd have to fight the urge to go back to sleep now. When I went back upstairs, the girls had gone and Joshua was peppering Marcus with questions as he watched him work.

"Joshua, Marcus is trying to work," I put a hand on Joshua's shoulder.

"No, that's alright," Marcus said between strikes of his hammer with his back to me, "He's fine."

I was standing at the stove when Marcus startled me by appearing in the kitchen with his toolbox, his blue jeans and dark skin powdered with fine white dust.

"All finished for today." He grinned as he passed through the kitchen. "We'll be back early on Monday, nine o'clock."

I managed a smile. "That's great, thank you."

Monique and Mary came sniffing into the kitchen.

"Are you staying for dinner?" I asked Monique absently as I stirred the pots.

Monique and Mary exchanged a stare.

"Sure," Monique said, smiling.

Matthew dominated the dinner conversation talking about the plans he had to build a fort in the small, sunbaked tree in the back yard, and fended off Joshua's interruptions, by which he demanded to be included in the project. We had planted that tree to shade the back yard, but the poor stunted thing hardly seemed to find enough shade for itself.

Henry was not enthusiastic about the idea of a fort in the back yard at all, and during an impasse between the boys, he turned his full attention on Monique, who had remained silent during the discussion. He asked her the usual questions about her home and school, and Mary and I interjected nervously. I just couldn't handle any unpleasantness right now, and I was desperately trying to throw him off the scent, but my fogged brain moved too slowly. I mentioned vaguely, without really knowing what I was talking about, that Monique was very involved in community work. It sounded wholesome.

Henry was intrigued and asked Monique, "What do you do?"

"Oh, lately I've been phone banking and hanging flyers for NARAL. It's a pro-choice organization," she said simply, and then took a bite of food.

"I know what it is," Henry snapped. "We don't support that organization in this household, and we certainly don't discuss that sort of thing at the dinner table."

"Are any of your kids adopted?" Monique asked him.

The bottom dropped out of my stomach. Mary glared at Monique hard, but Monique ignored her.

"What?" Henry drew himself up in his seat.

Monique repeated the question again, looking right at him.

Mary and I dropped our eyes and stopped eating.

"Nope," he said charmingly. "God blessed us with all three."

"Just because you *can* have your own biological kids, doesn't mean that you *have* to. You say that you don't agree that anyone should," Monique looked at Joshua, "refuse a pregnancy, and so I just wanted to know if that's just talk or if you have actually adopted an abandoned child."

Monique took a bite of food and waved her fork in a circle in the air before continuing, "Obviously, you haven't adopted a child with any sort of handicap, Down's, or crippling disease. But I guess you haven't even adopted a healthy, non-handicapped child, even though our foster care system and foreign orphanages are overloaded with them. So, I guess it *is* just talk. It usually is."

Henry's face turned scarlet.

"Your dinner is getting cold, Monique," I said desperately. "Eat your dinner."

"I find it interesting," Monique continued, completely ignoring me, and with an unfamiliar predatory gleam in her eye, "that pro-lifers don't object to all the born baby killing this country sponsors in the form of foreign wars for profit, the School of the Americas, and the theft of sustainable food production capacity by multinationals. Not to mention all of the American babies who die from poverty, lack of medical insurance and neglect. Pro-lifers only care about babies before they're born. After they come down the chute, their lives are subordinate to American financial and political interests."

Henry set down his fork and blew himself up twice actual size, focusing the entirety of his powerful gaze upon her. We all involuntarily shrank away, abandoning her. However, Monique did not change position nor lower her eyes, but just looked at him, frankly, earnestly. This made him blink and furrow his brow before drawing himself up again.

"Don't you think foreign policy is a little too complicated for a young lady your age?"

"Nope," Monique said, and resumed eating.

"Well," Henry took a bite and talked casually, dismissively, with his mouth full, "I think there are complexities that you don't quite understand."

"Really? Like what?"

The rest of us had been watching the exchange like spectators at a tennis match, not moving, not even seeming to breathe at all, but just looking at one and then the other as they spoke. We were all waiting for Henry to subordinate Monique. I guiltily wished for it as an end to this unbearable strain, but also dreaded it deep and heavy in my bowels.

Henry deflated himself, but raised his eyebrows as if he were unconcerned by someone so small as she, and took another bite before speaking.

"As I have already mentioned, young lady, I don't think that this line of conversation is appropriate for the dinner table."

Monique shrugged and smiled. Henry had backed down. Mary and I stared at Monique, sitting there untouched and smiling, for several moments before we forced our forks into our open mouths. Monique finished her dinner, still smiling, her smile seeming to say, *Still the champ.*

Henry was afraid of Monique. The idea of it, of Henry being afraid of anyone, stunned me. Maybe it was because she was black, maybe that pushed him off-balance. Maybe he was afraid that he would lose it and say something she would repeat to her parents, or at the school. Something had cowed him, and that was something I had never before seen.

When Monique came home with Mary on Monday, I found myself buzzing around her like a bee. I was happy and didn't sleep at all. I made them a cake. I poured myself some wine at 4:30 as I began to cook. Monique glowed and her naturally high spirits rose. We were all talking at once and laughing and the girls were trying to outdo each other. As a result, our conversation, in its hilarity, was getting more and more out of control. Or rather, Mary and I were playing straight to Monique's character, both of us enjoying Monique's outrageous statements and ribald talk. Then, something shifted.

"Isn't it crazy that the nuns are supposed to teach us about sex?" Mary yelled, laughing. "I mean, what do they know about sex? Their husband is a phantom without a johnson!"

"Though, from what I hear, the priests are having plenty of sex," Monique gasped, laughing also, "so maybe the nuns are too."

"I never before understood what the nuns meant when they said how wonderful it is when the Lord comes knocking!" Mary cried.

Even though I laughed, my smile faded. The hilarity was gone because I realized that Mary was in on it too, that she had been just hiding it from me. I was alone. Mary and Monique were talking and laughing together, and I was watching. Mary had left me behind.

"What do you know about sex, Mary Frances?" I angrily demanded.

"Oh," Mary imitated Monique's own mock sincerity, "only what those nuns teach me."

The girls fell over each other laughing.

"That is quite enough," I said, and left the room.

The sound of renewed fits of hilarity followed me as I went upstairs, my face hot, to check the progress of the tile.

"Hey there! What do you think?"

The kindness in Marcus' smile, and the momentary warmth of his hand on my shoulder brought tears to my eyes. How I longed to crawl into the sanctuary of one kind word. I opened my eyes wide to prevent a tear from falling, and smiled.

"The permanence of it makes me nervous," I said, and realized that it was true.

The other man working with Marcus turned around in surprise and laughed.

"It's too late to back out now!" he said.

There was a small patch in the shower where the pattern of the tile was taking shape, where, in my mind's eye, I could multiply it outwards and visualize it complete.

I stood in the doorway watching them for a quarter of an hour before I drew myself away. I wanted badly to lie down and sleep, but I couldn't with the men working there in the bathroom. It was in this way that my sleeping sickness was halted. I was still exhausted, but awake, and I spent my afternoons drifting like a ghost between the men working and my Furies.

I had already allowed the house to lapse into a controlled freefall of disorder, only partly arrested by the efforts of the housekeeper who refused to clean under the tarps, but now that the bathroom was ripped open I didn't bother myself with it at all. I had limped through gym workouts with Sally at first, then made excuses, and finally, I told Sally that I just couldn't do it anymore. Everything was falling away, but I was too tired to care anymore.

Then the remodelers were gone again. The corner unit bathtub was back ordered and wouldn't be available for another week, perhaps more. I gratefully renewed my naps, but set an alarm so that I'd be awake before the children came home. That first Monday, the boys were not yet home when Mary called. I could tell from Mary's tone that she could tell that I had been sleeping. Mary told me that she and Monique were attending an event after school and that they'd be late.

"It's a political gathering. It's not just Monique and I, but a lot of kids are going. It's for civil rights."

"How are you getting home?"

"One of Monique's friends is taking us home. I've got my cell…okay?" Mary asked impatiently.

"Oh all right. But please, try to be home at a decent hour."

"Okay, I'll try to be home before Henry."

Mary ran in, flushed and breathless, a half hour after Henry.

I was late with dinner again, Henry was talking at me as I threw it together, and Matthew was setting the table and complaining. Joshua had lost something important, I didn't have the patience to find out what, and he was turning over the whole house looking for it.

"I was out with Monique," Mary told Henry, throwing her backpack and purse on the couch, next to where he was standing in front of the blaring television, holding a scotch and waiting for the eight o'clock news cycle.

"You didn't come home first?" he asked, eyeing her belongings.

"Nope. A friend of Monique's drove us home."

The fast talking news reporter yelled at them in front of what she described as a "massive" demonstration in downtown San Francisco protesting against banks and corporations. It was still in progress, snarling traffic and requiring a large police presence to manage it.

My eyes widened as I realized that this was likely where my daughter had been that very afternoon. The reporters were showing scenes of marchers wearing black bandanas across their faces, scuffling and fighting with bystanders, and being thrown down by cops.

"Oh please!" Mary scoffed loudly from across the room, where she had reemerged. "Out of all of those thousands of people, a handful of dorks scuffle around, and that's what they show on TV as if all of those people were down there scuffling and fighting."

Henry's eyes were riveted on the screen in obvious dismay. It was the down side to living in San Francisco, he said. I looked up at Mary and Mary smiled at me, a smirking, defiant smile above crossed arms.

She's beyond my control, I mumbled bitterly to myself the following day as I hauled myself out of another numbing sleep. It was the only thing I had left, my motherhood, and now even that was slipping away. I nearly vomited from self disgust and then began to weep. I was surrounded by every good thing the world had to offer, but I couldn't care about any of it. I couldn't feel anything but my own wretched, gnawing discomfort, like an animal in a tiny zoo exhibit, pacing round and round, viciously biting herself because she lacked any other outlet for her dumb rage.

I continued to smile sweetly for the kids. I asked them all of the necessary and tender questions, though as I talked to them, I noticed myself talking from far away and looking at them, unseeing, through empty eyes. Could a shell, like one of those metal monkey mannequins in those animal experiments, could a shell be a mother, a real mother?

I wondered if the boys were even deceived. Mary, certainly, was not, but Mary could take care of herself. I couldn't stand the thought that I might be damaging my boys. Oh, to lay me down with a bouquet of lillies! That was my most guilty, secret and selfish wish.

Then, in the midst of these thoughts, and for reasons I didn't understand, Mary unceremoniously decided to let me in. It was just like that. Mary began to be herself in my presence. At first, I was flattered, as if I were again a schoolgirl being allowed to hang out with the popular kids. But then I realized the absurdity of this, and bit my nails to the quick with worry. Ultimately, however, I was too weak and numb to care for long and all I could do was to return to hating my weakness, and to mutely listen to those girls talk.

Mary revealed herself, in those weeks, not as the sweet and quiet but intense girl I had erstwhile known, but instead as an intense girl who pretended at sweetness and quietude. She and Monique talked about politics, morality, hypocrisy, philosophy and religion with a confidence and a passion that I had forgotten long ago, and they talked about sex in a frank, workmanlike manner so unlike my own feeling that I sometimes wondered if my parenting had had any role in the formation of Mary's character at all.

Mary and Monique, in their every conversation, in the darting meeting of their eyes whenever I spoke, in their veiled accusations and criticisms, continually nonplussed me and made me shake throughout my whole body with both longing and dread. Even when they had tired of me and wandered away, my mind compulsively retreated into a detailed and repetitive examination of my many failures, and everything

I did, everything anyone said to me in the course of my common day, confirmed my conclusions. I was a failed creature.

I sank further into a depression that the pills could not touch, and that I hid only with difficulty. I smiled, I told Susan and Sally how happy I was about the bathroom, I chatted with the teacher at Joshua's school, but my words resounded and reverberated inside the hollowed out shell of my head. I felt as if the skin of my being were tissue paper that a word could rend, yet it was completely insensible to any touch. I rambled around inside it like a solitary bee inside an empty hive. By the time the flowers began to bloom outside the front door, by the time I dutifully hid eggs for Joshua at Easter, my depression had transformed me into a shade. I was a spectator in my own home, in which everything felt separate from me, everything else alive and I already dead. If I did it, I caught myself thinking one day, if I did it, it wouldn't even be much of a thing to do, but rather it would be like finishing a thing already mostly done.

The Turnaround

I was staring dully ahead of me as I waited for Susan and Sally at the Powell Street turnaround. They had told me to meet them there and they were late. So I stood there watching the chattering, pointing, smiling tourists as they jostled for purchase behind the line where they waited for the cable cars. One after another, the red cable cars rolled to a stop in front of them, merrily jangling their bells. Each car disgorged a bolus of humanity from one side and accepted another in its place, and then, bells ringing, turned away to roll up the hill again. One after another the cable cars came and went, and yet the mass of people standing before them never diminished. Its colors shifted, its outline bulged, receded, knotted in little eddies, then compacted as it surged forward, but always continued, endlessly. I frowned at them as they looked past me, chewing, smoking, and laughing.

I was thinking about something Joshua's teacher had said to me. I had volunteered for her since the beginning of the school year, and still that teacher called me "Mom." It was that, married to something else the teacher had said, in passing, that struck me as insulting. I was sure the woman had no respect for me whatsoever.

I was thinking about this as I watched the human river pass before me, when a seaborn breeze raced up the hill from the piers between the cleavage of the buildings and blew my skirt up around me. As I pushed down my skirt with both hands, looking around to see if anyone had seen, a man bent down and pushed Play. A blast of trumpets sounded and a fast tempo remix of Cuban marimba filled every corner of my mind, crowding out Matthew's teacher, my floating skirt, the fact that both Sally and Susan were late. This annoyed me, this intrusion.

The man was dressed entirely in black, except for his unusual tap shoes. They were fashioned from a dull, well worn red leather, creased like the cover of an old book, and looked vaguely handmade in a European sort of way. In one motion the man drew a large board upwards in an arc above his head and threw it down so that it hit the ground like percussion on cue, and then he leapt upon it and began to dance. This got my attention. With the taps of his shoes, he beat a staccato rhythm that became another layer of percussion accompanying the music, all brassy brightness. For the first time, I realized that the sun was bright and hot, and everything around me began to vibrate with that same hot brightness. The crowd in front of the cable cars spilled outward and washed toward me. People slowed and stopped. Spectators soon formed an unbroken circle around a small clearing of herringbone red brick, a board and a dancer. The music changed from one rhythm to another, and, as if to announce the change, the man pulled off his shirt as he danced to reveal a smooth, rippled torso gleaming with perspiration. His skin was so dark that it seemed to contain another dimension shimmering inside it, and this, combined with the molded plastic perfection of his form, transformed him in the speed of his motion into a powerfully magical presence, a supernatural silhouette illuminated by the white hotness of the sun. As his shirt met the pavement and a drop of sweat fell from his face, the man doubled the cadence of his tapping feet, and the crowd erupted like startled birds, beating their palms and hollering. He skipped on tiptoe for an impossibly long time and then stomped, skipped again and stomped twice, each time in perfect cadence with the blast of trumpets, his arms telescoping outward like antennae, broadcasting the energy of the dance in traveling spirals into the crowd. Perhaps it was because of this cadence, or perhaps because I was standing so nearby, I felt myself drawn into his dance as a participant, rather than as a spectator. When he skipped, my heart skipped and when he stomped, my knees buckled ever so slightly as I felt the crash in my chest. Every time he crashed down into me and then spun away from me, I was overwhelmed by the release of my own powerful longing. It was what I had always looked for in Saint Agatha's Church and never found. I yelled and heard myself yelling. Then I noticed one particle inside me moving in a spiral upwards and I followed it until I exploded out of my being into the air high above before I disintegrated like spent fireworks, arcing downwards. I spiraled upwards and arced down again. I felt everyone moving, breathing, spiraling and arcing with me. It was then that the tapping rhythm stopped and the man's hand appeared in front of me. I almost laughed, waved him away, but instead, I met his eyes and accepted.

"Everyone can dance," he said as he wrapped his hard arm firmly around my waist and pulled me into him.

I relaxed my body and let it follow him as he stepped with me, back and forth, shifted, spun me to the end of his arm and drew me back to him. I was dancing. I laughed out loud when I realized that several hundred people were watching me dance and I was unashamed. It was I watching myself. At that moment, with all of those strangers as witnesses, I was not Mrs. Buchanan, nor Mom, nor any other label anyone could think of. I was a transcendent being becoming in that infant moment, self-aware. I felt his sweat, slick on my arms, warm on the front of my clothes, I could taste his breath, the salt of his work, and I gave myself over to it. And then, with one last explosion of drums, the music stopped and changed. He released me and the crowd applauded. Dollars dropped into the white painter's bucket in front of him as he swabbed his dripping face and took a long drink of water. The crowd was breaking up. I was crying.

"You've got it," a voice near me said.

I turned to see a very small wiry man wearing the shabby outfit of homelessness.

"You've got it," he insisted, regarding me with a steady gaze within which his pupils wobbled ever so slightly.

"What do you mean?" I asked, sure the man was mentally ill.

At the same time, I noticed with interest that I chose to continue the conversation with the homeless man instead of drawing away. Somehow, all the rules were suspended.

"I saw you," he said, screwing one eye at me knowingly.

"He was on TV," someone behind us told me.

Shifting Ground

I turned to see a pale, old man with a shock of white hair standing up from his forehead. He had pushed his shopping cart heaped with stuffed full sacks next to us, and pointed at the dancer, adding, "National TV."

"Hey man," the small man greeted him and then asked, "What was that program called? It was some kind of contest, or showcase for young talent."

"Nadine!" the old man yelled at a heavy set woman who scowled at me from where she stood, several meters away.

"What was the name of that program? The one?" he yelled at her again.

Nadine barked the name at him and resumed scowling.

"Yeah, that's the one. I wrote about him too. Published it."

"You write?" I asked the small man, not just a little surprised.

The man dug in the voluminous pockets of his sagging shirt and jacket and produced a sheaf of paper, folded in half and stapled together. It was a muddy photocopy of a collection of poems. On the front was the smeared image of a face that suggested that of the poet in front of a vague San Francisco skyline.

"Five dollars," he said to me as I took it from him.

I absentmindedly dug in my purse for the bill as I turned the pages. There was much about balance and perfection, unity and oppression, all scored by the shadow of want, deeply felt and clumsily expressed, which only underlined its pathos. Occasionally, beautiful gems of juxtaposed words that, alone, were poems entire.

"Will you really read it?" he asked.

"Oh yes, I think I will," I assured him.

The dancer began to dance again, and the three of us watched him together.

"Does he dance like this every day?" I asked the small man.

"Oh, no, it's different every time. He comes here, he looks at the weather, he checks out the mood of the people, the energy of the place. Then he picks exactly the right thing. He always knows."

"Atlanta!"

It was Susan and Sally, hurrying toward me.

"I was late," Susan said.

"And then we couldn't find you right away in this crowd," Sally said.

I turned to introduce them to my new acquaintances, but they, so easily dismissed, had already moved away.

"When we found you and saw that you were in trouble," Sally laughed and cast a glance over my shoulder toward the two men, "we hurried right over."

"No trouble," I said wanly, feeling my old self settling upon me like a blanket, feeling that brighthot energy receding, draining away.

As we walked by the white plastic painter's bucket, I stopped and dug in my purse. I didn't have enough money in the bank to give this man as much as he had given me, but I felt I had to give something. I dropped in every bill I had.

"Thanks!" the dancer called mechanically as he danced.

And then it was behind me.

"Are you alright?" Susan asked me after we were seated at a restaurant, smiling and cutting her eyes to Sally, "You haven't said two words since we got here."

I looked up from my hands. "I'm fine."

"Well, I'm starving," Susan complained and took off her scarf and suit jacket.

There was a white nametag on her shirt. It said, Ms. Susan Green. Sally laughed.

"Oh, this," Susan peeled it away and wadded it up, "I was at a meeting."

"I didn't know that you were a Ms.," Sally said, smirking. "Like the magazine."

"Well, of course," Susan said, ignoring the smirk.

"Really?" I said quickly, trying to head off another argument between them, "most people call me Mrs."

"Yeah," Susan said, "I always correct them."

"Oh, why bother?" Sally said, "It's not like it matters that much."

"It matters to me," Susan insisted. "I have my own name. That means patriarchy has died in my family line." She paused and gave us a mischievious grin. "I killed it. That's powerful."

"But your name is still your father's name anyway," Sally pointed out.

"My name is mine because I've had it my whole life."

"But then, your kids are Sloan, after their Dad. That's patriarchy."

"Only my son. Andrea is named after me. She's Andrea Green."

"I didn't know that!" I exclaimed.

"I think a lot of women don't say anything about the many ways they are treated with disrespect because," Susan glanced up at Sally, "deep down, they agree that they don't deserve it."

I turned over the food in my mouth. Juxtaposed in my mind was myself as I was, dancing at the Powell Street turnaround, and myself as the subject in the picture that Susan was painting, the kind of person who obsessed over what Joshua's teacher thought.

"Why do I have to make a lot of money at a job and call myself Ms. to get respect?" Sally demanded. "It really burns my bacon that everyone thinks that women who work are so great, and that I'm some kind of loser that they pat on the head and call a 'soccer mom,' as if that's all I'm good for, driving a minivan to soccer games."

Sally punctuated that image with a contemptuous huff before continuing.

"At that lunch we had at Atlanta's, you accused me of being jealous of you and you said that I wanted you to fail."

Susan's jaw tightened.

"I think you might be a little bit right, in my worst moments, and I'm not proud of that." Sally swallowed. "But you weren't right about everything. I don't like that you get more respect than I do, and that's what I'm jealous of. I really, really don't want a job or a career. My purpose in life is love. I care for my kids, your kids, Atlanta's kids, and when they're all grown, there will be a whole new batch running around. I'm the one everyone can count on to volunteer, to help out, to be there in a pinch. That's powerful too. This country would fall to pieces without people like me, and I like it. I like feeling needed, I like feeling dependable, responsible."

Sally took a deep breath to hold the space before beginning again. "I know you love your job, and I know you feel that you are doing something important, but I love my job too, and I'm doing something important too. And yours isn't more important than mine, and I don't think it's fair that everyone thinks it is. It makes me mad."

Susan opened her mouth to say something, but nothing came.

"I'm sorry for saying that your kids are suffering because you're going back to work," Sally continued. "I don't question Jeff's sense of purpose, or John's, or Henry's, so why yours? I know that you love them and you are doing your best just like I am, and none of us are perfect." Sally's voice cracked, and she stopped speaking.

Susan smiled with tears in her eyes and she reached out a hand to Sally across the table, which Sally grasped.

"You are such a good person," Susan said, "I guess that's why I wish you had more power in the world, why I try to push you to have more power in the world."

"I know," Sally said quietly and released Susan's hand.

"What you said about your purpose being love," Susan said, "Our culture has no respect for that and that's wrong. If I made you feel that I didn't respect that, I'm really sorry. I really am. That's the highest calling there is."

Susan paused before adding, "You know, this country could really use more people speaking the voice of love, because right now, the voice of greed shouts down every other thing."

Susan and Sally looked at each other a long moment and shared a smile.

"We always get sucked into these things and then we never eat while our food is hot," Susan said.

They both began eating, and the three of us ate silently for several minutes.

"Well, at least we have a choice," Sally said, "I mean, these poor Muslim women you see on TV already wearing their burial robes around everywhere. They aren't worried about whether they are a Mrs. or not, I'll tell you that."

Susan spoke with her mouth full. "Yeah, it is truly amazing that that kind of ancient oppression could exist at the same time as we are building space stations in orbit around this planet!"

"I know!" Sally practically yelled.

They were talking quickly to each other, relieved they could join together in judgment, create a bulwark against the Other. Neither of them seemed to notice that I was still there.

"Can I pay with a credit card?" I interrupted the two of them. "I just realized that I don't have any cash left."

I barely made it home before the kids. Mary and Monique came in arguing, which wasn't unusual. What was unusual, I noticed, was that I, myself, was at peace in the midst of it. They were ignoring me. They were saying things that I should have found offensive or threatening or disrespectful, but I didn't care. How was it that the girls made me chuckle now, when days before, I would have spent the entire day obsessively trying to cipher the hidden meanings relevant to myself as I bit my cuticles until they were all ragged, fire pink remonstrance?

Over the next days and weeks I noticed that since the Powell Street turnaround, the death of myself was something I accepted with a bemused calm, rather than a depressive collapse. The change was so instant, and yet so subtle, that whilst I was in the midst of it, I had moments of disoriented déjà vu when I felt as if I were living in two parallel realities, one anguished and one peaceful. And then, even the emotional memory of it, the anguished fitful protest of my being to the call of death, began to unravel entirely. The girls had not changed their words or behavior in any way, but in the same way that at the Powell Street turnaround all the rules had been suspended, somehow nothing pertained to me anymore.

Yet, as soon as I let myself die, something began to quicken inside me. Maybe it was the resumption of the rhythmic noise of the men working in the house. Maybe it was something working inside myself. But, something in me was interested, curious, seeking. I found the girls strange, fascinating and frightening, but also they excited me in a way that was almost indecent. Being around them made me want to take a lover.

The day the bathtub went in had seemed like three. Despite this, I could not sit still. I tried to relax, but my knees vibrated under the table with unspent energy and finally, I decided to wander upstairs. I was amazed to see it there in the "knowledge" corner, now almost entirely framed in gleaming black tile.

Marcus beamed at me. "Looks great, hey?"

I was smiling with such force, I was hardly able to make my mouth move to speak, and he laughed.

"It's wonderful," I said finally, "You didn't tell me that it was going in today!"

"It was going to be a surprise," he said.

As I drifted away, looking around the room that seemed to be so near completion now, Marcus turned back to his work. I regarded him with a cocked head. All that mystery about him between the girls, the secret of his life, gathered itself inside me, and I decided to ask.

"So, are you in school? Are you working your way through school?" I tried to avoid sounding as curious as I was.

"Nah, I didn't go to college. This is what I do."

"May I ask why you didn't go to college?"

"Sure. My senior year of high school, I got caught with a bunch of weed."

I tried to assimilate this information without visible shock.

"They threw the book at me, hoping to scare me straight, I guess. You can very well see," he said with an acid stare that I had never seen before, "how well that worked."

My mind was working very fast, but I could not decide what I was supposed to say, and I was finding it very difficult to hide my confused terror.

He smiled broadly and then displayed his t-shirt. The words, "Legalize It," were stamped across a graphic of a marijuana leaf.

I nodded in what I hoped was a sophisticated and knowing way.

"The truth is, it was pure civil disobedience. I think marijuana should be legalized. They should have given me an A in Civics instead of throwing me in juvie."

"Except that," I ventured, "even if marijuana were legal, it wouldn't be legal for high school age children."

"Point taken." He nodded. "But when little white high school boys get caught with a case of beer, they don't send them to juvie, do they? There's a reason cigarettes and alcohol are legal and marijuana isn't, and it ain't because weed is worse. It's racism and classism, pure and simple. It

Shifting Ground

allows the state to control undesirable elements—undesirable people—through selective enforcement."

Marcus said this with a fierce conviction that intimidated me, and I said nothing. I had never thought of it that way before, but I was afraid to say anything more. Marcus, apparently sensing this, threw up his hands.

"Oh, anyway, I should focus on my work."

I didn't move. I was thinking about Monique. This is where she gets it, I thought. From her brother. There was that other influence, of course. Perhaps that was what her parents were trying to breed out of her at St. Agatha's.

"Monique says she wants to be a political activist," I said to his back. "I'm not sure how someone makes a living doing something like that, but she seems to think she can."

"Yeah, she's into all that stuff. I don't know where she gets it."

I blinked. "I thought that you might be an activist yourself. You seem so," I searched for the word, "passionate about politics."

"Oh that's just being black, I think. Other people can afford to be unconscious, but as a black kid growing up, you learn firsthand on a daily basis about politics."

Marcus laid three more tiles, and then as he reached for more grout, he screwed up his lip.

"In school I was into science, mostly. I wanted to be a researcher and my mom made me memorize the periodic table of elements in grade school. I can still tell them all to you." He looked up long enough to smile.

"Why did you give up on it?" The question had left my lips before I realized how it sounded.

"I didn't give up on anything," his voice rose as he looked at me over his shoulder while he continued to work, "This isn't giving up. This is what I do. This is honorable work that's giving you something that you want, isn't it?"

I was a little shaken, but pressed on, "That's not what I mean. I mean that, if it is true what you say, that someone, or society, is trying to prevent you from having economic or political power; well, it seems they've succeeded."

The silence terrified me, and I almost fled, but then Marcus spoke. "I never had much taste for greed," he said quietly, and then he stopped working and looked at me.

I knew that he was looking at me in context, here in my multi-million dollar house. I was suddenly aware that I was his employer, that he was but one of several people working here today for me, inside and outside the house. I felt his judgment land on me.

"And, as for politics, it's just two different flavors of the same drink, no thank you very much."

"So," I continued, accepting his judgement, "good education and underfunded education, abortions or no abortions, civil rights or no civil rights, they're all the same to you? You don't care?"

"They are all outcomes of the same oppressive, coercive system that is run by the money held by a handful of white men. I boycott the whole system. I live outside it."

I felt my face flush hot with passion. I stood up tall, sure that I was right.

"But you're not outside it," I asserted. "There isn't a single location on the planet where you can live outside of a system. You participate whether you like it or not, and not voting is participating. You might as well work to change the system!"

"Oh, that's fine, coming from you."

He said this with that same acid stare, but then, apparently remembering that this was not an appropriate work conversation, he checked himself. He began to clean up to end the day's work.

I, however, had abandoned all of that. I felt that old feeling returning, that pulse of energy through me that I had felt at the Powell Street turnaround, and I found myself articulating opinions I hadn't realized I had, with a force and a precision I'd never imagined possible.

"Do you vote?" he asked me, stepping toward me.

"I vote in every election," I said quietly, defensively, unnerved by his closeness.

He stopped cleaning and set his lips, pressing them together and stared into my face, arresting my attention. "*You're* rich, *you* have a college education. Are *you* expressing your power in this world?" He took a step toward me. "Do you ever," he said slowly, evenly, still staring without blinking, "*even in secret*, vote for someone Henry doesn't approve of?"

"Sometimes," I said, my composure crumbling, the energy spinning away.

"In secret?" he whispered, moving steadily toward me now without breaking that intent, challenging gaze.

He leaned in very close to me, so that his lips were by my ear.

"We're not that different, you and I," he said with quiet fierceness.

I turned to look at him and he kissed me. He put his arms around my waist, bent me into him and kissed me like a sailor returning home, and I opened my mouth to him.

After he released me, my arms stayed suspended where they had circled his neck. He looked at me long and hard, like he understood something for the first time, and then he nodded at me, as a gentlemanly gesture of departure, or perhaps as one spirit's acknowledgement of another of like kind. Then he left.

I had clung to my composure until this moment, but as soon as he disappeared from the doorway, as soon as I could hear him descending the stairs, I began to hyperventilate.

He could have continued, I said to myself, shaking. I reached out for something to hold onto, but found nothing until I had backed up against Henry's highboy dresser. He could have led me into the bedroom and I would have had sex with him right there on Henry's bed. I was sweating and I opened the window, gulping at the fresh air.

I wouldn't tell Henry. It was best to forget it had happened, and if I saw Marcus again, I was sure I could behave as if it never happened.

Yet, when Henry came home, I couldn't bring myself to meet his eyes. Even though it was I who was wearing the scarlet letter, Henry annoyed me more than ever before. He came home late, as usual, and released upon me the events of the day, one after another, without waiting for a response. He poured down upon me an avalanche of words, sentences, paragraphs: I said, I think, I, I, I, I, and I. All of it was important, and he needed to let me know how he handled everything, how correct he always was.

Shifting Ground

I left the room where he was speaking to put away his laundry, then to do the dinner dishes, then to remind Joshua to brush his teeth, and he followed me with his words, talking loudly to be heard over the friction of my activity. I realized for the first time, as he followed me around, talking, that it wasn't even the content of the words that was important to him. What was important was the message that bound them, not only with each other, but also with the words spoken every other day, as well. As a headache began to form in the front of my head, it occurred to me that his words could crush bone.

I'm not allowed to have words. My words only make him laugh, even when they're not funny.

I mostly talked to myself. Every day, I had dozens of imaginary conversations, with him, my parents, Joshua's teacher, Marcus, Michael, strangers, acquaintances, and people I had never met. I said what I should have said. I said what I wanted to say. I talked about my plans, my ideas about God, what happened when you died, where I would be if I could be anywhere. I said things Henry would find silly, stupid or shocking.

Henry doesn't respect me, I realized, he does not respect me at all.

My face grew hot as I started the dishwasher. I thought that perhaps I would tell him about Marcus, after all. That would shut him up. I looked up at him in that moment with an expression that did, in fact, stop his mouth.

"Dad? Could you help me with something for a minute?" Mary called from the doorway.

Henry was distracted for a moment, looked back at me, alarmed, then quizzical.

I wiped my hands on my hips.

"Sure," he said, and left the room.

By seven-forty four the next morning, I was alone again in the house, waiting for Marcus. I was nervous about seeing him again, but not because I thought that something would happen. I was sure I could pretend that nothing had happened, and I was equally sure he would do the same. It was that Marcus knew something about me now that no one else knew. Being known, being seen. That's what made me nervous. As long as I remained on the edge of life, completely normal and invisible because of my normality, I didn't bother anyone and no one bothered me. Until Michael. Then the girls. And then there was the Turnaround. And now, perhaps Marcus too.

I wandered into the kitchen, poured myself a cup of coffee, set it on the coffee table, and sat down. It was only moments later that I was on my feet again, walking to the mantle to examine the objects there, then to the window to look out at the back yard. I descended to the basement to see if the laundry in the dryer was finished, and was nearly frantic to find it still wet. And it was only eight o'clock. I stood there in front of the agitating machines, biting my cuticles, waiting for the clothes to dry when I realized that it wasn't even the content of all of those mental conversations that mattered to me, but rather the meaning that ran through the weave of them. The meaning of them all was longing. All of them said, I want. The acknowledgement of the depth of my longing nearly slayed me. With clenched fists, I was thinking now, I want.

Want was a verb, was it not? Didn't it need an object? What was it that I wanted? What was it that took me to St.

Shifting Ground

Agatha's, only to be disappointed, to the mall, again and again, only to be frustrated? For the first time I realized why so many people smoked marijuana: to silence the voice of "I want." I would have gratefully accepted that drug just then, if only to feel a moment's peace, a respite from unbearable agitation. The machine finally cycled off and I leapt at it, folding the clothes with a quick, empty and mechanized glee. When the clothes were put away, I noticed that it was nearly nine o'clock. I unlocked the front door and escaped out the back. I wouldn't see him at all.

I was pretending to weed an immaculate flowerbed when Marcus appeared at the back door. He waved.

"I just wanted to let you know that I'm here!" he called.

"Okay! Thanks!" I called with an aggressive cheerfulness that was designed to keep him at bay.

Later, I was in the front yard again, avoiding Marcus, when the van dropped Mary and Monique. As they climbed out, I was thinking about something Monique had said. On the outside, she had said, we put on uniforms and knee socks for The Man, but on the inside, we are brewing revolution. Monique did have a flair for the dramatic, I thought, smiling to myself. Looking at the rows of blue and white uniforms, watching as Monique slammed the van shut upon them, I wondered if it were true. Were they rows and rows of revolution?

"Chocolate chip cookies!" I said to them as they followed me into the kitchen.

"You're gonna make me fat!" Mary complained, holding up a hand.

"That's the great thing about being a lesbian." Monique gave Mary a sarcastic smile as she took a cookie. "You don't have to be a slave to the male standard of beauty."

Mary sneered at her in return and took two.

"What's a lesbian?" Joshua asked.

I had forgotten that he was sitting quietly at the kitchen table, enjoying his cookies with milk.

The girls exploded in a fit of giggling. I opened and shut my mouth.

"It's a woman who likes other women," I finally said with determined calm.

"You like other women, right?" he asked.

"Sure," I said, ignoring the intensification of the girls' laughter, and hoping he wouldn't ask the natural sequential query, I added, "Do you want another cookie?"

"No," he said and cocked his head to one side. "So," he said, "you and Monique are lesbians. What about Mary? Mary likes women too, right?"

I sighed. "It's a particular kind of like, Joshua. Monique is a lesbian, Momma and Mary are not."

"What kind of like?"

The girls were now watching me in fascinated and silent amusement.

I retreated now, not sure that this conversation was appropriate. "It's a kind of like that I will explain to you when you are older."

"He'll just ask Matthew," Mary said.

"Or Henry," Monique said.

I noticed that I wasn't afraid that Joshua would ask Henry. "You know how Mary goes out on the weekends with Dave?"

"Yeah?"

"Monique goes out on the weekends with girls."

"Yeah, right!" Monique huffed.

Joshua stared at me, not really comprehending the distinction.

"If I ever get married," Monique said drily, "I'll marry a girl."

Joshua's eyes widened, "Oh!"

Matthew wandered in, drawn by the scent of warm cookies.

"Monique is a lesbian," Joshua told him with proud authority.

"No way!" Matthew said, turning to look wide eyed at her.

Monique smiled.

"That explains a lot," Matthew said, making a face at her and skittering around the arc of her punch.

"That explains what?" she demanded.

Matthew stuffed a cookie in his mouth, unconcerned. "I don't know. It explains why you're so…" He munched meditatively. "So *you*."

"I'm not so me because I'm a dyke. I'm so me because, unlike most people, I'm not a slave."

"Whatever," Matthew said.

"I don't do what I'm told just because someone tells me to. I don't want what they are trying to train me to want."

"Who is 'They,' dear? And what is it that 'They' are after?" I tried not to sound patronizing.

"'They' are the people in power, the one percent of white males who own and control most of the world's wealth. They want me to want my own slavery, to be obedient to my parents, then obedient to a boss man who will work me to death to make him more wealth, which he will then use to buy my political representation out from under me. They want to sharecrop me out and keep me quiet with cheap consumer goods. No thank you. The only choices in life, as I see it, are to remain a slave or to become a revolutionary."

"Or hit the lottery," Matthew suggested.

"Yeah, everyone and their mama thinks that they're gonna hit the lottery, but nine times out of ten, the only solution to a hard problem involves hard work."

"Give me the cheap consumer goods," Matthew said, grabbing another cookie.

"You don't even know what you're talking about," Monique said. "When you get older, you'll see. Your dad is rich, but Bill Gates he ain't. And you're not exactly a rocket scientist either, Mr. C in Math."

Matthew's face fell.

"You might just find yourself on the business end of this economy too, and then you'll change your tune."

Monique ate her cookie. "It used to be just the black people, but the underclass is getting bigger every day. Diversity for the underclass!" Monique crowed with laughter. "People are always talking about these terrorist sleeper cells," Monique went on. "The whole underclass in America is one big political sleeper cell, and someday someone is going to snap their fingers and wake them up."

I was fascinated by the idea of the political sleeper cell. I saw all of the legions of women like myself, like Sally, so obedient and industrious. The sequential turning of all of those individual tumblers would unlock revolution all over the world.

"The Man wouldn't let it happen," Mary said.

It sounded funny to me, to hear Mary talking about The Man.

"He would bring out the police, the CIA, the FBI, the whole thing, and now, you're probably considered a terrorist."

"That's why it's important to stay clean. I don't run with my old crowd anymore because I've gotta stay clean. If you're clean, they can't touch you, all the surveillance in the world can't stop you. You gotta be able to say, Let them watch."

"Yeah, watch this, baby." Mary made a crude gesture.

"Mary!" I only managed a mechanized shock that Mary ignored. I looked around my suburban kitchen and wondered at this talk of revolution, here. How funny it seemed, especially coming from my own child, so changed. I watched Mary's face as the girls talked and I wondered.

"Are you still planning on being a doctor?" I asked Mary.

Mary squinted and drew up her mouth in consternation. "I really feel, especially when we are talking like this," she said, "I really feel a strong…." Mary paused, searching for the word.

"Longing?" I asked, my nerves vibrating.

"Yes." Mary looked at me in surprise. "I've always wanted to help people, but now I also feel a longing to do something to change the world somehow."

"What did you want to be when you were our age?" Monique asked me.

The implication of Monique's casual question, that I had given it up, that it was too late, was all too clear, and it hit me like a blow. I blushed with shame as I remembered that, just yesterday, I had confronted Marcus with the same question.

"I hardly remember," I said. "Where has Dave been? I haven't seen him since last weekend."

Monique was looking from Mary to me with interest, her lips pressed tightly together.

"Are you still getting along?"

"Everything is fine," Mary said and turned away.

Later, when I was at the kitchen sink, ready to take my periwinkle colored pills, I realized that I didn't need them. I don't feel depressed, I said to myself, not at all. I dropped the pills back into the plastic bottle and drank the water without them. I felt like something was coming, something big, and I didn't know whether to be terrified or grateful. I was impatient for it to happen or go away.

"Maybe this is it," Sally suggested the next day over coffee in her kitchen, "the big thing you feel is coming is what you're feeling now, feeling better."

"But if this is it, why do I feel like it's still coming?"

"Well," Sally said, "maybe now that you have more energy, you just need to put it into something. Joshua's in school. What do you want?"

"Just me? I don't know. I just want…to do things, I don't even know what. I want to talk to people. I want to read things. I want to go somewhere and do something."

As I talked, I struggled with my shirt, yanked it away from my throat and pulled at my waist. "My clothes are too tight!" I exclaimed. "I think I'm gaining weight."

Tears of frustration welled in my eyes and Sally put her arms around me, chuckling.

"You are not gaining weight. You're as thin as a rail. I think you're just having yourself a nice little mid-life crisis, that's all."

I sat up. I always thought that was something only men did, with the women and the fast cars.

"What does my life mean? Did I make the right choices? What am I going to do now?" Sally said, ticking off the questions on the ends of her be-ringed fingers.

"Yes, yes," I said, my eyes opening wide.

"Just don't run off to an ashram," Sally said, patting me, "they won't let me call you there."

So it's all okay, I thought later. It has a label. There's probably a book on it in the library. I started dinner. The house was silent. I left the boys at Sally's, and Mary was with Monique somewhere. I went upstairs to look at the bathroom.

"We were just cleaning up," Marcus said.

He sounded apologetic. He knows I've been avoiding him, I thought. I looked at Marcus and our eyes met. He smiled gently.

"This is it," he said. "You'll be rid of us."

My heart full, I retrieved a mop. I mopped the floor, mopped us all out of the room, finally, and threw the new rug on the wet floor.

I opened the front door for them, and they passed out of it.

So cold. So cold with this man who has seen me.

"Marcus?" I said, halting him at the foot of the front steps.

He stopped and turned around and I threw my arms around him. The other man raised his eyebrows at me, but I didn't care. I squinted my eyes as I hugged Marcus and the other man disappeared.

"Thank you," I whispered.

He squeezed me in response, and then released me.

"Good luck," he called as he raised one hand from the curb before getting into the beat up company truck and turning the key. The truck sputtered and spat, and then panted down the hill out of sight.

I went upstairs again. I stood staring at the bathroom, but I couldn't stand still. I had an impulse to do something so ridiculous, so terrifying, I knew I must do it. I opened the door of the small balcony off my bedroom and stepped outside onto it, looking up at the side of the house. I dared not look down, but then I did. I began to hyperventilate and withdrew to the door. I knew there was a way—I'd seen Henry do it at Christmastime to hang up the lights. I closed my eyes and felt for that now familiar feeling of not being myself anymore, felt for the handhold and put one bare foot up on the railing. I nearly screamed as I hoisted myself over the roof's edge, trembling so violently, I found it difficult to crawl to the peak of the roof.

It took me a long time to fully open my eyes, but finally I forced myself to do it. My eyes opened wide. The little sliver of view I had from my windows was nice, but this was something else. I could see a wide swath of water, the rooftops like stairs up the hills above it, and an expanse of sky so large, it gave me vertigo to contemplate it. Anything was possible, I thought, just about anything. I watched people walking by on the other side of the street. I felt so conspicuous, so exposed, but no one noticed I was there. Everyone walked looking straight ahead. No one ever looked up.

I heard the front door slam. Mary and Monique were home.

Reluctantly, I climbed down. Climbing down was more difficult than getting up, but I was amazed to discover that it no longer frightened me as much. I was thinking about pouring myself a glass of wine as I closed the door to the balcony, but then I noticed that the house was silent. My body froze. It wasn't only unexpectedly silent, but there was also a strange tension in the air. Maybe that wasn't Mary coming in. I crept down the stairs clutching my cell phone, straining my ears to catch sounds of rummaging, of steps, of anything. As I reached the bottom of the stairs and crossed into the threshold of light spilling from the great room into the hall, I could hear Mary quietly talking. I sighed deeply and shook myself with relief. Mary was home and Dave was with her. That's all, I said to myself, it's only Mary breaking Henry's rules again. But, something about the way Mary was talking, the feeling in the room, caused me to pause. Instead of walking into the room and with some small qualms, I stepped backwards into the shadow of the door, spying on them through the crack.

"Well?" Dave asked with an imperious tone in his voice.

Now, I felt I knew this boy fairly well, but there was something unfamiliar in the way he spoke, in the bold attitude he held in his slight frame, that I didn't recall being a part of the quietly respectful boy I knew. I pressed against the crack of the door for a better view.

"Well?" he said again. "What is there to talk about? You've hardly even started yet. There really isn't anything for me to do yet."

They were always different with adults. I knew that, but the thought didn't calm the alarm growing in my belly.

"I've decided to have an abortion," Mary said.

I couldn't form thoughts anymore.

There was a moment of stunned silence.

"You can't do that," he said finally.

I quietly slid down the wall to the floor.

"I can, actually." Mary sounded sure, strong.

They're so different with adults, I thought again, staring at this daughter, supposedly mine.

"It's murder. It's against the church. It's the worst thing you can do."

"If it's not a life yet, it's not murder. What do you know about life? What does the church know about life? It's not in your body, it's in mine, and I *know*, it's attached to me, it's a part of me. If it were alive, *I'd* be the first to know."

Mary spoke quickly, confidently. She seemed to be repeating the knowing that she had discovered on her own before approaching this moment with the boy.

"Women create life, and women are born with the spiritual wisdom to make these kinds of choices. It's my choice." Her voice had a finality to it that made his face flush scarlett.

"Quit calling my son, *It*. He's a person created by God, who has a right to live. More of a right to live than you have a right to do what you want. You can't just kill a person just because you want to go to school. It's the worst sin there is and," he said, drawing his thin frame upwards and jutting out his pimpled chin, "I won't allow it."

Mary looked at him incredulously, then looked down at herself. Tears were streaming down my face now, and I knew just what Mary was thinking. She had chosen a boy just like her father.

He softened and came towards her. "I'll be supportive. Don't worry about that. I'll pay child support. He paused, satisfied with himself. "I'll try to go to a college nearby, and I'll come to see him every chance I get."

"I'm not ready to be a mother, and you're not ready to be a father."

"People do it all the time, and it seems to work out."

"It works out for who? The girls get fat and old before their time, they live with their parents or in some run down apartment. No one wants to date them. They drop out of school and, other than getting some guy to marry them, they're doomed to poverty for the next ten years until they can finally scrape enough time and money together to get a GED and go to community college. I'm not going to end up fat, poor and alone. No way."

"Well, you should'a thought about that before we did it."

"*You* should have thought about it. Do you really think you can *afford* a child?"

"I know a guy that has one and it doesn't cost that much. My parents are gonna buy me a new car for graduation, so I don't have to worry about that. Worse comes to worse, my parents can always help me out, like when I'm in college."

He looked down and licked his lips. "It won't be that bad for you, some girls get really good jobs after just a year at a technical college. A lot of jobs pay a lot without college, especially for someone smart like you. Maybe when I'm finished with college, we can get married, you know, when I'm settled."

Mary stared back at him, breathing deeply. "Okay. Okay. If you feel that strongly about it, if it's that important to you, then *you* can raise your son, who might, by the way, end up being a girl."

His face clouded, confused.

"I've already told you that I'm not ready to raise a child," Mary continued. "*I* want to go to college. When the baby is born, I'll nurse it for a couple of months and then I'll just start pumping milk, like professional women do. I'll get a job after school to pay you the support. Hopefully your parents will help you out a lot, because the support never pays for everything a baby needs, and then there's the childcare if you want to have a life. But then, maybe your mom will keep it for you so you don't have to drop out."

He just stared at her.

"If you withdraw your college applications tomorrow, and make plans to live with your mom for a couple of years while I go to college and work part-time to pay you child support, I'll have the baby. It sounds like fun, actually. I'll go to Stanford or Berkeley, and come home on the weekends to play with the baby. I'll take him for a month or two in the summer when I'm off. If you feel that strongly, then we could make it work that way. You raise your son and I'll go to school."

His mouth opened and closed in a fit of juvenile apoplexy. "But you're the girl!" he finally sputtered.

Mary smothered a smile, which twisted into bitterness. "Oh, so you just want a new toy. You want to dress up and pretend you're a daddy whenever you feel like it while the girl makes all the sacrifices. You want to pay a couple hundred dollars a month for the privilege of telling the girls in a bar that you've got a 'baby mama back home.' If that's what you want, I suggest you call the Big Brothers program, because you're not gonna be a big brother to a kid I raise."

There was a moment of silence.

"Well then, maybe it would be better if we gave it up to adoption."

"Oh, so it's *it* and *we* now! I'm not going to keep this pregnancy. I'm going to have an abortion. The decision is mine to make and I've made it."

"That's not fair!"

"You shoulda thought about that before we did it," her tone a mimickry of his.

"Well, you can forget about me! I'm not having anything to do with this!" he yelled.

"That's the first true thing you've said!" Mary yelled after him as he stomped out of the room and slammed the front door behind him.

Mary sat down on the couch and put her face into her hands, sobbing silently. I slumped on the carpet, behind the door, my face resting on my knees, sobbing silently also. Then I willed myself to sit up, I willed myself to stand. I wiped every trace of moisture from my face and straightened my body. She needs me now, I said to myself. I will not collapse.

I walked into the room, and Mary lifted her tear stained face in surprise. She was on her feet instantly, her eyes flashing.

"Don't even try to stop me," she said at me, fists clenched. "If you do, I'll run away and do it anyway. You can't keep me home from school—I'll just leave school and do it wherever it's legal.

She paused, her faced flushed and beautiful, before beginning again, angrily. "And you can go ahead and tell Henry. He can't even control me anymore. I'll find a way. I've thought about it and I've made up my mind. I'm not going to throw away my future, and anyone who forces a woman," she paused self-consciously, daring me with her hot, steady gaze to contradict this label she boldly applied to herself, "anyone who *forces* a woman to carry a baby in her body for nearly a year, give birth, look it in the eyes and then kill it in her heart as it is carried away from her, is a monster! I don't care how many pictures some woman says she'll send me. I won't do it and you won't make me do it. I'm the one that has to live with the consequences of this decision, not you."

She paused for breath, huffing, but staring at me to claim the space, prevent an interruption.

"And don't you dare say that I should live with the consequences of having sex. If I hear one more concupiscent hypocrite tell me that I shouldn't have had sex, I will scream until somebody's ears break! If you think I believe that you were a virgin when you got married, you must think I'm stupid, so don't even try to tell me you were."

Mary looked exhausted, and the fear and the fire had finally burnt out of her eyes.

After a pause that was long enough to become awkward I finally said, "I never said anything. I was just listening."

Mary's eyes dropped with shame, hiding tears. Finally she said quietly, "Are the good always weak? Is that how the world works?"

I grabbed my fierce tiger of a girl become woman and wrapped my arms around her, pulling her tight against my body.

"It will hurt me," I said. "It will hurt me deeply, but I'll go with you. I'll make sure that you are safe. I'll make sure that you're not alone when it happens."

I held Mary for a long time and had not yet released her when the front door slammed open and the boys ran in, breathless.

"The whole neighborhood is playing hide and go seek, Mom. It's not dark yet, can we stay out a little longer?" Matthew begged.

"Twenty minutes."

The boys ran back out, slamming the door behind them. Mary extricated herself from my embrace.

I placed my hand upon Mary's cheek. "Come on, help me make dinner. I'm late."

We worked silently in the kitchen together. We had a secret now. I avoided the moral question by focusing my mind on logistics. I was going to have to find a way to pay for it without alerting Henry. I'd have to withdraw it in chunks, pay in cash. Then I had a thought. While Mary set the table, I wiped my hands on the front of my jeans and went through the door of Henry's study. Glancing up, listening for him, I opened the drawers, all of which were unlocked except one. Vaguely I was aware that this exigency was merely an excuse to violate his privacy, that I had been wanting to do this very thing for a long time. I wasn't even surprised when the bottom left drawer revealed a crush of neat files, each of them representing some aspect of our household financial life. The confirmation of the lie I suspected enraged me.

I cocked my head. If our financial files were unlocked, what could be in the little locked drawer? Cash? A girlfriend's letters? A gun? I was determined to open it up. I retrieved a metal nail file from the bathroom and jimmied the lock. My hands were shaking as I opened the drawer.

Viagra? My eyes opened wide. Viagra? Henry is impotent? How is it that I didn't know? My eyelids dropped over my eyes with suspicion. Maybe he didn't buy it for me? I counted the number of pills left, checked the date on the label, and did the math. If he had a girlfriend, the relationship was chaste. In my anger, building over these several months, I suppressed a bitter smile.

I heard the garage door slowly cranking open.

I placed the bottle back where I found it and closed the drawer tight, so that, perhaps, he wouldn't even notice when he next unlocked it. I looked down at the open file drawer and slammed it closed. We shall meet again soon, I told those neat files.

Henry was walking in as I left the study.

"What did you need in there?" he asked.

"I was not aware that the entire room is forbidden to me," I said, breathing hot air in and out of my huffing nostrils.

That night, I was alone with that moral question. What Mary had said was probably true. Short of somehow jailing her, it was probably not possible, even for Henry, to prevent it. I knew that Mary would never buckle under again. There came a time when a parent could no longer prevent a child from sinning.

Of course, Mary didn't consider it a sin at all. Although I knew it was useless to remonstrate with her, I couldn't help but vent the frustration of my position, the position that Mary had put me in.

"I'm not trying to control you, Mary," I insisted, "Surely you know that I try to guide you because I don't want anything bad to happen to you."

"Yeah, exactly. It's all fear. It all comes from fear. And it's not just fear that I'm going to get hurt, either. It's also fear that I'll shame *you*, reflect badly on *you*, make your friends judge *you*. It was pure genius to get us into religion early, to control from within, but some of us are on to that scheme."

"Religion is not a scheme, Mary Frances," I scolded her.

"You only think that because you are still brainwashed by it. You can't see that it's a scheme to control you, but it is, and you let it."

"It doesn't control me, Mary, I control myself."

"If you control yourself, if you make your own decisions and think for yourself, why do you need to go every week to listen to some guy tell you what to do? What to think? If you really wanted only to prevent bad things from happening to me, you would have just taught me how to think things through so that I could make decisions that were right for *me*. For instance, to think it through and recognize that underage smoking and drinking are cool only because some greedy corporate bastards tell us it's cool. But no, you have to put on the full metal jacket of religious indoctrination. You just want to raise a miniature version of yourself. Well, I'm not you."

I watched with dread all of the pent up anger of her mouth shut tight adolescence rising to the surface in her reddening face, and like a bubble, it broke the plane of her consciousness and burst.

"I've seen your life and I don't want it," she said.

I could see that Mary was sorry for saying it the minute it left her mouth, but she didn't take it back. I turned from her with burning eyes and left the room, slamming the door behind me.

After we had not spoken for several days, Mary spoke to me about it, boldly in the kitchen as we were serving dinner. "Are you going to make the appointment, or shall I?"

It was futile, all the talk, all the arguing. I had already promised Mary, in that moment of unusual certainty, that I would be there, that I would help. So if it was a sin to help her, I concluded ruefully, my soul would just have to bear it. That night, I prayed until my eyes were closing, but I found no relief. The next morning, I made the appointment.

The event itself was anti-climatic. Mary was quite groggy on IV drugs. A nurse held one of her hands and I held the other. It was quick, and then there was a smear of blood and it was done.

"Is that…is that it?" I asked, incredulous.

"Just a minute," the doctor said and left the room.

"Yes, that's it," he said when he reappeared. "Mary will be taken to recovery now, about thirty minutes. The nurse will take her in."

The doctor shook my hand and left.

"That's it, baby," I said to Mary, who fluttered her eyes open and then closed them.

I thought I'd see it, but it had just been scraped and vacuumed away by a machine. I wondered where it was, what it looked like. We had seen an ultrasound picture, but it was hard to tell. This is my doing too, I kept thinking to myself.

"Is it…was it a boy or a girl?" I asked the nurse quietly, as another nurse wheeled Mary into the hall.

"Oh, honey, it didn't have any genitals yet," the nurse, who looked half my age, assured me.

The nurse, seeing my incredulity, retrieved for me a large and heavy, creased and worn paperback book, open to a large photo of a fetus floating *en utero*.

"Please come back this way," she said, as she led me back to the waiting area.

I looked at the picture as I walked. The caption below it read, "Foetus, Seven Weeks." The way they count the weeks is so confusing, I thought. Mary was nine weeks pregnant, but the fetus was seven weeks old.

I settled into a chair opposite the front desk and studied the photo. Crescent shaped, a primitive head with the eyes on the side, like a fish, and limbs, all four of equal length reaching out in front, together, it could have easily been some other kind of mammal: a muskrat, a cat, a pig. It was an impressionistic representation of a potential human, perhaps divinely created, perhaps divinely ordained, but not human, at least not yet. I turned back to the front and looked at all the pictures in order. The single celled organism in week one; the worm at three weeks; the tadpole with gills, a tail, and a heartbeat at four weeks; the reptile-like creature with four short legs and no mouth or nose at six weeks; the pig-like mammal with a tail at seven weeks; the primate at eight weeks; and finally, at the end of the first trimester, the curled-in humanoid with no neck, with eyes still on the sides and unisex genitals at ten weeks gestation. It was as if during development, a human went through all the other stages of evolution first. I handed the book back to a young woman with a blonde ponytail sitting at the desk.

"The one at twelve weeks is really starting to look like a baby," I said uneasily.

"A three and a half inch long baby that's still developing, I guess."

The blonde girl popped her gum and clicked the computer mouse in her hand.

"If it makes you feel any better," she said, not looking away from her computer screen, "twelve weeks fetal age is two weeks into the second trimester and 90% of abortions are done before that."

I, feeling a little relieved, went back to the recovery room and collected my own born child, took her home.

Mary slept off the drugs the rest of the day, and was subdued the rest of the week. I never saw Dave again. Perhaps to spare my feelings, perhaps to make sure that Henry wouldn't find out, neither Mary nor Monique ever mentioned it again, and life moved on. There was no outward sign that it had happened, but the far reaching everpresence of the event was illuminated by dozens of other signifiers. Mary had sought her own counsel, and had defied authority to act upon her own judgment. Not only that, but she had found her own judgment sound. For her, there was no going back. For her, the path ahead was emancipated womanhood, and nothing less. Mary began to speak, and what she spoke was a quiet rage, unchecked by filial duty, feminine modesty, or polite reticence.

It was astonishing to me to witness this change, to be privy to its inception, its course, its climax. To have this creature growing up in my home, a changeling becoming so unlike us, her parents, becoming herself. It wasn't the abortion that started it. It had been Henry's insistence on transferring her to St. Agatha's. By sending her to St. Agatha's to better control her, Henry showed Mary his fear that she could become someone other than the obedient young woman he was programming her to be. And, in showing her his fear, he revealed her own potential.

I was starting to think of myself as a new woman, as well. I still had mixed feelings about helping Mary with the abortion, but I was proud of the way I'd handled it. I'd practiced non-judgment, unconditional love and I'd supported my daughter during a difficult time at a moment when I myself had begun to feel useless.

It wasn't long before Mary's cell phone account was, once again, cancelled, and there were new restrictions. This time, however, Mary was not cowed, she did not become depressed, but instead wore these penalties as a badge of endured oppression that she would overcome. Mary knew that time was on her side. As for me, I was not agitated by this conflict. In fact, it seemed that the conflicted energy in my household more nearly matched the conflicted energy inside myself, and as a result, I felt more comfortable, more at home.

It was near the end of the school year when this heaving equilibrium splintered and blew apart, the pieces spinning off in all directions. A heavy rain had kept us in, and the humid house with its fogged windows was straining to contain the unreleased pressure of constantly sublimated conflict. Mary was reading a book on the couch, the boys were playing a board game on the floor, Henry was reading the Sunday paper, and I was drinking a cup of coffee as I watched the boys play. I marveled at how the surface of our lives belied the truth of them. This placid tableau, I thought, could be taken from the Rockwell picture book on our coffee table, but when you step inside it and live it, the reality of it is turbulent, oppressive, and unhappy. I thought it was funny how the raging storm outside was telling everyone our secret, exposing the truth of our family life for all to see.

Henry finished the paper, folded it neatly on the table and looked around with a restless sigh. His wandering attention landed on Matthew, as it habitually did now that Mary had become a force to be reckoned with.

"Matthew, have you finished your homework for tomorrow? You shouldn't be playing games if your homework isn't done."

"I don't have very much." Matthew glanced at his backpack across the room. "I can do it after dinner."

Joshua was looking from one to the other, apparently waiting to see if the game, which was just getting good, would have to be abandoned.

"Mary doesn't get straight A's by shirking her studies. She is setting an excellent example for you today, and you should take notice."

Henry was trying to give Mary a subtle compliment to release some of the pressure in the house, but Mary was angry and wouldn't allow it.

"I'm not doing homework," she said without looking up from her book.

"What are you reading?" I asked, trying to break it up.

"A feminist book," she said, and looking up at Henry, she added, "about how to fight against male oppression."

Henry's color deepened.

"Go get your homework now," he told Matthew.

Matthew, terrified by Henry's dark and contracted features, complied immediately, leaving Joshua to clean up the game.

Henry picked up the remote and turned on the television. A man was putting a ball in front of a hushed crowd. He is wishing he were playing golf, I thought. He is wishing he were anywhere but here, I thought, but then wondered if that last was, in fact, Henry's thought or my own.

"Will you play Matthew's side?" Joshua asked Mary.

Mary looked at him pityingly, but hesitated.

"I will," I said.

Mary gave me a relieved smile and continued to read.

"It's your turn, Momma," Joshua said.

It's just him. I don't want to leave the kids, only him.

I rolled the dice. I think I might hate him.

The phone rang and Mary got up to answer it. She came back into the room moments later. "That's Monique. She wants to come over. Is that okay?"

Henry pressed his lips together. I smiled and said it was fine.

"Do lesbians like playing games?" Joshua asked.

A laugh jumped out of my mouth.

"What?" Henry demanded, sputtering, his eyes wide.

"Lesbians are the same as other people," I told Joshua calmly, "and I imagine that some of them like playing games."

"What do you know about lesbians?" Henry demanded, directing his laser beam aggression at our six year old, now cowering on the carpet.

"Henry, your tone!" I admonished him. "You're scaring him!"

"Don't tell me to mind my tone," he said, raising his voice again. "I want to know what my six year old child knows about such a thing."

Henry's head snapped up when Mary came back into the room, followed by Matthew.

"What have you told this child about lesbians?" Henry demanded.

Mary's face grew angry and she opened her mouth to speak, but I interrupted her.

"This is not an appropriate conversation to have in front of Joshua, and certainly not in this tone of voice. You're frightening him!"

"Monique is a lesbian," Mary said quietly, calmly, "That's all. He knows that Monique is a lesbian."

"Monique is a what?" Henry spat out incredulously. "Why didn't anyone tell me this? I never would have allowed her in my house, with my daughter!"

Henry's voice dissolved in the face of an apoplexy that left him speechless.

"Monique is nice," Joshua said, and then shrank back into the shelter of my body.

"You stay out of this!" Henry snapped at him.

"That's enough, Henry," I said with an even toned passion that only hinted at the level of rage I was holding in check. Henry would not yell at my little boy, oh no he would not. I put my body between Henry and Joshua, and then told Joshua to run along to his room.

"No, I think he should hear this," Henry insisted.

"Matthew, take Joshua," I said as I shooed Joshua, patting his bottom.

Mary was staring at me with an open mouth, and open admiration in her face.

"You are not to see her ever again," Henry said to Mary.

Mary started to speak again, but I interrupted her.

"Monique is a good girl. She makes good enough grades, she stays out of trouble and she and Mary are friends. If you took the time to get to know Monique, instead of judging her, which is contrary to commandment by the way, you would like her as we do. She is a unique and good hearted girl."

"I will not have that abomination in my house," Henry raged. "Either you call her back and tell her not to come, or I will tell her myself."

"You may intercept Monique," I told Mary. "You can go to her house."

That is all the encouragement Mary needed, and she immediately turned to leave.

"You are grounded, Mary Frances," Henry yelled after her. "You are not allowed to leave this house."

"She is not grounded, Henry."

I stepped again into his path as the front door slammed behind Mary.

"I am not going to raise a bunch of little bigots," I said, raising my voice. "I may not agree with everything Monique says or thinks, or does, but, according to the example set by Jesus, I do not judge her. I accept her as she is and, just for your information, I like her."

"She is not allowed in this house, regardless," he said, holding his large frame in front of me, bearing down upon me, staring down at me.

I held my ground. "I don't agree to that. I won't support that. You will go to work tomorrow, and when you do, I will be serving cookies and milk to my daughter and her friend when they come home from school."

Henry pulled his great right arm back and cocked it behind his fist. In that moment, I met his eyes with my own eyes, blazing with the certainty that if he dared even once I would have him taken away in cuffs.

I double dog dare you, my eyes told him.

Henry's pupils contracted into a malignant stare as he dropped his fist and pushed past me, shoving me hard. I fell against the couch, but righted myself as the garage door slammed so hard it sent a concussion throughout the entire house. Then I heard his car engine revving as the slow, cranking garage door opener did its work, and finally tires squealing out of the driveway. I sat down, breathing heavily, feeling a little dizzy. Okay, I said to myself, that's it. I did it. I came out from under. Now to see what comes of it.

Henry came home very late, and came to bed after I was already asleep. I woke when he came to my side of the bed and put his hands roughly upon me. I pretended sleep, assuming he would give up, then recoiled when he continued, relentlessly. I pushed him away, revolted, but he grabbed my arms as he wedged one knee between my knees. He was absolutely silent as he shoved my legs apart. I used every ounce of physical strength I had to push against him and kick him as if he were a stranger. Grunting with effort, I tried to get my fingernails to his face, but he finally pinned my arms and then silently, resolutely, pushed on top of me, detestably into me. I cried out against the dry painful friction as he shoved himself into my body, but he ignored my pain. Wordlessly, silently, his odious heaviness worked on top of me, and then, without even a grunt, he withdrew and rolled over to sleep.

I hauled myself out of the bed and stumbled to the bathroom. I closed and locked the door and then vomited violently into the toilet. I collapsed against the sink, sobbing. Mucus mingled with the vomit and the tears in my hands. Then, a thought stopped my sobs cold. He had taken a pill to do this to me. He had thought about it beforehand and took a pill so he could do it. I leaned over the toilet so that I could throw up again, but nothing came. I spat a long stream of saliva and raised my eyes.

Before me, on the wall, I saw the beautiful flea market icon of the Madonna I had hung there. The Madonna's plump, unlined and childlike face was suffused with that painterly light suggestive of heavenly virtue and favor, and it was framed by a gleaming blue drape that covered her head. She didn't return my gaze, but kept her eyes downcast, her small mouth drawn tightly closed and pursed into a smile that promised serene contentment in exchange for obedience. She offered me no comfort at all. She was gilt and gleaming submissiveness; covered, silent, and impassive.

Suddenly my eyes flew open wide. The Madonna was wearing a hijab! I stood up straight and stared anew at the icon. She was wearing a hijab just like those poor Muslim women! My hand flew to my mouth and my stomach ached and ached. I thought about how my friends and I babbled about the "poor Muslim women" over there, far away in the Middle East, but I had never before recognized the poor Middle-eastern woman living inside my own heart. This Madonna, this antique, man-created ideal of womanhood had been imported like a relic into my home, into my heart! This! This beautiful Trojan horse was installed in me, as a model for me, a modern American woman! Submission, modesty, reticence, obedience, silence, all of these qualities solidified here, objectified into an image that has borne helpless witness to two thousand years of female subordination. This was no goddess mother, but a pathetic wire monkey mama substitute.

You are useless, I told her as I wiped the mucus, the vomit and the tears from my face. *Useless.*

I spent the rest of the night on the couch, not sleeping at all. I stared at the cold fireplace, the stacks of glossy home design magazines, and the large framed wedding photograph on the mantle in the dead glow of the streetlights illuminating the front window. I was still awake when the streetlights blinked out and the room filled with pink crepuscular dawn. Henry came to the table as usual, and when I did not serve him breakfast, he got up and poured himself some coffee and made some toast, completely unperturbed. I cycled through my routine without looking at him or speaking to him, cheerfully bundling the kids off to school.

As soon as I heard him leave, I ripped the edges of a brown supermarket bag and laid it flat on the kitchen table and then began scrawling furiously across its bare insides: *Henry loves me. It's dangerous to tell the truth. I don't know what is true. God is separate from me. God only lives inside churches.*

The priests know God better than I do. I need a man to survive. I have nothing important to do in this world. It's too late for me. I don't matter.

I paused, breathing hard, thinking. There was more. There had to be more.

I added: *I don't deserve love. I don't deserve respect. I must hide my power to be loved. I must obey to be safe.* More. As I wrote more, it was like peeling layer after layer of raw burnt flesh from my body: *I need Jesus to save me. I am fallen. I am lost.*

When the paper was covered with scrawl, I looked at the list, read it again and again, until the words became a blur that didn't pertain to me anymore. None of them were true.

"I renounce all of these things," I said, finally.

I picked up the paper bag screed and retrieved the flea market icon from the bathroom and walked into the living room with them. I took off the wall the large framed wedding photograph of me and Henry, turned it over, and smashed it violently on the mantle. I plucked the photo from the frame and walked quickly out the door to the back yard where I dropped all three items into the trendy and unused firepit built into the fancy stone back veranda. Standing over it and turning a match over and over in my fingertips, I closed my eyes. I release these beliefs, I said silently to myself and then waited to feel it happen. A little spinning sensation began in my insides and spread as a warm prickling throughout my body that made me lightheaded. It was that reverberating echo of the Turnaround. I opened my eyes and struck the match. The edges of the bag caught quickly, burning high and smoky, and the wedding photo was quickly blackened. The icon painting on heavy paper was the last to be devoured, sitting like a blue heart in the middle of the flame. I felt a mourning sadness to lose her, I did so love that beautiful face. As the flames closed in upon it, I shut my eyes.

I imagined the Madonna lifting up out of the flame, a blue angel flying free. Her hijab lifted off and fell into the fire and her long black curling hair flew outwards in every direction. I smiled in relief and joy as her burkha was lifted by an indecent breeze to expose her strong muscled legs that opened wide to let the wind cool and freshen her knees, her inner thighs, her furred pudenda that had been shut in damptight closeness for so long. Her enormous breasts bounced once as she turned in the air and disappeared. I opened my wet eyes and watched for a moment the snakelike traces of revived burn moving across the paper as it was stirred by the breeze. I fancied it looked like the tracings of an ancient language emerging from the charred fragments—a lost invocation inscribed in flame by a helpful, unseen hand. And then the breeze lifted and blew the gray bits and ashes. I stirred them as they blew and they lifted upward and fell lightly around the garden like a blessing.

I was still swallowing tears when I picked up the phone.

"Is Ms. Mara home?" I asked, willing my throat to open, to speak.

The voice on the other end chuckled. "No 'Hi Daddy' for me, huh? How do you like that?"

"I love you, Daddy." My voice, fulsome with emotion and need, had regressed to thick Georgian drawl. "But I need Mama."

My use of that word, the invocation of that relationship, which Ms. Mara did not allow under normal circumstances, communicated to him all that my words could not. He dropped the phone on the tabletop without speaking another word, and Ms. Mara answered within two of my anguished breaths.

"I've left him," I told her, gasping.

"Thank goodness!" Ms. Mara exclaimed.

"Now, tell me how to do it."

Esperanza

I.

"Mike? Will you give me my shoes? Oh God, I'm going to be late again!"

I fished one of Carol's heeled shoes out from under the dresser and smacked the bathroom door with it. She squealed. The bathroom door swung open and Carol's head appeared momentarily as she retrieved her shoe.

"I didn't say throw it!" She laughed as she retreated through the open door.

I threw in the second one and she squealed again as it hit the vanity cabinet door with a thud.

"I've got to run." She dashed out, grabbed her purse, and kissed me. "Don't forget. Don't work late tonight."

"Tonight?"

She stopped. "Did you forget our anniversary?"

"Oh! That's right, today is the tenth," I said. I wrapped my arms around her.

"Three months," she said, "only six more months to go for it to be longer than Kate."

"I wouldn't count that way if I were you, because...."

"Don't even say the name, the formidable."

"She's not really formidable, you might like her."

"I'm scared to death of her. I hope she stays wherever she is." Carol pretended to pout, kissed me and then pushed me away playfully. "I'm late! I'm always late now. See you later, here?"

"Yeah, here. We'll have dinner. In or out, whatever you want."

"Bye!" she called, her heels clattering across the marble foyer.

Three months with a practicing Catholic, who actually got me to sit in Henry's church not once but two times. I laughed softly under my breath. What was it with me and Catholic women? Carol...and Kate too. Kate was a lapsed Catholic. And there was that other woman I'd dated for a couple of weeks right after Kate, the one I picked up on New Year's Eve. She was Catholic, the daughter of Mexican immigrants. What if I were drawn to them because they all reminded me of Her?

At lunch, Henry picked up on my pensive mood. "You have to give me credit for my restraint," he said, "I haven't said anything for three months."

I gave him no encouragement.

"Come on. It seems to be going really well. Is it?"

"The sex is unbelievable," I said.

Henry coughed. "That's not what I meant," he said.

"She's a tiger. She's got those long nails, you know."

"Good God, man," he said shaking his head, "are you going to marry her or not?"

"I don't know," I said, meaning it.

"You think about it?"

"Yeah, all the time."

He smacked the food in his mouth, smiling. "What are you waiting for? What else do you need to know?" Henry asked, and then lowered his voice, "Don't tell her I told you, but she told me that she would say yes to a proposal."

I sat there looking at my hands, not eating, as this information integrated with the stories I had been telling myself. It filled in blanks. I wanted to be an honorable man. I didn't want to waste her love, her life, if I were not the man.

"So?" Henry asked.

"I'm not sure," I said, turning up my palms.

"Once burned, twice shy. You'll get over it. Just get over it. You're no spring chicken, you know."

"I know."

"Marriage is good for a man, especially a man like you."

"What do you mean, a man like me?"

"Oh," Henry deflected, "marriage settles a person. For instance, since you've been with Carol, you don't drink like you used to."

I granted him this with a shrug.

"You aren't moping around all the time. You work regular hours, you've been more productive, more organized. You don't think so much about things. You used to think too much. You're actually normal now, like you were when you were married before. That's all I mean, more normal, more yourself."

More normal. More myself. These words, clinging to each other like ying and yang, somersaulted across my mind's eye, so that I heard nothing else Henry said after them. These words hoisted themselves up and catapulted themselves from cannons of meaning. More normal! Being normal was what we were escaping, she and I, when we had moved to San Francisco so long ago. The rules weren't going to apply to us. I became normal?

We had wanted to do something risky, we were going to change the world. But then we were offered the opportunity to sell ourselves to make wealth for others in return for what seemed like a lot of money to a child of five and twenty. It was the opposition of the dream of the spirit to the dream of the body. We wanted both. We were going to beat the man who wanted to use us up, we were going to make our money, build our security and then abandon him. We were going to come out on top of the pyramid scheme.

I'm not sure I had ever developed a clear picture of what it was I wanted to do. It was something big, of that I had no doubt. I saw myself, driving with Ez in that Oldsmobile across the entire length of this nation, certain that I had no limits. Something idealistic, yes. In that too, was a denial of limits. Something that it was a pleasure to do, and left me time to do other pleasurable things. Something challenging, something that forced me to grow. Myself, heart wide open, eyes on the horizon.

And then, all of the small, necessary tasks reigned in my horizon until I could see only the following week stretched out across my day planner, and the necessity of always competing barricaded my heart and narrowed my eyes. I was rich and successful, but I was a completely vanquished man, a species of creature utterly foreign to me.

I didn't voice any of this to Henry. He probably imagined that I was still deciding whether I would propose to Carol next week or next year.

I called Carol mid-afternoon and told her what Henry had said at lunch.

"What's wrong with being normal?" she asked. "Normal is good. I mean, what's the alternative? Abnormal?"

"I don't know. It seems like there should be something else."

"Like what? Normal people work, get married, have kids, see friends, have fun on the weekends. I'd love to win the lottery and quit working, of course, but other than that, I really can't complain. I've got a steady job with full health benefits, a great apartment, a great guy. Maybe someday," she paused, chuckling to herself, "someday far, far into the non-threatening future, I and that great guy might have some great kids. Sounds kinda good, doesn't it?"

"In a way."

"What do you mean, in a way?"

"Well, I definitely wasn't happy before I met you, and I'm happy now."

"Happy is good."

Happy is good, I was thinking as I left the office early. I was fingering a summons, turning it over in my fingers as I walked. I had gotten a ticket weeks ago and had nearly forgotten all about it. I was going to stop by the Hall of Justice and pay it off before I went home to take Carol out to dinner. Poor thing, what had she gotten herself into, trying to normalize a man like me?

I stopped at my usual coffee shop to fortify myself with a latte. I passed under the vintage diner style coffee cup sign into the coolness of the franchised neo-Italian interior and stood behind a line of people stretched before a young woman with crew cut, orange hair. I glanced away from her as I ordered, trying to avoid staring at the large, machinery metal stud protruding from her lower lip. Like a word that hides, elusive, on the tip of the tongue, and is finally found, I said to myself, Does it do any good?

I stumbled out of the coffee shop, asking, Does it do any good? I bumped into people on the sidewalk, asking myself, Does it do any good, all of this happiness, this baby making, these friends, this fun on the weekends? It seems like I should be of some use to something other than these things. Be of some use to the dream of the spirit that I bartered to support the oligarchy's status quo.

It was in that moment that I was pushing against the glass revolving doors of the Hall of Justice, as I watched the sun bounce, one, two, three times off the planes of glass as they moved, reflecting my body traveling through them, that I saw her. I saw her on the other side of the glass behind my own reflection. I did not blink for fear that I would lose her and I followed the doors back around to the outside of the building without losing sight of her. I stood there in front of the revolving doors as people pushed around me, watching her walk away from me in those high, high heels of hers that still left her short of middle height. I watched her walk with her shoulders carried high, her buttocks moving under pressed slacks. I watched her because I didn't know what else to do. If I went to her, what would she say? I willed her to stop, and then I was terrified when she did. She tossed her head into the breeze that scurried past the building and moved her thick hair away from the black sunglasses that covered her eyes. She raised her wrist and looked at her watch. Then, she stopped moving. She knew. She looked up, looked around for me, and then she found me. We stood there for two breaths looking at each other and I knew that with her, there would be no dissembling. I ran to her.

In a moment my arms were around her, bending her to me, and I leaned down to bury my face in her hair. She was wearing a different fragrance, but underneath it I could smell her own familiar warm skin scent. She pulled away from me and took off her sunglasses to wipe her eyes while I kept my hands on her, touching her shoulders, moving her blowing hair from her face.

"My God, how fine it is to see you," I said.

She didn't speak for a long time, but finally, she met my eyes and then took a deep breath. "I was going to call you," she said, wiping her eyes again, "I have been trying to work up the courage to call you, but…." Her voice failed and she turned up her hands.

"I'm not going to ask you all the questions you know I want to ask," I said.

"I thank you for that."

"At least not right now."

She laughed, and that steadied her.

"Do you want to sit down somewhere together?"

She nodded her head and smiled a dazzling, wide open smile that illuminated her entire face.

As we sat outside at a café table on the sidewalk, I watched her talk. In her pinched nose, her high cheekbones, her wide full mouth, I could see the fat faced dirty tomboy girl who used to challenge schoolboys to wrestle, the mortified early blooming adolescent who sat next to me in middle school mathematics, and the beauty I came to love in my teens, sister, friend and lover in that moving mouth, those waving, glossy red nails.

Ez stopped talking and smiled at me indulgently. "You're not listening to anything I'm saying, are you?"

"I'll start listening when you start saying something that matters."

She looked at her hands. "For instance?"

"Why did you disappear like that?"

"Isn't it obvious? It was hard enough to leave, but to leave and stay gone." She pursed her lips, started again. "I needed some distance. It had to be done and I needed some distance to do it."

"I still don't understand why."

"Let's not talk about that now," she pleaded, "I explained it to you for years before I left and you never understood. Maybe someday you will, but don't let us talk about it now."

I exhaled. I watched her fingertips retreat from mine, reach up to smooth a stray curl from her face. Her still lovely face.

"So, like I said, I was working up the courage to call you," she said, "I had only seven months or so left to do it."

She met my eyes.

"Last Christmas Mami told me that if I didn't figure everything out and call you and set everything right by this Christmas, she was going to call you and invite you over herself."

"She misses me!" I cried with joy.

"Of course she misses you. You can well imagine what I went through that first Christmas with the divorce just started. Everyone asking about you, wanting to know why, whether you were coming back. Then, last Christmas, the reality had set in, but that just made them more determined. So, Mami gave me her ultimatum."

"I went back last time and slept on my father's fold-out, saw Josephina, everyone from school."

"I know," she said quietly.

So, she knew everything about me. Josephina probably told her everything about me, while I was in anguish, not even knowing where Ez was. It wasn't fair and it annoyed me.

"Don't be annoyed. I told you. If you had known where I was, you would have called, come, yes?"

"Of course."

"That's why you couldn't know. I needed time to rebuild my life, from nothing to something. I needed time for it to take hold, before I saw you again."

"Are you with someone?" I asked, finally.

She nodded. "Not the same one," she said quickly, knowing that the one she had cheated on me with was a sore point. "His name is Beassè. I would introduce you, but he's still in Paris. I go back and then we come back together."

"Paris?" She doesn't even speak French.

"That's where I've been."

I opened my mouth and then closed it.

"You wouldn't believe how fast I learned French. I guess I imagined that I would get a job picking grapes and immediately become a part of some revolutionary society. Instead, I was miserable and lonely, sitting in cafés and studying all the time." She smiled wanly. "And then I met Beassè. Can I say that? Do you mind too much?"

"I mind some."

"Try not to mind, and I'll try to give you time to get used to it, yes?"

"Yes," I said.

"So, I'm here to get a new place. I've just got a *pied a terre* that I had from before, one room in a house. We'll need something bigger."

She said *pied a terre* as it should be said, and that addition to her already prodigious verbal repertoire was very sexy.

She took my hand in hers, her eyes liquid. "Would you like to see it? We could catch a streetcar and you could see it."

Do I want to see it? As if I could say no.

We took a streetcar to the Castro and she walked quickly, holding my hand, pulling me along. She chatted in a constant stream about her Paris apartment, her new Buddhism, and her scribbling, as she called it.

"I always thought you'd make a great writer," I told her.

She pulled me into a doorway and then up a long flight of dark stairs. There was a phone booth at the top of the stairs; inside it sat a rotary telephone atop a wooden chair. A boy of about four squealed and ran past us wearing only a pink tutu.

"Esperanza's home!" he yelled.

Ez smiled and led me down the hall to a closed door at the end.

When she opened it, the threadbare hallway carpet gave way to gleaming wood floors. A spill of light from far windows illuminated the hallway behind us as we walked in and shut the door.

I was overcome with curiosity.

"I took the carpet up," she explained, "and painted."

The walls were her own Cuban yellow. Pillows in a dozen colors mounded on top of a plump duvet on the king size bed that dominated the room.

"I always wanted one," she said. "A king-sized bed."

I didn't recognize a single object or piece of furniture in the room. I eyed everything as she led me to the terrace. She flung aside sheer white drapes and opened the glass doors to a balcony filled with tropical plants blooming red, orange and yellow.

"I let them use my room as a guest room when I'm away and they take care of the plants," she explained.

The setting sun coaxed the petals of a night blooming jasmine open, and the wet, heavysweet scent drifted between us. The low, orange sun glowed in her face as she talked and her eyes sparkled with a wild feral beauty.

"Ah look," she breathed "the sun is setting."

I reached behind her head and twined my fist in her hair at the nape of her neck.

"Oh, yes," she said.

I crushed her to me in every knowing way we had built, touching each other those many years. Undressing her was exquisite, discovering every familiar part of her again, discovering the new ring piercing her navel. As we fell onto the bed, a stray thought needled me.

Was this the bed where she was first unfaithful to me?

Her hands moved differently. There were ways that she wanted mine to move differently. I was still moving to the same rhythms, but she was moving to others, unknown to me.

It wasn't the same, and experiencing it when it wasn't the same made it harder to remember all the times it was.

"Ez?" We were lying side by side in the middle of that monstrous bed, our heads cradled together.

"Yes?" she answered sleepily. Always that feline sleepiness after sex.

"Let's not again."

"Yes." She understood perfectly. I wondered if she had brought me there, knowing that it wouldn't be the same, knowing that it would cure my want.

We lay there silently together, staring up at the canopy hanging from the ceiling.

"This guy you are seeing," I started.

"Beassé."

"Yes, Beassé. Is it serious?"

Ez laughed. "I seriously respect him. I seriously enjoy being with him."

"You know what I mean."

"I just don't think like that anymore. The only thing that is serious to me at this point is having children with someone, and no, I'm not going to have children with Beassé." She was still grinning.

"So, he's just some young stud."

"He's not *just* anything. And he's young only if you think of us as still young."

She moved her head away from mine, onto her own pillow.

"Beassé and I, were are young. You, I'm not so sure."

"Now you're just being mean," I said.

"I'm just saying what's true, but it has been a long time since you have wanted to hear what's true. Why repeat myself?" She mumbled this last and flopped over onto her belly to look at me. "Why all the questioning?"

"I was just wondering how much he will mind."

"Oh!" Esperanza rolled over again in a fit of laughter. "Don't feel guilty on his account. Make yourself miserable about it as I know you must, but don't do it because of him!"

"He won't mind?"

"He's not...how do I put it? It's not part of his philosophy of life to be possessive. Yes. Beassé doesn't care about owning anything."

She closed her eyes.

"Well, one's philosophy of life and one's feelings, or what happens to one," I was forced to abandon the third person with an exasperated sigh. "Your life doesn't always conform to your philosophy of it." It was painful to say it here, now.

"I know," she said without opening her eyes.

The room grew darker.

"You paint a rather crass picture of sexual fidelity," I said, privately acknowledging to myself the ridiculous hypocrisy of my complaint. In that moment, whether it was in my place, or hers, Carol was waiting for me.

"I trust him to be careful with his health and mine, but otherwise, why should I care who he makes love to in the hours he calls his own?"

"Fidelity is not about merely owning. It's a desire to keep a certain intimate way of relating only between two people. It creates intimacy."

"I think that people who create intimacy only with difficulty need exclusivity. Beassé and I have an extraordinarily intimate relationship with each other and with others, as well. It's a higher order relationship, in my opinion. It involves far more vulnerability, far more trust, than mere controlling fidelity."

"Some people flee from intimacy through infidelity."

"True," she said without passion. "Cheating on a faithful relationship destroys intimacy, but remaining true to an open one creates it. Beassé and I never pledged to be faithful, and therefore it isn't possible for us to be unfaithful, except with each other."

She had me. I didn't agree that sleeping around was some higher order relationship. I didn't buy that one bit. But she was still true to Beassé, and I was a cheater, no question about it.

"I try to be an honorable man."

"If you have to try, you've already failed. Actually having illicit sex is merely a physical completion of a spiritual infidelity that already exists."

I thought about this. "There is a woman in my house waiting for me," I confessed.

"Yes?"

"I imagine that the cell phone in my jacket pocket over there has been vibrating itself to pieces for the last two hours."

She didn't say anything.

"I was going to marry her."

"What?" She sat up on one elbow, her face flushed with color.

"I was going to marry her, move her into the house on twenty second, and start having babies."

"*No te creo!*" Ez was sitting up now.

"Henry set me up with her…,"

"Henry!" she spat.

"Henry set me up with her, a woman from his church, and I was happy and productive. Henry said that I was back to my normal self."

"Normal self!"

Ez jumped out of bed, and her breasts moved side to side as she pushed one punctuating finger at me as she spoke. "You are so feeble that when you die, an angel is going to have to come all the way down from the clouds and carry your limp spirit all the way to heaven."

"Or to hell," I offered.

"Can't you do anything for yourself? Can't you think for yourself?" She was yelling now. "Or will your pablum life have to be spoon fed to you forever?"

She threw a pillow across the room. It hit the wall with a thud and sent some family photos clattering to the floor. Then she stood still and raised her palms in front of her. "It's none of my business. That was the whole point of that exercise. It's no longer any of my business."

As she picked up the photos, she mumbled to herself in Spanish about how she shouldn't allow herself to get sucked into my shit. I waited.

"But, as your friend," she said, and raised a finger at me, "I cannot stand by and see you destroy yourself like this. This is not you!"

"Why is everyone always trying to tell me who I am?" I yelled back.

"Because you so obviously do not know! You just stand around with a collar around your neck and a leash in your hands, waiting for someone to tell you who to be. You were miserable when you were alone because you had no one there to tell you who to be." Ez slammed the bathroom door behind her.

I laid there on my back watching a fading slant of light cross the ceiling. Ez emerged dressed, and wearing lipstick, and I realized that I was still naked. I gathered the sheet around my waist and peered around in the deepening gloom, looking for my clothes. Ez turned on a small stained glass lamp.

"We still feel young," Ez said, "but our lives are nearly half over."

"I plan to live to a hundred."

She ignored me.

"The time has come to think about what these lives could mean."

"What does yours mean now?" I asked her.

She sank into a chair. "I'm still working that out. So far, I've only figured out what it isn't." Her voice rose. "But, at least I am trying. At least I'm still alive."

I sat on the edge of the mattress and struggled to put on my pants. I felt a strange paralysis overtake my limbs. My brain seemed to be working very slowly. Ez stood in front of me and grasped my head in her two hands and drew it toward her, nestled it against her belly. She stroked my hair. "Go home to your woman," she said, waggling my head affectionately between her hands.

"Carol," I said.

"Go home to Carol. I'll call you when I get back." She slapped my cheek twice with firm affection, and in that way, dismissed me.

Shifting Ground

Outside on the sidewalk, I started to move in a direction I thought would take me home, but I became disoriented. In one day, I had been home, a faithful almost fiancé with Carol, at work productive and normal with Henry, and then in bed with my ex-wife, who had said to me, out loud, every renegade thought I'd had since she left me. In the dim halo of light cast by a streetlamp, I collapsed, dizzy, to the sidewalk. Several people walked quickly by.

The next morning I didn't stir until the late morning sun assaulted my face. I sat up with a start, but then remembered it was Saturday. It had been an ugly night. I had a headache and that same groggy disorientation that you get from liquor, except that I hadn't had anything to drink. Was it really true that I had slept with Esperanza, and then made Carol cry for several hours before I fell into bed?

I had to go into the office. This was becoming a nasty habit, this leaving in the middle of the day and not returning. They probably thought I was cracking up. Maybe I was cracking up.

I was standing in line for a latte at my regular coffee shop near the office thinking about this when Henry walked in. He was wearing those ridiculous Scottish looking clothes that golfers find so fashionable.

"What are you doing over here?" I greeted him.

Henry cut in line beside me. "I'm just dropping some dry cleaning on the way to the club. What about you?"

I inclined my head in the direction of the building, "Oh, just going in for a few hours."

"Good for you, Mikey," he said, carrying his coffee out.

II.

Henry dropped the ball on the grass and squinted up at the noon sun. His companion was finishing a tale to which Henry had only been half listening. He felt the breeze across his face. He would have to slice it a bit. He changed the club in his hand for another and his companion stopped talking. He returned to the tee across the uniform perfect, clipped close greenness of the grass. He stamped his feet and the grass gave with a satisfying sponginess. With two fingers, Henry placed the ball on the tee, gazed down the long lane of green stretching out straight before him, and sighted the fluttering flag distantly beckoning, like a promise. He relaxed as some muscles became smooth while others tensed, and Henry's sharp arrow's gaze held that fluttering red promise prisoner, willing the ball to follow also. He drew back and completed a perfect swing, watched the ball fly in a perfect arrow's arc, heard his companion whistle as they watched it, and then opened his mouth as the ball, mid-flight, deviated ever so slightly. That slight deviation multiplied as it traveled, and Henry could hear God calculating the speed, the trajectory, the mathematical implications of that tiny angle that spoiled the arc, the numbers scrolling across Henry's eyes as it flew, winked once, and then disappeared into the rough.

Henry cursed under his breath.

"Wanna hit a provisional?" his companion asked him.

"Nah, I saw where it went. It was just inside."

The man maintained a sympathetic silence as he addressed his own ball and hit a lovely drive. The ball flew, bounced on the circle of greener grass and rolled away from the hole several more paces before coming to a stop. The man smiled and put away his club. As they rolled slowly alongside the neatly sheared line of vegetation, Henry was pointing.

"Over there, Joe, by that dead tree," he said.

"They need to take that out," Joe said absently, "what an eyesore."

"Stop here," Henry said and alighted while the cart still rolled, "I'll only be a second."

"Don't you want to just drop a ball here? I don't care."

Henry almost said yes, but then his brows knitted in angry determination. Henry didn't need anyone's damned charity. "No, I'm gonna go in there and get it out," he snapped. Henry stalked across the grass and stepped across the threshold of the vegetable kingdom. "I'll have it in the cup in two," he called.

"Yeah, yeah." Joe sighed lazily, stacked his feet on the dash, and took a swig from a metal flask.

Henry turned away and entered the wall of vegetation growing under the canopy of trees. Keeping his eyes trained on the ground, he waded through the surprisingly thick undergrowth. He held his club in front of him, sweeping it ahead of him as he advanced, exposing skittering insects and spooking small creatures that scuttled in all directions.

He stood up and stretched his back, which had begun to ache. Maybe he wouldn't find it after all and Joe would have his chuckle. A rustle in the undergrowth caught his eye, and Henry spotted the white gleam of the ball only a few steps away.

He lifted his eyes and turned around to see if there was any hope of a shot out of there. He turned around again, completely bewildered. Dark forest stretched interminably in all directions. He turned back around toward the direction he had come. "I've come a little farther than I thought," he muttered as he pocketed the ball.

His socks were getting snagged in brambles, and after only a few steps, he found himself completely mired in a large growth of suckering, thorny vines. He hacked at them with his club, advancing slowly. Once on the other side of the vines, he came against another growth of vines.

"This is not the way I came," he muttered and started around it. Perhaps the angle of his retreat was just a little off. He looked to the left and to the right. The entire landscape was littered with large, fallen trees and rotting logs, brambles, thorny vines, and massive evergreen trees weeping to the ground.

He must have gotten completely turned around. If he went too much farther, he would get completely lost. That would be just great.

Henry found himself back at the thorny growth he had hacked through with his club. He was walking around in circles! By now, he was sweating and starting to itch. Resigned, he exhaled loudly, and felt for his cell, but it wasn't there. A small arc of panic began to turn in his belly.

Some distance away, he spied something that looked like a path. Henry oriented himself with the dismembered thorn patch and counted his steps, assiduously traveling in a straight line toward the path. Twenty-two steps. After he had been walking through forest for fifteen minutes by his watch, he realized that the path was not taking him back. What time had he gone into the rough? Henry had no idea. His sole purpose now was getting himself out.

Henry prayed that Joe had fallen asleep and had not, in fact, alerted the local police department that Henry was lost. The path was made by someone, and so it must go somewhere. It was a golf course, for crying out loud, not a wilderness park in Montana!

Henry deferred worry and allowed the cadence of his feet, the steady beating of his heart and the regular huff of his breath to lull him into a meditative resignation. After some distance, Henry found himself getting winded. He looked behind him and was astonished to see that he was traveling uphill, and had been doing so for some time.

After hiking uphill for another fifteen minutes at almost a run, his back and his legs ached for real, and he was breathing like a marathon runner. He was getting nowhere and he was not going to be able to go much farther like this. He was hungry, thirsty, thorn ripped, itching, and his clothes were soaked with sweat. He was losing his resolve. He was even hoping that those smirking goons at the club would find him.

The ground finally started to level off again, but Henry could see an even steeper grade ahead of him. Defeated, he looked around for a log to sit on and catch his breath and saw, a little way off the path, the ruin of a building. He made straight for it.

Some old cottage, he thought, though the fallen stonework made it look like the keep of a castle.

Henry let his golf club fall from his shoulder and slide through his fingers as he carried it before him. He settled himself on the stones of a ruined window frame, resting his arms on the wall. He wasn't even thinking about Joe now, or the game, he was just grateful that his breathing was returning to normal, and that he had a moment to figure out what he should do next. Some ants were building an enormous hill complex in the middle of the ruin and comfortable on his throne, Henry became absorbed in watching their exertions. After poking one mound with a stick, he smashed it. Then, he saw another group of ants walking in a long line, struggling to climb over a low place, and so he piled some sticks and built a bridge for them. This made him feel calmer.

Then a familiar, creeping uneasiness sent ripples of alarmed flesh up his back as he heard one word.

"Come."

Reluctantly, Henry raised his eyes to her blazing blue vividness, right there in front of him, sword raised high. He fell back against the stone, clambering over it in his panic. He jumped up, howling. Something had bit him hard. A large spider scampered across the stone seat and dropped off the back of the wall into the underbrush. Henry's wild eyes glanced behind him. She was gone.

Henry put his hands on his knees and willed his hyperventilating breath to steady. Maybe it was the poison taking effect. Dear God, he was going to perish lost in the rough of the fourth hole of the local country club, murdered by his own insanity. His tale would become internet legend.

It was brighter behind the wall. Puzzled, Henry took a few steps forward. The forest wasn't quite so dense here. There seemed to be a clearing ahead and Henry made straight for it. He blinked as he stepped into the bright noonday sun.

"Are you gonna hit that thing or what?"

Joe was looking at him impatiently.

"Yeah, sure," Henry mumbled, looking around bewildered.

It seemed nothing at all had changed in the hours he was gone. Was he going completely mad? He absentmindedly drew the ball out of his pocket, rubbing it like a fetish.

"Couldn't hit it outta there, huh? I told you," Joe drawled.

Henry dropped the ball on the grass, but couldn't care about hitting it yet. "Give me that thing," Henry demanded.

Joe handed him the flask. "You're buying me a drink at the club after I ruin your handicap."

III.

The sun had just begun to set on another Saturday spent in the office when Henry burst in, as excited as a child.

"Come on, Mikey," he urged me, "we just have enough time to get to the course before the sun sets."

"You know I don't play golf, Henry, and anyway, there isn't enough time."

"We're not going to actually play. Hurry!"

His excitement was infectious. I trotted behind him to his car.

His tires squealed in the country club parking lot. I trotted behind him again as he raced to a golf cart, and before I was comfortably seated, he took off at full speed, bouncing across the fairway, nearly losing me altogether.

"Are you going to tell me now?" I hollered over the wind, the squeaking of the seats and the whine of the electric engine pushed to its limit.

"Something happened. I'm not sure what. But I found this cottage in the rough and I want to show it to you."

"You want me to look at a cottage on the edge of a golf course?"

I was annoyed, disappointed, and yet inexplicably unnerved. There was something about the look in his eyes that made my spine tingle with anxiety. I kept looking at him as I bounced on my seat, gripping the flimsy frame of the cart to keep myself from falling out of it entirely.

"The ruin of a cottage, a long distance into the rough," he yelled, "It's a bit of a hike, but you've got tennis shoes on." He looked over at me a little sheepishly. "It could have just been me. Maybe the sun, I got overheated. It just seemed like I was in there forever and then Joe, that guy I play golf with, seemed to think I was only gone a couple of minutes." Henry slowed down the cart and was training his eyes on the edge of the rough with manic intensity. "And then there's the sun," he said, his eyes still searching.

"What about the sun?"

"I was hiking around for hours and when I came out, the sun was still in the same place, it was still straight up. Not to mention that I came out right where I went in after being lost."

"So, the story you're telling me is that you got lost at the golf course?"

"I know it's ridiculous. And I got bit by one mother of a spider."

I focused my eyes in front of me and kept my mouth shut.

Okay, we must be getting close," he called and slowed down to a crawl, his eyes manically searching, "look for a dead tree."

"That guy you golf with drinks pretty heavily. You have any today?" I asked.

"Yeah, some," he replied absently as his eyes continued to search.

I laughed to myself.

The light was starting to fail, but I trained my eyes on the brush that was sheared straight at the edge of the fairway. When we got to the snapping flag of the fourth hole, Henry stopped the cart.

"Where is it?" he muttered to himself as he turned the cart around. "They must have taken it out."

We drove slowly again along the line of rough, looking again for this dead tree or its stump.

I saw nothing that even suggested that a tree had been removed. There were no vehicle tracks, no disturbed earth or brush and absolutely no stump. The light was failing as we again reached the flag of the fourth hole. "Come on Henry, let's go home."

He shook his head as if dazed, but acquiesced. As we backtracked, he kept looking at the rough.

"Are you okay?" I asked him as we returned the golf cart.

"Of course I'm okay, I just don't understand what happened to the stump, that's all."

"Do you want to get a drink? I could use a scotch," I said.

I sat down at a small table near the massive, carved oak bar of the club lounge and ordered us two Lafroiags as he stood in the doorway calling home on his cell.

"Everything fine?" I asked him as he sat down.

"Of course," he said, his mouth a tense line across his face.

"Let's get some food," I said, my stomach lurching with hunger.

"Order for yourself. I'm not hungry."

"So what exactly happened?" I asked.

"Just what I told you. We were playing golf…" he began. The waiter interrupted him.

"I'll have the chicken wings and some fried cheese," I told the waiter.

"Good God," Henry said.

"You said you weren't eating," I insisted and the waiter left with a smirk.

"Just forget I said anything," Henry snapped.

"When did the spider bite you?"

Henry sighed. "Right before I found my way out."

"And the building? Could you see it from the fairway?"

"No. I told you, I had been hiking for hours before I found it. I was hiking around, I found the ruined cottage, the spider bit me and then I got out. End of story."

"And the other guy didn't think you were gone that long."

"He spoke to me as if I'd been gone a few minutes."

"Then, it follows that you were not hiking around for hours. Not even that guy would mistake minutes for hours."

"But I was filthy and soaked with sweat. I had gotten stuck in thorns. I was a mess. How do you explain that?" Henry raised his voice to an uncharacteristic squeak and several men turned to look at us.

I looked at the unmarred whiteness of Henry's golf sweater and his creaseless golf pants.

"Your clothes are hideous, but if you call this a mess, I can't help you."

Henry looked down at his own clothes and with shaking hands, took a long drink of the scotch. The ice rang like little bells against the glass until he set it down again. "Jesus," he said.

"What does this mean?" he asked, looking up and staring past me.

"It's probably nothing," I said.

"Has anything like that ever happened to you?"

"Me?" I laughed. "Sure. Mostly when I was younger and it was always chemically related."

"Maybe the spider did get me before I got lost and I just got it mixed up."

He pushed his glass away. "I probably shouldn't be drinking now," he said in a small voice.

"Maybe not. Here, have a cheese stick."

He looked at me dubiously as I held out the basket to him, but he took one.

We polished off the food and then sat there for an hour talking about everything but golf.

"How are things at home?" I asked casually.

"Fine." He said it a little too loudly and drew himself up over me.

"Speaking of," Henry said, "I should go."

Henry insisted on driving back to the office to drop me off. He was fine, he said, and anyway, he had had much less alcohol than I. I didn't point out that he was the one seeing things.

On Monday, Henry was at his desk early and smiling amiably with the rosy-cheeked, scrubbed freshness of a Sunday school boy. He seemed to have shrugged off last weekend as a mere irregularity. We went to lunch at The Slanted Door, like we did before Young Jones quit, and we drank a toast to the associate who was working overtime, filling Jones' shoes.

Henry did seem fine, but that creeping anxiety I had had at the golf course never quite left me. His smile was too ready, it was stretched too tight. I watched him and I willed him to say something, to talk about it, but he said nothing and every overly animated word warned me that I shouldn't either.

It's probably nothing, I said to myself as I bent my mind to the task of jousting with federal bank regulations and didn't notice the rest of the day pass until the lights went off in the secretary's station outside my office.

I didn't see Henry all week, but I was too buried in work to think much of it. On Friday morning I finally asked my secretary.

"You haven't heard?" Joyce asked in a conspiratorial whisper.

"Heard what?"

"She up and left him. As soon as school was out, she took the kids back East and served him right here in his office. She's gone…."

Before Joyce had even finished her sentence, I was out of my door on my way to Henry's office. He was there. He had probably been there all along. He was sitting behind the mass of his desk, which supported a nearly equal mass of paper and open volumes. His own bulk rose behind this bulwark and he was wearing large black-framed eyeglasses I had never seen before. I could see by the way he looked at me, impervious, that he knew why I was there.

"You going to The Door?" I asked him.

"Sure."

The sound of his voice knocked the wind out of me. It was small, as if everything that was Henry had been sucked out of it.

"I'll meet you here at noon," I said.

"Make it twelve thirty," he said, and gave me his best facsimile of his old grin.

Later, we walked in silence, waited in silence, ordered the usual. I searched for something to say, scrolling through topics and then rejecting them—the kids, whether he'd heard from Atlanta, the lost cottage. I didn't want to talk about work.

"I saw Esperanza last weekend," I said finally, "and it's over with Carol."

He looked up sharply, the expression his own self, resurrected, and I was so relieved I launched into the whole story. He was, in turn, surprised, disapproving, then shocked, then amazed.

"What does this mean?" he asked finally.

"I think it means that the rest of my life is about to start," I said and felt strange saying it, because I didn't quite know what I meant.

"With her?" Henry spat out.

"No. I mean, not in the way you mean. With her in my life? Sure. Her family as my family? I've already had marathon telephone conversations with the whole lot of them. Live with Esperanza? No. That's clear."

"What, then?"

"I'm moving in a direction that is not determined by my relationship with anyone," I said and squirmed inwardly, remembering Esperanza's too clairvoyant critique of my helplessness.

"Esperanza's back," I started again, "and I'm still restless. It wasn't her I was waiting for. I feel some sort of calling...."

I bowed my head, waiting for Henry to make a dismissive comment, but it never came. I looked up at him, unnerved by the silence that I felt rather than heard, and saw something that made the hairs on the back of my neck bristle, like a dog's. Henry's face was pallid and his chest heaved in small bursts as he stared without blinking past me, through the world I was looking at, looking at something else I couldn't see. He sat motionless, following something with his eyes, seemingly insensible that I was looking at him, that I had spoken to him.

"What are you looking at?" I asked him. When he didn't respond, I repeated the question and angled my face into the trajectory of his eyes.

Henry started back, tipping his chair and upsetting his water glass, staring at me with wild eyes, as if seeing me there for the first time. Then, as his eyes focused on me, he blinked several times and licked his lips. He reached for his water glass, but discovered that he had spilled it into his plate of food. He finally abandoned the pretense that nothing had happened.

"What did you see?" he asked me, his hands shaking.

"What do you mean, Henry? Nothing. I mean, I was just sitting here talking to you, and then...." I lifted my palms.

"And then what? That's what I want to know."

"Don't you know?"

"I want to know what *you* saw first."

"I didn't see anything except you," I struggled to characterize it, "staring into space. You didn't seem to know I was here. You didn't hear me talking to you."

"What did you say?"

"I said something about how I felt a calling."

"I heard that part."

"Then I asked you what you saw, because it looked like you were looking at something."

"You didn't see it?" Henry licked his lips again, "Her?"

I looked around. "Which her?"

"You would know," Henry said, and then jumped when a waiter appeared at his elbow to take the glass and clean up the spilled water. "Jesus," he said under his breath.

After the waiter left, I asked him, "Does this have something to do with that cottage and what happened?"

I don't know why I asked him that, because it didn't make any sense, except that the wild and hunted look in his eyes was the same.

"I don't know."

"Well then, just tell me what it was you saw."

Henry heaved a sigh. "I saw a woman in a long blue gown, the kind one associates with angels or fairies, that sort of thing. She floats rather than walks." He looked up at me and I maintained my most earnest poker face. "And her long hair also floats, as if every part of her is suspended with some power."

"You *saw* this? With your eyes?"

He nodded gravely. "And that's not the worst of it. She looks right at me and I know she's here for me. She challenges me to do what I'm supposed to do."

"Which is?"

"Some part of me knows, but I can't put it into words."

I cocked my head. "You talk like this isn't the first time."

Henry shook his head, not looking at me. "It's happened before."

"Did this start after the cottage thing?"

Henry shook his head slowly again no.

"I can't believe you didn't tell me that before!"

"I'm sorry I told you about the cottage. I thought the cottage was real. I thought it was something I could show you and then, somehow, everything would be explainable, but...."

Henry released a wincing shrug, still avoiding my eyes. "Now you think I'm really nuts," he said.

"Did you," I paused, but then forged on, "Did you tell Atlanta? Is that why she left?"

"Oh no. I have never said anything to anyone, except you."

A new thought occurred to me, a renegade, irrational idea. "You say that it's a kind of angel who calls to you. Why not just go?"

"What?" Henry yelled and drew back as if scalded. "Get up from the table in the middle of lunch and follow a specter?"

"Well, you're not eating your lunch, you weren't doing much good here. Maybe it's not even a physical kind of following. You said that part of you knows."

"I can't believe you are even suggesting such a thing. You don't even believe in angels, and you're telling me to follow it around, if that's even what it is."

"I'm just saying, why be afraid of it? See a doctor, sure, but there are different ways of looking at this, and they're not all bad."

"I've already got an appointment with a doctor. Maybe I have a tumor."

"You said you know what it wants. Maybe you should just say yes."

"I don't want to have anything to do with it," Henry said angrily, "I didn't expect to hear this kind of rubbish from you. I'm sorry I told you."

We sat in silence for a few minutes and the waiter quietly laid the bill on the table and left.

"It's a tumor and they'll just cut it out," Henry said.

After I was back in my office reading over a memo Alicia had prepared earlier in the morning, I was astonished by the advice I had given Henry.

"Follow it," I chided myself under my breath. But then, maybe I would say yes.

Now that I knew about Atlanta, and even about the Blue Lady, as I now called her, Henry didn't hide from me anymore. He was at my elbow all the time like a needy child, and I understood why. I remembered how it was for me, but for him it must have been a thousand times worse. The difference between him and me, however, was that I could never shut up about Esperanza, and Henry wouldn't talk about Atlanta at all. So, I found myself in the uncomfortable position of spending an inordinate amount of time with Henry, not talking about anything relevant to his life. We talked about work a lot and that bored me.

We were playing golf at his club one Saturday, or rather, he was playing golf and I was standing by, for this was the compromise we had worked out, and talking endlessly about banking subsidiary companies and the federal regulation of them, when I couldn't stand it anymore.

"To be honest, Henry, I just couldn't give a flying fuck," I said, exasperated.

Henry stared at me.

"At first, it was a challenge, just to survive and compete. Then after I became partner it was a challenge to manage it all, to keep all the balls in the air. And now, at this point, being rich is supposed to satisfy me, but to be honest, I just don't care about any of it anymore."

"What does that mean?" Henry asked, looking a little frightened.

"I'm not sure," I said.

"It doesn't mean anything," he said confidently, "It's just a phase."

"How are you feeling?"

"Work is going fine."

"No, how are you feeling? You had an appointment with a doctor, right?"

Henry glanced down the fairway. "He says that it was just stress, and I'm taking something for it. Problem solved."

"How is everything going with Atlanta? Is that wrapping up?" I asked.

Henry drew back with a physical aversion to the question and stared at me. "I'm hitting her with everything I've got," he finally said, viciously pushing out each word.

"Are you sure that's good for your stress?"

"This will not stand. It's a bad example for my children if I buckle under and allow it."

"Is she back?"

"She flew back for a court appearance, but she says that so long as I'm still in the house, she's not coming back. Supposedly I'm supposed to be out of the house by the fifteenth, but we'll see."

"That's only a few days."

"I know when it is," Henry snapped. He turned away to tee up his ball.

As I watched him check the wind in the treetops, sight the hole, address his ball, I couldn't help feeling that Henry had become his own worst enemy. As soon as I thought this, I recalled that conversation we had had, it seemed like years ago, when I suggested that Henry should empathize with me, should think about what it would be like if Atlanta left him. I would be dead, he had said.

I realized that he made no allowance for deviation, that he allowed no room in his being for compromise, that he stacked up all of his goblins and opposed them by force to keep them at bay. This was a battle of life and death for Henry.

Weren't there other kinds of death, though? I wanted to say this to Henry as he silently swung and watched his ball fly. Perhaps Atlanta was dragging him to his death, but perhaps it could be a fine and good death that would make a better man of him.

I realized that I was talking to myself. Where was the part where it all made a better man of me? Where was my Blue Lady now?

ATLANTA, GEORGIA

I.

I looked out of Ms. Mara's kitchen window, watching the shadow pattern of the swaying apple tree as it stirred in a stiff summer breeze. I marveled at how I had forgotten the light. I had forgotten the Georgia sunlight, how it seemed to slant, even at high noon, how indirect, how polite and rounded it was, like the words out of people's mouths. I came every year to escape the cold San Francisco summer, and every year I was surprised that I had forgotten the light. That harsh California sun baked away the memory of it, perhaps, so pale and deferential it was in comparison. I was comforted that although the memory of it was baked away over the long year that I was out West, I always returned to find it still here, still patiently waiting, solid with quiet permanence.

I washed the dishes, each one by hand, in my mother's chipped porcelain farm sink. I looked out of the window into her backyard, unchanged since my girlhood. In the center were those old Gravenstein apple trees, thick with apples, growing round and ripe. Underneath, in a hammock, with her big toe touching the grass, moving the hammock lazily to and fro, was my daughter, growing round and ripe also. Her hair, the length of it now cut off to cool the back of her neck, bounded upwards in loose, glossy black spirals as she bent her head over a book. That girl had powers of concentration that could bend spoons. A bomb could go off right next door, and Mary would merely turn her page. Just like her grandmother.

My earliest memories were all of my mother, Ms. Mara, reading, writing, shuffling pages. She gave me blank pages to shuffle also and to scribble on to quiet me, to purchase one more hour of uninterrupted work. She loved me, I was fairly certain of it. No, I was sure she did, in her own cerebral way. I guess when I married Henry, I thought I was making a match that opposed as opposite the cool rationality that ruled my youth. I rinsed the bowl in my hands, and stacked it face down on top of the other clean dishes filling the drain rack.

I knew virtually nothing of my mother. Her parents and her family, if she had any, I had never seen. Beyond her curriculum vitae neatly laid out in the printed bios and book reviews, her history was a family mystery. But I saw the traces of it in her inability to hold me, in her inability even to hold my eyes, and in her unwillingness to respond to the word, Mother. She was not on a first name basis with this world. She was, and had always been, to me and everyone else, Ms. Mara. I watched Ms. Mara say something to Mary as she passed her to come in the house.

There was something new this time, though. During the course of my life, this woman had never changed. She looked like a woman of forty at twenty-five and there remained, immutable. At sixty, her barrel chest took in great gulps of air and pushed it behind her words with the same force she had at thirty, her hands were two hydraulic hinges that made men nervous, and she boasted that no dentist had ever breached the surface of one tooth. Yet, when she opened her front door and came out onto the porch early on that first morning we arrived, clutching a sweater around her waist though it was already seventy-eight degrees, I was shocked by the sight of her nearly six foot frame squashed small, thinned, shrunken and bent, as if she were struggling to support a great invisible burden. I never thought it possible that this woman would ever age, would ever change, could ever be touched by any force of nature, yet the evidence that she had stood apparent before my eyes.

"Atlanta, you want that I dry?"

Ms. Mara had come in through the back door, and now began to dry dishes. I looked at her out of the corner of my eye and smiled into the sink as I continued to wash. I noticed the tension that began in my shoulders creep upwards into my neck, my jaw, the tension, the frisson, of conversing with Ms. Mara. It was a kind of nervous tension that attended the constant strain of repressing and sublimating all emotional connection, defending against it. I suspected that if those gates were opened, the intensity of that released energy would consume us both in a combustive flare.

"She sure has gotten pretty," Ms. Mara said, looking out the window at Mary. "You make pretty ones."

"Pretty, but terrible too," I said, laughing. "She is all her father and you. She has none of me in her."

"Yes, but there is some of *her* in *you*."

She said this as she said everything important, without looking at me, still drying the cup in her hands. It was her way of congratulating me, of telling me that she was proud of me, of my strength. Tears pricked the corners of my eyes and I grabbed another dish to wash. I had never in my adult life cried in front of Ms. Mara and couldn't imagine what would happen if I did. We passed several minutes in silent contemplation of the back yard out of the windows.

"If there's anything else you want me to do, I'll do it," she said.

"Everything is getting taken care of," I told her. "He's supposed to be out of the house in a couple of days, and when that happens, we can go home and finish it all."

Ms. Mara didn't say anything, and it occurred to me that she didn't want us to leave. This too, if true, was surprising. Perhaps after thirteen books and sixty some years, she was finally learning to enjoy having others around. Another thought occurred to me.

"Do you think about retiring?" I asked.

She was silent for several moments. "Do I think about it? Yes. Do I think I could bear it? I'm not sure what I would do with myself."

"Your garden here is a full time job by itself, Ms. Mara, and you could still write at home. What with the internet and all, the only thing you'd miss is the students, and you complain about them all the time."

"Sounds like you are arguing the case. Is there some reason you want me to retire? Do I look infirm?"

"Oh for pity's sake," I said, astonished anew at how she could pierce my thoughts, "forget I said anything." I continued to wash the dishes.

"Why do you think I should retire?"

I hadn't really analyzed it before I said it, but now I knew why. This was the happiest I'd ever seen her. Ordinarily, while she was home during our visits, there was always present a certain impatience, a wanting to get back to it. This was yet one more parallel with Mary. It was the same antsiness, always leaving or wanting to leave. But there was none of it now, for she was drying these dishes, one by one, as if she could continue doing so forever. I liked it.

"You seem happy at home now. It's nice to see you happy."

"Whatever do you mean Atlanta? I've always been happy."

My hands stopped washing. I'd always thought that Ms. Mara's unhappiness was a premise of our lives that we all, the three of us, were in tacit agreement upon.

"To be honest," I said, as I pulled the stopper from the sink and wiped my hands on my jeans, "that comes as a complete surprise to me."

Ms. Mara fixed her heavy lidded bug eyes upon me and then raised them in righteous amazement. Then she wrinkled up her full lips and pressed them together as a veil of rationality settled upon her features. "Perhaps, Atlanta, you and I have different definitions of what happiness is, or feels like. I think that entirely possible now, given what you have said. To me, the greatest happiness I have found in my life is applying myself toward the furtherance of ideas that are important to me. I cannot imagine a higher and better use of my gifts."

"But don't people have phases in life? I mean, I don't pretend to have gone though so many, but I feel that I am going through one now, and I have never before seen you change at all, not one scintilla, and maybe it's time you did."

She was afraid of the life of the heart, I thought, and once again, I wondered what it was that made her so afraid to open that door. I had imagined everything from mundane nuclear family insults to horrific ordeals, but she had never given me any reliable indication of the truth of it.

It didn't really matter, the cause, I supposed, but I felt a resolve in myself to get to the bottom of it, the effect of it. If I had the courage to face my own demons, my hero, my unfailing, unflinching, unbending, workhorse of a mama should be able to, as well.

So, I said it.

"You don't have to tell me why. I don't even know why I just said that, because I know very well that you will tell me nothing true about it. It doesn't matter why, Ms. Mara, but the fact is that you are afraid of love, of loving and receiving love, and I'm afraid it's killing you. That's why I want you to retire. I want you to live the life of love, and live a long time. I want you to stop being afraid."

"I'm not afraid of anything, Atlanta. I really do not know what you're talking about."

She had put away the towel and now faced me, though, unable to meet my eyes, she looked slightly away as she spoke to me, glancing back at my face with each fresh phrase.

"Then why must I call you Ms. Mara? Why never Mama, even when I was small?"

She flinched. "You know very well. I have explained this enough times. It's a question of identity and gender politics. I didn't want to be confined in this culture's definition of a mommy, and frankly, I don't think you have been much improved by allowing yourself to be shoehorned into it. Although it's impolite at this juncture to point out that recent events have made this point all too clear, I feel that I must mention it, since you press it."

Ah, the divorce. I almost was drawn into a heated discussion of that offered red herring, but then I stopped myself. I knew better. Three some decades of struggling with Ms. Mara had well prepared me for this moment.

"My life and choices aside," I began, "we were talking about you. You have many fine ideas, but you are using them to avoid your fears. I am not deceived, and I seriously doubt that I'm the only person who sees it."

It was at this impasse, as we stood staring at each other, or rather, as I stared at her and she stared at my right cheekbone, that we both noticed Mary standing in the frame of the open back door, her first finger marking a place in the book held at her side.

"Mary!" Ms. Mara welcomed her with relief, "Perhaps you can settle this question with your mother. She's gotten this ridiculous idea in her head that I am some kind of fearful creature quaking in her shoes, that I'm afraid to…." Ms. Mara raised her hands in exasperation, so loathe she was to even speak it out loud.

"Afraid to love and receive love," I said.

"Whathaveyou," she replied dismissively and drew herself upright. "You arbitrate. Do I strike you as being a person who is afraid?"

I smiled because I knew that Mary didn't play favorites. She would take the question seriously. Mary drew up her mouth and rolled her jaw, as if she were testing the question with her tongue. This she always did when she was too far inside the privacy of her own mind to notice that she was doing it, this very unflattering gesture.

"If there were a tiger charging toward me and I needed someone to stand their ground in the face of it to protect me," Mary said to Ms. Mara, "I would want it to be you."

Ms. Mara stretched her lips in a triumphant grin and folded her arms.

"But I can see it," Mary added, looking directly at me before she turned back to her grandmother, "I suspect that for you, Ms. Mara, there are things more terrible than tigers."

Ms. Mara's complexion blanched at this traitorous conduct from the one she considered her own, her skipped generation real daughter, and she turned and left the room.

The idea of Ms. Mara so upset that she fled unnerved me, but Mary just shrugged.

"She asked," she said, and laid her book face down on the counter as she reached into the fridge. "I almost hope that Henry does get some kind of new delay," she said. "It's kind of interesting this year, with me grown, and the three of us together. There's always magic in threes."

We stood looking at each other, and I noticed that Mary looked right back at me—she, unwounded, met my eyes unafraid.

"Do you see it too, or is it just me? Do you see how she is changed?" I asked.

"I see it," Mary said, "I actually started noticing last year, but this time, it's pretty obvious."

Mary smiled at me with raised eyebrows. Then, with a glass of milk balanced on a plate of food in one hand and her book in the other, she disappeared out the back door.

I sat down at the kitchen table and put my chin in my hands and stared at the apple green walls. Matthew breezed in then and began to dig in the refrigerator.

"Where d'ya get that?" Joshua asked Matthew as he passed him in the doorway carrying out a slab of banana and vanilla wafer pudding on a plate.

"Fridge, second shelf, in the back," Matthew said behind him as he walked into the living room to plant himself in front of the television.

"Hi Mama! Can I have some pudding too?" Joshua asked.

"Of course. Do you want me to get it for you?"

"Nope. I can do it."

I watched him with pride as he struggled to put the heavy glass casserole dish on the counter and then to stand on tiptoe to reach a spoon into it. He smiled at me as he carried his plate into the living room, leaving the dish with the spoon in it on the counter.

I heard Daddy teasing the boys before he too appeared in the kitchen.

"Do we have any iced tea made?" Daddy asked me.

"I think so," I said.

"Do you want a glass?" he asked me as he lifted a pitcher from the refrigerator.

"Sure."

"I'm just telling you now," I said, looking at my hands, "just so you know, that Ms. Mara and I have had a fight."

"Oh boy," he said with a chuckle in his voice as he sat down opposite.

"No, a real one, about something real. She just turned around and left and I'm not sure if she's talking to me."

I was terrified that I had gone too far with her, that I was lost. That she would finally wash her hands of me was something that I had lived in terror of my whole life.

Daddy took a long draw of his tea and set down the glass before smiling at me gently. "You know how she always says that she had only one child because of the population explosion?"

"Yeah?"

"Well, it's a good thing for that population explosion that her first one was a girl, because she would have kept on pushing out babies until she had you."

I watched my fingers as they skidded across the chilled sweat of the glass and made it cascade down the sides in tiny rills.

"Your mother loves you like nothing else in this world. She would walk through fire for you."

I blinked my eyes hard and watched the rills roll down.

"Then why can I not feel it?" I asked.

"You know very well why that is. Maybe not the details, but you know."

"Do you know? Really know?"

"Of course I know. You know I know."

"And yet you hear the things she says, the stories she tells, and you don't say anything."

"She's a stubborn woman, Ms. Mara, and if you mean to bring her to heel, you have your work cut out for you." He looked past me, his grey eyes squinting between his heavy graying brows and broad nose at the idea of it. "That would be something," he said.

"I don't know why I have to press it now," I said, rubbing my eyes.

"It doesn't matter," he said, reaching out and patting one of my hands firmly with his hand, still heavy and strong. "You are good. You go ahead and trust your instincts because your instincts will be good ones." He paused. How are you holding up? I mean, generally?" he asked me.

"I'm okay," I said, pushing my hair from my face. "I thought I might miss him, or more likely, miss being married, but I find I don't. Maybe it's because we are out here, or maybe because he is being such an ass about it, I feel like it's just a chore that must be managed."

"Maybe the grieving will come later," he said, rising.

He bent down to me and gave me a firm, sideways hug before he placed one of his hands on the top of my head, as he'd done when I was a child. He was still behind me, talking to me while he stroked my hair when Mary came in, put her dishes in the sink, and ducked into the back hallway.

II.

The last thing Mary wanted was to listen to the too loud volume of a mid-afternoon monster movie with her brothers, and she wanted to steer clear of whatever her mother and grandpa were talking about at the table. She just wanted to bury herself somewhere and organize her thoughts. She had started reading some of the Existentialists in the spring, and now, with nothing else to do, she was making her way through Ms. Mara's collection. Skirting Hegel as too difficult, she had just finished a heavily edited collection of essays explaining Marx, which she needed to return. She ducked into Ms. Mara's study. The room was dim behind heavy drapes, cool, and smelled of humidified paper. She didn't bother to turn on the light. She was just going to trade the Marx volume for another one.

"Which is that?"

Ms. Mara's voice was loud in the silence of the room and Mary jumped. She turned around with one hand on her chest, breathing hard. "You scared the crap out of me!"

"This is my study."

"In the dark? How can you see, anyway?"

Ms. Mara looked at her from behind round spectacles, which gleamed in the single beam of light slanting in through the heavy curtains. "I've worked in this study for four decades before you arrived this summer Missy, I see just fine." Ms. Mara bent over her papers.

"Are you in here," Mary addressed the top of Ms. Mara's bent head, "because you're mad at me?"

Ms. Mara looked up, pen still in hand. "I asked, you answered. It was fair enough."

"But you're annoyed."

"I didn't like your answer, but that wasn't one of the rules, that I had to like it."

"But you *feel* annoyed, I can tell," Mary replied, "and I just hope we can all talk about it. Mom is upset."

"That's not a surprise." Ms. Mara said, and began to read again.

Mary turned to the shelves, looking for the empty space in the rows of spines.

"Which is it?" Ms. Mara asked again. "Let me see it."

Mary held out the book to her and Ms. Mara raised her eyebrows approvingly as she leafed through the table of contents.

"Can I ask you something?" Mary said.

"Of course."

"Is Mara your real last name?"

"Oh for crying out loud, Mary."

"I just want to know. My friend says I'm black."

"What does your friend know?"

"Well, she's black and she thinks she knows."

"Mara is, of course, my real last name because I make it so, and that's all that is relevant."

"It's relevant to me, though," Mary insisted. "I just want to know how you were born so that I know who I am, that's all."

"You are who you think you are. Period. Who you are is for you to decide and no one else. DNA means nothing."

"But people always say, I'm this, I'm that, and they ask me what I am, and I can't say exactly."

"Those people are identifying with something they didn't choose for themselves. You are more free, you can choose. When people ask you what you are, tell them whatever you want."

Mary rolled her jaw.

"Now, if you love bright colors and hot weather, if you love African drums and dancing, that's just wonderful. Adopt all things African for yourself and cherish it, but don't worry about whether you have any African blood or not." Ms. Mara paused and smiled to herself. "And if some one hundred percent African fellow over there loves Gaelic and bagpipes and just can't get enough fog and beer, then by all means, he should adopt all things Irish to himself. It's the affinity of spirit that matters."

Ms. Mara handed the Marx book back to Mary, and turned again to her papers.

"If you lie about who you are," Mary insisted, "then you aren't letting people get to know you. You keep them at a distance."

"Bah! It's not a lie, Mary, as I've explained, and I'm connected or not, as I please," she said. "All these philosophy books you are burning through, they all say the same thing: that we have to think about everything in an organized way, that it is all rational, when there is nothing whatever rational about it. Life is completely irrational, and the desire, the intent, to shoehorn it into a rational structure limits it. I need no other justification for my system of belief than my own preference. That's the point that Stirner should have pressed. We need not lead an animal life in order to avoid spooks, because, of course, the hedonistic life is a spook. Everything is a spook. The trick is to choose your spook carefully. I'm comfortable with my spook, and that is all I care to say about it."

"Except that," Mary said, her face flushing, "in the same way you say the spook of rationality limits the lives of others too much, perhaps your spook of separation limits you in a way that you will find intolerable."

Ms. Mara's pen audibly dropped from her fingers onto the table. She cocked her head at Mary, the angry line of her mouth turning into a narrow smile.

"I don't know what you and Atlanta think you are doing, but whatever it is, it is pointless. You are a smart girl, Mary, but you don't know anything about real life. You don't know what I've seen."

"Tell me what you've seen," Mary said.

"Bah!" Ms. Mara huffed again. "I will never speak of it, and certainly not to you."

Ms. Mara picked up her pen once more and bowed her head over a page. Mary replaced the Marx and scanned the shelves for another.

"Stirner," she breathed. She pulled a volume from the shelf and turned to leave.

"Kinship of the spirit always transcends that of the blood," Ms. Mara called after her just as Mary reached the door. "Kinship of the spirit can then become that of the blood, and that transubstantial mystery is one of the most beautiful that life offers us."

Ms. Mara began to jot some notes.

III.

Mary emerged from the hallway looking flushed. Before I could ask where she had been, she made a face at me. "Mama, are you going to spend your entire afternoon in the kitchen?" Mary demanded.

"I'm too nervous to do anything else," I confessed. I had been chewing down the jagged cuticle on my right index finger before I spoke, and I now returned to working on it.

"She's not as mad as you think she is," Mary said.

"You talked to her?" I sat up, my stomach knotting.

"She's not that mad, but she's on to us, and on the defensive."

"What do you mean…us? I'm not doing anything," I said, my breath quickening.

"Don't be a chicken." Mary laughed. "This is only the beginning."

I went back to biting my cuticle.

"The problem with her," Mary said, sitting down at the table opposite me, "is that she's too smart. Just when I think I've got her going in a certain direction, she says something really cool and fascinating…."

"The red herring."

"The what?"

"The red herring. With me, she always tries to provoke me. I guess with you, she says something cool. But anyway you look at it, she is the master of control."

Mary rolled her jaw, and I could tell that she was thinking herself a match for it, the little strategist. I eyed her as she stared out the back window. She had such a fine profile, all fine bones and creamy tanned skin, and I liked her new short corkscrew curls.

"Will you keep Buchanan?" Mary asked suddenly. "I mean, after the divorce is final. Will you keep Buchanan or will you go back to Mara?"

This question took me completely by surprise. The divorce had so completely eclipsed my future, I couldn't imagine anything beyond it. "I have no idea."

"If it were me, I'd change it."

"Really?"

"I'm actually thinking about changing my name, myself. It doesn't have anything to do with the divorce or Henry.

I'm thinking about changing my last name so that it's not patriarchal."

Ms. Mara strikes again, I thought.

"What in the world would you change it to?"

"Mara, maybe," she said, "Continue the female line."

I had no idea why, but this idea, the idea that Mary would go over my head in this way and forge a connection with Ms. Mara, on Ms. Mara's terms, made me furious. Tears smarted in my eyes and I pressed my angry fingertips together.

"It's all just ideas," I said angrily.

"Ideas drive everything."

"Dead ideas with a cold heart," I spat, tears stinging my eyes. I got up from my chair and bolted outside.

Squinting against the sun, I stalked under the shade of the apples and then continued beyond them, to the back of the yard where I couldn't be seen from the house. I headed round the ancient rugosas sprawling like trees, their petals on the ground like great crimson tears, and ducked inside the back arbor. I stood in front of the old wood bench built in the shade of two tremendously large climbing roses covered in bloom, fuming impotently, looking at those roses and hating them. The roses—their deep pink generosity exuding a moist, sweet scent—merely stared back at me, gently nodding and smiling. I sat down on that bench where I had hid when I was a girl scribbling in a journal and drew my knees up. Why did I care that Mary wanted Ms. Mara's name? That was how it was supposed to be all along, the three of us named Mara, and Mary's daughter after. I remembered what Susan had said: Patriarchy has died in my family line. I guess that's what

Ms. Mara had thought when she named me after herself instead of after Daddy. What a terrible disappointment I must have been to her! Somehow the idea that I was a disappointment didn't make me sad, but rather it struck me as consolation. What truck did I have with her wounds? What were they to me?

Yes, at some point Mother decided that she did not like the game this world was playing and she picked up her skirts and left. She maintained an unlisted number, screened her calls, pulled her drapes, sent out line edited messages as her only interchange. In a word, she'd lost faith.

Just like Henry. The moment someone decides they need to control the world around them is the moment his faith is utterly lost to him. Henry spoke endlessly of his faith, but in truth, he had none. How ridiculous I am. I married Henry to get away from her.

I wasn't stupid. I was educated, and I'd lived with Ms. Mara for nearly two decades and had been exposed to a radical view of the world. I never said 'yes sir' without question. I had my reasons to love God even though I had never really believed in Him, at least not as a creature, as a man in the sky who judges. The reality of it was that the warmth of Henry's superstition was a thousand times more comfort to me than the cold and critical eye of Ms. Mara's ideas. Her ideas! I felt imprisoned by them. I was, every day, the too slow student in Ms. Mara's classroom of ideas.

Yet, the warmth I thought I'd found in Henry's Christianity was so tissue thin, so insubstantial, and so, I hate to think it, but so it seemed, insincere, that I found myself unsatisfied. There was a too bright intensity to Sunday cheerfulness, a studied cordiality to Sunday conversation, that belied real intimacy or love, and I knew that this cheerfulness, this solicitousness, this cooperation stopped at the boundary of our church and it made me wonder. If that love stopped at the walls of the church, if the helpfulness, the kindness, evaporated as we all got into our cars and went out into the world, wasn't that just like Ms. Mara's separation, only extended outward ever so slightly? If love drew value boundaries, was it real? If I'd left the church to join another, or to become heathen altogether, would I find myself outside?

When I saw those people screaming threats and insults outside abortion clinics—they screamed at my child now, every time I saw them, I saw them screaming at my child—or screaming at gay people—my dear Monique—or screaming at the whole world over the radio waves that radiate outward to the entire universe, cursing the entire universe with their telegraphed contempt, I wondered, who were they talking to, if not to themselves? Who were they talking to, if not to God? It was, of course, God who was shrinking into the depths of her down jacket, her eyes downcast as the jeers rained down upon her. It was God who was supported by two burly women who held her securely by the elbows and hustled her inside the clinic, leaving her persecutors outside, howling. Did not Christianity's prophet say that what we do to the least of us, we do to God? But no one ever reads the Bible anymore, they just consult it like a lawyer's book. They flip flip flip to find a word or a phrase that they can use in an argument to justify their hate, their weakness, their power over, because it is far easier to play lawyer with the Bible than to live it.

I bent my forehead to my knees and sighed deeply. I tried to live it, I did. I was still angry about Mary's abortion.

Angry at her for making it necessary. Angry at this world for making it necessary. Angry at my inability to do anything about it all. And then that damn boy had gone and told everyone about it just to shame her.

I ground the heels of my hands into my eyeballs until they ached. I still hadn't decided whether we were going to change churches or not. If we changed churches, we'd have to change her school again. Mary didn't care. She wore it like her little badge of courage and she had her long list of Internet friends to support her.

But I cared. A ripple of fresh shame ran through my body as I remembered that scene after church at St. Agatha's, a couple of weeks before school was out. I had left Mary in the foyer while I rounded up the boys to leave. When I came back, a number of people were watching Mary and a mother from the school, Mrs. McKee, as they argued with raised voices.

"If you were serious about putting an end to abortion," Mary was saying to her with her jaw aggressively thrust forward, "you would open that big purse of yours and help create a world in which children are welcome and women aren't *punished* for having them. You would pay for college education and childcare, and health care; you would support young women. But no. You find it much more *convenient* and *satisfying* to stand in front of a clinic and scream at frightened sixteen year olds for free. You say you love babies, but you love your money more."

I looked at Mary in horror, but she ignored me, thick in her rage. She picked up her purse from a bench where she had dropped it. "I am never coming back here," she said and turned her back and stomped away toward those big double doors, still crammed with people.

"The culture of death wins again," Mrs. McKee said to Mary's back, loud enough for Mary to hear.

Mary wheeled around, much to the surprise, I think, of Mrs. McKee. Mary's cheeks were bright red, her eyes like lasers, as she stomped back to lean into the woman's face.

"You say that your culture is a culture of life, but that's a lie. It's a culture that is eagerly awaiting suffering and mass death. You won't even admit to yourself how much you long to watch me suffer for saying no to you. Well, I would rather be 'left behind' to suffer with the Hindu child than to be sitting next to you as you stuff your fat face with ambrosia, and enjoy the spectacle of our suffering from your cloud." Mary's face contracted into an expression of disgust as she looked around the bright and humming foyer, "It's all so ugly."

She wheeled around a second time and stormed out the front door.

The woman didn't acknowledge what Mary had said, except to recoil when the word *fat* was applied to her. After Mary had stomped away, the woman just sniffed and turned to me. She looked me up and down, as if to judge how much of this was my fault, and settled her face into an expression of pious pity.

"God help you," she said, then turned away.

Of course I'd counseled Mary to love and forgive and all of that, but I couldn't help feeling the same rage! And it was that day, the day that I danced at the Powell Street Turnaround that I realized there was something else, that there was a third option beyond saved and damned, religious and not, and I had to find a way to live it. What is it that took me back to the bosom of the altar? So far, I didn't think it was anything more complex than not wanting to be alone. I didn't want to be alone, again, floating adrift in a relativistic universe, free and terrified.

I stretched my legs out, covered my face with my hands and sighed into them once before letting them fall.

A bee circled my head, no doubt thinking me a strange flower, then traversed the length of me to explore a virgin blossom just opening near my feet. The breeze stirred my hair, lifted it around my face and I pushed it behind my ears. My anger was spent and that disappointed me. I plucked a rose in frustration and held it before my face. I was going to tear it apart, but the perfection of it stayed my hand. It was heavy in my cupped palm, a hundred petals arranged perfectly, evenly, in an unraveling spiral around a central disk formed of tiny petals, each bending inwards, all glossy deep cerise and without blemish.

I don't remember closing my eyes, but I rather abruptly found myself walking in that desert. I could hear no sound and no breeze stirred my hair. In a strange reversal, I was holding a picked apart rose as I followed a trail of petals that lay on the silt before me and stretched beyond where my eye could reach. As I came upon each one, I picked up the petal, still cupped and glossy, and placed it around the rose's green eye, where it found its place and held it. I did this for some time and I was so intent on the task of it, so mesmerized by the goal of putting together the rose, that I didn't notice where I was going. As I picked up yet another petal and placed it on the flower's edge, it seemed to me complete. I looked up to confirm that there was not another ahead of me waiting, and I was astonished by the great roar that came from where the silt gave way to the sea. I woke to find my mother's pink rose still cupped in my palm.

"Can I sit with you?"

I was startled and blinked my eyes. Matthew had found me.

"Sure," I said, and made room for him on the bench.

He sat down and I handed the rose to him.

"Mom?" he asked, as he turned the rose in his fingers.

"Yes, Matthew?"

He had something heavy in his heart and I could see that I would need to be patient. I made myself comfortable and smiled at him, my boy who seemed to have grown a foot in one month. Surely, the exterior stretch was stretching him inside as well.

Matthew didn't say anything at first, and then he started to pick apart the rose in his hands. He kicked at the fallen petals with a toe as he twirled the naked corolla between his thumb and finger.

"Are you angry at someone? Did you and Mary fight?" I asked.

"No." He tossed the spent corolla onto the lawn.

I looked up at the canopy of leaves, waiting. I reached up and plucked another flower, inhaled its fragrance, and handed it to him. He shook an insect from it, smelled it, and began to pull it apart also.

"Mary's smart," he began and then paused, his eyes all juvenile insecurity, "and Joshua is...oh so creative and sweet!" Matthew waggled his fingers in the air in mock imitation of the way adults fuss over Joshua.

"Yes?"

"What am I?"

I rubbed his shoulder. "You are whatever you want to be."

"Everyone says that," he complained.

I knew just what he meant. I looked up at the canopy of leaves again as I thought about it. "Well," I said, "if you could imagine yourself exactly as you want to be, not in any future time, or in any past time, but right now, what would you be?"

"What do you mean?"

"Well, for instance, your clothes are too small now, right? And perhaps you would prefer to be a boy who has new clothes that fit?"

"Sure."

"Well, what else? Imagine the perfect Matthew now in the summer before his eighth grade year."

Matthew looked at the second rose in his fingers, now also bare corolla that he held by the stem. I fancied I saw the fallen petals rising up in a dancing spiral of breeze and arranging themselves around it. I looked at him and remembered myself.

"Strong," he said.

"Is that all? He has new clothes that fit and he's strong?"

"Yeah."

"Then step into it, Matthew. Step into that boy in your mind's eye and become him, make it so."

Matthew looked at me then, and perhaps for the first time saw me as someone other than his Mom, someone more than just a Mom.

"So, if I'm ever feeling not strong, I just imagine myself strong."

"And any not strong is only part of the process of being strong, I think." I gazed again upwards. "It's like there are two versions of you, and they are playing tug of war with your self. So, every time the negative side pulls you over there, you've got to pull back as hard as you can and the most powerful way to do it is to just say that you've already won. You can be swimming in your own weakness, but if you insist that you are strong, eventually you will be."

Matthew drew his eyebrows together.

"Use the force, Luke," I said to him in my best baritone.

He smiled bashfully. "Can I ask you—" He paused. "Can I ask you what the perfect you is?"

I felt myself color, but then when I thought about how I could put it into words, I pursed my lips with surprise. "Strong," I said.

He met my eyes and nodded.

We sat there on the bench talking then until the sun began its slow summertime descent and the gentle call of the cicadas began. We didn't talk about anything commonly thought of as important, but rather like intimates, sharing our thoughts as they occurred to us. What a good, good, beautiful creature he is! I brushed a lock of hair out of his eyes.

"Do you want to go in and help with dinner?" I asked him, standing up.

Ms. Mara was in the kitchen cutting up vegetables when we went inside. Matthew went upstairs.

By way of greeting, Ms. Mara said, "Atlanta."

Her tone said this: I know that you are engaged in your usual emotional gymnastics, but I, as you very well may see, remain unaffected, and await your pleasure.

"Hello, Ms. Mara," I said simply.

I washed my hands at the sink and walked toward the living room where I could hear Daddy and Joshua chatting. I found them both on the floor with some crayons and Mary sprawled in an armchair with her book.

Mary looked up when I came in. "Ms. Mara in the kitchen?" she asked.

"Yes," I said.

Mary closed her book. She was going in for another sortie. I exchanged looks with Daddy as Mary got up and dropped the book on the seat cushion. I was glad to have no part of it.

A half hour later, Mary reappeared with a triumphant expression on her face. She sidled up to me on the couch.

"Just don't ask direct questions. That tips her off. Reveal secrets about yourself, talk about your feelings and then wait for her to say something," Mary said and then recounted the entire conversation they had had about men.

Oh, is that all one need do? I thought sourly to myself. Look at her grinning at me and congratulating herself.

"Good God, Mary," I hissed so that Daddy couldn't hear, "she lies. Her little parables mean nothing. It's pure Uncle Remus. If you want to think you've got something with Ms. Mara that I never had, you go right ahead. But five years from now when she starts contradicting herself, when she tells you a story about having had only one boyfriend, or ten, to make some other point, you'll find out that it's all fiction. She's just making it all up to illustrate some *idea* she wants to impress upon you. That's it, that's all."

Tears smarted in the corners of my eyes for perhaps the tenth time that day. I was ready to go home, though I knew I'd find no comfort there either.

Mary began to argue that this was different, when the phone rang next to me. I picked it up and handed it directly to Joshua, who was still sitting on the floor, coloring.

"Hi Daddy!" he said, "I had a great day, but Daddy, I'm ready to come home now."

I left the room to avoid the awkward moment when Henry would try, through Joshua, to bring me to the phone for another round of threats on the heels of entreaties.

I was sitting on the porch biting my cuticles when Mary appeared.

"You can tell your mother that I will be moving a few things into an apartment tomorrow," Mary repeated in Henry's intonation.

"Thank God. We'll go home as soon as I can get a flight."

The lawyer will call tomorrow to tell me the news. I'll check flights right after dinner. I lifted my index finger to my lips to bite the cuticle, but finding none there, moved to the next.

"Oh yeah," Mary said as she sat down on the front steps. "Dinner is in fifteen minutes."

We listened to the cicadas singing that seesawing song about the heat. Mary was smiling as she disturbed the dirt in front of the porch steps with her toes. Still satisfied with herself, I supposed. Thinking that within a few days she had it all figured out.

"I was seventeen once, you know," I said to her. "I was smart and eager and determined to get information out of her...."

"It's not that I'm smarter," Mary interrupted. "Maybe I am, maybe not. I'm saying that it's time. She's different now, you said so yourself."

"Not that different."

Mary sat silently with her chin in her hands, staring at the setting sun, and rolling her jaw.

"Are you ladies coming in to dinner?" Ms. Mara asked through the screen door.

"Can we eat on the porch?" Mary asked, "I hate to move, it's so hot."

"I've already got the table set," Ms. Mara said, holding the door open for us.

"Ms. Mara doesn't feel the heat, of course," I said.

"What is that supposed to mean?" Ms. Mara demanded, coming out of the door several steps.

"You know what it means," I said, and I felt that now familiar feeling of falling forward come over me, that feeling that the rules are temporarily suspended.

"Five minutes," she said, turning to go inside without us.

"By the way," I said, "Henry called to tell us that he's out, and so we'll be leaving as soon as I can get a flight."

The way I said it sounded sharp to my ears, and Ms. Mara stopped the arc of her movement, her weight in her heels.

Mary sat up straighter, immediately alert to the energetic shift between us.

As Ms. Mara again turned to go back inside, Mary blurted, "I think I'm changing my name to Mara."

"Really?" Ms. Mara turned back.

"I forbid it," I said, my body snapping to attention. "I have already told you that I am against the idea and you may not do it so long as you are a minor."

Mary squared her body in front of me. "Why do you care so much? You're divorcing Henry, why should you have his name? We could, all three of us, be Mara. The boys would still be Buchanan, like Andrew and Andrea's parents."

The idea that Mary would give Ms. Mara what she wanted, what I never gave her to punish her for what she never gave me, made me furious.

"Why should I want to wear the name of someone who abandoned me?" I demanded. "She told me in a hundred different ways that if I made myself smart, educated and strong I would get her approval, her love, would get everything I want, but it was a lie."

As soon as I said it, the anger evaporated and in its place, inconsolable grief that I could not contain. I was insensible to anything else that anyone else was doing or saying, but was aware only of my two palms over my face and the effort to force my constricted, aching chest to heave breath in and out. I felt someone stroking my head. I wiped my face with my hands and looked up to see my daughter's face in front of me, suffused with such a beautiful and gentle compassion, that I felt like sobbing anew. I put my arms around her and drew her to me.

"Oh, I have not been a good mama to you," I said.

Mary held me tightly and began to cry also. "You've been a great mama," she said.

I wiped my face again and added, "You've seen the training I've had."

Mary laughed softly. "It's not that hard to open up, once you decide you want to, I guess."

As if by agreement, we both looked up at Ms. Mara. She was backed up against the wall of the house, both of her hands held out to her sides, as if searching for support, staring at the two of us without blinking, mouth open in disbelief. She seemed so small, shrinking into the corner of the porch, and I was overwhelmed with compassion for her.

I knew then that I already had what I needed, and it astonished me that I didn't need it from her. Indeed, I felt complete in myself. That's what the Turnaround had been about all along. It wasn't about my mother, or my father for that matter, although for a long time, it was easier to think it was. No one can save you. You have to find it in yourself. I got up and Mary stood next to me. I stared at Ms. Mara long enough for her to feel it. I knew she felt it, my completeness. She could choose any way she pleased. I was not going to make any more demands of her, for as large as she was, she was far too small to carry the collected detritus of two thousand years of fractured feminine archetype.

"Let's go in to dinner," I said to Mary. I put my arm around her as we walked across the porch to the door. I paused in front of Ms. Mara, but as she did not move, we passed on. Just as we opened the screen door Ms. Mara huffed loudly.

"I'm sorry I was not the kind of mother you wanted," Ms. Mara said, her tone defensive.

"It doesn't matter," I said, smiling gently, and I meant it.

"What in the hell do you want from me?" she demanded angrily.

"I want you to be here with me," I said, "That's all. Be *here* with me, you stubborn old woman."

That's when Mary leapt into the wormhole that led into the depths of her grandmother's heart, the place where the ideas and the feeling met.

"Ideas, by themselves, are dead," Mary said. "People read your books not just because they contain good ideas, but because you write them with such passion. It is in that intersection where your power lies."

"I don't see what that has to do with anything," Ms. Mara complained.

"Bring that partnership into your lived life."

Mary and I watched Ms. Mara think until Mary interrupted her.

"I'm going to start calling you Grandma, whether you like it or not."

Ms. Mara's eyes darted to meet Mary's. "Too much, too fast. I can see your point, Mary, but I need to think about it, work it out…."

"Does a rocket reentering the atmosphere go slowly?" Mary asked, "No, Grandma. It's time for you to come in for a landing, so strap yourself in."

Ms. Mara's complexion darkened, "What makes you think this world deserves our gifts, Mary?"

"It's not a perfect world, I'm not saying that," Mary said, "but the paradox of it is that if we withhold our gifts the world becomes less worthy of them…." Mary stopped and looked significantly at me, and I understood her.

"But if we give them freely, we heal the world and make it worthy," I said.

I drew myself upwards, squared my shoulders, closed my eyes and took one step forward and enclosed her two elbows in my arms, pressed her elbows into her body as I embraced her. Her body tightened in alarm, but I held her huge frame securely.

"Everything is going to be okay, Mama," I said.

Mary enfolded her from the other side and I felt Mama's muscles, one by one, release and let go.

"I don't know what this is." Mama started stammering like a child, filling the space with words to crowd out her nervousness. "I don't know what this means."

"What do you want it to mean?"

She looked back and forth between us, helpless to stop the tears that were streaming down both of her cheeks.

"Alright," she choked, "alright. When I was about five years old, I was found walking down a dirt road in my underpants and I didn't speak for a long time. I grew up in an orphanage bearing the same last name as the orphanage director. I have some memories that I don't like very much. There were also some ugly details that people knew at the time but no one told them to me."

We drew back, our arms still around her, waiting.

She looked at her hands, "The name, Mara, I chose it when I went off to college on a scholarship. I was at a party one night, and a good-looking boy asked me my name. Well, I was already studying the old goddess lore, and Mary Mara is what popped out of my mouth. That's what I've been ever since. What else do you want to know?"

When we stumbled into the kitchen together, arm in arm and tear stained, the three of them, Daddy, Matthew and Joshua, looked up from their almost emptied plates. I could imagine the picture we made and it made me laugh, and then the two Marys, the old, stubborn one and the young one, began to laugh also.

"I think those women have been dippin' into the sherry," Daddy said, but he smiled at me with just enough sparkle to let me know he was pleased.

I don't know whether it was the prospect of facing Henry, or the prospect of facing a real relationship with Mama, but I didn't sleep at all. There was no dread, strangely, on either account, but rather a girl's excitement. Someone had told me once that anxiety was just excitement put together with fear, and that if you took away the fear, you were just excited.

When we bustled around the following day, preparing to leave, Mama followed me around, watching me as if she were not sure what would happen next. She still flinched when I called her Mama, but I could tell from the way she turned up her pressed lips afterwards that, somewhere in there, she liked it.

It seemed scarcely possible, but I had the kids in the rental car on time.

"Oh yeah," I said, as I made a last minute scan of the house, "I have a new cell."

I wrote my number on a pad next to the phone. Then I paused. I looked up at Mama as she stood in the doorway watching me write, and then wrote in neat block letters above the number: ATLANTA MARA. I laid the pen down next to the notepad and then followed Mama out onto the porch.

When I threw my arms around her neck, I noticed that the usual tension in my shoulders was gone. I smiled at her and she met my eyes for an instant before looking at the car, where Daddy was leaning into the windows, entertaining the kids.

I laughed and started to go down the steps, but she grabbed me. She seized each of my shoulders in the vise grip of one of her huge hands and she held me tightly as she drew me in. "I'm proud of you," she whispered in my ear, and then released me and turned away.

As I stumbled down the stairs I thought wonderingly, I have a Mama. I have a Mama!

The Yellow Sundress

I.

It was completely disorienting to return to the office, plow through a stack of paper, eat lunch with Henry, and return to the echoing chill of a neglected house to heat up spaghetti in the microwave and eat it in front of the television. It was disorienting to return to this life after I had seen Esperanza. When my mind wandered, I fantasized about other lives now. Maybe this was mid-life crisis. Maybe if I were married I would fantasize about twins with large breasts in fast cars, but as I was not, my fantasies took a more settled turn. I would marry someone younger, with freckles, and fur on her legs. We'd move to a farm and have children. Or I would work part time and write a book, or at least, read one. Join the Peace Corps. I could still do that. Surprise everyone by getting myself arrested protesting something.

It was true that all of these fantasies featured a beautiful, young woman, but I knew that she was not what I was seeking. A young man, who knew nothing of life, always had an eye out for another woman, a new woman. He was busily creating memories because he felt he didn't have nearly enough yet. I was full to bursting with useless memories of conventional used up days, and I wanted to try my hand at building something more meaningful. Knowing that, and saying it to myself made me feel more like a man than I had ever felt in my life.

So, now what? I asked myself every morning as I knotted the tie at my throat. What did a man do with the days of earned manhood left to him? Life was too short. Just as soon as you started to understand the big things, it was almost time to get ready for retirement and death. Of course, I was being a bit maudlin and melodramatic as Esperanza claimed I was wont to do, for I was supposedly at the height of my social power, but there was truth in it, this exigent press of time in the middle years.

It was at this juncture that they came back from Paris. Esperanza and the other one, who she claimed was eager to meet me. She actually put him on the phone. He sounded sincere enough, or maybe that was just his painfully slow English and Frenchie accent. I was imagining him as I was driving over: young—even though she said he wasn't, I couldn't imagine him as other than too young—stylishly pale, tousled and unshaven, thin in his low slung designer jeans, affected, fey. I experimented with several versions of self satisfied smirk as I drove. You can imagine my surprise when I saw him sitting outside with her, when he stood up taller than I, and I met him, a broad shouldered brown skinned man, his cheeks, nose and eyelids washed with dark freckles, his eyes age creased, his smile and grip easy and secure. I was a man meeting a man. I looked at Esperanza and she raised one eyebrow at me as she smiled to herself.

"This is Beassé," she said to me.

"Beassé," she said to him, "This is Mike."

"As if you could be any other." Beassé laughed deep in his throat, which resonated warmly. "I've heard so much about you, I feel as if I know you already."

I released his hand. "I wish I could say the same, but Ez doesn't tell me anything anymore."

I was prepared to dismiss the stylishly fey one, but this Beassé, large and easy, made me uncomfortable.

"You must be hot," Beassé said so very slowly, smiling in his uncreased pale linen shirt, eyeing my suit, rumpled from a day at the office.

It was at that moment, of course, that the dam broke between my shoulder blades and a small torrent of sweat ran down the center of my back and pooled in the waistband of my briefs.

"No," I said, "not particularly."

"It's not usually this hot this time of year, is it?" he asked, enunciating each word.

"No. The coldest winter, summer in San Francisco, etcetera," I said impatiently.

Esperanza spoke to him in rapid French, no doubt explaining the reference to Twain, perhaps explaining me.

"Do you want some sangria?" Ez asked me. "We got a whole pitcher. Here, have some sangria."

I accepted a glass. It was a damn fine sangria, tart, and freezing cold with crushed ice rather than rocks. It refreshed me and put me in a better mood.

"I know you are supposed to drink the cider here, but I only like to drink it warm when it's cold out. Heat means rum, lemonade, or sangria," Esperanza declared before she took a long sip. She was babbling and I wondered what that meant.

I took a long swallow. The frosty hillocks of ice stubbornly gripped the side of the glass even as I returned it upright in my hand. The sangria hillocks were dreaming Kilimanjaro, yet melting along the edges and already beginning to slip. I looked up to find Beassé's eyes upon me. He did not avert his gaze but smiled again, a slow and genuine smile. That annoyed me.

I looked at Esperanza and she began babbling again. She talked about all of the inconsequential events of their trip over, the crying baby, the smelly fat guy, the bad food.

"Even in first class." She widened her eyes, heavy with khol, before waving her fingernails and continuing about the food, and the poor prospects of the major airlines generally.

This I could not tolerate, this blithering. Who is this person? I jammed my fork into my water glass in search of a chunk of ice to roll around in my mouth. Beassé excused himself. The two of them exchanged looks before he turned away. As soon as he was gone, Ez grabbed the fork out of my hand and winged it out onto the sidewalk. Our neighbors stared at her in surprise.

"I don't know why I should care about your approval! But I do, dammit. Can't you like him a little?"

The people around us returned to their crepes. A passing waiter quietly placed a clean fork next to my left hand.

I looked at her staring at me and took a drink of sangria. "I do like him, Ez. I like him only too well. I don't know if I can do this."

"Sure you can," she said, "I know you can. You were my brother once, before husband. Be my brother again, make an effort."

I raked a hand through my hair. When I looked up, Beassé was excusing himself through the patio. Ez smiled at me encouragingly. He smiled at me as he sat down. I looked at Ez and then smiled in return. All of us now smiling at each other.

"Have you ever been to the U.S. before?" I asked. My thighs were knots of tension underneath the table, and I could feel fresh sweat breaking out on my scalp. I scowled at the sun.

"I went to UCLA for a year on exchange," he said, taking, it seemed, five whole minutes to speak the phrase.

"Really!"

"Oh, Beassé speaks French slowly too." She laughed, and the two of them relaxed a little as couples do when they are silently enjoying a shared story.

"What do you do?" I asked, exhaling slowly, trying once again to make that effort.

"I do my best to be in this moment," he said.

I looked at Ez and she poured herself more sangria.

"I mean, what do you do, as work?" I asked.

There was a terrifically long pause that made me tense, that made Ez visibly tense, despite her efforts to appear relaxed, but he floated in it in that damnable nice and easy way of his for an eternity before he raised his eyes to mine.

"I am a lover," the man said, with apparent sincerity.

Heat flushed my face. This man had just told me that he made a living by fucking my ex-wife, and had done so with all the sincerity of an earnest schoolchild. Fuck this. I rummaged in my pocket for loose bills so that I could leave.

Esperanza began laughing hysterically, waving her hands in the air. Twice, she began to talk, but was so overcome with mirth she couldn't speak at all. Beassé just looked at me and then at her, apparently completely confused. I found a bill and dropped it on the table, but Ez finally stopped laughing and, with one hand on my arm, began talking to Beassé in rapid French, saying something that made him smile. They were both stifling laughter now.

"He means that he loves people." She giggled again and put a hand to her mouth. "He's not referring to anything *nasty*. He means that his proper job description is a person who loves and serves others, someone who creates community."

"What? Who hires someone to do that? Is this some weird new religious thing?"

"No, I do not believe in God. No one hires me. I have no master. I do not worry about making wealth. I do things that are necessary, but that do not come from any institution that provides a salary. For instance, I overstayed my visa and spent a couple of years creating public vegetable gardens in San Francisco. I worked with the Alice Waters foundation there and then helped start a school program in Chicago. I was in Chiapas for awhile, but I learned more than I taught. I lived in Zucotti park with Occupy. I organize, I give free workshops, these sort of things. I give, and I know that, in giving, I will always have what I need."

"Who, exactly, is it that provides for you?"

"Oh, people I have known and lived with all over the world."

"We have a word for that," I said, making a wringing motion with my hands.

Ez shot me a look.

"Oh yes, you Americans have a word for everything don't you? But whose word is it, Monsieur Davis? Is it really yours? Or are you, as a good little…" Beassé paused and looked at Esperanza.

"Dutiful Producer of Wealth," Ez told him, as she eyed me.

That was *our* phrase. I inwardly fumed.

"Yes, as a Dutiful Producer of Wealth," he continued, "are you merely saying what you have been taught to say, repeating the words without thinking, like a grammar school child? If you die today, what is your life? How can you add up your life? As a lawyer, you make corporations, make *filiales*, *capital-risques*, you make and move around money, mostly for and between rich, white American men. This is what your life has been used for so far. Can you really look at me in my eye and tell me that your work is what the world needs? That your life is more important than mine? Your work more important than mine?"

For Beassé to speak this many words took an interminably long time, and although the words were sharp, they were spoken sincerely and without aggression, so that if I were to raise my voice at him, as I wanted to do, I would be the asshole. A fresh river of sweat broke down my back. I took a deep breath and swallowed the fist in the mouth I wanted to give him.

"Most people have to earn a living," was all I said.

Ez took my glass from me and refilled it.

"I know what you mean when you say earn," he began, "you earn money to pay for your life. But doesn't that strike you as *pass*é? It seems to me primitive. I earn my living by making a contribution. I try always to contribute more than what I earn, for I have little need for things. This is very different from the conventional way in which you allow them to value you, they put a price tag on you and then they try, against your will, to wring out more work than the number on the tag. This struggle seems to me to be between animals and I want no part of that."

"Don't think you would get a job as the managing partner at the firm," I said.

"Whenever I hear the economists talk about how people need jobs," he continued, relaxed and amused, "I cannot help but think that is the last thing they need! People need work, something to do, yes! But a job? *Mon dieu!*"

"That's all fine and good for community building or whatever," I said, "but where the rubber meets the road, in actually producing things even you would value, say, life saving medicines, people have to work in a job."

"There is a difference between earning like a child, and earning like a grown up human being," he replied. "When we were children our parents said to us, if you perform the following tasks and do what I say, I will give you money to spend and we agreed and we felt very satisfied with ourselves. When I grew up and became a man I left my parent's house. I did not want to trade in one father only to gain another, which is what happens when we work to earn a living, in the way you mean. The young person agrees to obey the man with a job in exchange for money. He has traded one father for another one."

"And the alternative is?" I asked, not expecting an answer that made any sense.

"The alternative is to live life without fear. Instead of saying to yourself, I need money to survive, you say to yourself, to what use do I wish to put myself? Then, you either find a place, or you create it if it doesn't exist, working in partnership with others. People who make medicines can operate the company together, define their goals together, and apportion the money earned as they all see fit. There is nothing sacred about the American way. Farmers and teachers and mothers are the most important workers and they earn the least. Useless executives running good companies into the ground make hundreds of millions that they waste only upon themselves. Money should always be put toward the best and highest use. It should be in a flow that is constant."

A string inside me vibrated with something I recognized but my searching mind couldn't identify it. It made me unaccountably sad. I couldn't do anything but look at them for several moments.

Esperanza pressed her lips together in tacit agreement. I looked down at her fingers twitching with excitement, her fingers that were professionally manicured and carried expensive rings that flashed in the high hot beams of late day autumn light. I wondered what this was about, her and him.

"See," he began again, "if you approach the world with your hand out, then other people are in control of your life. But if you become a free man and make your own life, you do not allow yourself to be used. Another person does not use you for their own purposes, like a slave. You work in partnership with others toward common goals."

"Do you understand now?" Ez asked breathlessly. "The change is only one of mind, but it makes all the difference. He's a one man creative force."

"I was a corporate slave become a completely free man, without country and without master. I am a snail, I carry my home with me," Beassé said.

"And he creates a home where there was none," Ez said quietly.

"Is that what he does for you, Ez? Are you a creative force now?" I asked, my sadness now turned to anger.

"I still work for the money," she said defensively "but I'm not afraid to quit. Now, as for what he does for me, Michael, you know very well what he does for me. He is my partner as you were. He hasn't found work here to do yet, we are just arrived. As far as I'm concerned, he doesn't have to make any money at all and I've told him so."

To hear her talk about him as her partner smarted. I had stepped too far out of line, and she had disciplined me. I sat there chastised, wounded, and annoyed, not looking at them. I was trying to make the effort, but it wasn't easy. After some moments, I realized that what annoyed me more than anything about this line, this *carpe diem* shit, was that he was living the life I always said I was going to live, but never did, and it was obvious that she was with him and not with me for precisely that reason.

I lifted my glass to drink, but found it empty. I felt miserable for being a failure and even worse for hating this guy because I had failed . Esperanza reached out and held my hand, which I had abandoned helplessly next to my empty glass on the tabletop. She knew me, and it was so good to be with someone who knew me and understood. That was what mattered. Beassé held her other hand, and she chatted with him, filling up the space.

"Well, in my work at the firm," I offered, completely out of context, "I guess I'm the father figure, the one in control that you complain about," I said to Beassé. I was thinking of the way I had made Young Jones tremble last Christmas. "But at least that means that I'm serving myself and my own purposes, according to your definition."

"*Est vrai?*" he asked, "If that is true, then you are a fortunate man." He lifted his glass to me.

"Do you really feel all that powerful, though?" Ez asked me sharply,

I took my hand out of hers. The answer, of course, was no. In fact, I felt completely helpless much of the time. I couldn't even run the new goddamned copy machine they'd installed on our floor last winter.

"Is this really how you would choose to live? Is this your dream, or is it someone else's compromise that you shoved yourself into? You have to wear a suit, you have to find business, you have to behave yourself, keep your mouth shut, and be who they want you to be to get business, you have to work long hours. These things are masters too."

Sweat was breaking out on my face now, and I peeled off my jacket and took off my tie.

"Ah, leave him alone now." Beassé laughed at Esperanza as he poured the last of the sangria into my glass. "Let him relax after a long day."

Esperanza looked at him and then looked at me and then laughed.

He changed the subject, started talking about something—I didn't register what it was. It was something warm and soothing, like perhaps a story about summertime in a far off place, that occasionally made Esperanza chuckle and I chuckled with her. I wasn't even having real thoughts I could hang onto. My brain was paralyzed, drifting, and thinking about something a great deal with no participation from my conscious mind whatsoever.

I don't know how it happened, but I liked him now, really liked him. He did have some kind of magic. Somewhere, over the course of the last hour, I had accepted him as part of her, of what must now come with her, and instead of fighting him, I allowed the third line to complete itself as we made a triangle together. Their shoulders relaxed and they leaned in together and leaned in towards me and we all talked in Beassé's own easy way for another hour until the sun was falling out of the sky and the chattering night time crowd started filling the foyer and crowding the bar, waiting for seats.

I said goodbye to them at the sidewalk, they walking up 16th, and I turning away in the opposite direction. My head was so full of thoughts that I almost missed her, sitting several tables away from where we were on the patio. I wasn't sure at first, because she looked like Atlanta Buchanan, only better. She was still thin, but somehow her body was bigger, more substantial, and her familiar gentle reserve had more presence; it, too, carried more weight. She was wearing a simple yellow shift and sandals, and her face was tilted to accept the slanting orange rays of sunset beneath her wide brimmed sun hat. She looked like an antique Parisian postcard overpainted in red and gold watercolor hues.

"Atlanta?" I addressed her from the sidewalk, "Atlanta Buchanan?"

She lifted her eyes and then creased them in a smile that I instantly recognized as hers.

"Atlanta Mara now," she reached out her hand. "It's so nice to see you."

Her hand was small, soft and warm. I leaned against the chair opposite her after releasing it.

"How are you?" I asked, on one hand conscious of our awkward relation to each other, through Henry, and on the other hand, not feeling that it mattered, "It seems like it's been so long since I've seen you."

"Yes, in a divorce it seems that the friends get divided up as well, doesn't it?"

I silently wavered, feeling the awkwardness and the not mattering, at the same time, and then she decided.

"I was just going to leave, but if you'd like to come sit down, I can stay," she said.

"Oh," I deferred, conscious of my sweat soaked body, "I just left there, actually. We were sitting just over there."

"Really? It's a wonder we didn't see each other. Who were you here with, if I may ask?"

"Esperanza and her new boyfriend, if you can believe it."

"No!"

"Yes, but it wasn't so bad." And I felt, at that moment, that it wasn't so bad at all.

"Don't go," she said cheerfully, her hands busy with her pocketbook, some papers. "I'll go pay the bill and come out."

Atlanta Mara. This was Henry's ex-wife. And yet she wasn't really Henry's ex-wife, but someone else entirely. I waited there with my hands in my pockets, watching the door. Several people moved aside for her and that hat as she emerged, her ruby lips, it seemed to me freshly painted. We turned and walked past the sunset, in and out of the shade of buildings and she put on a pair of tortoise shell sunglasses and smiled at me again. She looked so tremendously good. It was interesting to notice that I'd liked her, not suddenly, but in the past tense, as if my liking were a presence that had been standing quietly by all along.

"Henry picked up the kids after school," she said. "This is his weekend."

"Ah," I said. It hadn't occurred to me to wonder about the kids. "How is that going?" I asked.

"Badly," she said, "but we all do the best we can."

I'm hitting her with everything I've got, Henry had told me.

"I'm getting my Masters," she said, lifting the papers. "Meanwhile, Mary is trying to get early admission to Berkeley. We'll both be checking the mail for our admission letters." She laughed a high, musical laugh.

We walked aimlessly, talking about her plans. I told her about Esperanza. I exaggerated a little just to make her laugh. It was getting dark now, and Atlanta swung her hat by her side as we walked. Everything sparkled, as if the carpet of the night sky were laid down upon the concrete of the city and each open door we passed presented us with new sounds and smells, in succession as if they were presents opened merely to amuse us two.

This was a date. The thought occurred to me as we ended up back at the big intersection at Mission Delores, which squatted heavily on its steps and stared at us from across the street.

"Where do you want to go?" I asked.

"What's down there?" she asked, pointing to the narrow alley next to the old Mission.

I shrugged and we jaywalked toward it. We followed a chain link fence heavily planted with shrubbery until there was a small gap. The gap revealed an enclosed garden area adjoining the Mission. We walked a couple of feet more and stopped opposite a large break in the shrub barrier. The garden area was, in fact, a very small graveyard, absolutely still and silent, illuminated by a strange light. It looked like a movie set. Dominating the space was a white statue of Mary, supplicant, the moon upon her like a spotlight. The gravestones in front of her leaned and seemed to be praying also. For what? I wondered briefly, then laughed at myself. What meaning shall I project onto these materials, these stones? Longing? Quest for meaning, guidance, salvation? No. Tonight they shall be only stones heaving upon shifting material Earth. This city is built on landfill, after all. My eyes left this scene and were drawn instead to Atlanta's profile. She was gazing at the statue of Mary with an expression I couldn't read. I asked her what she was thinking.

She seemed embarrassed by the question, and paused, her eyes drifting back toward the churchyard before she answered, "I don't think I will ever look at her in the same way again."

"What do you mean?" I asked as she turned away toward the street.

I think she was pretending that she didn't hear me, for she continued to walk away from me, her hips swaying meditatively. The churchyard had put me, too, into a meditative mood. Seeing Atlanta ahead of me, silhouetted in the nightlife lights and the headlamps from an occasional speeding car made me wonder about this building, built out in the wilds to teach the savages the way of the Father, now crowded in on all sides by speeding post-Modernism. I turned and took one last look at the anachronistic tableau—for it seemed to me in this moment that this was all that was left of the Father's way, this streetside tableau, like a museum exhibit memorializing it here—and followed Atlanta.

When I emerged from the alley, she had already turned the corner and was mounting the first steps on the front of the mission in the shadow of the overgrown trees rising along the sidewalk. Many times I had seen couples stopping what they were doing there on those steps as they mutely followed me with their eyes, waiting for me to pass, but tonight we were alone. Atlanta seemed deep in thought as she ascended the steps and wandered from one column to the other, touching them, moving in and out of the moonlight like a lonely Ramaytush shade. She turned to me briefly and allowed the shadow of the massive church door to swallow her. I followed.

As I slowly ascended the stairs, I felt a kind of creepiness, a dread attached to that haunted collonade, and then she leapt out at me and grabbed my shoulders.

"Boo!" she said, and I did jump.

Shifting Ground

She spun away from me laughing a deep throated laugh. That first touch captured the attention of every nerve in my body and I watched her as she skipped across the portico and pressed herself against the stone doorjamb of the massive door. I inhaled the scent of bergamot lingering in the air where she had been and regarded her for several moments before I turned and pressed myself against the doorjamb opposite. Her eyes glittered in the darkness as we stared at each other. I crossed the space that separated us and pressed my body to hers, staring down into her eyes. I put my hands on her shoulders, expecting her to lose courage, to now turn away, but instead she turned her face to mine and offered me her mouth. I quailed for a moment, thinking of her as Atlanta Buchanan, but her mouth was still there, insistent and swollen with promise. I kissed her, unexpectedly but happily surrendering. One's life doesn't always conform to one's philosophy of it.

There was nothing insecure, nothing restrained in her kiss. My God, she was a fully open flower, stamens glistening and I, become now wanton, pushed my hands into her hair as the momentum of the gesture pressed her body against the cold stone. Instantly, she was panting her sweet hot breath into my face and kissing me again and again, making soft mewling sounds against my cheek. Footsteps passed rapidly on the sidewalk and I covered her mouth again with mine and pushed her farther into the shadows. Her hands were everywhere, urging me on, and I pushed into the yards of fabric crushed between us as she cried aloud. Driven both by terror and longing, I continued to do the things that made her toss her black hair and cry out. I stilled her cries against my shoulder and my lips as I frantically scanned the steps, the sidewalk beyond. Then, the long, slow ache of her teeth biting into my right bicep and the sight of one erect nipple silhouetted against the city lights beyond closed my scanning eyes to everything but her.

It wasn't until we were safe, sitting side by side on those steps, she lying back and staring up at a tiny patch of stars visible through the treetops, that I thought, I will be having lunch with Henry on Monday. I will want to see her again and again. She seemed to understand, but also seemed completely unconcerned, herself. Well, she was through with him. That was the thing. She was through with him and I was not.

"Don't you worry about Henry," she said, wrapping her body around me. "It will all work out somehow. I'm sure of it."

II.

Michael walked me back to my car. I wasn't sure what had made me so confident that everything was going to be fine. It was a little like the feeling I had right after childbirth, all three times. I was so full of joy, it was just impossible to worry about anything.

"Will you call me?" I asked him coyly when he walked me to my car, and then I stared up at him through my eyelashes.

A wave of emotion visibly shook his body and rolled into his face as he crushed me to him, and we were again, tongues and hands and eyes, like teenagers, completely heedless.

Shifting Ground

The following glorious days, we spent every moment together we could manage, while maintaining the dual fictions that I was still single and that Michael was still Henry's loyal friend. It no longer bothered me when Henry tried to bully me over the financial settlement, or constantly requested last minute changes to visitation schedules. Nothing bothered me. It was all beautiful background music to secret time spent with Michael. We carved it out of his afternoons. We stole it for weekend dinners when Mary stayed home with the boys. We luxuriated in it on weekends that Henry had the kids. I had forgotten what it was like to be in the presence of someone who treasured every word I said, who was charmed by my every gesture.

"You're having sex, aren't you?" Mary said to me on a Friday, as she lounged across the kitchen counter while I made dinner.

My body froze in momentary panic before I could casually lie. "I don't know whatever you are talking about, Mary Frances," I said, straightening myself over the chopped vegetables.

It was a good effort. I had been seeing Michael for only a month, and I didn't want to give up our perfect secret easy lovemaking. Not so soon.

"Don't Mary Frances me," she said. "I'm not stupid, I've got eyes. I just can't figure out who it could possibly be."

She said this last almost to herself, and then continued.

"Regardless of what any of us think about the divorce, it's final, so, technically, there's nothing wrong with it. And just because Henry isn't seeing anyone, that doesn't mean that you have to be a nun. And I know you won't go back."

She seemed to be repeating out loud her own thoughts, and I disciplined myself not to interrupt her or to defend myself, but let her finish.

"You're happier, that's for sure, and easier to live with."

There was a long silence then, and I resumed cooking. Perhaps just letting it go there was the best thing.

"I won't tell, if that's what you are worried about," she said to me.

She wasn't going to let it go. "No, dear, that is not what I am worried about. I know very well that it will be strange for you kids when I move on...that I have moved on. I guess I was just keeping it to myself for now because that is easier for everyone."

"But, you're lying to us."

Yes. I didn't like to lie, but I couldn't see how I couldn't. Michael needed time to figure out what he was going to do about Henry, about the firm. Mary wouldn't tell, but the boys would very naturally talk about Mama's new boyfriend.

"Please understand that there is good reason," I said, "for now. The boys are too young, and it is too soon to be introducing them to someone I'm seeing. And I don't really, technically, lie to them. I do say that I'm going out with friends."

"I want to meet him. I won't tell and I want to meet him," Mary said.

"Alright," I said, raising my eyebrows in resignation, "alright."

It still thrilled me to hear his voice on the phone, every time. I always got butterflies when I called him, and I lay on my bed like a schoolgirl when we talked at night. I could hear him smile, see the little corner wrinkles as he smiled. I could feel his mood, his presence, and it made my heart so full that I wanted to sing out loud some cheesy showtune from *Oklahoma!* or *The Sound of Music.* Did he love me because I was so crazy or in spite of it? For sure, he was a little afraid of me. Although he denied it, he was still reeling from the shock of our first date. He often looked at me with a bemused expression on his face, like, what in the hell is she going to do next? And the truth is, I never know until the time comes to do it.

I called him to tell him about Mary. Getting him to commit to a day, to schedule it, was a task made more difficult than usual by the fact that he wasn't overjoyed that our secret was unraveling so quickly. We were not going to break it off. I was pretty sure that he wanted to get married, and I had to find some way to steer him in another direction, because I would never marry again. At some point, he would have to tell Henry, and they would have to sort all of that out at the firm. I wished it could be otherwise, for his sake, because I knew how he loved his inertia. But he would have to give it up.

"Make him choose!" Sally said when I called her about having Matt and Joshua over for dinner next weekend, the appointed meeting date between Mike and Mary.

"We know. He knows," I said. "It's only been a month, and he needs a little more time."

Time was running out and everyone knew it. Sally asked about Henry, and we ended up spending a whole half hour unpacking the latest salvo of paper from Henry's lawyers. I was so tired of fighting over money, but on principle, I wanted my fair share.

"Maybe you'd just be better off paying him to go away. Give a little so that the whole business will end," she said.

"I tried that. Then he just fights for more."

"He doesn't want it to end," she said with deadpan conviction.

"We're divorced, but I don't think the process of the divorce will ever end."

Shaking off thoughts of Henry, I called Michael on his cell to confirm that Sally could watch the boys. I could tell that he was still at work because he affected that distant business voice of his and responded to me in monosyllables.

"So, you're meeting Mary and I next Friday. I'll make reservations if you tell me where you'd like to go."

"We can talk about it next week," was all he said.

I was starting to lose patience. "Are you going to be on time tonight? Are we still going tonight? I don't want you to be late, Michael. It's really important that you are on time, okay?"

"Yes, that is still happening as scheduled," he said, and then added with a businesslike emphasis, "I'll talk to you later."

I hung up, eyes rolling with wonder at how a man's supposedly unbearable ardor and longing could vanish on a whim. What in the world made that mind work?

III.

I was sitting at the bar at The Slanted Door with Henry when Atlanta called me on my cell. My body was instantly saturated with perspiration as I talked, with Henry staring right at me, waiting. She was calling me to solidify plans to meet with Henry's daughter next week and to confirm the plans we had that night, when Henry's ex-wife—my girlfriend—can meet my ex-wife, no less. Jesus.

"Alisha," I said casually, as I holstered the phone.
"She's still at work?"
"She'll have your office someday."

I shouldn't have put so much effort into dissembling; Henry's mind was completely distracted. We had been talking and talking, but clearly we were not talking about what was on his mind.

"What do you think?" Henry asked me.

He had been talking about his legal battle with Atlanta, a subject with which I, of course, was already well acquainted. Because I was constantly on the verge of telling Henry about Atlanta, or at least wanting to, constrained only by the fact that I had no idea what would happen next, I felt myself in no position to advise him.

He complained, as always, when I offered him no solid opinion.

"Your divorce didn't seem this difficult," he said.

"We didn't have kids and we didn't fight over the money. It was rather like surgery—unpleasant, but quick and clean, and with uncertain prospects for recovery, at least for me." I tried to simulate my own maudlin attitudes, but couldn't pull it off. I laughed nervously instead.

"You don't talk about her anymore," Henry said.

"I told you I wouldn't," I said and took a long drink.

"That never stopped you before."

I could hear him thinking it. He knew I was seeing someone.

"I see her sometimes," I said quickly, "I'm seeing her tonight, actually."

Henry was visibly surprised, but then shrugged.

I looked at my watch. "I have to leave soon," I added.

"Hey, you could take me with you!" he said.

His usual, confident joviality was affected, and the last syllable dropped into uncertainty. He couldn't even sustain it for seven syllables. Something was wrong, he was clinging to me, but he wouldn't tell me what it was, and I was afraid to ask.

"Oh, it's just Ez and me. She wants to talk to me about something," I said.

Henry raised his finger to order another scotch. I waved away the waiter's inquiring glance.

"Oh come on," Henry said.

"I really have to go soon."

Henry tapped his index finger on the table as he stared at it. He was holding me there. For what, I couldn't imagine, but I was getting impatient and was looking for any opening.

"I didn't get to where I am today by being a weakling," he said.

This statement had the air of something important. I sighed and allowed my weight to settle back into my chair again. We were actually getting somewhere, but I wasn't sure I liked the sound of it.

"She left me because I wouldn't change," he continued, "the divorce is final, she's not coming back." He tapped his fingertip again. "So, what good would it do for me to change now, anyway?"

More comfortable now, I leaned forward.

"And if I allowed myself to hop down that rabbit trail and entertained all of these loosey goosey thoughts, I'd lose my edge, and I might not be able to get it back. Then where would I be? No, to be a competitor, you've got to keep your blade sharp."

"I'm bored with competition," I said. It was the first true thing I'd said.

"It's competition that has made this nation great," Henry asserted. "The cream rises to the top. If that doesn't happen, you just have milk, mediocre milk."

"That's crap and you know it," I said, "It's the products of privilege that rise to the top, and there are plenty of blobs of cream stuck down under the milk. And anyway, I'm not sure that exploiting poor people all over the world, destroying their democracies, selling arms to blood thirsty dictators, and grabbing everything of value for ourselves is what I would call the works of a great nation. If that's what I'm working so hard for, I think, perhaps, a vacation is in order."

I finished off my drink and swished the ice at the bottom of my glass.

"Well, if that's how you feel about it, maybe you should go be a commie in North Korea and see how you like that."

Henry always retreated to that old saw.

"I prefer to remain in my own country and fix the problems we have here."

"Like what? What, exactly, are you doing to alleviate America's woes?"

He had me there. Pretty much nothing, aside from the occasional check to someone who sends me something through the mail, someone who was actually doing something.

"Very little," I said.

After a long pause, Henry said, with an exaggerated dubiousness, "My therapist says that the Blue Lady represents something and wants me to meditate on it."

Henry was seeing a therapist? I was stunned. This was what he'd been wanting to talk about, but he had to wait until I had lost an argument with him to do it.

He snorted a laugh, to make it clear that he thought such notions ridiculous, to distance himself from the whole business, and took another drink of his scotch.

"What do you think?" I said anyway.

"I think I need to get rid of the therapist."

A predictable response, but the door was open.

"Do you still see it…her?" I ventured.

"Nah, the doctor changed the medications I'm taking, and so far, so good."

"Don't you ever feel," I ventured, "that we're working and fighting, just so we can work and fight some more? We're just sitting outside Troy, exhausted and miserable and blood stained, looking forward to another day of work and blood?"

"But they got in, didn't they? They eventually got in."

"For what?" I yelled, exasperated, more at myself than at him, "For no good reason."

Early retirement. A big house to raise kids in. A new kitchen, where on the weekends we can lean on a marble countertop and entertain our friends. Health insurance. Nice vacations when we can find the time. I was reminding myself of all the reasons why I'd chosen the security of corporate life.

But what about a little house with a bite sized mortgage in a funky neighborhood, where, as the sun sets on a Wednesday afternoon, neighbors sit around my flea market kitchen table and kick at the edges of the linoleum peeling up as they laugh at my jokes. Someone who knows how to play, has time to practice, starts playing a guitar, or maybe I have a piano. There are kids, maybe mine, running around, hollering at the injustice of being tagged It. It's a very conventional type of happiness, but I'd take a conventional happiness over my old conventional unhappiness any day. Plus the earned bonus of not having to bear the weight of being a part of a repressive system that exploits others to buy my lifestyle.

So deep in my own thoughts, I wasn't really paying attention to Henry until that familiar crawling dread stopped my chattering mind cold and I looked up at him.

He cut his eyes toward me when he felt mine upon him, but then cut them back to what he was looking at. I looked in the direction of his gaze and saw what I expected to see. Nothing.

Henry licked his lips, tried to look away, dissemble, but found himself unable.

"You see her, don't you?" I said.

He nodded.

"Well," I replied, not even sure what I was saying myself, "What is it? Quick, think. What does she make you think of?"

"Not of any woman I know," Henry stammered.

"What do you mean?" I asked.

"She's...fierce. I feel like she could destroy me."

"Does she have a weapon?"

"She carries a sword, but it's not...she doesn't want to kill me exactly."

A fine and good death, I thought to myself, that makes it possible to live.

Henry took a long drink with shaking hands. She was gone.

I was fascinated by the Blue Lady, I would follow wherever she led, and it was frustrating that the only access I had to her mystery was through Henry.

IV

I was perched on the edge of a red velvet bench seat in the foyer of the restaurant, compulsively pulling down the hem of my skirt and fiddling with an untouched lemon drop cocktail as I waited for Michael. I was desperately praying that he would get here before Esperanza found me, shaking like a nervous puppy. I shrank into my seat when she walked in. She was just as I pictured her—one of those short curvy women who are built for those little red slip dresses—which she was wearing with a pair of strappy red heels. She didn't see me at first, but rather marched right up to the hostess and asked for her table. Her companion, surely this was Beassè, followed behind her at a more comfortable pace, and then lounged at her side, looking around with an air of pleased expectation.

Esperanza shook out her thick hair, a completely unselfconscious gesture of enjoyment, clearly enjoying it's weight, her sense of her own beauty. She turned to say something to Beassè, but then she noticed me staring at her. I looked away. The hostess found the reservation and led them past me.

I brought the heel of my hand to my forehead. Stupid, stupid, stupid! That was the moment in which I should have stood up, extended my hand and said, "Oh, you must be Esperanza Cuellar. I'm Atlanta Mara." She'd known it was me, too. And now she knew that I knew. How many self-possessed Cuban women have come in here accompanied by a French speaking black man? She'd know that I sat out here on my hands in the lobby waiting to shuffle in behind Michael, who, last time I checked, was still in his car. It became more pathetic by the second! Where was Atlanta Mara of the Powell Street turnaround?

I drank the entire cocktail in one gulp, as a tight faced lady swaddled in designer fashion watched me in horrified silence. I stood up, and marched past the distracted hostess into the restaurant rehearsing my unrehearsed and easy confidence.

Thank God they were sitting with their backs to me. I walked around to his right to face her.

"Pardon me," I said as they looked up at me, "I'm Atlanta Mara," I said, extending my hand, "and…."

"I knew it!" Esperanza said loudly, "I almost said something."

"It occurred to me…" I began again.

"Sit down!" she said. "Right here next to me. Where is your drink? What are you drinking?"

In a moment, I was sitting next to her. She pulled me close, put a glass of wine in my hand and before I knew it, I was fielding rapid fire questions. The miracle of her was that I didn't even feel plain next to her. She didn't make me feel plain, but included me in her brightness.

So, this is how it is with Esperanza, I thought to myself. It's no wonder.

"It was really embarrassing to come in here without Michael," I confessed.

Esperanza dismissed the idea with a wave of her hand. "You call him Michael? Hmm, that's interesting," she said.

Beassè was watching her and smiling to himself. He smiled at me, as if we shared a private joke. In my nervousness I didn't even notice myself downing an entire glass and now I was already tipsy and they were pouring me another.

"Oh, no, really," I said, pulling my glass away, "I don't usually drink."

Esperanza just laughed and overcame my puny gesture, filling my glass overfull. I had to sip from the edge before I could lift it. She did make me feel puny, in a funny way, like the adult child of a doting mother. It was funny because it wasn't a gesture of dominance, but rather of generosity.

Over Beassè's shoulder, I saw Michael hurrying through the dining room. He reached us, his eyes pleading me for mercy from across the table before he said anything.

"I'm so sorry, really I am. I meant to be on time, but I just couldn't get away," he explained breathlessly to me, hardly acknowledging Esperanza or Beassè.

"She's fine," Esperanza told him. "Have a glass of wine Mike, sit down."

Michael sat down next to me and said nothing. He just kept staring at me, scanning my face for repressed rage. He was breaking up our jolly energy and so I finally turned to him, took him by the chin with one hand, and put the other hand on his thigh, high up, and kissed him deeply, tongue and all. After I released him, he looked around the restaurant, at Beassè and Ez, who were grinning at him, and didn't blink for several minutes.

After we ordered our meal, Beassè started a conversation with Michael about cooking. He was saying that it was its impermanence that made it the highest form of performance art, like the sand paintings Buddhist monks make and then sweep away. Michael was listening to this with an attention that surprised me. As for myself, I had done enough cooking for a lifetime and had no interest in sand paintings. I turned to Esperanza.

"May I ask why you divorced?" I asked Ez. "You seem to like each other so well, even now."

"He doesn't talk about it?" Esperanza asked.

"No, except once, before I knew him well, but he was… it wasn't clear."

"He was drunk, you mean." Esperanza hawed loudly.

My question continued to float in the air as Esperanza sipped thoughtfully at her martini. "I'm a little disappointed that he didn't make up some story about what a beast, *un gorgon*, I am," she said. "Well, we were childhood sweethearts, of course. I met him when he was a silly boy, but I loved him anyway. We were going to be mavericks, he and I, which meant that we were going to somehow manage to get ourselves out of Florida," She smiled wryly. " We married right away because everyone told us not to and we had so much fun."

"Did you get out of Florida right after?"

"Oh, yes, we both went to San Francisco and became hippies. We quickly found that being a hippie in the Haight was a little like joining 4H in Missouri. We weren't mavericks anymore. So he went to law school and I got an MBA."

Esperanza rubbed her fingers in a way that told me that she used to keep a cigarette between them.

"The rest of the story is boring. I got a job at a start up, and he got a job at a law firm. We always said that we would do it just long enough to pay our school debt, make a little life. Then, he bought a BMW. Then we had to go to dull *soirees* and smile at dull, little, pasty men and their dull, little, pasty wives and we had to find them all fascinating."

"I was a dull, pasty, little wife," I said. "and I was never fascinating."

"It is more honest to be dull in a dull life," Esperanza said. "But I don't believe it, that you were ever dull. Look at you." She waved one hand.

I was both surprised and embarrassed and glanced toward Michael. He was still talking about cooking.

"So," Esperanza continued, "I couldn't stand listening to those guys, with their big, donkey laughs, talking as if what they were doing was *important*. Pretending that manufacturing stacks of paper actually meant that they had become something better than other people, that they deserved more than other people. It was all a silly, child's game, but they girded themselves for it as if it were an battle of mythical proportions! Ez raised her arms in imitation of a Wagnerian opera singer.

Esperanza caught Michael's eye. He was dividing his attention between what Beassé was saying and what she was saying.

"I'm not saying anything I haven't said to him a hundred times," she said mostly to him. Michael turned back to Beassé and she turned back to me. "I refused to participate." She tapped her imaginary cigarette on the table. "Then, Mike became pasty too and I lost him. He likes to pretend that he doesn't know why I left him, but he does. I left the year after he became partner at that firm."

Esperanza tossed her chin in the direction of Michael's building as if it were an unsavory person.

"I fled," she said quietly, only to me, "with another man."

Shifting Ground

Esperanza checked my face for signs of shock, but I betrayed none. I had already known about this part of the story, for Henry had crowed about it several times. Henry had seen Esperanza's affair as an example of the tide of sin, danger, and upheaval non-believers are prey to.

"Now, I don't want you to think me a hypocrite. I don't imagine that what I am doing is important. I know it isn't. If the company I work for now went bankrupt tomorrow, it would be forgotten the next day by everyone except all of us who must then find a new job." She lifted her fierce eyes and looked straight into mine, "but at least I know it's not important.

"I know that many people are looking for meaning now," she continued, "and I know that there is some good to be made of me, but I wonder if it's necessary for it to happen at work, if work needs to be so important."

I had not even thought of this possibility, that work wasn't important. I leaned toward her.

"For me," Esperanza shrugged and made a face of casual dismissal, which must be borrowed from Beassè because it looked so foreign, so European, "I wear it lightly. I don't worry about work. I do it, then stop, and go home. I quit for a while sometimes, travel, write. I don't much care to get more or be more. But then I get promoted anyway, despite myself.

I kept looking at her, wanting more.

"For Beassè, work is everything. He never says anything, but I wonder what he thinks when I come home late from work, carrying a shopping bag from a fancy store. Maybe I am too attached to the beautiful life, too *assouvire*, to look for something meaningful."

She raised her eyes to mine again, but this time they were not fierce but were instead unsure.

"What do you think?" she asked me.

"It makes me so glad to hear that someone like you shares my secret weakness," I said.

"Someone like me?"

"You know what you are!" I laughed. "So strong in every way."

"But is it really weakness to be uncertain?" I thought out loud. Or was this notion, instead, a red herring I was forced to accept at a level of my being so fundamental to myself, that I was no longer at liberty to examine it. Blundering headlong forward without considering the alternatives, without reading signs, without tracking consequences. That's not strength, but ignorance. "Moving forward is a process," I concluded out loud.

"*Vraimant!*" Ez said, She interrupted Michael and said something to Beassè in French before turning back to me. "I told him that you are a smart woman. You say the same kind of thing he does. A process, yes."

"It has always been this way, I think," Beassé responded, "but when everything is staying the same, the process is so slow, we don't notice it. Now that everything is changing so fast, it's all we can do to run and keep up with it."

"Work and money seem to be in the cross hairs of this so called process, more than anything else," Michael mumbled.

"Michael is practically a socialist now!" I blurted. I don't know why I said it, except that all of this talk of work reminded me of the kind of thing he and I talk about. I've never heard him talk like that with anyone else. I checked

Michael's face. He seemed to be shrugging off Esperanza's scrutinizing gaze.

"Is this true?" she asked. Her expression was insecure, and I realized for the first time that she had been assuming that Mike's relationship with her was primary, that she had greater claim to him. I shared something with him that she did not, and this was a threatening novelty to her.

"I don't know if I'd call myself a socialist," he said, taking his usual middle road.

"You want state owned banks!" I said, "and single payer health care. You think essential services like the internet and cell phones should be owned only by regulated non-profits or cooperatives. You want worker owned companies, and you support a constitutional amendment declaring that corporations aren't people!"

A smile crept across Beassé's face, "Does he now?"

"That's not socialism," Michael insisted.

"You wouldn't believe the stuff he says about his own clients," I said.

Esperanza was watching us talk with an expression I couldn't read.

"So, you finally came around," she said, not even looking at Michael, but at her glass, and then took a drink. "Why are you still working there?"

"It's none of your business why I'm still working there, is it?" Michael snapped. Esperanza looked up sharply. "You have always pretended that you were the more enlightened one, but your family were all imperialist one percenters in Cuba and you're all still one percenters in spirit, even if you're the only one with the bank account to prove it."

"The Revolution has been long over, Mike," she replied, quietly.

"God love 'em, but as soon as Castro and economic justice went in, your family got out."

"My uncle died, and two cousins were imprisoned," she said, her voice raising. "We were lucky to get out. Look at them now. You can go to jail just for saying the wrong thing, and *nada funciona*!" She was upset and retreated into the Spanish.

Michael replied to her in Spanish and I only caught the words, America and U.S. I didn't know he spoke Spanish.

"If it weren't for the fact that the U.S. cut them off and were always trying to stage coups against Castro from day one," he continued, "it would be a completely different place!"

"Oh, yes," she said, "typical liberal apologist argument against a repressive, murderous regime. I can't believe I'm hearing this from you."

"Yes, me. The reactionary one," Michael said. "Look, just because you're banging a revolutionary, doesn't mean you are one. Walk your talk, Ez, and then you can talk to me about where I'm working."

"Excuse me," Ez said and got up. Her eyes were shining with tears, whether of rage or hurt, I couldn't tell. She retreated towards the front of the restaurant.

"Sorry," Michael said to Beassé.

"Oh, no trouble at all," he replied with that same expression of casual dismissal on his face. "Her feelings about Cuba…they are very mixed."

I thought that perhaps we would move on to something else now, and I tried to think of something, but then Michael kept talking.

Shifting Ground

"It's just that those constant comments of hers are really getting to me," he said.

"Yes," Beassé said.

"How does it work, her and you?" Michael asked him with a raised voice and Esperanza's sweep of his palm.

"We are all...very mixed," Beassé replied and then laughed at himself.

I got up and went to the bathroom. I found Esperanza there, as I thought I would. She took out a tube and pretended to perfect her lipstick when she saw me.

"I was hoping that maybe I could help smooth things over," I said.

"It's not necessary," she replied airily, "Mike's just mad that I was talking to you about him, that's all."

I didn't think so, but I didn't want to start an argument.

"We all just need another glass of wine," I said cheerfully, hoping that she would just agree and shrug it off.

"He's annoyed, he'll get over it, and then we'll be fine," she said.

That assumption of primacy again was irritating.

"You know, I think that sometimes when you're talking to Michael," I said, "I think you're really talking to yourself."

Esperanza met my eyes in the mirror. "I'm fine, if that's what you came here to find out."

When Esperanza came back to the table, she behaved as if the argument had never happened.

"We should do this again," she said.

"Yes, we should," Michael said.

"No, I mean it."

Michael glanced at me.

"Oh, don't worry about her," Esperanza said, "She's fine."

I wasn't sure if I should take this as a compliment or not, when Ez smiled at me with closed lips. It is the kind of smile that is shared between equals.

Michael looked at me and then back at Esperanza before he said, "Sure, okay."

"You are truly not mad at me for being late, for arguing with Ez?" Michael asked as we crossed the foyer alone.

"No."

My mind was completely elsewhere.

"You are an amazing creature," he said, breathing out, and caressed my hair.

I shivered as we stepped out into the steady evening breeze and Michael wrapped his arm around my shoulder. I wasn't cold. I was stimulated, excited. Every nerve in my body was crying for touch, everywhere. I moved my body under his arm like a cat and he slid his hand down my back, caressed the small before dropping to my swaying butt. I looked up at him from under heavy eyelashes and parted my mouth. He grabbed me and dragged us underneath the shadow of a tree.

"Now, please, now," I cried, kissing him, so wanton I could no longer see clearly.

"Here? We'll be arrested."

"My car," I breathed, running my hands everywhere on him, on me, "It's there."

I glanced down the block, and then pulled his hand as I ran toward it. I kissed him again while I fumbled for my keys and then opened the back door.

He hung back, standing discretely away as I clambered in the back.

"It's a residential street, Michael!" I exclaimed, amazed that he continued to fret about policemen.

"Do you get into this? Are you an exhibitionist?" He was still looking around.

"Other people are neither here nor there to me right now."

I was laying myself down in front of him, arching my back.

"Not so irrelevant if they are tapping at your window with a flashlight," he said.

I bared my breasts in response.

As he sank down onto me I thought to myself, how often do we actually *sleep* together after?

Shifting Ground

I.

Mary didn't wake up until she heard her brothers screaming. Before that, there had been a regular pounding sound, like a giant heartbeat, or like someone running, slowly, down a long hallway. She dreamed she was running down the hallway of her house, but then the hallway ended and the pounding went on. That's when the shaking started and Matt and Joshua started screaming. Her bed shook up and down as she sat bolt upright. She knew that she should be afraid, that she should be doing something, but she was only excited, as if it were an amusement park ride. The planet itself was heaving her around and all she could think was how huge, how awesome it was! She watched as the top drawer of her dresser shook open, and the television on top of it bounced off and crashed down onto the floor. Then the shaking stopped. No winding down, no slowing. It just stopped.

She leaped out of bed and ran to her door, reaching it as Matt ran into the hallway at the top of the stairs.

"We just had an earthquake!" they yelled at each other, as Atlanta came running to the top of the stairs.

"Outside," she commanded. "Where's Joshua?"

Matt turned sideways to reveal Joshua clinging to his back, and Atlanta picked him up. Everyone came outside at the same time. All of the moms carried their youngest ones, and the older ones, like Matt stood around trying to look cool.

A posse had formed, with Jack's dad in the lead carrying a big wrench and some other tools. They headed straight for Atlanta.

"Is everybody alright?" Jack's mother threw herself into Atlanta's arms, smashing their kids between them.

"We're alright Sally, we're all here," Atlanta said, completely calm.

"Tons of stuff at our place is broken, the Carraway's across the street too, but those are just things. Who cares about things!"

Jack's mom kept blabbing while the posse moved on to the next house. Mary wanted to go with them, to see if someone had a cell phone. Maybe she could sneak in the house to get hers. She was thinking about Aidan, her brand new wonderful boy. She was wondering if he were worried about her, if he were outside like this, maybe trying to call. I wish he lived closer, she thought helplessly, I could just walk over.

"Holy shit, we just had an earthquake!" Monique yelled in Mary's ear, making her jump.

"No kidding," Mary said, punching her. "Where did you come from?"

"I was out running, and as soon as it happened, I ran over here. The houses seem alright. I tried to call home, but the phone lines are jammed."

Shifting Ground

"Oh jeez! Can I use your cell?"

"I just told you, the lines are completely jammed."

"Someone's getting through, or it wouldn't be jammed," Mary replied, taking the phone from her. She dialed Aidan's number, imagining him answering it, willing it to go through. The insistent beep of the jammed line assaulted her ear.

"That sound is so friggin' annoying," she muttered as she hit redial, only to hear it again.

"We'll be havin' aftershocks," Mo said, grinning at her. "Is that what you're thinking? Get Aidan over here for that?"

Mary punched her again, but Monique had a point. Mary hadn't thought about it before.

"Can you imagine how great it would be to do it during an aftershock?"

"Yeah," Mary said, thinking about it, wondering now how she and Aidan could make it happen, maybe later when everything had settled down. Still busy, still busy. Damn!

"Hey," Mary said, "I wonder if text would work?"

She tried, "R U OK?"

It seemed to go through. Then, that wonderful little two beep sound for a return message.

"Mary?"

Her hands were shaking.

"Y. We R OK. U?"

"OK. Broken stuff. Mess. ILU. Wanna C U."

"What's he sayin'?"

Monique leaned in to look over Mary's shoulder, but Mary edged Monique away as her thumbs flew over the keyboard about the aftershocks.

301

"They're the same as we are," Mary said.

"Well, don't use up all my messages," Monique complained. "Anyway, I can't stand still. Let's go walk with all those guys."

Mary stifled a giggle at Aidan's response as they went over to join the posse.

II.

Sally was talking to Susan and Jeff in the middle of the street with all four of their kids. She was giving them the full update. She was really wound up. I tried Michael again on my cell, one, two, three, times.

"Mama, can I go over with them?" Matt asked me.

"Of course," I said, "Don't go anywhere else without checking first."

Joshua clung to me as I sat on the steps of our front walk. I tried Michael again. He lived high on that hill up on all those sticks. Had all those sticks held? That house was Ez's house—I felt sure that it would have held together. Still, I wanted to hear his voice. John returned from his survey of the neighbors with a large group in tow, including Mary and Monique. They met Sally and her group in the middle of the street and conferred.

"Everybody is alright for two blocks in both directions!" Sally yelled at me, "They're now going to go house to house, checking the foundations and turning off the gas. We should wait to go in until we're all checked!"

I gave her a thumbs-up.

"Matt is coming with me," she yelled and I nodded back at her.

"Do you want to go with the kids?" I asked Joshua.

He lifted his head from my shoulder, looked up at me mutely before shaking his head and returning to the safety of my shoulder. I pulled him tighter.

"You're alright," I said.

"I hope Daddy is okay," he said.

The thought had not even crossed my mind. Henry was always okay, always the same. He had solidified in my mind more as a thing, a reality, rather than a human being.

"I'll try to call him, darling, but the lines are jammed," I told him as I dialed.

Sally walked back into the middle of the street with several other parents and every child under the age of 13, dragging two hockey goals to lay crossways on the street, and some other toys. There was almost a party atmosphere on the block, everyone out and chatting. Someone had retrieved a radio and several people in lawn chairs were gathered around it. I finally gave up hitting redial for Henry and tried Michael, too, for good measure.

"I'm sorry baby," I said to Joshua, stroking him, "I'm sure he's just fine. He's big and strong and smart, and he's just fine."

An older model red Volkswagon sedan moved very slowly down our street, and the people standing in the street parted for it as it approached. It stopped one block up, before the bolus of kids playing in front of the houses on our block. An African American woman jumped out and began walking purposefully down the sidewalk on our side, looking for someone as she walked. She must have been up early, because she was well dressed in a skirt suit, stockings and pumps. Sally noticed her too and looked at me because she seemed to be coming straight towards my house. When she came close enough that I could see her face, I realized that she must be Monique's mother.

"Are you looking for Monique?" I asked her as she approached my front walk.

"Yes!" she cried, "Have you seen her?"

"She was just here. She's with Mary and some folks who are checking the houses. She's completely fine."

"Oh thank God," the woman said as she collapsed on the stairs a few stairs below us, "she went out running, and didn't come back. I tried to call her…."

"But the lines are all jammed," I finished for her. "They're fine."

"Thank God," she said again. "I'm Paula Wilson, by the way."

She extended her hand and smiled. I shook it and smiled back.

"I'm Atlanta Mara, and this is my son, Joshua."

Joshua turned his head on my shoulder to stare soulfully at her.

"Say hello, Sugar," I prodded him.

"Oh, it's alright. He's all shook up, I'm sure."

I laughed at the unintended pun and she laughed with me.

"You look like you were halfway to work," I said.

"I was just leaving when it hit. You ever been in one before?"

"We were here for Loma Prieta. Have you heard how big this one was?"

"No, I've just been looking for Monique. It seems like a pretty hard one though."

Shifting Ground

Paula peeled off her jacket.

"There's no way those kids will be in school today, and I don't want to be driving across any bridges anyway."

"Oh, you're a teacher?"

"Nah, I work at Berkeley."

"Oh really!"

"Yeah, we used to live up in Oakland, which was closer, and we tried to find a house in Berkeley." She threw up her hands. "If you think housing is high over here, you should go look in Berkeley. She made a whistling noise between her teeth.

"It's a long commute, but I can't give it up because of the college benefits. I'd do anything for a cheap college education for my kids."

"So, Marcus could have gone to college cheap?" I didn't mean to say it out loud, but I just couldn't believe it.

"You know my son?"

I blushed. "Well, he helped to remodel my bathroom. Monique suggested it."

"Oh, of course."

"He's a fine young man. A lovely person," I told her.

She smiled a pained smile. "I know he is."

"And I think it's really wonderful how you are raising Monique. Not every parent could be so open minded and accepting."

"What do you mean?"

"Well," I paused.

I was unsure now. Maybe it wasn't something they talked about with strangers. But I already said something and I couldn't just leave it.

"You know…Monique is such a remarkable girl and I just think it is wonderful how you allow her to be open about her orientation...and in a Catholic school no less. It's so healthy and functional."

She stared at me while I said this and as soon as I finished, she carefully draped her jacket over her arm and stood up.

"Excuse me," she said as she turned down the stairs.

Monique and Mary had just walked up the sidewalk with Jeff's group. Paula looked down at Monique as she descended the last stair. I couldn't see Paula's face, but Monique looked stricken.

"I'll see you at home," I heard Paula say to Monique and then she turned up the street.

Monique stood there unmoving, her mouth open.

"What did you say to her?" she demanded.

"She didn't know?" I asked, incredulous.

Monique sank down on the sidewalk, put her head on her knees, and then wrapped both forearms over the top of her head.

"No wonder!" Mary yelled and threw up her hands, "I knew it! That's why you keep your mouth shut with the nuns! I should've known that Ms. In Your Face was full of shit!"

"You don't understand!" Monique wailed from under her arms. "You don't understand the pressure I'm under with them all the time. It's only with them! Oh my God!"

Monique stood up and ran down the street toward the bay.

"Should we go after her?" Mary's anger had turned to concern.

"Give her some space," I said. "She'll come back."

Jeff came up behind Mary to check the house. The ground started rumbling again just as they started up the stairs. Everyone out in the street stopped what they were doing. The cement under me shook and Joshua started crying into my hair as he squeezed my neck tighter.

"It's just an aftershock, baby," I soothed him. "It will only be a minute. See? It's over already."

I looked down the hill and saw Monique far below, clinging to a light post. She let go and started off at a full run again.

III.

My lungs were aching and I had to stop. It wasn't that I couldn't run anymore. I could run much longer than that. It was only that the terrible squeeze in my chest kept coming up, choking me. I was gasping for air. I put my hands on my knees and cried again. Run and then cry, run and cry, all the way through Sausalito. Usually I turned around when I got close to the Golden Gate Bridge mess and all the traffic, but today I ran on, around, and right up onto the bridge. I wanted to run on the street part, but there were cops around and I couldn't tell if they were trying to close down the bridge or limit access or what. I skedaddled onto the pedestrian part, making myself inconspicuous.

Part of me knew what I was doing up there. Yeah, I knew. But I was pretending I didn't. I just kept running, not thinking about anything, completely numb. Finally, exhausted, I stopped next to a suspender. It was four cables like great metal ropes stretched next to each other to make a column with nothing but air between them. I turned my back to the slow moving cars to shield myself from dumb questions. Far below, waves like tiny white commas pushed away from me toward Alcatraz Island. Quick, quick, up and over. It would have to be like that. Yeah, I was thinking it out loud now. It would have to be quick quick, no standing up top and wondering because I'd lose my nerve and get myself arrested. I looked at the little barrier only chest high in front of me. It would be so easy if I could be quick about it. I grabbed one of the cables with my right hand. It was too big to get my fingers all the way around and the twisted metal felt dry and cold in my palm. The metal was vibrating with the wind and the cars and the strain of holding up the bridge. The wind whipped my hair forward and then back and around, blowing my tears all over my face. The little white commas kept moving away, away below me. I looked at the little shelf below I'd have to clear, and then to the cable I'd have to use to hoist myself up. The dull paint that sealed those twisted tight cables was the color of dried blood.

I'd never have to go home. I would never have to hear what they would have to say about it, what *she* would have to say about it. I would never again have to hear the nuns talk about me like I was dirty, other people talk about me like I was diseased. No more talking heads yelling about my gay agenda. As if just wanting to have a normal life like everybody else was an agenda!

"I just wanna be!" I screamed at the bay, my spit hitting my face as the wind brought it back to me. "I just wanna be!" I screamed so hard my voice cracked. Those stupid tears again. Quick quick up and over. I grabbed the barrier without really seeing it, felt for a foothold. Quick quick up and over. Found it and hoisted myself up so that my feet were up top. Now to jump and clear the shelf. Quick quick. And then the wind whipped my hair around so hard it stung my face. I lost my balance and pitched forward, pivoting on the tips of three fingers that slipped around the cable. Blinded by my blowing hair I reached out with my other hand and grabbed only air.

I dug in those three fingertips and flung myself towards those cables with my outstretched arm, and my elbow wrapped around one of them just as my toes began to slip. I caught glimpses of cement near and water far away and I struggled toward the cement. I wanted to live! I hung there on those two cables, partially suspended over the abyss like some crazy scarecrow for several minutes before I could find solid footing and stand again. My hair blew backwards, and I saw in front me the placid bay waters sparkling in the sunshine and a plane crossing the sky. I felt stupid. I wiped my face and jumped down.

"What the hell were you doing up there?" a man yelled at me from his car passenger window.

"I just lost my balance," I yelled back at him.

An older white dude in a BMW. Somebody's dad. "Are you okay?" The man got out of his car. Someone honked at him and he impatiently waved them around. He came and stood next to me.

"Sore," I admitted, rubbing my battered arms. "That was stupid, getting up there just for a better view." I gave him my most obedient smile.

"Tell me your phone number and I'll call your parents," he demanded.

"No, thanks. I'm good," I said, still trying to sound cool.

"Maybe I should flag down one of these officers," he threatened.

"Just mind your own business and I'll take care of mine."

"You're a child. You are my business and I'm going to take you home."

"I'm not getting in a car with a stranger!"

"Okay, I'll call a police car for you."

The bridge started shaking with another aftershock.

"Get in!" the man commanded and I did.

I made myself small in the leather passenger seat, which made crunching noises under my sweaty legs.

"Put on your belt," he commanded and locked the automatic locks.

He drove slowly across the bridge.

"You know," he said, "it wasn't so long ago that I wanted to do what you were doing."

"You?" I looked at him. He had clear blue eyes with the sort of crows feet you get when you're kind. He was somebody's good dad.

"But now," he continued, "I feel as if I am the most fortunate man in the world. Everything can turn on a dime." He nodded at my disbelieving look, "Believe me, on a dime it can all turn around."

"What would you say if you found out your kid was gay?" I wanted to know if he really was a good dad or not.

The man pursed his lips. "Well, I can't imagine having to be told like that. I mean, I can't imagine not knowing. We'd have a relationship where, when he started thinking about it he'd say, you know, I think I might be and I'd say that's okay, don't worry about it. Like that."

"So you wouldn't care?"

"I wouldn't be upset about it, if that's what you mean."

As we approached the end of the bridge, he asked me where I lived. There was no way I could go home. Not yet. "Go right. I'll tell you."

I'd go to Mary's. Maybe they'd be mad at me too, but not that much. They'd take me in.

IV.

I would have to tell the girl's parents, of course. Make sure she got help and maybe if they knew what she almost did, they would be more understanding. Maybe. With some people you never knew. When she told me to turn up the hill, I realized that the girl lived on Atlanta's street. Her parents probably knew Atlanta.

"Stop here," she said.

It was Atlanta's house.

"You don't live here," I said.

"No," she admitted. "It's my friend's house."

"Is your name Monique?" I asked.

Her eyes opened wide.

"I'm Mike, I'm here to see Atlanta."

Her eyes opened wider. "You're the mystery boyfriend?"

I laughed softly. "I guess so."

Monique covered a smile with her hand and we stared at each other for a moment.

"I'm going to have to tell Atlanta about what happened," I said.

"Damn," she said, pushing the fingertips of both hands against her forehead. "Alright. Whatever."

Mary was a little surprised to see us both at the door. Beyond, I could see Atlanta's sons, some other kids and some neighbors gathered around a TV watching the earthquake coverage.

"He's the mystery boyfriend," Monique told her.

"I know!" Mary blurted, and then assumed an air of cool maturity, "I'm sorry Mr. Davis, but I don't actually know where she is. She's probably on the roof."

"On the roof?" I exclaimed.

Mary just rolled her eyes.

"Don't leave this house," I said to Monique sternly.

Monique cut her eyes to Mary and nodded meekly.

"What's with him?" Mary was asking as I backed out of the house, onto the walk.

"Atlanta?" I called. "Atlanta!"

A head popped over the crest of the roof. "Mike? Oh hold on! I'll meet you there!"

Atlanta appeared at the front door, closed it behind her, and threw her arms around me. "How's your house?"

"What the hell were you doing on the roof?" I demanded. "Has everyone around here gone nuts?"

"Thinking."

"When we just had an earthquake? When there are still aftershocks?"

She laughed. "The aftershocks are very mild now." She looked at me with exaggerated patience. "Look, yesterday, when it was highly likely that we would have an earthquake any minute, you weren't worried about it at all. Now that we've had one, the pressure has been released and there is little chance of it happening, you're scared! That makes absolutely no sense! I'm safer on the roof today than almost any other day!"

I felt my face flush, and threw up my hands. "I have been terrified for you for hours. I fought my way across town with a cramp in my stomach. I had a horrible feeling that I had to get over here right away to save you, and I find you up on the damn roof!" I sat down on the front steps and told her about Monique.

"I guess it wasn't me you were rushing over here to save," she said, her eyes moist with tears. She squeezed my hand.

"I think she's okay now," I said, "She was off the barrier by the time I got there. I think she had already changed her mind."

"Well, that's something, at least."

"Have you heard from Henry?"

"Yeah, he got through on the ground line and talked to the kids. His building is fine."

The front door opened and a couple came out with two boys. Both of them were smiling cat grins at me. Atlanta blushed. The couple stopped in front of us, waiting.

"This is Michael," Atlanta said. "Michael, this is Sally and John, and their sons, Jack and Steven."

"*The* Michael? Well!" Sally said.

"It's a common name," I said.

"But you add a special kind of lustre to it, or so I've heard," she replied.

John bumped into her and took her arm.

"It was nice to meet you," he said as they continued down the stairs with their sons in tow.

"Yes, very," Sally called. Atlanta snorted a giggle.

"Should I go now? I just wanted to see you, make sure you were okay."

"No," she said with quiet determination. "It's time."

We went inside together. The news was still on, but the boys were gone. Monique and Mary were on the couch, but they weren't watching TV. Mary's arm was wrapped around Monique's and she held Monique's hand in her lap. They had been talking and they looked up at us together as we came into the room. Atlanta sat down on the other side of Monique and put both of her arms around her. I sat down next to Atlanta.

"We love you," Atlanta said to her.

Fresh tears welled in Monique's eyes and slipped down her cheeks.

"We love you," Atlanta said again. "Do you have any idea what it would have done to us to lose you? To be watching them talk about you on the news? Any idea? You are our girl, part of our family too and you may not do something like that."

Monique hid her face in Atlanta's shoulder and cried real tears and Mary held her from behind.

"Your parents love you too and they'll come around. We'll all get through this together."

We sat there like that with Atlanta talking to Monique until she stopped crying, and then we turned off the TV. We were all still watching Monique, and Monique wriggled.

"I'm fine," she said.

"We need to start thinking about dinner," Atlanta said, breaking up the emotion in the room. She turned to Monique. "Do you want to stay or do you need to go home now?"

"I'd rather stay," Monique said, "I know I have to go sometime, but not yet."

"Alright," Atlanta said. "Shall I make some pizza?"

Monique looked up at her with pure gratitude. "Can I help?"

Matt and Joshua sauntered in.

"Boys? Do you remember Michael?" Atlanta asked quickly.

"Yeah," Matt said. "Dad's friend."

"Well," Atlanta bobbed her head in affirmation and looked at Joshua, "Now, he's Mommy's friend too."

Matt's eyes opened wider as he looked from me to her. Joshua just smiled at me.

"How do you feel about that, Matt?" she asked.

I wondered what he was thinking. Maybe replaying all the times we had seen each other, maybe especially the golf day. Finally, he looked at Atlanta. "I think it's fine. A little weird but fine."

"Weird, okay?" Atlanta asked, a little worry in her voice, "or weird weird?"

"Weird he'll get used to it," Mary said.

"Yeah," Matt said, "Like that. It's alright."

My cell rang. I mouthed, "Ez" at Atlanta as I walked out onto the back veranda.

"I can't believe I got through," she said breathlessly. "How are you? The house? Have you heard from Atlanta?"

"I'm fine and the house is fine, I think. Atlanta and the kids are fine. I'm over here, actually. We're all going to have some pizza together."

"*No te creo!*" Ez laughed. "That's great! She lives in Sausalito, right? Up Pine?"

"Yes...what are you thinking?"

"We'll come over."

"Uh, I think I'd better ask Atlanta first."

"We'll bring food, it'll be fine."

Esperanza hung up on me before I could say anything else. I went back into the kitchen.

"Um," I said, scratching my head and speaking quickly, "Esperanza and Beassè are coming over. She said it and hung up on me before I could say anything. I could try to get through to her again."

Atlanta stopped kneading the pizza dough in her hands and then resumed. "They're bringing something, I hope."

"They said they were bringing food."

"Great," she said simply, looking at the kids. "We're gonna have a party!"

"An earthquake party!" Matt said and Joshua whooped. "Michael's ex-wife and her boyfriend," Mary said to Monique.

The girls opened their eyes large at each other and giggled.

"You'll like them," Atlanta said.

Mary leaned in close to Atlanta and lowered her voice. "Have you talked to Henry about Miami? About Ez's idea of inviting us all to Miami?"

"Well, no, Mary. You know very well that there is a major stumbling block to that plan. Michael and Henry need to have a talk first, and then we'll see."

"It would be so cool to go to Miami," Mary said.

"What about Miami?" Matt asked.

"A friend of ours thought we could go there for Christmas, maybe. It's just an idea," Atlanta said.

"Would Daddy go too?" Joshua asked.

"Maybe," Atlanta said brightly while she chopped carrots for a salad. "This Christmas you have with Mommy, remember? But if Daddy wants to come to Miami too, he can. We'll all have to talk to him about it."

What a tightrope she had to walk with the kids, I thought, always having to pretend that she was friendly with Henry. Then, Atlanta turned to me. "Actually, it would be a lot better than him being here by himself and pretending that it's okay. It would be great for the kids to have both of us during the holidays. There's really great golf resorts there, right? He could go to some golf resort. Why not?"

Is she serious? My shock must have registered on my face because she began speaking quickly as she turned away and dumped the carrots on top of some lettuce in a bowl. I guess I'm talking to Henry *this week*.

"You'll see. It will be like with Ez and Beassè. We'll all wear him down, he'll relax and we'll all be friends."

Jeeze. Assuming I did talk to him this week and he didn't murder me...I guess he might be reasonable about it. It was true that he had been beaten. He was unraveling in ways I'd only hinted to Atlanta about. But, the idea of Henry ever becoming a member of our happy band seemed to me ludicrous fantasy. I hadn't told him about us precisely because I couldn't even imagine just how bad it would get. Now the boys know. Time's up. I had my back to her as I poured out two glasses of wine.

"Can Monique and I have a glass of wine?" Mary asked.

"No," Atlanta answered.

"Schoolchildren in France drink it every day, for crying out loud. I'm nearly eighteen," Mary complained.

I could feel Atlanta pause, and so I stood there with my back to them, the bottle suspended in mid-air.

"Oh, alright," she said, "half a glass each."

I poured out two more.

Atlanta was checking on the pizza and the boys were cuing up a video when the doorbell rang.

"That can't be Esperanza," I said.

Atlanta laughed. "It's like Grand Central Station around here!"

We could hear Joshua run to the door and then whoop with joy.

We came out of the kitchen, all of us, Atlanta and I, Monique and Mary, all of us holding wine glasses, to see who it was. Henry stood there in the foyer, frozen with an arm around each boy, staring at us open mouthed. Then his face turned a deep scarlet.

"What is this?" he yelled. When no one spoke, he stammered, "I don't know what this is!"

The boys backed away from him. Henry turned and fled out the front door, slamming it behind him.

Atlanta held out her arms to the boys. I ran after Henry.

"Stay away from me!" he yelled as I followed him down the steps, "Stay away from me or by God, I'll kill you!"

"It wasn't an affair, Henry. You were divorced."

"But you! You!" he screamed, turning on me.

I stopped. He was standing in front of his car on the street, the red Bentley GT SuperSport he'd bought himself last year, and I was on the sidewalk. He would have to take a couple of steps to hit me. Adrenaline pounded through my entire body. It had been a long time since I'd been ready for a fight. It felt good.

"This isn't ideal, obviously," I said, interrupting him, "but this conversation had to happen for those kids."

The mention of the kids made him blink and deflate one notch.

"You're hurting those kids," I said, "Matt and Joshua asked about you all morning, they were so happy when you got through, and they were so excited to see you just now and what did you do? You scared the shit out of both of them."

Henry swallowed and glared at me. "What the hell do you expect me to do? When I see you here, in my house?"

"It's not your house, Henry," I said. "You're not married to her anymore, and dragging out the financial litigation forever won't change that."

We glared at each other.

"What do I expect you to do?" I continued, "I hope I can expect you to accept it for those kids. I didn't set out to get together with Atlanta, but it happened, I love her and I'm not going to give her up." I walked toward him a step. "I know what to expect, but I guess I keep hoping, that you'll let go and give it up because you have to, Henry."

And it seemed so clear to me in that moment that I was right. His visions, his illness, his divorce, his problems at the firm, all of it had been Henry breaking. He was being broken too, just like the rest of us, whether he liked it or not, and he was doing it the hard way. I wanted to explain this to Henry, to shake him by the shoulders and show him how much better it would be for him to allow himself to be broken, but when I met his eyes, they were narrowed, unblinking aggression.

"You've always been...not entirely a man...not a reliable man," Henry said, his mouth screwed in distaste. "You're some kind of sick free agent. I should have known that I couldn't rely on a man like you." He took a menacing step towards me.

"It wasn't one of your reliable men that you took to the golf course to see your ruined castle. You didn't tell any of them about the Blue Lady. Those tales were reserved for the free agent."

"Of course you would use that against me!" He retreated to the car again.

"I'm not using anything. I'm just helping you to understand me, and yourself. I love her. You can't make me give her up and we have to find a way to live together in a healthy way for those kids."

"You always described your divorce," Henry said slowly, enunciating each word with venom, "as quick and clean. Your break from the firm will be neither." Henry walked around and opened the door to his car.

"Those kids wanted to see you!" I yelled at him, standing opposite to him now, on the other side of the car gleaming under the streetlight.

"We will never see each other again," Henry said before slamming the door shut and roaring away.

A very dramatic last word, but we would likely see each other plenty, I thought. A strange feeling crept into my belly, however, as I watched his taillights spin around the corner. A feeling that maybe in some sense, he was right.

I sat down on the steps. I wanted to let my limbs relax again, and I wanted to give Atlanta space to say whatever she needed to say to the boys. I wanted to give her the chance to lean out the front door and suggest that maybe I should go home. I waited for Esperanza.

"What a day!" Ez hailed me from the sidewalk as she and Beassè walked up, arms loaded with market bags.

"You have no idea," I said, and told them about Monique, about Henry and the rest of it.

They sat down next to me on the stairs.

"What do you think is going on in there?" Ez asked.

"I don't know," I said.

"What should we do?"

"I don't know."

"Well," Ez slapped her thighs as she stood, "There's only one way to find out."

She picked up her bags and turned up the stairs and Beassè followed. There was no good reason for me to wait outside, so I went in behind them. When we opened the door, I heard Edith Piaf on the stereo and smelled basil and garlic. Esperanza smiled widely at me. "I knew it," she said and marched through the living room.

When we got to the kitchen door, all four kids were pulled up on stools behind the counter, watching expectantly as Atlanta pulled a pizza from the oven.

"Hi darlin'!" she said to Ez as she set the pizza down.

Atlanta gave Ez a kiss on each cheek, and then Beassè. She looked at me over the kids' heads, her expression a question, and I raised a hand and mouthed, "Okay."

V.

After dinner, my kids were watching a movie, but I could see that Monique wasn't watching it. She was just sitting there with her chin in her hand, staring somewhere beyond. Mike was talking to Ez and Beassè, so I walked over and took Monique by the hand.

"Come with me," I said.

When we got to my bedroom balcony, she said, "No friggin' way!"

"It wasn't a good idea the first couple of times I did it, I admit, but now it's perfectly safe—see the rope and the handholds? You're an athletic girl, you can do it."

I shimmied up, and she followed. Once we were settled up top, her mouth dropped.

"I see what you mean," she said.

Yes, it was best at night. Everything all lit up for Christmas all the way up to the sky and spread out for miles.

"I don't know why it's different," I mused, "maybe it's 'cause gravity is just a tiny fraction weaker, or maybe 'cause you have so much of the world piled on top of you when you walk around on the ground, but when I'm up here, I feel so light, I can think."

"Everything is so small," Monique said.

"Yes. For instance, right now do you care what your mama thinks about lesbians? Up here?"

Monique looked at me and then looked out again. "It's strange, but, not so much. I'm gone in six months anyway. She can cut me off, but I can work, right?"

It was impossible to put it into words, so we stopped talking.

"What do you think about lesbians? Really?" Monique asked me.

My first thought was, judgment is against commandment. But then I realized perhaps for the first time, why it makes no sense. You judge a thing, something finished. But people are never finished, are we?

We're trained to think of ourselves as a thing, as a product. We put ourselves on display to be judged, approved or rejected. We even say out loud that we "market" ourselves. And in the same way that the shopkeeper turns the chipped edge to the back, we hide our loneliness, our pain, our fear, and when we do, we hide ourselves as creatures in process. Unknowable, we cut ourselves off from others and from life. What Monique wanted me to do was to judge her in this way.

"I think lesbians are lovely," was all I said.

"I don't think your priest would agree."

"Priests are creatures in process, just like us."

"I go to Mass because I have to. Why do you go?"

"The church and I have come to an understanding. I'm not sure what it is, except that it is what I say it is."

I sighed. "I pray, but I don't imagine that I'm putting in a request to someone big up there somewhere. Praying is a communication with the universe...."

"With the universe?" Michael asked as he scrambled up the roof, cursing, "I must be nuts," he said as he swung a knee up over the edge.

"I mean, communicate with energy somehow," I said, moving over to make a place for him, "I think that we're always whispering to those little strings of energy, and they, rather impersonally, oblige us."

"What are you *locos* doing up there?" Ez called from the balcony below.

"Stargazing," I said, gazing at Michael.

"Discussing the String Theory of Spirituality!" Michael said.

"I should get home," Monique said.

"You feel ready?" I asked her.

"This is my world, right? I'm ready for anything."

"We'll be down in a minute," I called down to Esperanza, who was watching Monique climb down.

Michael stayed there with me. Sitting on the roof still held so much power for me, I wanted to feel its vibration a little longer. We nestled our heads and breathed together as we gazed out across the bay.

I saw Monique cross the street in front of my house. Once on the other side she looked up for me and raised her fists in a victor's salute. I raised my fists in return. She left one hand in the air for a moment and opened her palm to me. Then she turned up the hill at a run.

CHRISTMAS

I.

"*Ya lo veo*," Esperanza's mother said, knowingly nodding, as soon as she saw my Mama, who had come down from Atlanta and was now standing uncomfortably at the front door of Ez's family house in Coral Gables.

Ez and her mother spoke in rapid Spanish and Ez laughed loudly.

Ez's mother reached up and grabbed Mama's giant arm.

"You are a dark old lady like me," she told Mama. "You come in the kitchen and I'll make you a special Cuban drink."

Mary Mara allowed herself to be manhandled by this woman half her size, and looked back at me as she was led away. Daddy gave me a hug and then followed them. Ez smirked as we watched them disappear into the kitchen and then leaned in to me, talking behind one of her hands. "Apparently, Mami took one look at little Mary and thought…you know, that…," Ez giggled, "she wasn't a gringo's daughter."

"Not Henry's?" I laughed.

"But now, after seeing your mother, she knows you are an honest woman."

We both laughed at the importance of being an honest woman before Ez went back to the kitchen.

I needed some coffee. We had flown in last night, battling Christmas Eve crowds. We had slept in, but I was still exhausted. Mary and Monique were napping upstairs. Matt and Joshua had slept on the plane and seemed to have a supernatural level of energy. The boys were so wild, I didn't want to take Josephina up on her offer to watch them, but she insisted. She especially loved the wild ones, or so she said. I went to the back window to check on them again.

They were out back with Josephina and her sons, playing on a yellowing lawn under a setting sun. An old swingset slumped in a corner, ignored. Joshua chased Josephina's younger son, who was about his age. I couldn't remember his name. Matt threw a football with the older one, home from college, who didn't seem that interested in playing. All boys, although Ez's sister and her girls were driving in from spending Christmas Eve with the husband's parents.

I simply must learn all of the names before dinner, I resolved as I watched the kids play.

All I could see of Josephina now was her broad bottom. She was digging in a small shed, tossing one, two, three, four balls back over her head before she stood up and closed the shed door.

Joshua yelled, "Balls!" and the two younger ones began kicking them immediately.

They were fine, just like the last time I'd checked.

Beassè handed me a steaming cup of coffee.

"You are a mind reader!" I exclaimed.

"And I didn't let her put in the sugar." Beassè chuckled.

I laughed. Ez's mother would put in three or four spoonfuls if you let her have her way.

Wonderful smells were coming from the noisy kitchen and it was making me hungry. I had already offered to help cook several times, but had had no luck.

"I confess I don't know what to do with myself, with no kids, and no cooking, on Christmas Day," I told Beassè.

"Relax," he said.

"Are you good with names?" I asked him.

Monique and Mary came into the room. Monique followed the smells toward the kitchen, while Mary threw herself, slumping, into a chair by the front window.

"What's with her?" I asked Monique as she passed me.

"What do you think?" she replied and then disappeared through the kitchen door.

Such melodrama! I thought. Mary's boy, Aidan, hadn't gotten his early admission letter yet. So what if he went to Berkeley or to another school? She was fretting over nothing. Well, she'd put up with plenty from me, and so I had no choice but to be patient with her. I smiled at good, good Beassè, who was talking to me, telling me everyone's names.

Ez came out of the kitchen, wiping her hands on an apron, which she then took off. She and Beassè exchanged glances as she passed by and then she sat down on the couch by herself. She dropped the apron on the coffee table and picked up a rum drink that wasn't hers and took a sip of it. She leaned back, raised her legs and piled her tall shoes, one on top of the other, on the table next to the apron.

What was it about Esperanza? She was so tiny, but wherever she was, as she moved along, space bent itself around her like a neutron star. She was pure potential. When I was with Esperanza, I felt anything could happen.

Esperanza was looking at me and Beassè, and then through us. Then, she saw me staring back at her and dropped her eyes, which then slid to a horizon somewhere near the tops of our heads. To where is her mind flying? I wondered.

II.

Atlanta was staring at me. She was listening to Beassè talk, but she kept looking back at me. I looked at Beassè. He was used to my moods, and unimpressed. He just kept on talking to Atlanta. Jesus! I think he might actually be trying to seduce her! Look at him, so charming, so smooth. I waved one hand at the idea and took a drink. Atlanta's eyes shot back to mine, but I betrayed nothing.

Atlanta had been good for me. She made me think about things I hadn't thought about in a long time. Her—with her roof sitting—trying to piece together the meaning of life, and faith, and love. The really big stuff. I had been raised to believe that only God knew the meaning of life. It was out there, up there, and much too big and complicated for the likes of me, so what was the point? It was much easier to wave a cigarette around and pretend that cynicism was sophisticated.

Whenever I thought about the big stuff, I thought about Cuba, which was funny, because I didn't think about

Cuba at all when I was actually in Cuba. I was just thinking about myself and leaving Mike. I'd gone to Cuba because I wanted to see my roots. I thought that seeing our old family house would somehow give me some kind of idea, or closure, or clue that would allow me to feel alive again, feel like I could think of something new again.

But now that all of that was over, I thought about Cuba, or rather, about Fidel. However we Cubans felt about him, we all claimed him. Fidel was family. He was the distant family member that everyone endlessly talked about behind his back. He had his sympathizers and his critics. Jealousy, love, pride, disappointment, anger, decades long grudges, it was all there.

Fidel and I had a lot in common. Both idealistic and both failed in exactly the same way. We'd both lost faith, taken the easy road, and lost everything that really mattered. But, unlike him, I was now awake to all that. I don't know why I cared, but it broke my heart that Fidel had refused to bend.

Napoleon said that in a contest between might and spirit, spirit always wins. Fidel had known that in the old days. It won in the jungle against terrible odds. He didn't win the revolution *por la fuerza*, and the moment he began to believe he did, the revolution died and mere petty dictatorship took it's place. My family hated him because he took everything from them, but I, born in America, didn't remember the old life, what was lost. As a fellow idealist, I was just curious. Maybe my family's losses could have been worth it, maybe it could have worked. The terrible tragedy of Fidel's failure is that we'll never know if it would have worked—a voluntary, democratic sharing of resources—a utopia! He had an entire island of people willing to try it, but he strangled his own child fresh from the womb. Now, in reaction to him, they will all abandon the dream as soon as he is dead. It's a tragedy of monumental proportions.

I drained the glass of liquor I was holding, felt its burning tracers through my body.

Oh Fidel, I addressed him in my mind's eye. Fidel! I demanded his attention. Do you remember? When you were hiding in the jungle with the taste of dirt in your mouth, the sounds of hundreds of men heavily loaded with lead for you, looking for you, near to you, you were never truly afraid, were you? You may have had a knot in your stomach, three days excrement pent up, but deep in the core of your being you were never afraid. Even as they closed in upon you, celebrated your certain death, you never in your heart feared the death of the revolution because you knew that spirit would vanquish the force of flesh, that the force of flesh was a chimera, convincing in its sound, in its reverberation, but nevertheless so insubstantial you could almost pass your hand through it, through them, and then you did. Now look at yourself! I admonished him. You have become the shadelike specter of force of flesh yourself, and nothing more. What is there left to do now but die and let it all die with you.

Not me. No, not me. Maybe instead of shopping, and getting my nails done, and fretting about remodeling an outdated kitchen, I'd quit my job and go on the road with Beassè. I'd just say out loud to whatever energy is out there, the "universe" as Atlanta called it, that I wanted to be of some service. Perhaps if I did that, something will happen. Beassè says that if I have faith, something always happens.

III.

I dipped a spoon or a fork into what Rosa was cooking enough times that I was finally thrown out of the kitchen. I went to find my chair and sat down in it, next to Ez, who was on the couch. Oh, it still felt so good—threadbare, broken in and sagging.

"Will you open this for me?" Joshua held out a Mexican made Coca-Cola in a glass bottle with a pry off top. I fished my keys from my pocket and opened it. Joshua smiled at me. If only we could tie that kid's smile to the electrical grid! I swatted his butt and he ran from me squealing.

I was suddenly overcome with so much gratitude to all of these people here in this house, so much love for them all.

"You know," Ez picked up an apron from the table and folded it, "after I left you, that was Elijah's recliner."

I laughed and wiped a tear that had slipped down my face.

"I'm serious!" she said and tossed the apron down. "No one sat in it and it just sat there empty, waiting for you."

She smiled at me warmly, and I could tell by the flush on her cheeks that she had already had plenty of rum. We sat there together, just watching everyone else come and go.

"So, you said that you wanted to know where I went," she said, "when I left you."

I sat up straighter.

"I went to Cuba."

"Cuba?"

"Yes, supposedly to reunite with long lost family members, but I had no interest in seeing any of them. I know you thought that I left you for another man, but that's not true. I left him too. "

Ez's fingers twitched in that way they did when she has had a couple of drinks and craves the cigarette she no longer smokes. I waited.

"I promised Mami that I would see her sister right away," she continued, "but instead I checked into a hotel like a tourist and got very drunk in the bar. *Terrible.* The first and second nights both. And I took two men, one each night."

I shook my head in my hands.

"Do you want to hear it or not?" she snapped.

"Okay, alright," I said before I could stop myself.

"The third day I just wandered around like a phantom. I wanted to see everything. I walked all over Havana, and hitched rides when I couldn't walk anymore. The third night, I was sitting outside a café in front of a small plate of greasy food, feeling sick and drinking bubble water. I was just sitting there, too sick to eat, looking at everything. Looking at the uneven streets, the boney mutts everywhere, the skinny women in sagging dresses, once fine, the crumbling façades of the buildings, the rusting cars. Everything was in a state of decay, falling down, falling apart. The whole country seemed to be held together with safety pins. And yet," she paused, "people were walking down the street holding hands, they were laughing at the table next to me, someone was playing a guitar in an open window *arriba*, and those rusted cars chugged by crammed with people going somewhere!" Ez banged her fist lightly on the table.

"I looked at them, these *pobres*, and I thought, 'Jesus! What resilience! What beauty! What strength!'

Ez took my glass from my hand and took a long drink.

"I was just sitting here just now thinking about how he—Fidel—lost his faith in his own ideals as soon as he came into power and could actually do it. ¿Estraña, no?"

"No," I said.

Ez pursed her lips.

"Sure," I said, "The minute somebody has any power, the first thing they think about is losing it. So, they spend all of their time protecting it."

"But, why couldn't he just have had faith that the same coincidences, the same providence that delivered the country to him would continue to protect it? That whatever the people voted for, it would be part of the process of the revolution, even if it didn't fit his idea of what was right? That if the revolution really was right, then no one—not even America—could destroy it? It seems to me that a dreamer and an asthmatic who somehow vanquished an entire power structure with just a handful of people, a couple of guns, and some duct tape, would somehow understand that."

Esperanza's voice had risen with righteous indignation. What was this really about?

"If he did that," I said settling back into the chair, "he would qualify as some kind of ascended master of consciousness, because that's a level of faith I don't think this world has seen much of. Ghandi is world famous for a reason."

IV.

Mom was right, I was moping. How can you fake being happy when the one thing you want more than anything in the world might not happen? Mo and I had snuck some drinks but they didn't help. I didn't want to be a drag on everyone, but I just couldn't help it. When Beassè and Mike left the room, I knew that Mom was talking to Esperanza about me because they were both looking at me. They talked and then they looked. Ez was nodding. Why couldn't they just leave me alone?

"Can I sit next to you?" Ez asked.

Her face was red from all the alcohol. It took all my self-control not to roll my eyes.

"Sure," I said, not at all sounding casual.

"I was in love when I was your age," she said. "Mike and I knew right away that we were meant to be, that we would get married."

I didn't say anything because, obviously, they weren't meant to be if they got divorced. I wondered how much longer I had to pretend that I didn't think she was full of shit.

"You don't think we were meant to be, but we were," she said. "Sometimes our ideas of what is meant to be aren't perfect enough. Our divorce is part of our relationship, it's a bridge to a new phase of life for us together."

I watched her and she smiled to herself.

"You know, your mother is an amazing woman. Somehow she understands this. Not very many women are secure enough to be here." Ez looked at my mother. "Look at her over there."

I looked. She was standing next to Ez's Uncle Ernesto. Her skin was only a shade or two lighter than his, and when she laughed, all her front teeth showed white. I was sure I'd never seen all of her teeth before. It was so funny to see her with them, all the shades of brown, looking so international. In Sausalito, she had always seemed so white, so suburban, but she fit in perfectly here. Ernesto had made his very own Mojito recipe and was pouring it for a big group: Atlanta, Grandpa, Ez's parents, Ernesto's sister and Ez's cousin, Ermelinda.. They made Grandma come over and take a glass, and Mom put an arm around her, crunched her in with everybody else. They all crashed their glasses together, and Mom drank hers down in one gulp as the rest of them cheered. She was a beautiful, ripe, free, talking, laughing creature, who I was seeing for the first time. She had made this happen. She decided she wanted it and she'd made it happen, and realizing that made me want to run to her, clasp her hand in mine, tell everyone that she was mine, my own mother.

Ez had been watching me. "Life is messy, Mary, don't ever expect it to be otherwise. Your mother divorced your father. I understand that is painful, but would you deny *this*?" She looked back at the group of them and raised a hand emphatically. "Embrace the messiness, Mary. Don't imagine that you have to understand everything, just know in your heart that it will turn out perfectly, and it will."

I could tell that this was one of those moments when someone was telling me something important, something I would remember and use, like a tool, over and over, and I sat quietly, letting it sink in.

"Say it," she said, "it will turn out perfectly."

"It will turn out perfectly," I said, and I did feel somehow lighter, happier. I could imagine getting in my car and driving away from him, I could imagine it happening and being okay. It was all going to be okay. I loved him, he loved me, and it would turn out perfectly.

Ez patted my cheek firmly and walked over to Uncle Ernesto, calling, in her imperious way, for a glass.

I loved all of them. At that moment, I had no fear anywhere in me. No fear of losing Aidan, no fear of being on my own, no fear of being wrong, stupid. I just loved, and my heart burst with love, and I wanted to tell Aidan all about it.

My phone rang. Aidan. When I lifted it to my ear, I could hardly speak.

"Hey gorgeous," he said.

"I was just thinking about you, I was just dying to talk to you," I said to him, almost sobbing, and then throwing caution to the wind, I said, "I love you." And then I said it two more times, "I love you, Aidan, I love you so very much."

He made that deep animal chuckle he makes when he's deeply pleased and embarrassed at the same time.

"I got in," he said.

"What?"

"I'm going with you. They sent the letter to my dad's house. I got it today."

I burst into tears, and I could tell that he was choked up too.

"I can't wait for you to get back," he said, his voice thick and husky. "I want to touch every part of you, I want to do that for a very long time."

By the time I got off the phone, my face was hot, my eyes swollen and I was breathing the heavy, greenhouse air through every pore. I wandered out the front door, touching every person I passed until I was standing on the sidewalk.

Shifting Ground

The leaves of a banana towered above me and gleamed in the moonlight. The leaves of trees hung suspended, motionless, in the still evening. A rusting gate, the concrete sidewalk, a broken wood fence picket, they all seemed to be one thing, carefully balanced and arranged. Even the vigorously growing dandelion and escaped lawn grass growing from every bare patch of earth seemed placed just so. Everything gleamed with a light that was not reflected, but instead came from within. Every surface seemed completely alive, vibrating with life. I felt a little dizzy, mesmerized by the night, the overpowering damp scent of jasmine and the feeling that my own boundaries were dissolving into that vibrating aliveness. It was all so beautiful and so perfect that I reached out one index finger to disturb it, like the surface of a pool of water. My finger touched only the warm live air. At my feet, a vigorous violet colored flower pushed up from a broken piece of curb.

I turned. I could see them all, Ez, her family, Mom, Mike in his easy chair, and Monique yak yak yaking in the front window of the house, illuminated like a theatre, they too, part of it and vibrating with life. If only Henry could have let it happen, if only my Dad could have been here too, rather than in his self imposed exile. In my mind's eye, I took him by the hand, brought him here. How could he not want to be a part of this? Stubborn, I said to myself and smiled at his stubbornness because it was his. I love you Daddy, I said to him. I listened, but I heard nothing, so I went up the walk and inside. Aidan was coming! I giggled as I leaped over the threshold.

V.

Four thousand miles away, a red SuperSport shot down the freeway in an unwavering trajectory, the long line of the guardrail underscoring the scorching red and orange sunset breaking over a dark ocean. The freeway steamed in an unusual Christmas heat wave, and the hard, hot sunshine drenched the red car in its light, yet the face of the driver set above the square set shoulders remained in shadow behind the visor. The car sped over the hot pavement relentlessly, as if it were a salmon pushing upstream, as if the car were pushing against and defying the magnetic force of the Earth itself. The driver shifted in his seat and the grim line of the mouth became illuminated by the slanting sun before it opened in shock and surprise. The hands lifted from the wheel as if from something hot, returned, gripping, and, as if to avoid an invisible obstacle, the red car swerved sharply to the left and then to the right, its tires screaming. The cars speeding toward it and behind it swayed crazily in a ballet of avoidance, and as two of them skidded to a stop in the gravel margin, the red car broke through the guard rail, vaulted, and like a toy, spun once in the air, glinting, before it disappeared behind the embankment.

The paramedics who scudded down past the broken guardrail found the car on its top, the driver suspended by his belt, his blood pooling in the hood below him. The touch of four hands releasing him opened his eyes, and Henry squinted against the sunshine. A paramedic shifted his shadow to fall on Henry's face.

"Do you know your name?" the paramedic asked as his companion furiously worked to rip the shirt, stop the blood.

"She was in a whirlwind," Henry murmured in a barely audible whisper, and blinked tears from his eyes wonderingly.

The paramedics exchanged glances, their hands slowed.

"She was in a whirlwind and she held out her arms to me."

Henry sighed, and the life went out of his face. The four hands released him, the shadow passed, and Henry's eyes stared into the sun without blinking.

VI.

I could have sworn I heard someone call me Mikey. I looked around but there was no one there. The adults were all sitting down now, talking and laughing on the other side of the room, next to a television playing a black and white movie with the sound off. Mary's young man was going to Berkeley and the two girls were holed up together in the corner talking. The boys, overtired, were running up and down the stairs hollering with the other kids, and no one was telling them to stop. The room was full of noise, everyone was ignoring me, but it was unmistakeable. Someone called me Mikey.

It was then that Ermelinda called Atlanta to the phone. Atlanta made a silly face at me as she passed and I watched her disappear into the hallway, and then reappear at the end of the plastic corkscrew tether of the old style handset. I saw the color leave her face as she glanced at me.

    When Atlanta sank to her knees, I just knew.

Epilogue

Just when I think it is over, Michael shifts his weight on top of me and brings a giant rolling wave back around to crash into me again, carrying me far out into the ocean, crashing back and rolling out, again and again. It is too much to bear and blinded, ears ringing, I throw my arms back to grasp the iron headboard and pull against it as I sink my teeth into his shoulder, sobbing. He holds his ground against my flailing body, driving my sobs deeper into my throat before his body tenses, still and shuddering, and he moans into my hair. I float gently downward, back into myself, as he winds his fist in my hair and presses his face against mine, moaning one last time. Rolling on our sides, Michael's eyes, large and moist with adoration, meet mine and then he strokes my face, my hair, and then my face again with both hands, and then we are kissing deep in our mouths. I laugh with pleasure and then he laughs. He pulls me tightly against him and murmurs in my ear before he falls heavily asleep.

It's been a long time since we've seen each other. When Henry died I needed space to grieve and to think it all through. I wanted to be clear for Michael, to be the gift for him that he was to me.

It took a long time to figure out what Henry had been to me. Once he was gone and I no longer needed to oppose him in my every thought, fight against him, in and out of the courtroom, I had to let him in. I had to acknowledge that there was a reason he had been the center of my being for such a long time. He was part of what made me who I am. How could I be anything but grateful for that? I finally let him in enough, loved him enough, to say goodbye. I said goodbye not only to him, as a man, but also to his security, his certainty, to his assurance that he could always take care of everything for me.

In doing so, I said okay to my own frightening chaos. If it's true, that inside chaos resides unthinkable possibility, I want to experience that. The possibility of world peace. Why not? The possibility of healing the world, healing myself? They are the same thing.

I want to be a part of a worldwide caliphate of real faith free from mere obeisant submission to human authority. We who define faith not by possessing control over others, but by relinquishing it. We who are infinitely connected, not closed, who are transient and embrace death. We carry our chaos with us into our day jobs, into the post office, the PTA. We ravel, we weave into the warp, the woof. The checker, the bank teller who touches us finds themselves mouthdry with existential longing. At night, the sidewalk warps just a little under our feet, objects nearby shift imperceptibly, then back, fracturing the world each time. An inaudible, low decibel, rolling wave screams and screams, a cry from underground that brought down the Bay Bridge, that sends rocks skidding down Mt. Tam, that breaks all of your glasses. That scream is breaking us too.

As you listen to this, you blink and this moment passes away. The cadence of the present moment presses relentlessly on. It does not pause. It does not skip. It's gone. It's gone. It's gone again.

For me, each of these tiny deaths are not cause for fear nor nostalgia, but are doors to new landscapes, new ways of being, remade anew each moment. I stand, suspended on a sliver of firm ground between a void behind and another in front without fear, at one with the flow of life in this moment. What every kind of happiness has in common is love for this moment.

The chilly night breezes in through the windows and sends gooseflesh rising up my back. A car passes. Someone laughs and then I hear low voices talking on the sidewalk below. I sigh. If I leave now, I'd get home by eleven. It's a school night and Mary needs her sleep. As I dress quietly in the glow of the streetlight outside, Michael's eyes flutter open.

"Do you want me to walk you to your car, Darling?"

"No. You sleep. I'm not afraid."

THE END

Acknowledgments

My deepest gratitude to my extended family who have been rock steadfast in their encouragement during the writing of this book: Lorie, Brett, Juanita, Simon, Melissa, Will, Andrea, Arne, John and Jen, Bruce, Jenny, Tamara, and Tamara and Len, Sue, and all the rest of the gang back in Sellwood. Thanks also to the even wider group of friends and family who are standing ready to order this book the minute it is released. Thank you all for your support. I'd also like to thank Clayton and Louisa for your intellectual companionship over these many years. Thank you also to Ian Koviak (bookdesigners.com) for designing a fantastic book cover based on my father's design. Special thanks to Ruthann and Mark, Susie, Greg and Julie, George, Regine, Alia, Jennifer, and Carole for your long friendship and faith in me. And thank you to the women who have cared for my children, without whom this book would not exist—Sianny, Ilze, Christina, and Natalia. Hugs to my children, Elie and Esme, who refill my cup every day and remind me to laugh. And a big kiss to Cael who has been this book's most enthusiastic partisan. I love you all.

About the Author

A.Z. Zehava is a writer, permaculturist and activist. She lives in Amsterdam, and Portland, Oregon with her family. This is her first novel.

Made in the USA
Charleston, SC
10 April 2014